The Monk's Disciples

The Monk's Disciples

Jeffrey Robinson

LITTLE, BROWN AND COMPANY

A *Little, Brown* Book

First published in Great Britain in 1997
by Little, Brown and Company

Copyright © 1997, Jeffrey Robinson

The moral right of the author has been asserted.

A CIP catalogue record for this book
is available from the British Library.

ISBN 0 316 87968 1

Typeset by
Palimpsest Book Production Limited,
Polmont, Stirlingshire
Printed and bound in Great Britain by
Creative Print and Design (Wales), Ebbw Vale, Gwent

Little, Brown and Company (UK)
Brettenham House
Lancaster Place
London WC2E 7EN

This book is for the wonderful Milly Marmur and for the late Dr Julius Marmur, a man with the soul of a poet, whose work in 1958 first indicated the double helical nature of DNA but was neglected because the Nobel Prize-winning magnitude of its significance was not yet appreciated.

Alberik (1622–1684), French Benedictine monk falsely credited with having formed the basic tenets of genetics.

Translated from Latin entry in *Lives of the Benedicts*

Prologue

The airlines do it to me on purpose.

I know they do because they know it's me.

My guess is that they have my name flagged in their computer, because it doesn't matter how many people are on the plane, it can be almost empty, but as soon as the person at check-in types in B–A–R–O–L–O, V–I–N–C–E–N–T, the computer automatically spits out a boarding pass with a seat pre-assigned next to a numskull.

I can spot him a mile away. He's the guy with the green and yellow checked pants, bright red golf shirt, matching baseball hat, blue seersucker jacket and lasso tie, who is non-stop chewing Chiclets and is always 'Glad to see ya'. So, as soon as he gets on, I start staring out the window because I know from experience that the instant we make eye contact the numskull is going to tell me his name, grab my hand to shake it, tell me where he's from and demand, so what do you do?

The problem is, if I say I'm a lawyer I'm stuck for the entire flight because he's going to want free advice. Okay, I admit that I always carry my business cards with me, just in case. Okay, I also admit to having a few business cards handy in the pocket of my bathrobe at home because you never know if the guy knocking on the door is someday going to need an American lawyer in England who specializes in insurance claims. But free advice? No. That's not the way it works.

Once I cottoned on to the fact that the airlines were out to get me, I went in search of an occupation for which no discussion is possible. Now when someone on a plane sneaks past my defences with, 'So what do you do?' I tell him, 'I'm in scaffolding.'

I even know how to say it in several languages. It's *échafaudage* in French, *baugerust* in German, *impalcatura* in Italian and, as I once had to employ, *byggnadstallning* in Swedish.

Trust me, no meaningful dialogue is possible.

Which is exactly what I was counting on the night I came back from the States and the numskull rushed on at the last minute. I was feeling especially sorry for myself since I'd just spent two weeks with my boy Johnny who lives in New Jersey with his mother. He and I hung out at the shore – you know, down in Ocean City – ate junk food, stayed up late and one night I took him to a bar in Sommers Point where they had go-go girls. He's only fifteen, so I made sure they weren't topless or anything like that, and all he had to drink was a Horse's Neck – you know, ginger ale with grenadine syrup – but I figured it was time he did stuff with me that he could never do with his mother or the jerk she lives with. It's a male bonding thing. We played miniature golf, we went bowling and one afternoon when it rained we saw three movies. A couple of nights we went to a driving range to hit golf balls and then he got in the batting cage with an automatic pitching machine and spent an hour knocking the stitches out of baseballs. Another night I heard there was boxing over in Ventnor, so we drove up there and I took him to the fights. I showed him where I almost got arrested thirty years ago in Atlantic City, tossing Salvo washing machine tablets into the fountain in front of Chalfont Haddon Hall – the soap bubbles up and if you throw enough of them in the suds overflow for half a block – and then I snuck him into Bally's so he could play the slot machines. He won eighty-five bucks. He wanted to blow it all as a down payment for a windsurfer but I told him to save his money and staked him to it myself. That set me back a bundle. But he windsurfed every day at the beach and must have been pretty good because a couple of seventeen-year-old girls started paying attention to him. He liked that. I just sat there on the sand, far enough away to give him some space, and gloated. I also bought him a new pair of Reeboks and stuff for his computer. I got him a game he wanted called Inter-Galactic Rollerball – what do I know – and a bunch of CD-Roms, including one that has every phone number and street address in the entire USA. After that I got him a new modem, which he swore he needed because his old modem was too slow and the new modem would make everything work a hundred times faster, especially when it came to accessing the

Internet, and anyway, he said, he could even send faxes with it. Frankly, I didn't have a clue what he was talking about.

When I finally returned him to his mother, Johnny asked how come he couldn't live with me in London. I wanted to tell him the truth, because your old lady thinks that living with some out-of-work trumpet player is a better deal than living with me. Instead I made a lame excuse about this being best for him. That made him cry. When he started, I cried too. I promised him that as soon as he graduated high school he could come to London to go to college. He liked that so we both stopped crying. Then his mother said, no you can't live in London, even though she's English, and I said, yes you can, which only made him cry again.

So there I was, in a really foul mood, thinking to myself that someone at American Airlines must have screwed up because the seat next to mine was still empty. Except, just as the crew was about to close the door, a numskull charged on with both arms full of junk he'd bought at the airport and a suitcase that could never fit under a seat.

No prize for guessing where they stuck him.

He took all my stuff out of the overhead bin so he could bulldoze his garbage in and then he nearly fell into my lap when he sat down.

And all this time I was being very obvious about staring out the window.

Except, I could see his reflection as he buckled his seatbelt and launched into a speech.

Putting on my best scowl, I buried my nose in a copy of *Boxing Illustrated.*

He was a middle-aged Englishman who was kind of spooky because he never stopped staring straight ahead. It was as if he was transfixed by the little paper doily hanging over the headrest on the seat in front of him.

And he just babbled on.

Either he didn't care that I wasn't listening or he didn't notice.

He said he'd almost missed his flight up from Washington because he was late getting to the airport because he hates driving on the wrong side of the road, which means he would have missed this flight to London – which would have been perfectly fine with me – and as long as we're on time getting out of Kennedy, hopefully, we'll get into Heathrow on time because it's a short connection for the flight to Marseilles and he can't miss that because he's finally getting even with everybody, settling old scores, and he doesn't even give a damn if they sue him.

Hey, the instant I heard that, I reached inside my pocket, grabbed one of my cards and handed it to him. I said, if you ever need an American lawyer in London, I'm your guy. I said, I take a cheque or a cash retainer as an advance against one-third of the settlement. I sort of mumbled, I only keep half of the retainer as an honorarium just in case, you know, on the outside chance, we lose. And then, in my most confident tone of voice, I said exactly what I figured I needed to say to clinch the sale. 'Helping people to get even is my specialty.'

Still not looking at me, he began asking all sorts of questions, mainly about patents, which is something I know nothing about.

Except, I didn't tell him that. I said, sorry, no free advice. Cut-rate, yes. Free, no. Then I slipped on my eye shades and after a while I fell asleep.

Except, the next morning when we got into London, the numskull shook my hand several times and promised to ring me.

'I really want to get even.'

I reassured him, 'It's what I do best.'

He never once looked at me.

I never got his name.

Chapter One

Someday, I'm going to get even with the son-of-a-bitch who invented lamb vindaloo.

Where the hell was the Alka-Seltzer?

Why, hello, Mr Barolo. Patel always gave me a big welcome whenever I made the mistake of going into his restaurant. *Why, it's so nice to see you again.*

With half-closed eyes I fumbled through the medicine cabinet.

Why, Mr Barolo, can I offer you a glass of vintage Bulgarian vin rouge while you're perusing our extensive and extremely well-planned menu?

A bottle of aspirin tumbled out. Then my Old Spice after-shave smashed in the sink.

Perhaps I might recommend the lamb vindaloo.

Through the fog in my brain it dawned on me that the Alka-Seltzer wasn't there because it was in my night table, where I'd left it the last time I'd eaten the Sunday night special at Patel's Taj Mahal of the India Gourmet.

Taj Mahal.

It's a store front.

India Gourmet.

It's a contradiction in terms.

I felt my way through the dark apartment . . . crash! . . . and banged into two dining-room chairs that I was keeping in the hallway because I don't have a dining room.

Damn.

Limping back to my bedroom, I yanked at my night table drawer and spilled everything onto the floor. The box of Alka-Seltzer landed at my feet. Except, now I didn't have any water.

I mumbled out loud, 'The hell with water,' popped one of the tablets into my mouth and started to chew.

Jeeezus, that stuff is awful!

Except, when I finished the first tablet I chewed a second one.

Uch!

Patel's food was the Indians' way of getting even with the British for the Raj.

Why, Mr Barolo, I hope you have enjoyed this evening's dining experience.

Taj Mahal of the India Gourmet.

I slipped back into a tormented sleep.

Gourmet, my ass!

When I was a kid growing up in Brooklyn, my mother used to force a home-made concoction down my throat that tasted truly horrible. Except, it always made me feel better. So I stayed in bed all day Monday, cringing at the smell of mallow root, cranesbill root and bistort, all mixed together with a couple of dozen drops of water. I forced it down, then chased it with a swig from the giant bottle of castor oil that I keep in the fridge. Nothing has changed over the years. It's still a ghastly potion. But by five on Tuesday morning I knew I'd live long enough to get my revenge on Patel.

I put some water on the stove to boil, tossed in a chamomile tea-bag – I learned about herb teas from Louise – poured it into a 'Souvenir of Antwerp' mug that I'd picked up in a junk shop a few days before and moved into the living room.

Weaving my way past the thirty-five chairs I had there, lined up in rows like an auditorium – each a different size, each a different style, making up about a quarter of my entire collection – I checked the answering machine to see that there were two calls. Both were from Henry, my Australian secretary who hated the name Henrietta. Last month she called herself Pru. The month before she called herself Allison. These days she was Suzannah.

I didn't listen too closely – it was something about a guy named Bickerton – because all I wanted to do was watch a couple of videos. I sorted through a stack of tapes, found the first Liston-Clay fight, threw it into the VCR, crawled into a Victorian high-backed wing in the second row, put my feet up on a little early twentieth-century bentwood and spent the rest of the morning pretending it was February 1964.

Miami was where the fight was. The USS *Norton Sound* somewhere in the South China Sea was where I was. All the black guys on the ship were rooting for Clay because they knew how good he was. All the white guys were rooting for Liston because they hated black guys with big mouths and Clay had a big mouth. Except, I knew Clay would win. There was never any doubt. So I laid off nine hundred bucks at 6–1. Imagine that. They gave me 6–1 on Clay just because he had a big mouth. What a night. Seven rounds later, he was the champ and I had nearly five and a half grand in my pocket.

Watching that video was almost as good as my mother's elixir.

When the fight was over I went back to sleep, got up around noon and felt okay enough to ring the gym to ask if Hambone had bothered to show up. Charlie surprised me by saying yeah, that Derek 'The Hambone' Hannover had not only gone through his long workout routine but he'd also gone three rounds with one of the guys, taken some punches and stayed on his feet.

I said to Charlie, 'Will wonders ever cease,' re-ran the tape and watched the Liston–Clay fight again.

Half the money I won on the ship that night was wired home to my mother. Two grand went into my college fund. The rest sat in the bank for more than four years, until I blew it on a ring for Louise.

I was still in bed, now with my nose buried in last week's copy of *Boxing News*, when the phone rang. I couldn't be bothered reaching for it. The answering machine clicked on and a few seconds later I heard a voice say, 'So? Are you there or not?' It was Henry. 'This is Delia.'

I mumbled, 'What happened to Suzannah?'

She demanded, 'Where are you? Still not picking up, eh? I guess that means you're not coming into the office today. Well, I'm going home. There are messages for you. That fella Bickerton rang again. He wouldn't tell me what it's about yesterday and he wouldn't tell me what it's about today. He keeps saying you'll know. Yesterday I told him if he wants to retain you he has to send you a retainer. I thought that was a good idea seeing as how the phone bill came in yesterday and the electricity bill came in this morning, the printer is running out of toner and we need a box of fax paper. He asked how much and I said a thousand pounds. He didn't so much as blink. I mean, obviously, I couldn't see whether or not he blinked because he was on the other end of the line but when I said a thousand pounds he said, I'll do it. Just like that. I figured I should start at a thousand pounds and settle for five hundred but he was willing to go for it straight away . . .'

I tossed my *Boxing News* aside and threw a pillow on top of my head.

Maybe I should sue Patel. If this was America I could take him to court for trying to poison me. I could sue him for loss of earnings.

After a while I started to fall back to sleep.

I thought about phone bills. Electricity bills. Fax paper. My eyes were almost shut.

Pru. Allison. Suzannah. Delia.

Burp!

Chapter Two

Wednesday I felt like going to the office, if for no other reason than because Wednesday is when my copy of *Boxing Week* arrives from the States. So I shaved and showered, stepped into a suit, opened the windows to air out the flat and made my way down Portobello Road to the tube at Notting Hill Gate. Five stops later, I got off at Oxford Circus, climbed up the stairs and walked through the back streets of Soho, taking my time because the weather wasn't too bad. Which is one of the best things about living in England. After a few years you learn to disregard the weather so that, unless it's truly miserable or truly beautiful, everything in between becomes not too bad.

My office is on the second floor of an old building just off Wardour Street, above a Chinese restaurant. The hallway usually smells of eggs and stir-fried fish but One Hung Lo – his real name is Lance but it feels intrinsically wrong to call a Chinese guy Lance – knows better than to try to pull a Patel on me. From the hallway I can walk directly into his kitchen and at the far end there's a big round table where he lets his special friends eat. There's no menu – you get whatever the chef happens to be doing – and more often than not, the people who share the table with you don't speak English. But that's the first place I think of when I want to impress someone with how well I'm connected to the *lo mein* mafia. Just as good, if I phone down to order something, he likes me enough to deliver.

Across the street there's a betting shop where I've got a credit balance, thanks to the fact that the Cypriot gangster who runs it doesn't know as much about boxing as I do.

Next door is a little deli. Barney and his twin brother Bernie, the two old guys who have owned it since Moses used to eat there, have finally gotten it through their lead-lined yarmulkes

– because I've spent the past four years drumming it into them – that you never put mayo, catsup and lettuce on a pastrami sandwich. And because I don't like their mustard, I brought a big jar back from New York a couple of trips ago and they keep it on a shelf just for me with my name on it. Pickles they've got knocked – they probably have the best assortment of pickles in England – but the quality of their blintzes leaves a lot to be desired. They refuse to believe there's a difference between blinis and blintzes. Someday I plan on teaching them how to make a proper knish, but that will take time because they're so damned stubborn.

There are plenty of Italian restaurants in the neighbourhood but I go to a joint five minutes down the block called Giovanni's because he comes from Naples which is where my grandparents came from.

And Charlie's gym is a fifteen-minute walk in the other direction, just past Tottenham Court Road. I keep my three fighters there because it's an okay place and anyway Charlie gives me a deal. He and I speak the same language, even though his people came from Turino and northern Italy isn't the same as southern Italy.

So that's my world.

Lots of lawyers need fancier addresses and maybe they also like to eat in better places, but I've got everything I want right where I want it. I'm a pastrami and Pabst Blue Ribbon kind of guy who maintains his own hours and figures there's no shame in that.

It suits me just fine.

Except, maintaining my own hours doesn't suit Henry.

'I've been ringing you for two days,' she barked the moment I stepped in. 'You don't return any of my calls. How am I supposed to know if you're dead or alive?'

I looked at her dumpy frame wrapped in a flowery dress, black-rooted blonde hair and wire-framed granny glasses, and told her, 'When I'm dead I won't come to the office. Any mail?'

'Maybe you should start with your phone messages. Don't get excited. There's only one. That bloke named Bickerton.'

'Where's his number?'

'He didn't leave one.'

'Why didn't you ask?'

'Because he said you'd know what it's all about.'

I didn't. 'So if he calls back, get a number. Find out what he wants. Ask him. Tell him I mainly do insurance. Also make sure he knows I don't practise here, that I do American stuff.'

'I told him all that.'

'What did he say.'

'He didn't.'

'And you don't know what he wants?'

'He wants to retain you.'

'What for?'

She exhaled really loud to show me she was getting annoyed. 'When he rings back, you ask him.'

I tossed the messages onto her desk. 'I'll take the mail whenever you're ready.'

'I'm ready.' She handed me the bills from Monday and Tuesday. 'Today's bills aren't in yet.'

Neither was *Boxing Week*.

My own office, just behind hers, is a cramped room with two of my best leather chairs facing my old wooden desk. My favourite, high-backed judge's seat, is behind my desk. I picked it up for next to nothing at an auction when they emptied out an old courtroom in Bristol. Behind that is a window with a view of another window in the building behind ours. One of my walls is lined with legal books, most of them out of date but all of them leather bound which helps decorate the office. The wall opposite has my eight boxing trophies lined up on a glass shelf sitting just under my Law School diploma. On what little space there is next to the door, I've hung a framed original poster from the Louis-Schmeling fight.

Talk about unforgettable nights. I've got that one on tape, too. June 22, 1938. It only took the Brown Bomber two minutes and four seconds into the first round to destroy the great white hope of the Master Race. I've watched it a hundred times because those two minutes and four seconds sum up one of the things I love most about boxing – it's better than real life because the good guys sometimes win.

The phone rang.

Henry got it, blurted out, 'You should live so long,' then shouted to me, 'Your friend the jerk.'

That meant Hambone. 'Don't tell me you've gone to Charlie's two days in a row?'

In his rolling Jamaican accent he explained, 'I was doing my road work, Vince, and this bloke in a black cab nearly run me down.'

'What do you want me to do?'

'Can you sue him for me?'

'You mean, so you don't have to fight in three weeks?'

'Aw, come on Vince, he almost killed me.'

'Phone me when he succeeds and I'll make your mother a rich woman. Until then, get over to Charlie's and start punching something. I'm warning you, three weeks from now this guy's gonna to pin your ears back.'

'I'm at Charlie's now.'

'You start punching something. I'll see you when I see you.'

Hanging up, I reminded Henry, 'Bickerton. Get his number and I'll call him after lunch.'

'Lunch? You just got here.'

'Well, now I'm outta here.'

I love hanging out at Charlie's, sitting on the top row of the wooden bleacher that runs along the far side of the smelly basement, watching fighters go through their paces. The noise is right. The smell is right. It takes me back to a gentler time.

Charlie found Hambone for me when he was just sixteen. A tall, strapping kid with chocolate skin and dark wild eyes, he quit school because some shyster promoter promised him six big money fights. He got beat in the first two and the promoter dropped him like a hot potato. Except, the promoter didn't give Hambone his contract back. It meant the kid was stuck. He couldn't make any money if he didn't fight and if he did fight, everything went to the shyster promoter. A friend of Hambone's brought him to Charlie and when Charlie heard what kind of a jam he was in, he called me. I not only extricated Hambone from his contract, but signed him up to a fair one and installed him at Charlie's. That was two and a half years ago. Since then he's had six fights and won the last four. What little money I've made with Hambone I've reinvested in him and my other two fighters. I've got a young featherweight from Ghana named Sterling. And I've got a kid from North Africa named Khalid who should probably be a bantamweight except he eats too much. They're both just starting out. I've managed to convince Sterling to stay in school for another year, even though he hates it. Khalid quit before I met him but I found him a job through this Arab guy who runs a restaurant, a fellow Giovanni knows, so at least he can train a couple of mornings a week and earn some money waiting on tables the rest of the time.

The deal is, I spend just enough to see what kind of promise they've got and then, when they're on the way, I sell them on to some promoter, take my profit and find a few more young kids who might have a shot. Over the long run I've made a few bucks. Once in a while I hold on to a fighter, the way I've hung on to Hambone, because I reckon he might just go somewhere. Which is when I invariably lose whatever money I've made.

Charlie agrees that Hambone could be the one. Believe me, I'm due. And I trust Charlie. He reminds me of an old Irish priest I used to know. The guy who boxed my ass into church.

It was back in Brooklyn. The cops picked me up one afternoon, hanging out, smoking Lucky Strikes with Fat and Guido on the boardwalk at Coney Island. I was like, maybe, fourteen. They shoved us into a squad car but instead of dragging us back to school – I went to Abe Lincoln over on Ocean Parkway – they brought us to a Police Athletic League gym at the end of the King's Highway. The cops were Italian, which meant they sort of looked after us, but the priest was an Irish guy named MacNamee. I figured that meant he should be looking out for the Irish kids, except there weren't any Irish kids in our neighbourhood. It was Italian and Jewish. Which was all right with me because the Irish kids, like the ones who lived in Flatbush and Bed-Sty, were always looking for trouble. Not that the Jewish kids were pushovers. When you picked a fight with them you had to be careful because some of them were pretty big and anyway, there were more of them than there were of us.

The thing was, growing up in Brooklyn taught you that there are times in life when you make a stand and there are times in life when you strap on your Keds and accelerate home. If you made it through your teenage years without getting your nose busted six times, it was because you learned that lesson. And every smart kid from Brooklyn carries that lesson with him for the rest of his life.

Anyway, the cops dumped us at the gym and MacNamee

challenged each of us to one round. He said, if anyone could knock him off his feet, the cops would take us back to the boardwalk and buy us lunch. But if he decked us we had to go to church every Sunday for a month. He was a parish priest at St Margaret Mary on Exeter Street which is sort of the dividing line between Brighton Beach and Manhattan Beach. Well, I was cocky enough to want to be a big shot, you know, to be the first kid on my block to beat up a Mick priest, so I said, yeah. He took off his collar and I took off my shirt and we strapped on some gloves.

And he beat the crap out of me.

He knocked me down. I got up and he knocked me down again. I got up a second time and he let me have it a third time. When I tried standing up this time, my legs were like Jello. I fell flat back onto the canvas.

He grinned, 'See you Sunday.'

I snarled, 'Fuck you . . . Father!'

I reneged on going to church but I kept coming back to the PAL gym. Father Mac taught me to keep my left hand higher and to stay off my heels. I learned to jab and I learned to hook. But most of all he taught me how to throw a real deadly uppercut.

About eight months later, I got back into the ring with him and when the bell sounded I shot out of my corner. His hands were too high. I faked right and, with everything I had, landed a left uppercut smack on the bottom of his jaw, draping him across the ropes. He gave me the most flabbergasted look I have ever seen on any human being. I pointed at him with my left glove and screamed, 'Now you know that I know.' And the following Sunday I walked into St Margaret Mary and sat in the front row where he couldn't miss seeing me. It was the first time I'd gone to church since I was ten years old.

If only Hambone had an uppercut.

I watched him go a couple of rounds with one of Charlie's no-hopers. Then he and I sat with Charlie for a little while to talk about his upcoming fight with Pretty Boy Davey McGraw, a kid from south London who had a pair of very fast hands. Charlie wondered if I'd invest a few quid in a friend of his named Moe Moses who specialized in getting guys up for a big fight. Charlie swore he could make a difference. I'd never met him but I'd heard about him and from what I'd heard, I wasn't a big Moe Moses fan. Anyway, I didn't have the spare change. I said I'd have to think about it.

By the time I left Charlie's, it was around one thirty. Not having eaten for two days I was famished, so I strolled back to One Hung's, found a seat at the round table in the kitchen and worked my way through a plate of lemon chicken and a huge bowl of crab meat soup. I kept asking myself, does Hambone really have what it takes? After lunch, I thought about checking in on Giovanni, maybe having an espresso with him, but I decided no, instead I'll have some fun and call the schmuck who's handling a claim I'd put in against British Airways for clients in the States. You know, just to bait him for a while.

Upstairs, Henry greeted me by waving an envelope in my face – 'He sent it!' – then hitting my chest with the first edition of the *Evening Standard*. 'He sent it. He really did. But wait till you see this—'

'Who did?'

'Bickerton.'

'Sent what?'

'The retainer.'

Sure enough, inside the envelope was a Barclay's Bank cheque made out to me for £1,000. It was drawn on the account of Dr L. Roger Bickerton at a branch in Brighton. There was nothing else in the envelope.

'He sent it. But wait until you see . . .'

'No note. No nothing.' I told her, 'Call information and ask if there's anyone listed in Brighton with his name.'

'You can't phone him.' Henry pushed the newspaper at me. 'And he won't be phoning you again, either.'

She was pointing to a small article on page two. The headline announced 'Scientist Missing – Apparent Suicide'. The story read, 'Dr L. Roger Bickerton, former head of the European Research Project's Eastbourne Laboratories, has apparently committed suicide by taking an overdose of sleeping pills, then jumping into the sea on the Channel Island of Guernsey. His car was found early this morning abandoned on a cliff at Point de la Moye, on the southern tip of the island. According to police there, a note was located inside the car alongside an empty bottle of sleeping pills. Dr Bickerton became an outspoken critic of Government cutbacks in science and technology when he was made redundant six months ago. His body has not been found.'

'Jeeezus.' I carried the cheque and the newspaper into my office and threw myself into my chair. 'A guy I don't know phones me, wants to put me on a retainer, sends me a cheque and kills himself.'

Henry was standing in the doorway. 'What do we do now?'

I looked at my watch. It was two forty. 'What we do now,' I said, as if it should be obvious, 'is deposit this before the bank closes.'

Chapter Three

When I got home there was a message on my machine from Greta. All it said was, 'Dinner?'

So I rang her at the gallery and when she answered all I said was, 'Salmon steaks and garlic pasta.'

She answered, 'Garlic at your peril.'

I said, 'I'll take my chances,' and when I hung up I ran out to the supermarket to buy salmon, fresh garlic and a bottle of mouthwash.

In weaker moments I sometimes thought that Greta Eccleston and I were a number, but whenever I asked her if we were, she'd insist, 'We're not a number, we're simply two old friends who sometimes share a rucksack.'

I'd remind her, 'It's called a sleeping bag.'

She'd remind me, 'We don't sleep.'

We met about seven years ago when she was working at Christie's auction house in the furniture department. I never bought any chairs from her – she was way out of my league – but we got to know each other and long before we started discussing rucksacks, she was already offering me a professional discount to entice me to put some of my chairs up for sale. She left Christie's about a year later to manage Rose-Morrow Fine Arts on Cork Street and there, too, she was friendly enough to say that I could have whatever I wanted at the usual dealer's discount. Except, I don't understand modern art and the only thing I collect, besides chairs, is souvenir mugs.

She's a nice-looking woman, an inch taller than me, with dark blonde hair and one of those square-cut Scandinavian faces. She once told me that her grandmother was Danish, although Greta was born and raised in England. Anyway, where I come from

Danish means prune pastry. Probably no more than a couple or three years younger than me – I never asked her age and she never volunteered it – she'd dumped her husband somewhere along the line. He had something to do with pension funds and now, apparently, lives in the Dordogne in France with his teenaged secretary and her only slightly older mother. I know she's got a son who's a doctor and a daughter who's married. God only knows, she might even be a grandmother. But we don't get personal about stuff like that, even though we get extremely personal about other things.

Not that I wouldn't mind meeting her kids, it's just that she's always wanted to keep that side of her life to herself. And I guess that's okay with me. She's defined the way we maintain our friendship and I like her company enough not to want to let anything get in the way of that. In fact, we've been very careful about our friendship right from the beginning. I must have known her for two or three years, and been out to dinner with her fifty times before it ever dawned on me that maybe she was waiting for me to take things to the next step. I kept telling myself, there's nothing broken here so why fix it? I guess, looking back, she felt the same way because the day I phoned her at the gallery and suggested we change things, she was just as surprised as I was to hear myself suggest it.

As soon as she picked up the phone I asked, 'How long have we known each other?'

She didn't recognize my voice. 'Who's this?'

'It's me,' I said. 'So how long have we known each other?'

'Oh, hello, you.'

'Hello, you too. Now, how long have we known each other?'

'What a funny question. I don't know. How's two years, four months and three days? Why?'

'Because I think it's time we had an affair.'

She laughed. 'You mean, right away? In my office? What about all those people walking by on Cork Street?'

'Stop joking.'

'Aren't you?'

'No,' I said. 'I'm not. You're the woman I most want to have an affair with.'

'Oh . . .' She dared, 'When?'

'Tonight? Tomorrow night? Whenever you want. My place. Your place. Wherever you want.'

She couldn't help but giggle. 'How about in the middle of the afternoon in some third-rate hotel?'

'It is the middle of the afternoon,' I reminded her. 'Hold on for just a few seconds, while I look in the Yellow Pages under sleazy hotels.'

She came back with, 'They're probably all booked at this hour.'

'Then let's go to Claridge's.'

'You know what?' she told me, 'I like you when you're silly.'

But I needed her to understand. 'I'm serious. Come to my place after work.'

'To see your etchings?'

'I don't have any etchings.'

'Well, then, to see your chairs?'

'No. To have an affair.'

'Can we have a drink first?'

'And dinner first, too.'

'Oh. Drinks and dinner and an affair. Sounds like quite a programme.'

I told her, 'See you at eight thrity.'

She showed up at quarter to nine. 'My mother always lectured me that a lady must never appear to be over-anxious.'

I handed her a glass of champagne. 'Here's to our affair.'

'Oh yes, our affair.' We clinked glasses. 'Actually, if we were going to have an affair, well, we should have had it a long time ago. Right when we first met. That's when affairs are best. The first time you meet.'

I reminded her, 'We met in a crowded auction room between lots 106 and 107. Just imagine how expensive it could have gotten if the auctioneer mistook passionate groans for a secret bidding signal.'

'Sold to the lady on her back at the side of the room.' She took a long sip.

I suggested, 'We've known each other long enough now.'

'But we're friends.'

'Isn't that to our advantage?'

'Well . . .' She shrugged. 'I'm not sure. Sometimes I think it would be more exciting, more passionate to have an affair with a perfect stranger.'

'You mean like someone you meet changing planes in Kansas City?'

Her eyes opened wide. 'Did you?'

'Wishful thinking,' I conceded. 'Anyway, affairs with strangers are out of the question at my age. I suffer from xenophobia.'

'Inflammation of the what?'

'No, that would be xeno-itis. This is phobia, fear of.'

'Fear of xenos?' She assured me, 'If I ever saw one, I'd be absolutely petrified.'

'Xeno,' I explained, 'is Greek or Hungarian or Latin for foreigner.'

'Strikes me that Greeks and Hungarians and Latins are foreigners. Need I add, so are you.'

'Except in Athens, Budapest, the Vatican . . .' I bowed, 'and Brooklyn.'

She asked, 'Why are you afraid of Hungarians?'

'Foreigners meaning strangers,' I said. 'Like in France. Everyone thinks the French hate tourists. Not true. They're xenophobic. They hate everybody they don't know, even other French people.'

'Now you're adding French people to the group.'

'Only foreign French people.'

'Well then . . . if strangers are out of the question,' she said, 'why didn't we sneak off just after we met? When we were no longer strangers? Or, why didn't you come along while I was still married? That's supposed to be the most exciting.'

I stared at her. 'Is it?'

She paused. 'You probably won't believe this . . . but I never had an affair while I was married. Did you?'

'No.'

'Honestly?'

'Honestly. Louise . . . my wife . . . she did, but I didn't. Frankly, when I look back, I don't know why I didn't. Except, I guess, I never got around to it.'

'Too old-fashioned,' she said. 'Although . . . maybe if we'd had an affair while we were married it would have saved both our marriages.'

'You mean, together?'

She smiled coyly. 'Alone may be more convenient but together is better.'

We finished the bottle of champagne, I started making the smoked salmon pasta and, when I suggested a second bottle of champagne, she said, sure, why not. She set the table in the kitchen and I lit a candle. We ate our pasta and drank our champagne and every time I looked at her, she smiled.

'You're laughing at my pasta.'

'You're a good cook.'

'I'm Italian. Of course I'm a good cook. So why are you laughing at my pasta?'

'I'm not,' she assured me. 'I'm laughing at you.'

'What did I do?'

'You've thought of everything, except violin music.'

'Itzhak Perlman was already booked.' I shrugged, 'Maybe I should have asked my neighbour for advice.'

'Why? Does she play the violin?'

'No. She just has affairs.'

'How do you know?'

'I use the word affairs casually. For all I know she plays world-class gin rummy. It's just that I see loads of men hanging around at all sorts of hours.'

'You're such a gossip.'

'It's intellectual research,' I pretended. 'You see, I have a theory. I think that everyone thinks that other people always do it more than they do. Like my lady neighbour. She's an overly hormonal twenty-five-year-old, so I reckon that she . . . you know . . . has more affairs that I do. In fact, I'm convinced she's doing it all the time. Especially when I'm sitting here watching television, wishing I was having an affair.' I gave her my best pout. 'Then again, she might be thinking I'm having affairs all the time, especially when she's sitting home watching television, wishing she was having an affair.'

'Or playing over-hormonal gin rummy.'

'That's right,' I said. 'So if my theory holds true, it could mean that no one's having any affairs at all.'

'That's your theory?' She started to laugh. 'When I was in school, my best friend Nicola . . . well, I always thought Nicola was the hottest number alive. Just after I got married, she confessed to me that she thought I was.'

'And neither one of you was, right?'

She made a face. 'Wrong. She really was. I was too scared.'

I nodded firmly. 'Proves my theory.'

'No it doesn't.'

I refilled her glass. 'No, I suppose it doesn't.'

We finished dinner and sat right where we were, with the candle casting long flickering shadows against the white tile walls. 'Let's have an affair,' I said.

'Oh yes, our affair.'

'Tell me, without thinking, right off the top of your head, three things you'd want to find in the perfect affair.'

'Only three?'

'You tell me the first three things on your list and we'll see if they match the first three things on my list.'

'All right.' She toyed with her glass then took a sip. 'Let's see . . . my three are . . . a man who likes to make love on rainy Sunday afternoons instead of watching football. And someone who likes to make love outside at night, you know, in a field somewhere. And . . . why not . . . making love to a total stranger.' She stopped. 'Now you.'

I nodded. 'Okay. My three things are . . . one, someone who likes roses. Two, someone who adores jazz piano, you know, like Teddy Wilson. And three, someone who loves to cuddle in a soapy bathtub by candlclight.'

She was surprised. 'What a romantic.'

'What's wrong with romance?'

'*Au contraire*.'

I purred, 'I love it when you talk dirty, like that.'

'I just never figured you for being such a softy.'

'Sorry.' I confessed, 'I wouldn't watch a soccer match in bed on a rainy Sunday afternoon. But I would watch boxing. Personally, I'd rather make love on Sunday morning. You know, put some moody Tony Bennett music on the stereo, and then have breakfast afterwards. Or even during. As long as you don't mind sausages rolling into your slippers and scrambled eggs doing terrible things to your pillows.'

She cut in, 'Sounds to me like during is out.'

'I'm afraid,' I went on, 'so is making love in a field. I'd forever be worried about someone walking a dog. Or a buffalo stampede.'

'How about,' she wondered, 'making love on a beach?'

'You mean like Coney Island on a Sunday in July?'

'Well then, how about at night? Along the water's edge?'

'What, and drown when the tide comes in?'

She toyed with her glass. 'Why did you ring me today?'

'Because I want to have an affair with you.'

'But our ideas of what constitutes the perfect affair don't match at all.'

Eventually I conceded, 'Maybe not.'

For the longest time we sat there not talking.

She was the one to break the silence. 'It probably wouldn't work, you know.'

There was another long silence before I said, 'We're different, you and me. We started off by being friends.'

She said, 'I wouldn't want to spoil that friendship.'

And I said, 'Neither would I.'

She reached over to the candle, to get some wax that was dripping onto the table.

I poured what was left of the champagne into our glasses, then touched my glass to hers. 'Here's to friendship first.'

She took a sip. 'It's getting late.'

I smiled and told her, 'I'll call a taxi.'

But she didn't move. 'It could ruin our friendship.'

'Well . . .' I had to admit, 'It would definitely change our friendship.'

She stared at me. 'It's late.' Then she wanted to know, 'Instead of ringing for a taxi, would you walk me home?'

'Yes.'

'Why?'

'If that's what you want . . . that's what friends are for.'

'And if we were kids in school,' she asked, 'would you carry my books?'

'Happily. All of them.'

'And if we were lovers . . .' her voice got very soft, 'would we still be friends?'

I told her quietly, 'I hope so.'

She took a deep breath and slowly stood up. 'Have you got more candles? This one is burning down.'

I took her hand and, just like friends, we went into my bedroom.

I was still racing around trying to clean up before she got there when the bell rang.

'A present,' she said, smiling, when I opened the door. 'Close your eyes.'

I did.

First she kissed me softly on the lips, then said, 'Now open.' I thought she meant my mouth, so I kept my eyes shut and showed her my tonsils.

'No. Look.' She was holding a souvenir mug a few inches in front of my nose. 'Like it?'

'Hey.' There were three broad stripes – blue, black and white – and written in gold in the middle stripe was Tallinn – 1219. 'This is terrific.' The weirder the place the more I liked it. 'Where the hell is Tallinn?'

She came inside and I shut the door behind her. 'Estonia.'

'That makes everything perfectly clear,' I said. 'And what happened there in 1219?'

'It was destroyed by the Danes.'

'This is something they celebrate?'

'They don't make up mugs for just any old occasion.'

'How come you know so much?'

'Geography and history are my best qualities.'

I put my arm over her shoulder and assured her, 'Frankly, those are not the first things that come to mind.'

I served the garlic pasta – and made a point of putting the mouthwash on the table next to it – then the grilled salmon. She talked about the gallery and I told her I had my eye on a George the First walnut veneered armchair – 'It's great, with carved cabriole legs and ball and claw feet' – and after dinner, after we did the dishes together, she crawled into my arms and whispered, 'Take me to bed.'

Later, as she lay next to me, she whispered, 'Nine hundred quid.'

I told her, 'You're expensive but worth every penny.'

'Your chair, you idiot.'

'Oh.' I pretended to be surprised, then suggested, 'I was right.'

'About what?'

'Geography and history.'

She slowly moved her hand along my stomach. 'I know the difference between north and south.'

'You seem to.'

'I was very good at geography.'

'How good?'

'This good?'

'All right, so let's have a geography quiz. What about Guernsey?'

She gave me a strange look. 'I'm trying to get romantic again, and you ask me about Guernsey?' She put her face up to my ear and went, 'Mooo.'

'Not the cows, the place.'

'What are you talking about?'

'I've never been there.'

'Me neither. But why . . .'

'I guess, 'cause I never got around to it . . .'

'Not, why haven't you ever been to Guernsey? But, why are you thinking about that now? Does it have anything to do with a sudden lack of blood in the brain . . . ?'

'No . . . it's a client . . . I don't know, it just sort of dawned on me to ask. How far away is it?'

She shook her head. 'My husband used to ask me to talk dirty. You want me to talk geography.'

I opened my eyes wide and grinned. 'Try me.'

She lifted the sheets to peek under them as she told me, 'It's the Channel Islands. You can fly there. I'd guess it takes about an hour.'

'How would you drive there?'

'You wouldn't. I mean, you obviously couldn't drive across the English Channel, but there are ferries . . .'

'So it's not exactly the easiest place to get to.'

'Speaking of easy places to get to . . .' She moved closer.

'I was just hoping you knew something about it.'

By this time she was under the sheets. 'This is north . . . and this is south.' She asked, 'Your geography quiz . . . am I passing?'

I easily convinced her, 'With flying colours.'

Chapter Four

Greta offered to drop me off. It was part of her routine. The first few times she stayed over I'd suggested I go with her to Cork Street and walk to my office from there. Except, she never wanted me to do that and never told me why. So now each time she stayed over, I got out on Regent Street.

I gave her a peck on the cheek goodbye – 'Thanks for the mug' – and cut around Broadwick Street, stopping at a newsagent's to pick up a stack of papers. I expected to find an obit somewhere on Bickerton. But there was nothing in the *Mail* or the *Guardian*. The *Telegraph* and the *Independent* both had blurbs in the news section saying that his car had been found with a suicide note inside, but neither went into very great detail about him. So I turned to *The Times*, convinced that if an obit was going to be anywhere it would be there because people were always dying in *The Times* who never seemed to die in other papers.

And, sure enough, there it was.

Dr L. Roger Bickerton, the 58 year-old-scientist, was the head of the European Research Project's Eastbourne Laboratories until six months ago. Born in London, Bickerton had a successful academic career, first at Cambridge, then at the Haute Ecole des Etudes Scientifiques in Paris where he published a radically revisionist study of the statistical analysis which formed the basis of Gregor Johann Mendel's controlled pollination experiments. He was rewarded by being named assistant to the late Professor Etienne Cesari whose work at the Institut Pasteur secured his international reputation. Bickerton however remained in Cesari's shadow until his mentor's death in 1980. Following a failed marriage,

Bickerton returned to England in 1981 to spend three years as director of the Nestlé-Needham Laboratory at Cambridge before being appointed head of the Eastbourne Laboratories. Highly acclaimed inside a relatively small branch of the scientific community and virtually unknown in wider circles, for much of the past two years, Bickerton had been critical of Government cutbacks in scientific research funding, a stance which resulted in his early retirement at the end of last year. Under the heading of 'Forced Resignation' he described his departure from the ERP in a letter published in the *New Scientist* as 'a bitter personal defeat'. Those sentiments were echoed in the note reportedly found in Bickerton's car at Point de la Moye, Guernsey, Channel Islands, where the police are labelling his death a suicide. His body has not yet been recovered from the sea.

That was all. No photo. Nothing else. I didn't understand what he did for a living but at least now I knew where he went to college.

At the office, I handed the obit to Henry. 'Look what I found in *The Times*.'

She yelped, 'Crikey,' and followed me into my room. 'Now what do we do?'

'About what?'

'About your client.'

I reminded her, 'You mean, my late client. What do you want me to do?'

'How about trying to find out who this bloke is?'

'Was,' I corrected. 'And as long as his cheque clears, I figure I already know as much about him as I'm going to.'

She stared at me.

Instead of getting into a lengthy discussion with her, I reached for my active cases folder and read out loud the label on the first file. 'Michael and Paulette Hartley v. British Airways.'

'What about the reason he hired you?'

I found the lawyer's name and number, then grabbed my phone hoping she'd take the hint. 'If he calls again ask him.' But as soon as I said that, I forgot the lawyer's number. So I started to dial my own because I knew if I hung up she'd take it to mean that we could keep talking.

'And you preach to me about responsibility.' Turning on her heels, she walked out of my office and slammed the door shut.

Supermarkets are a wonderful place to meet people, especially fellow Americans because Americans talk to strangers in supermarkets, which is how I met Michael Hartley.

It was a few years ago in my local Safeway. I was buying tuna fish. Hartley wondered why I preferred tuna in oil instead of tune in brine. I said because oil is good for your heart. He said he preferred brine because fish don't swim in oil, they swim in salt water. That started us talking. It turned out he was from Tennefly, New Jersey, sent to London by a company that imported European electronic goods. I told him my ex-old lady lived in New Jersey, that my boy was growing up just outside Patterson and, of course, he knew the area well. So after he took a few cans of tuna in brine, I handed him my card and said, if you ever need a Yank lawyer in Britain, call me.

The next thing I heard from him was last month when he sent me a fax about this problem he and his wife were having with British Airways. They had a confirmed booking London to Chicago and got bounced. Adding insult to injury, BA charged them overweight for showing up with five suitcases, but never bothered to bounce the suitcases. Somehow, three of their suitcases wound up in New Zealand and the other two were sent to Rio.

It reminded me of the old joke of the man checking in for a flight to New York. He tells the person behind the counter, I want this bag to go to Los Angeles, this bag to go to Buenos Aires and this bag to go to Hong Kong. The clerk says, that's impossible, sir, you're flying with us to New York. And the guy says, yeah well, last time I flew with you to New York this bag went to Los Angeles, this bag went to Buenos Aires and this bag went to Hong Kong.

To make the Hartleys' experience all the more complete, only four of their five bags ever reappeared and when they did, they were half empty. The locks had been ripped off and several things were missing, including some important family papers. Of course, the airline denied any liability. They always do. The only compensation the claims' department was willing to make, besides repairing the damaged bags, was the standard pittance they hand out, based on weight, regardless of the actual value of any missing items.

A lowly assistant wrote to the Hartleys, explaining that because they checked in five bags, ownership of the fifth bag would have to be assigned either to husband or wife. He conceded that the overweight payment would be reimbursed. However, the missing bag would be deemed to be part of the designated passenger's fourty-four-pound limit – despite the fact that the airlines have pretty much done away with the weight limit across the Atlantic, in favour of simply permitting two bags per passenger – and the amount of the airline's liability would then be appropriately *pro rata*, because that's what it says in some obscure international treaty that was signed in the days when flying boats were only just making it across the pond faster than Lindbergh.

It was pure double-talk.

The airline was also contending that because the Hartleys had not provided a detailed list of the contents of each checked bag or in any way arranged to insure those contents separately before checking in, they could not pay for anything allegedly taken out of the bags while in transit. Although the lowly assistant 'deeply regretted' any inconvenience, he said he felt certain that 'the enclosed cheque for £298.60 is fair and just compensation'. The last paragraph of his letter pointed out, 'Therefore, no further action will be taken by us in this matter.'

In other words, take it or leave it.

Well, I have a singular aversion to being bullied. Furthermore, I don't believe that everything in life can be so neatly boiled down to two options. So when a big company gives me that take it or leave it crap, I remind them that there's a third choice which goes, I'm about to shove it up your butt.

Not a lot has changed since my days in Brooklyn, except now I wear ties.

Hartley was savvy enough not to cash the airline's cheque and instead got in touch with me. I wrote one polite letter stating the grounds for Hartley's claim, and got a polite form letter back from some in-house lawyer named Whitten, restating his company's refusal to consider a bigger payout. I then wrote a not-so-polite letter, informing Mr Whitten that the Hartleys were represented by an American lawyer who had no intention of suing them in Britain but would kick ass in the States where juries hate airlines.

Last week, I guess it was Tuesday, I got a letter from Whitten, who was 'extremely pleased' to inform me that BA had decided that, in this instance, a goodwill gesture was appropriate. Although he insisted that the airline was in no way acknowledging liability, considering its desire to maintain a warm relationship with frequent fliers such as the Hartleys, enclosed was a cheque for £350 to settle all claims, past present and future.

Again, cash it and the game is over.

I returned the cheque by messenger with a note that read, 'You're joking. And just in case you doubt our intentions, you have five working days to make a realistic offer before I file suit.'

On Friday morning, a conference call came in from Whitten and some fellow named Drummond who introduced himself as a senior commercial manager for international client affairs.

Because I believe that, generally speaking, the bigger a man's title the smaller his genitals, I treated him accordingly. 'The only thing my clients are interested in,' I said, 'is your money.'

'We take a more pragmatic view.' He explained, 'We're interested in our continuing relationship with our clients.'

'Same thing,' I said. 'It's called, pay up and keep a friend.'

'That is precisely what we are doing. And I believe that £350 is fair compensation, all things considered.'

'All things considered,' I reminded him, 'two of your five days are gone.'

He paused for a moment, then suggested, 'Mr Barolo, I repeat that we are concerned about our relationship with the Hartleys, so, all right, in the name of additional goodwill, we would be willing to throw in enough Air Miles to give the Hartleys each an upgrade to Club Class on their next full fare economy class trans-Atlantic ticket. I sincerely hope you will agree that this is an amicable settlement. But I am afraid that this is our final offer.'

'No kidding!' I reached into my top drawer to turn on the tape recorder that is hooked up to my phone. 'Final offer, huh?' I love that line because it's about as meaningful as a teenage boy

promising his girlfriend, we don't have to go all the way. 'Oh . . .
what the hell.' I needed to separate Drummond from Whitten.
'I know you guys are under a lot of commercial pressure.' I put
on my most sympathetic voice. 'I suspect you must get this stuff
all the time. I know it's not easy. You're in a very competitive
market, so you want to do the right thing.'

'We certainly are,' Drummond said. 'And we certainly do.'

This was a good game – I loved it – called divide and conquer.
'Well . . . listen . . . I have to agree that the easiest thing would
be to settle amicably. I mean, I'm sure we all have better things
to do with our time. And maybe if we stay friends . . . well, you
understand . . . maybe next time I fly to the States I won't
put me next to the numskull with the lasso tie. You know the
guy I mean?'

Drummond forced a polite laugh. 'I do believe I have
seen him.'

I dangled the bait. 'Yeah . . . but neither of you have to sit
next to him because both you guys get upgraded. I mean, you
guys fly first class, right? Apparently, passengers in first class
get very good service.'

He took it. 'Mr Barolo, something tells me we can indeed
settle this in a mutually acceptable manner.'

Whitten cut in, 'I think we're getting off the track . . .'

'A lot more legroom up in first class. Better food, too.' I tried
not to overplay my part and sound too naive.

Drummond must have figured he was dealing with a sucker
because he started using big words. 'Mr Barolo, indeed there are
certain amenities we are occasionally inclined to make available
to various preferred clientele. If, the next time you fly to the
States, you'd be interested in discovering just how good our
first class service is, perhaps you would give me a ring . . .'

What fun. 'Are you saying I could become part of that
preferred clientele?'

'I'll let you have you my direct line so that . . .'

Whitten tried again. 'Perhaps we should settle the Hartleys'
claim . . .'

'I think that's what Mr Barolo and I are doing.' The
senior commercial manager for international client affairs was
obviously a take-control kind of guy . . . which was exactly the
wrong tactic in a contest like this. 'Because you're being so
reasonable about this . . . and I personally appreciate that . . .

here's what I'm prepared to do. If the Hartleys will settle for
£350 plus the appropriate Air Miles to assure their upgrade,
and you would be gracious enough to accept from us an upgrade
to first class on your next trans-Atlantic flight . . .'

'I'm afraid that . . .' The solicitor was increasingly nervous.
'I think we have to keep these things totally separate . . .'

'Aw, come on, fellas . . . if you can just come up with a few
more dollars. I'm in a spot here. You see, my clients already
said no to £350 and if I'm going to convince them to accept
a settlement, which I would like to do . . .'

Drummond wanted to know, 'How much is a few?'

'Gee . . . I don't know . . .' This wasn't a fair fight because
both of them were still wearing short pants until they got their
driver's licence. 'You're putting me in a tight spot. Why don't
you just tell me what you think would be equitable for . . .' I
stressed, ' . . . you know, for everybody concerned.'

I could hear Whitten cup the phone, trying to warn off
his client.

But Drummond was the sort of fool who thought he knew
better than his lawyer. 'I'm sure we could stretch it to £400.'

'Hmmm . . .' I calculated out loud, 'Let's see . . . that's, what,
just over . . . $600?' Then I wondered, 'How many pounds
is $750?'

Whitten said, 'I think we really need to stick to . . .'

Again, Drummond cut him off. 'Is that what it will take to
settle this?' He paused to tap the numbers into his calculator.
'Just shy of £500.'

'Do you think that would be asking too much?'

'Shall we round it up to that?'

'We've come a long way, you and me, Mr Drummond. So . . .
you're offering £500, plus the upgrade miles for them, and if
they accept that, what did you say you'd do for me?'

'No, wait,' Whitten insisted, 'this just isn't . . .'

'What I said was . . .' I could hear from Drummond's voice
that he was already gloating with victory, ' . . . if your clients
will settle for £500 plus the Air Miles that will give them an
upgrade to Club Class, I will throw in an upgrade to first class
for you the next time you fly to the States.' Now he lowered
his voice, as if he was letting me in on a secret. 'I will even
give you the name of a consolidator, you know, a bucket shop,
where you can get the cheapest ticket on the market. Then,

you let me know when you want to fly and I'll book you in first both ways.'

'You have to understand,' Whitten was desperate, 'only the cash and the Hartleys' Air Miles can be written into the settlement agreement and anything else you discuss with Mr Drummond is strictly between you and him.'

'This isn't going to be one of those space-available things . . . you know, my upgrade. I can fly any time I want and the upgrade is good?'

Drummond answered, 'As long as the Hartleys settle this now, your upgrade is assured.'

I asked Whitten, 'And a settlement on those terms would be acceptable to you?'

He hesitated. 'Well . . . let me say that . . . I can only put into writing . . .'

'Aw . . . come on guys, I need to be perfectly clear what the deal is.'

Drummond said, 'You can expect written confirmation this afternoon.'

'However,' Whitten persisted, 'said written confirmation will not contain anything in addition to the settlement with the Hartleys.'

'So how do I know if I get the upgrade?'

'You can take my word for it,' Drummond said. 'If your clients settle it this way, right here, right now, you will be taken care of. That's the deal.'

The last step was to make certain that the solicitor was okay with this. 'Mr Whitten? Is it a deal?'

He agreed, quietly, 'Yes, it is.'

That's when I went with my uppercut. 'Actually, fellas, I suggest you take your £500 offer and add another zero. And when I hang up, Mr Drummond, ask your lawyer to define the term corrupt solicitation. By the way, did I mention that my phone conversations are taped? Gee, I'm sorry, it must have slipped my mind. I don't know if any of this will stand up in a British court, but I'm sure it won't do much for your job security or your learned friend's reputation with the Law Society. You see, it's illegal for him to be party to any deal like this. And he just was. So I'll expect your cheque for £5,000 to settle the claim, with no other stipulations, on my desk within three days. Otherwise, guys, see you in an

American court with an American jury. Oh . . . and . . . have a nice day.'

The two on the other end of the line were furious. But that was their problem. Anyway, with my one-third cut of the settlement I could pay for my own upgrades.

So now their three days were up.

I dug through the Hartley file again and dialled Whitten's direct line. As soon as he answered, I said, 'I suppose you explained the facts of life to your pal Drummond.'

He knew who I was right away. 'What do you want?'

I chided, 'It can't be my charm, so it must be my accent. I still haven't seen your cheque.'

'I have nothing whatever to discuss with you. Your tactics are absolutely repugnant. I have reviewed the matter with the other solicitors in my office and we are of the unanimous opinion that if you were a British solicitor . . .'

'But I'm not. And your time is up.'

I could feel the animosity oozing out of the phone. 'I believe a cheque was posted to you yesterday afternoon.'

'The old it's-in-the-mail trick, huh? Well . . . that's all right, Whitten, I trust you.'

Getting even for my client was the purpose of the exercise.

'I assure you the feeling is not mutual.'

Sticking it to an airline made victory all the sweeter. 'See you around the Law Society . . .'

He slammed down the phone.

'Gotcha!' I said out loud in triumph. 'Henry?' I shouted, 'Henry . . .'

'I'm Delia.' She came in waving a large manila envelope. 'And wait till you see what just arrived in the post.'

'Five grand?'

'How did you know?'

I took it from her and read a letter from Whitten which stipulated that the enclosed payment was being made without accepting responsibility for any loss or damage to the Hartleys' goods and as a final settlement for all claims in this matter. There was a lot of legal mumbo jumbo – after all, the poor guy had to do something for his pay cheque – but there was no mention anywhere of frequent flier miles for the Hartleys. Oh well, Whitten and Drummond had to save face somehow.

It was too early to phone Hartley in New Jersey and tell him the good news and until he said okay, I couldn't cash the cheque. So I shoved it in the little safe under my desk, sorted through the rest of the mail – nothing of any interest – and phoned Charlie. 'Hambone show up today?'

'Yeah, he's here.'

'Okay, I'm on my way over. Then I'm going to Giovanni's, I'm celebrating. You want to come along?'

'Who'd you beat?'

'British Airways. KO. Second round.'

'It's got to be an early one because I've got the accountant in today.'

'If you've got an accountant it means you're making too much money which means you're overcharging me. I'll be there.' I told Henry I was going out for lunch.

'It's only ten thirty in the morning.'

'It's an early lunch.'

'What about Bickerton?'

'He doesn't eat lunch any more.'

Chapter Five

I could have been a contender.

'*Chutzpah*,' he barked at me, landing a left in my face.

'What does that mean?' I ducked under his follow-up right.

'You call yourself a Brooklyn kid?' He jabbed twice and missed.

'I am a Brooklyn kid.' I moved in, trying to pin him onto the ropes.

'Then how come you don't know words like *chutzpah*?' He circled left.

'What is it, some sort of Mick expression?' I planted my feet, waiting for his left hand.

'It means guts. It means nerve.' And out of nowhere his right hand slammed into the side of my face, sending me sprawling onto the canvas. 'It means balls.'

I lay there, trying to focus my eyes as he towered over me. 'What's that word?' I somehow struggled to my feet.

He moved away, drawing me into the centre of the ring. I threw a left hand that glanced off his shoulder. And then his right crashed into my head again, and I went flying back onto the canvas.

I landed with a terrible thud.

And now my eyes wouldn't focus.

'Jeezus!' All I could see was his outline, standing there, towering over me again.

'Get up,' he called.

My legs refused to work.

He yelled at me again. 'Do that!'

I couldn't clear my head.

'The word is *chutzpah*.'

It wasn't until many years later that I understood Father Mac wasn't only teaching me how to box, he was also teaching me how to get through life.

When I was sixteen and thought about quitting school to turn pro, he wouldn't let me.

'Go back to school.'

'What for?'

'Do that!'

When I was eighteen and graduated from high school and wasn't sure what I wanted to do – and anyway didn't have the grades to get into a good college – he got me into the Navy. My dad was gone by then . . . I didn't really know him anyway . . . and my mom was weeping so much the morning I was supposed to leave that Father Mac wound up taking me over to Floyd Bennet Field, which was a small naval air station in Brooklyn. He stayed with me all morning until I got sworn in, and stayed with me all afternoon while I waited for a plane that would take about twenty of us to boot camp in Virginia.

While we were sitting around, he asked me what I was going to do when I got out of the Navy.

'What are you talking about? I just got here.'

'Now's when you should start thinking about what comes next.'

'You mean, like boxing?'

'No, I mean like college.'

'Four years is too far down the line for me to think about now.'

'No it isn't.'

I didn't want to argue with him, so I said, 'Okay, I'll think about it.'

He looked me straight in the eyes. 'Do that.'

And because I didn't want to disappoint him, I added, 'I promise.'

Boot camp wasn't as tough as I thought it would be. I hated marching and I hated all the Mickey-Mouse-like standing inspection while some jerk with white gloves strolled through the barracks looking for a speck of dust we somehow missed. But I signed up for the boot camp boxing tournament and walked away with the middleweight title.

That turned out to be a stroke of luck because the training division executive officer, Commander Kelly, had boxed at

Annapolis and he took a liking to me. Around the time when assignments started coming down, he called me into his office and informed me that the Navy intended to send me to electricians' school. I told him I didn't know anything about electricity and cared even less. He asked if I'd rather stay at the boot camp as a physical training specialist. I said it sounded better than being called Sparks, but if it meant I had to exercise all day long, I wasn't sure I wanted to do that either. He said, trust me, I said I did, and right after boot camp when all the other guys in my squadron left, I wound up becoming part of the permanent crew.

I figured Commander Kelly was just being friendly. Instead, he was getting me in shape to fight in the Training Command championships. I won the middleweight division in six rounds. Then he entered me in the Atlantic Fleet championships and I took the middleweight crown there in four rounds.

At one point, I happened to mention to Commander Kelly that I was thinking of going to college when I got out and he helped me enrol in a Navy correspondence course which got my high school average up. I finished that in six months, then took a college entrance exam. I got accepted to the Navy's college-by-correspondence programme and began with freshman English and sociology. At the same time, Commander Kelly convinced me that while I could count on the GI Bill to help finance college when I got out, I had to put some money away for a rainy day. So I went to the Credit Union and opened a savings account which I called my college fund. That first Christmas I noticed a miscellaneous deposit of $25. I figured someone must have made a mistake so I reported it to the Credit Union. They checked their records and said it had come in from someone called John MacNamee. I phoned him and asked how come a guy who'd taken a vow of poverty had a spare $25? I asked if he was helping himself to the poor box. He laughed. Then I wanted to know how he knew about my college fund account. Again he laughed. It took me a while to figure it out but the only other person who knew about that account was Commander Kelly. So I went to him and asked him how long he and Father Mac had been plotting behind my back. Now he laughed.

I have never trusted two Irishmen since.

*　　　*　　　*

I'd been on station just over a year, not counting boot camp, when Commander Kelly announced that he was putting me into the inter-service nationals. I was all for it. Then orders arrived for him. He was getting command of a ship. I told him I'd miss him. Instead of saying he'd miss me, he invited me along. Except, by this time, I wasn't sure I ever wanted to leave Virginia. I'd never been in better shape, I was boxing semi-pro in town . . . picking up fifty bucks a fight for my college fund . . . the food wasn't bad, I was really starting to enjoy my courses and I was only half a day by train from home. Even though I still had to put up with some Mickey Mouse, I was kind of a local star.

Also there was a girl in town named Rosemary who had a car and she was pretty hot stuff. She and I were shacking up on weekends and I guess, like all nineteen-year-olds, I was worried that if I moved on I'd never find another girl who did what Rosemary was willing to do.

Commander Kelly promised me that if I stuck with him I'd be the fleet champ and that before my hitch was over, I'd get a crack at the inter-service nationals. Except, there wasn't any billet on board for a physical training specialist and that meant I'd have to retrain into another field. He suggested I give electronics a shot, but that still didn't interest me. So it looked like I'd stay in Virginia, until about two days before he shoved off, when he announced that he'd gotten me assigned as a personnel clerk. I didn't know anything about personnel, and didn't know anything about being a clerk. But he said I didn't have to worry about that because he'd already done enough lying for me by filling in a whole bunch of official forms proclaiming me a trained typist. I told him I'd never typed anything in my life.

He said, 'Sign this,' and handed me a form he'd already signed that included the line 'Typing skills' and the little block ticked off 'Yes'.

I wondered if we'd get court-martialled together. He assured me we would. So I signed.

Typical of the Navy, no one ever asked again if I could type and all the time I was the ship's personnel clerk, I never had to type. I was assigned the extra duty of ship's physical training specialist and I spent most of my time getting the crew in shape.

Actually, my first four months of sea duty were spent in the shipyards in Baltimore, while the Navy turned AV-11 into AVM-1 but kept the name, the USS *Norton Sound*. She'd been commissioned in 1943 and spent World War II in the Pacific as a submarine tender. Later they converted her into a seaplane carrier. In 1949 the 'Snortin' Norton' was transformed into a seagoing guided missile test platform. Now she was being equipped to test and evaluate the Typhon air defence system.

I figured we'd stay in the Atlantic and was kind of hoping we might eventually sail into the Med because I didn't know if I'd ever get to Italy any other way, but the Navy had its own ideas. With a skeleton crew, we slipped out of Baltimore on a shakedown cruise south, went through the Panama Canal, then headed up the Mexican coast to San Diego, where we picked up the rest of our crew and sat for two months waiting for the Typhon missile guys. In the meantime, I won the San Diego Naval Training Centre middleweight championship. I never went more than two rounds in any of the six elimination contests that got me into the finals, although the day before the last fight, a couple of salty old Chiefs – leftovers from World War II suggested that it would be a friendly gesture on my part if the fight went exactly six rounds. I was odds-on favourite, which meant they'd get next to nothing for betting with me. And even though the other guy was an okay fighter, he was a hothead and the worst thing a fighter can do is lose his temper because when his temper goes, his control goes with it. So they weren't going to win anything betting on him. The base bookies were saying it would be over in three. However, round six was coming in at 5–2.

At first, the Chiefs hinted I could expect part of their action if it went six. Then they said they weren't asking me, they were telling me. That's when I went straight to Commander Kelly. He said if I could prove my case, the Chiefs would wind up court-martialled. I said I had no way of proving it, except to let the fight go six and take whatever hand-out they felt I was entitled to. Or, I could finish the fight in under six and maybe get my legs broken. He said, there's a third alternative, which is to fight your best fight and challenge them to take their best shot.

So that's what I did.

I climbed into the ring on the night, waited for the first

round bell, flew out of my corner – just like Louis going after Schmeling – screamed out loud, 'Welcome to round six,' and knocked the poor bastard out with my second punch.

The Chiefs were still looking for me a few weeks later, but by that time the USS *Norton Sound* was chugging west on our way to Hawaii.

Father Mac kept writing to me about life back home, about my mom – she wasn't feeling so good but he said the doctors were taking care of her and he checked in on her whenever he could – and reminded me that no matter how difficult it might be to keep the faith in the midst of temptation, he was counting on me to remember what it meant to be a good Catholic.

I wrote, I go to Mass.

He wrote back, that's not the only thing I'm talking about.

Of course, I knew exactly what he was talking about. But I couldn't tell him that in San Diego I'd met a Mexican girl named Juanita who knew even more than Rosemary and in Hawaii there was a girl named Martina who didn't know what Juanita knew but almost.

Father Mac also asked in his letters if I was going to confession.

I told him, 'There's no priest on board.'

He reminded me, there were plenty of priests in San Diego, and there were plenty in Hawaii, too.

I told him, 'I'll try not to let you down.'

He answered, 'Try not to let yourself down.'

Even though I forgot about confession more often than I remembered, and didn't always make it to Mass, the following Christmas another $25 deposit showed up in my college fund.

There wasn't much Mickey Mouse on board ship because staying afloat and staying alive was a full-time job. But the Navy was still too clubby for my taste.

A lot of the guys liked hanging out together. In Virginia they went to bars together and got drunk together. In San Diego they went down to Tijuana together and picked up whores. It was the same thing in Hawaii, a lot of drinking and whoring. But I was getting it on regularly with Martina and when I wasn't with her I was digging into my correspondence courses. I was also sparring a lot. So instead of hanging out with the guys, I just went about doing my own thing. Except, some of the guys

resented it and every now and then one of them would try it
on with me, accusing me of being the current Mrs Commander
Kelly. In the beginning I refused to let it get to me. But after we
left Pearl Harbor and set sail for the Gulf of Tonkin, I finally
got fed up. I put out an open invitation to the ship's crew to
settle scores. I said I'd step into the ring with any one of them,
regardless of what weight they were. No one came forward. So
I extended the invitation to any two of them, any weight and
at the same time. Again, there were no takers. Which, looking
back, was probably just as well.

But the ribbing stopped.

We spent the next seven months, three weeks and two days
in the Gulf of Tonkin. The rocket crew kept firing Typhons
all over the place, although none of us ever saw any real action.
At least, no one shot back at us. Except, I did see a helluva lot
of other ships sailing past and tens of thousands of airplanes
screaming over our heads.

I won the Pacific Fleet championships in seven rounds and
the inter-service South-east Asian championship in nine. I got
to visit the Philippines and Japan. When we were scheduled
to rotate home, Commander Kelly announced that we weren't
heading back to San Diego the obvious way, which meant east,
we were going back 'the Navy way' which, for some inexpli-
cable reason, meant west. So I also got to visit Thailand.

We were just making ready to sail from there to Trincomalee
in Ceylon when a telegram came from Father Mac to say that
my mother was dying. Commander Kelly got me a seat on an
Air Force tanker going up to Tokyo and while I was hanging
around base ops, trying to get on the first thing smoking east,
some Air Force sergeant walked up and told me he'd seen me
box. It turned out that he was the guy drawing up the flight
manifests and when I told him about my mother, he said he'd
take care of me. Within twenty-four hours I was landing at
Travis Air Force Base near San Francisco, where the guy in
Japan had already booked me on the next plane to Washington.
But that wasn't leaving until the following morning and when I
phoned Father Mac he said there probably wasn't much time
left. He said he'd already given her last rites.

So I went commercial into Kennedy and took a taxi to
Coney Island Hospital. As I walked into my mom's room, she
opened her eyes, saw me there, gave me a big, warm smile, and

while I held her hand and told her that I loved her, she just
sailed away.

Father Mac found me standing next to her bed crying.

A few days later he and I buried her. My cousins were there
and so were my aunts and so was my only uncle, and so were
all of my mother's friends. But Father Mac's Mass wasn't for
them. It was for me and my mom, and as I sat there in the front
row looking at her coffin and listening to the way he spoke about
her, I realized it was for him too.

My Aunt Rosa said she'd take care of my mom's stuff.

And my pal Guido had a cousin who was a lawyer who knew
my mom and he said he'd consider it a privilege if I'd allow him
to settle her estate. He handled all the legal things and never sent
me a bill. Ten years later, when he got busted for fraud and I was
one of the junior guys in the Brooklyn District Attorney's office,
I worked out a plea bargain for him. It was probably a conflict of
interest and I guess I should have told my boss about it, but I
figured I owed him one. Anyway, the only thing my mom had
besides the apartment was a joint bank account – she'd put it
in her name and mine – with all the money I'd won on the ship
the night Cassius Clay beat Sonny Liston. She never spent a
penny of it.

The Navy called it compassionate leave and Commander Kelly
didn't seem too much in a hurry to have me back, so I moped
around Brooklyn with Fat and Guido. One night, Father Mac
and I went to the fights at Madison Square Garden, and on
the way back he reminded me that he was hearing confession on
Saturday afternoon. I didn't want to disappoint him, so I walked
all the way down to St Margaret Mary and waited until my time
came. I never intended to go into a lot of detail about what my
life was like, but I was willing to 'fess up to a few minor sins –
occasional sloth and temporary bouts of coveting – except, he
came right out and asked me about sex. I couldn't lie to him so
I told him yeah, that I'd had some girlfriends. He reminded me
of when I was a junior in high school and was messing around
with Frannie Lavorno who was a senior. I'd been too scared
to tell him but she was too scared not to, and named me as
the culprit. When I went to confession that following week,
he was waiting for me with both barrels. I don't think I have
ever felt so guilty about anything since. Although, even after

she confessed that first time, Frannie Lavorno and I kept doing it and I didn't worry about her soul because she wanted to keep doing it. Except, every time we did it I couldn't get it out of my head that I was letting him down. That created a lot of conflict. She felt guilty and he was disappointed and both were my fault. I kept hoping to figure out how I could have Frannie Lavorno and absolution, but to no avail. My soul was only saved when she went off to college. Although Father Mac kept me dangling on the noose a long time before he was willing to say that I'd repented.

Now I had that same uncomfortable feeling.

Instead of going into detail about Rosemary or Juanita or Martina, I told him the problem was that the Navy didn't provide enough cold showers. There was a long pause before he told me, 'I am not going to lecture you about human dignity. You're no longer fifteen years old.'

I tried joking, 'Instead of doing a lot of small confessions between now and then, can I wait until I get out of the Navy and sort of do a really colossal one?'

He didn't find that funny. 'You will have to do what your conscience tells you to do. And when the time comes you will not have to answer to me, you will have to answer to God and to yourself.'

I whispered to him, 'I'll see what I can figure out.'

He whispered back, 'Do that.'

And I walked out of there feeling so damn guilty about somehow having let him down, yet again, that I actually spent the next six months staying celibate.

Except, after a while, the Navy ran out of cold showers.

Chapter Six

Charlie Ruggiero was a contender.

Back in the mid-1960s, he showed some real promise as a welterweight and probably would have gotten a shot at some sort of title. He might even have won the British Belt, which isn't much but it's better than nothing. Except, he couldn't keep his shorts on. He'd been scheduled to fight a loser named Ringo Casey. The idea was to make it last seven or eight rounds – there was no doubt that he could have knocked him out in three but he needed the ring time – and then take a shot at the London champ, Kenny Tannenbaum. But one night after some heavy drinking, Charlie wound up in bed with Casey's wife and the next morning when Casey stumbled in – God only knows where he'd been – Ringo swore he'd kill Charlie. He got his chance in the ring. And the no-hoper with the horny wife proceeded to beat the crap out of Charlie. Apparently, Casey went home after the fight and also beat the crap out of his old lady, for which he wound up doing a year. After that he disappeared, so did Mrs Casey, and Charlie opened a gym. He never got another chance.

Every now and then he'd get some promising kid in to train there, but the really big guys – Bruno and Benn, Eubanks and Naseem – were all too young to have heard of Charlie and by the time they were coming up, the boxing game had become the boxing business. So Charlie slogged on with a second-rate gym for second-rate fighters, which didn't bother me because Hambone was better than second rate and even if Charlie had an accountant, he was *paisano* which meant his prices were negotiable. Twice I even managed to pay him in chairs. I owed him something like £450 and paid it off with a Yorkshire ladder-back armchair that he'd seen in my hallway

– his wife wanted it – and a copy of a Jacobean oak hall chair that now lived behind his desk. He got a good deal because if he had to buy those chairs today they'd cost him over a grand. I got a good deal too. They cost me £225.

'How you doing?' I banged Charlie on the back.

Almost thirty pounds heavier than he'd been in his fighting days, he had a full head of white hair and wore half-glasses that were constantly falling off his broken nose. 'Look at this kid.' He pointed to the young black guy sparring in the ring which took up most of the gym's floor. 'What do you see?'

I watched the kid dance around his sparring partner, then told Charlie, 'I see a kid who's afraid to get hit.'

He nodded slowly. 'I knew you'd say that.'

'What, you were hoping for another Sugar Ray Leonard?'

He held up both hands. 'A guy can always dream.' He pointed back to the ring. 'His name is Bingo.'

I reminded him, 'Rhymes with Ringo.'

'I wish you hadn't mentioned that.'

'Where's Hambone?'

He motioned towards the far end of the gym, where Derek was wrapped in a sweatsuit, pounding on the heavy bag. He didn't see me, so I let him pound away.

About ten minutes later, Charlie called out to someone, stopped the sparring match with Bingo and put one of his fighters into the ring with Derek.

I sat with Charlie for three rounds, both of us sprawled across the top row of the bleachers. He kept saying, if Hambone can't keep his right hand up, he's going down. And when the sparring session was over I told Charlie if Moe Moses was available, I'd stake Hambone to two weeks.

'I'll phone him,' Charlie said, and promised, 'You won't regret it.'

We waited for Hambone to shower, then the three of us walked over to Giovanni's. I had pasta, Charlie had a steak, Hambone had a steak and pasta.

'So tell us about the second round KO,' Charlie said.

'I'll go you one better. Listen to this.' And I told them both about getting a cheque from a guy who turns up dead the same day.

'Was he one of your regular clients?' Charlie asked.

'Never heard of the guy.'

'How come people I never heard of don't send me money?'
Charlie wanted to know. 'What are you doing about it?'

'What's to do?'

Hambone cut in. 'You think somebody knocked him off?
Vince, if you're in any sort of trouble, you let me know and
I'm right there for you.'

I patted him on the back. 'I'm not in any trouble. But
thanks.'

'So,' Charlie wanted to know, 'what did you do with the
cheque?'

I looked at him. 'Hey.'

'Good old Vince.' He slapped me on the back, then leaned
forward, 'Whatever keeps you amused.'

'What do you mean, amused?'

'I mean . . . you know . . . amused. You're thinking about it,
so you're amused.'

'I'm not thinking about it, I'm telling you about it.'

'Same thing,' Charlie said.

Even Hambone agreed. 'He's right, Vince. If you're talking
about it you're thinking about it and if you're thinking about
it, you're amused.'

Charlie patted Hambone on the back. 'We rest our case,
counsellor.'

I told Giovanni to bring some espresso and give me the
cheque because his friends were giving me a headache. Instead
he showed up with a bottle of grappa. He and Charlie
both downed a glass. I stuck with the coffee. Hambone
had pie.

When they left I nursed a second coffee with Giovanni, told
him the story of how some guy sent me a cheque then turned
up dead and asked him what he thought.

'You gotta know the bloke, right?'

'Wrong.'

'You sure?'

'I'm sure I never heard of the guy before.'

'That doesn't necessarily mean you don't know him.'

'Since when is logic an Italian strong point?'

He poured another grappa for himself but I begged off.
'What . . . you never met a guy and didn't know his name?'

I stared at him. I met a guy and didn't know his name.
I mumbled, 'Son of a bitch!'

'So?' Giovanni raised his glass. '*Saluto.*' He nodded. 'You figured it out, huh?'

I sat back and started to grin.

The numskull from the plane.

'Amusing?'

'What amusing?'

'You look amused.'

'What is this "amusing", the word of the week?'

When I left, instead of going back to the office, I found a taxi and took it to Fleet Street.

I wasn't amused.

I was curious.

Chapter Seven

Three weeks after my mom died, I rejoined my ship in Cape Town, South Africa. We were docked next to a British frigate and when Commander Kelly heard they had a couple of hands on board who could box, he challenged their CO to a night of it and we built a ring on the helicopter deck at the stern. For the next few days, wherever you looked, someone was making book. It meant there was going to be a pile of money riding on these fights.

The *Norton Sound* fielded seven guys but the Brits had one of their guys drop out, so when the programme got Mimeographed, there were only six listed to fight. Except I wasn't one of them. Our middleweight entry was someone called Carlo Panati.

'Who the hell is he?'

'He's boxing for us,' Commander Kelly told me.

'He's not on our ship.'

'But you are,' he said. 'They never saw you before so they don't know who you are. But they might know your name which means we'd never get any odds. So we put down someone else's name . . .'

'You mean, I'm going in as a ringer?'

He grinned. 'There are three ways of doing everything. There's the right way. There's the wrong way. And there's the Navy way.'

So Carlo Panati stepped into the ring that night a 2–1 underdog. I had a couple of bets on myself and was part of the overall ship's pool. Three rounds later I was $1,600 richer. Luckily we slipped out of port before the Brits figured out they'd been had.

There was nothing to spend the money on coming up the

African coast. Anyway, I was hoping that when we got to the Med we'd do a turn starboard and I could blow it in Italy. But Commander Kelly said Italy was out of the question. The closest I got was Casablanca, Morocco, and there wasn't much to spend it on there either, except I bought myself a camel saddle. It seemed like a good idea at the time.

From there we circled around northern Spain, and were just hugging the coast of France when one of our four huge Babcock and Wilcox boilers blew. With it went our scheduled stop in Cherbourg, which I'd been counting on because I wanted to see Paris. Instead, we limped on up to the Irish Sea and wound up sitting in a shipyard in Liverpool for nine weeks.

With nothing else to do, I checked out the local boxing scene. There was a heavyweight running around the country in those days named Henry Cooper who was talking big about someday taking on Cassius Clay. Because of him there were a lot of young hopefuls looking for their shot in all the other classes too. I could have gotten fights every week, except there was no money in it and I already had enough amateur trophies to last me. My only interest in climbing into the ring was to fatten up the college fund. But beating up some local kid just to pick up a $25 purse was no longer my idea of how to spend a Saturday night.

We had bases all over England so the USO was there too and when it looked like we were going to be in town for a while, they set up dances for us. The swinging sixties were happening, but that was in London and I was in Liverpool. The Beatles might have made the place famous, but they got smart and left. I was stuck there so I started showing up at the USO's dances.

That's how I met Louise.

She came to one of the dances with some of her girlfriends. A tall, thin fifteen-year-old redhead with dark eyes and high cheekbones, I spotted her the minute she walked in and danced with her all night. A couple of nights later she invited me to a party. We wound up in the back seat of her father's Morris where things got hot and heavy, but at the last minute she said she couldn't go all the way with me because she was a Catholic. I tried to convince her there really wasn't much difference between a triple and a home run, but she didn't understand baseball. Anyway, by that time, she was too scared to stay in the car. The next night we crawled into the back seat again and the same thing happened. It wasn't long before I was starting to think that Liverpool and I weren't made for each other, except the following week she invited me home for a Sunday lunch and introduced me to her mother and father. They were okay and they fed me pretty good and the week after that they asked me to go to church with them. I said yes, because it was kind of nice being in a country where I didn't know anyone and being invited into a family situation. Except, my back seat sessions with Louise – which were happening every night – were driving me nuts. I didn't know how, but I was sure this was all Father Mac's fault.

I did, however, learn a few things while I was hanging out in Liverpool – that underpants are knickers, that knickers are plus fours, that undershirts are vests, that vests are waistcoats, that garters are suspenders and that suspenders are braces – and all the time I kept reassuring Louise, it takes practice to master a foreign language.

Just before we left Liverpool, I took some of that money I'd won in South Africa and bought a gold chain with a gold heart hanging on it for Louise. I bought a silver picture frame for her mother and because I didn't know what her father liked, except warm beer, I gave him my camel saddle. I promised Louise I'd come back and get her as soon as I finished with the Navy. She promised she'd wait.

She was on the dock, crying, as we pulled out.

When the *Norton Sound* sailed into Baltimore and I got my mail, there were thirty letters from her.

I was twenty-two when I demobbed and I guess right up until I walked down the *Norton*'s gangplank for the final time, I had every intention of going back to Liverpool. But on the train ride up to New York I started thinking about her and me and about what I really wanted. For the first time, I wasn't sure if I was in love with her or in love with her letters or just obsessed with finishing what we'd started a hundred times in the back seat of that car.

And now I was also worried about school.

I'd been accepted at Brooklyn College and they were taking me as a second semester sophomore. I kept thinking that if I didn't show up when the new term began in ten days' time, they'd somehow cancel the deal.

By the time I arrived at my Aunt Rosa's place, I'd convinced myself that I knew what I had to do. I wrote to Louise and said I was staying in Brooklyn. I asked her to join me. Three weeks later, a letter arrived from her saying that she'd met someone else and that she wished me good luck. I thought I was prepared to handle that. Except, I was devastated. Father Mac tried to console me. Except, I wasn't in any mood to be consoled.

At one point he said, 'That's what you get for toying with your emotions, like that, and losing control of your physical dignity. And toying with her emotions too.'

I lost my temper. 'What the hell do you know about love?'

He snapped back, 'I never took a vow not to love.'

That semester, I failed economics and only barely passed English and psychology.

I wrote to Louise that I was waiting for her.

Instead of getting myself a summer job to help finance my junior year, I wound up going to summer school to keep my grades high enough so that I could stay in school.

Louise never wrote back.

The following winter I met a Jewish girl name Emma and she helped me get my grades on track. Father Mac spent a lot of time reminding me that even if Emma wasn't Catholic, I owed it to her to keep away from temptation. I never told him that over Christmas break I got Emma pregnant and had to use part of my college fund to pay for an abortion.

I was boxing on the varsity team, and doing pretty well in the inter-collegiates, until Emma and I broke up. I wrote again to Louise. She didn't answer this letter either. When it came time to enter the national championships, my heart wasn't in it. I got beat in the fourth round of my first bout. Louise was too far away to blame, so I blamed Emma. But now I just blame me. No *chutzpah*, as Father Mac would say. Still, I owe Emma a lot because she helped me get through college, then encouraged me to think seriously about going to law school.

I told Father Mac what was on my mind and he arranged an interview with the Dean of Brooklyn Law, who accepted me there and then. With that in the bag, I floated through my last year of college. But I was in for a rude awakening when law school started. It was much tougher than I ever imagined it could be. Also, my college fund was just about dry and the GI Bill wasn't enough to live on. I worked out a deal with Brooklyn College and signed on as a part-time assistant boxing team coach. Except, I had classes all day and needed to spend most evenings in the library. In the end there just weren't enough hours in the day to study and also to earn some money, so I had to quit coaching.

The Archdiocese kicked in a small stipend in the name of some scholarship I'd never heard of – I always suspected Father Mac invented it to help me – but when I looked at my bank balance at the end of my first year, I was broke. And no matter how I played with the numbers, I began to realize there probably wouldn't be a second year.

That's when Louise showed up.

One day, just like that, someone knocked on my door, I opened it and there she was. I couldn't believe it. My little friend of fifteen was now twenty. I wanted to say, how come you never answered my letters, except within minutes we were in bed and stayed there for two days. When we finally got around to talking, she told me that after I left Liverpool her mother started calling her a whore for longing after a sailor. Her mother kept saying, you'll see the sailor boy's not coming back. All Louise could do was cry, 'But he promised.'

Shattered that I didn't keep my promise, Louise quit school intending to go to London. But she was then only just sixteen and her parents wouldn't let her leave home. So she got a job in Liverpool, working in an insurance company, and stayed there until she was eighteen. Finally, one day after work, she simply walked over to Lime Street Station and climbed on a train for London. She knew a guy living in Pimlico who was trying to be a musician, banged on his door that night – arrived just like that – and moved in with him. She stayed for a couple of years, working in offices, until one morning she woke up and found him dead of an overdose. She helped herself to whatever money he had lying around the apartment and moved in with a girl she knew in Wimbledon. She enrolled on a secretarial training course, learned how to type and take shorthand and soon found work again, this time at Lloyds of London. For a few months she had a fancy address in Chelsea, living with some guy in the insurance business, until one morning she woke up and found another guy in bed with them.

That's when she got it into her head that she wanted to find me. It took a year or so before she had enough money saved, but like the day she got on the train for London, one day she just took a bus out to the airport and got on a plane for New York.

And here she was.

She said, 'I didn't know what I was going to find.'

I said, 'You found me.'

And she stayed.

Father Mac did not approve. Yet he got Louise a job as a teacher's assistant in the Archdiocese. We ran into a minor hurdle after about a year when the Bishop heard that Louise and I were living together in sin and dictated, either we had to get married or she had to quit her job. So Father Mac married us.

Between what she was earning and the GI Bill, I squeaked through law school. I then spent four months studying for my bar exam, and passed it first time around. Father Mac helped me get a job in the Public Defender's office where I worked for two years before I grew sick of helping guilty kids get off and transferred to the District Attorney's office. I worked there another two years before I grew sick of sending innocent kids to jail.

I'd just past my thirtieth birthday, Louise was twenty-five, and we were now trying to start a family. I probably would have stayed in Brooklyn for ever except two things happened within a week of each other that changed my life.

On a hot and sunny Monday morning in August 1975, Louise walked into my office in tears. She said she'd just been to the doctor. She said he told her she could never have children. She said because of that she wanted to go home to Liverpool. I calmed her down and promised that we'd do everything we could to prove the doctor wrong. But nothing I did after that could change her mind about going home.

Four nights later . . . it was well after midnight . . . in the middle of a terrible rainstorm, someone started pounding frantically on our door. I got out of bed, spotted two uniformed police officers through the little spy hole, unchained the door, unlocked it, and opened it. They were there to tell me that Father Mac had been murdered.

The next thing I knew I woke up in Coney Island Hospital. They said I passed out. But it must have been worse than

that because I was there for a couple of days. And while I don't
remember much about the next two weeks, I do recall checking
myself out of the hospital because there was no way in the world
that I was going to miss his funeral.

I can still remember the Mass they held for him at St John's
and can still hear the Cardinal's lamenting voice as he spoke
about the man who'd been my second father and my only
brother. I can still feel the rain as it poured down on my
face as I stood at the foot of his grave in Most Holy Trinity
Cemetery. I can still feel the mud under my feet and smell all
the beautiful flowers at the side of his coffin and see that huge
cross on the top of it.

I can still feel his hand in mine, guiding me.

I will forever still hear his voice.

Do that!

When I learned that two Puerto Rican kids had been arrested
for his murder, I went to my boss and demanded that I get the
case. He said no. So I went over his head, all the way up to the
DA himself. I said, 'Either I get the case or I'm gone.'

When he said no, I quit.

The case was assigned to Assistant District Attorney H. Lowe
Stevenson – we used to joke that the H stood for hard-on –
whose father was a partner in one of those ultra-WASPy Wall
Street law firms. He had a degree from Cornell and a wife who
wanted him to go into politics. In their minds, the ADA's job
was supposed to be some sort of stepping stone. Except he once
confessed to me that he only accepted the job in downmarket
Brooklyn because his father didn't have any pull in upmarket
Nassau County and commuting into Manhattan, where his
father could have gotten him an ADA post, was too much of
a hassle from Garden City, where he lived with Mrs Hard-on
and their 3.2 WASPy children.

I understand now why they didn't let me handle the case.

I will never understand why they gave it to him.

Reading the indictments against the two kids made it sound
open and shut. They'd broken into the rectory to see what they
could steal. Father Mac found them there and challenged them.
They stabbed him nine times. The knife was covered with their
fingerprints and when the cops finally caught them, the clothes
they wore that night – covered in blood that matched Father

Mac's – were hidden under their beds. And just so that no one could have any doubt, one of them had the nerve to be wearing Father Mac's chain and cross around his neck.

At their arraignment, I sat in the back of the courtroom and heard their lawyer plead not guilty. I later learned that their attorney had offered to plea bargain but that Stevenson had refused. Instead of putting them both away for twenty-five years for manslaughter, he was grandstanding to send them to the chair for murder one. It was a totally dumb thing to do. A bird in the hand is always worth two in the bush. And anyway, juries in those days didn't send kids – even Puerto Rican kids – to the electric chair.

At their trial, I sat in the back of the courtroom listening to Stevenson explain, with absolutely no passion, how these two had stabbed Father Mac. I mouthed the words 'nine times'. But he never said that. I waited for an expert witness who would describe to the jury how these two had subjected Father Mac to horrendous physical damage. But he never called anyone to testify to that. I wanted to see the jury's faces when Stevenson showed them the autopsy photos. But he never showed them any photos. I couldn't figure out why he never referred to the victim as a priest – he kept talking about John MacNamee – until I realized he didn't have any Catholics on the jury. Here he was, trying two people for the murder of a priest, and he'd consciously eliminated Catholics from the jury. I later learned that he was thinking that Catholics would never go for the death penalty.

I sat in the back of the courtroom listening to their attorney vigorously tear into the police handling of the case.

I watched Stevenson in his summing up make fundamental errors of fact.

I watched the defence attorney in his summing up completely destroy what few points Stevenson had scored.

I sat in the back of the courtroom to hear the jury find them both not guilty.

The next morning I stormed into Stevenson's office.

'What the hell, old boy,' he shrugged, 'can't win 'em all.'

I broke his jaw.

Two weeks later, Louise and I moved to Liverpool.

I had no idea what I was going to do when we got there. That

I couldn't earn a living as an American lawyer in Liverpool, because there was virtually no American population and almost no American business, didn't seem to concern Louise. She wanted to go home, so now we were there.

We spent the first few weeks getting settled – I got reacquainted with her parents and met all of her relatives – and by the time the family welcome wore off, which was pretty fast, our savings had also drained up. One of her cousins found her a job as a secretary in a catering firm and helped me rent a storefront that would serve as a law office. I painted the walls, bought a second-hand desk and some chairs, bought a second-hand typewriter, hung out a shingle that said American Attorney-at-Law, wrote letters to every company in the area that might conceivably do business in the States, wrote letters to every American law firm in London that might conceivably do business in Liverpool, put my name on the US Embassy's list of American lawyers in England, and sat back, waiting for something to happen.

At the same time, I started hanging around gyms looking for boxers.

I did a little work for an insurance company that needed to settle a claim in Texas, and I promoted a few fights. But that insurance company only had one claim in Texas and I never managed to get more than a couple of hundred people into my fights because the boxers I found weren't interesting enough.

We struggled on like that for three years, until the strain of trying to make a go of life in Liverpool was just too much. I told Louise that we had to face the truth – it wasn't working – and that the time had come, at least for me, to go back to New York. She said she wasn't ready yet. And I might well have left, except that's when she got pregnant.

The doctors who said it couldn't happen never came up with a good reason why it did. Although, frankly, I'm glad that it did because at least for a while, we lived in the glow of John MacNamee Barolo.

When the baby was a year old, Louise started saying that, yes, maybe we should go back to the States. I didn't hide the fact that going home sounded good to me. Then she changed her mind and said we could compromise. She decided that halfway between Liverpool and Brooklyn was London, so for a while we lived in London. We found a place in Westbourne

Grove, not far from where I live now, I got another office – painted it, hung out my shingle and wrote more letters – and started looking again for fighters.

She and I made it all the way to 1986.

That's when one day, straight out of left field, Louise announced that she was having an affair with an American musician she'd met while we were still in Liverpool. I was flabbergasted. She said she was in love with him and wanted a divorce. I sat there dumbstruck. She and Johnny moved out that weekend and the next thing I knew, she and Johnny and the musician had left Britain for New Jersey.

It took me years to get over Father Mac's murder. I eventually learned how to survive without Louise. But I am still not over missing Johnny.

Frankly, I don't really know why I've stayed in London. Sure, over the years, I've made some friends. And I've managed to build up a small law practice. And every now and then I find a boxer with *chutzpah* who might someday be a contender. But I guess the only reason I stay – at least the only one that makes any real sense to me – is that the older I get the more I realize that life is sort of like being at sea on the *Norton Sound*.

Staying afloat and staying alive is a full-time job.

Chapter Eight

Back in the mid-1960s, when the *Sunday Chronicle* had a huge circulation, someone christened Harold Lamb McBride 'the ogre of Fleet Street'. It was a reputation he plainly cherished. And he went out of his way to encourage it after the *Sunday Chronicle* folded and he moved on to spend five drunken years reigning over the now defunct *News*.

A Scots Catholic who never forgave the English Protestants for what they did to Queen Mary, he drove reporters harder than anyone ever had and took enormous pleasure in berating them when they didn't return to the office covered in blood, automatically assuming that they hadn't done enough digging. He refused to hire women except as secretaries because he believed that reporting was a man's business and when he was forced to give in, he infuriated his token female reporters by insisting they stick to stories about cooking and babies. When they objected, he fired them for insubordination. Although, in that respect, he was very even-handed because he took equal pleasure in firing male reporters for insubordination.

He autocratically redefined the tabloid business, bringing 'in your face' journalism to Britain, while steering both of his papers further down market than anyone had ever imagined either could go. Although he was eventually out-tabloided by the *Sun*, the *Mirror* and the *News of the World*, he was the man who showed them how to do it. His front pages were loud and his sports pages were robust. The chip on his shoulder was huge, he feared no one, relentlessly took on the pompous and almost certainly helped to bring down at least one government. He was an old school editor who ruled with an old school iron hand. And both of his papers made more money during his tenure than either did before. Even though they both, eventually, went bust. In the end, he was an old school editor who could never come to grips with new school journalism.

We used to bump into each other at Charlie's place, where McBride spent a lot of afternoons getting drunk after Fleet Street left him behind. Then Laddy Caldwell phoned and that was McBride's second coming. They'd met back in the *Sunday Chronicle* days, when photographs turned up on McBride's desk of someone looking suspiciously like Caldwell in handcuffs being spanked by a black hooker. In those days, Caldwell was a Tory backbencher who seemed ripe for promotion. McBride ran the photos with the man's face blacked out and a caption reading, 'Is this conservative enough for the Tories' front bench?' It prompted a call from Downing Street asking, off the record, if the gentleman in question was Laddy Caldwell. McBride responded by running a front page story recounting the gist of the phone call, ending uncharacteristically with a firm denial that the gentleman in the photo was Caldwell. His plan was to send the Labour Party off on a witch hunt, which is exactly what happened. They blitzed the media with accusations, naming several of the Tory party's kinkier members as the mysterious gentleman in handcuffs.

An accidental consequence of the affair was Caldwell's eternal gratitude. He never got promoted to the front benches, but McBride's mendacity gave Conservative Central Office the chance to let Caldwell off the hook by promoting him to the House of Lords. When Caldwell then bought Herald Newspapers . . . twenty evening tabloids spread across Great Britain . . . he made good on the debt he felt he owed McBride. Now, as Executive Editor of the Caldwell-Herald Group, McBride rationalized his partnership with the English upper classes by reminding anyone who bothered to ask that his loyalty only ran as deep as Caldwell's overdraft.

His office was in an ancient walk-up, just down a small lane, around the corner from where the Press Association used to be. Technology had taken the papers away from Fleet Street, the real estate developers had moved in and instead of buildings with the day's latest editions framed in the windows, the signs now read 'To Let'. Except for the Caldwell-Herald Group. Ironically, the ogre of Fleet Street was now the last resident on the block.

Once inside the paint-chipped front door, after risking my

life walking up the rickety stairs, I found a receptionist too busy talking on the phone to ask who I was. Instead of waiting, I pointed to the door behind her and stepped through it into a large room where a dozen people were sitting in front of computer screens, clicking their keyboards, making me think that an infinite number of monkeys given an infinite amount of time still couldn't teach me how to use one of those things.

At the far end of the room was a glass enclosed corner where I spotted McBride leaning back in his chair, facing away from the newsroom. On the wall behind him, in a heavy gilt frame were the words, 'GET USED TO THE SEWERS BECAUSE THAT'S WHERE POLITICIANS ARE AT THEIR BEST'.

I knocked on his door, heard him growl, 'In,' and asked, 'Are you really this busy or are you just glad to see me?'

He looked up from behind a desk covered in newspapers and files. 'Slumming, are we, counsellor?' He had a huge face, with dark, glaring eyes, not a hair on his head and large floppy ears. The corners of his enormous mouth were turned down into a permanent scowl, made to seem all the fiercer by a bulbous nose covered in tiny red blood vessels. He pointed to a chair that was covered in newspapers. 'You can either put them on the floor or sit on them.'

I moved the papers to the floor, sat down, then pointed to the computer terminal at the side of his desk. 'Can you bet a horse on that thing?'

'No. But you can probably book a package tour.'

'You . . . a closet nerd?'

He gestured towards the newsroom. 'Full of wankers going blind in front of their screens. It's not a newspaper office, it's a travel agency.'

'How much for a cheap flight to Majorca?'

He wasn't amused and changed the subject. 'How's that Hannover kid?'

'Coming along. Charlie wants to stick Moe Moses on him.'

'He's the best.'

'You think so?'

'I know so. He's a miserable bastard but it's always best to have a miserable bastard in your corner instead of the other fellow's.' Something in the newsroom caught his eye. 'That,' he bellowed to a young guy walking past the office door. 'There.'

The fellow stopped, looked around, obviously didn't understand and asked McBride, 'What?'

'That.' He stared at the table along the side of the room where a coffee machine sat in the middle of empty cups and back issues of newspapers.

Following his gaze, the fellow asked, 'Coffee?'

McBride confirmed, 'Yes, Mr Greystone the Third. Coffee.'

I suddenly understood. 'Not for me, thanks.'

'Keep the pot full,' McBride growled.

Greystone stared at him. 'The pot? Oh, you want me to take care of the coffee. Sure.' He kept nodding. 'No problem.' Then he dared, 'Anything else?'

'Nothing.'

The young guy went to deal with the coffee pot.

McBride began shaking his head. 'Mr Greystone the Third is the son of Mr Greystone the Second who is some sort of media mogul in the mailroom at the BBC. This, then, is an English journalism dynasty. Mr Greystone the Third even studied journalism. They all study journalism. But they can't cover a murder without getting sick, can't get quotes without a press conference, can't spell without their damned computer programs, don't have ink in their blood and can't keep the coffee pot full. It's a wonderful world we live in, counsellor.'

'You think young lawyers are any better?'

'I don't believe in them either.'

'How come Mr Greystone the Second didn't hire Mr Greystone the Third?'

'At least one of them is too smart.'

'Speaking of hiring relatives . . .'

'My mistake wasn't to hire a relative,' he snapped, 'it was to hire a teenaged girl.'

'They're called women now.'

McBride scowled. 'Did you come by to lecture me on being politically correct? Because if that's why you're here, I'll show you politically correct . . .'

'I came by to find out about a guy named Bickerton. L. Roger.'

'Who he?'

'He was head of something called the European Research Project in Eastbourne.'

'Eastbourne? Wait a minute.' McBride found a telephone buried under some papers and dialled a number. Without introducing himself, he told the person who picked up the line at the other end, 'Bloke's name is Bickerton. Spelled the way it sounds. Involved with the European Research Project on your patch. Have we ever run anything on him?' He listened, then announced to me, 'You're too late. He's dead.'

'I know.'

He barked into the phone, 'Fax me whatever you've got,' hung up, took a deep breath, leaned back and stared at the ceiling. 'Moe can make a difference. When's the fight?'

'Two weeks from tomorrow night.'

'Who's he up against?'

'Davey McGraw.'

He thought about that for a minute. 'Something tells me he's fast. Can your kid punch?'

'When he thinks he's ahead he can. But when he gets behind, he backs into the ropes. He fought a no-hoper named Goodman Floyd a couple of months ago. Except the no-hoper slugged him in the first round and Hambone spent the next five hanging onto the ropes. He can take a million punches all doubled up like that but you don't win rounds taking punches. I kept screaming to him to get off the ropes, but he's got a stubborn streak. It's inexperience. He got lucky in the sixth. Floyd walked in with his right hand down and Hambone nailed him with a left hook. It was a real sucker punch.'

'They used to call that style.'

'I call that stupid. It's not the way he's going to make any money in this game.'

'He got a payday coming up?'

'If I can get him past McGraw, I might be able to arrange something. One, maybe two more fights down the line. But first he's got to get past McGraw. Then we'll see.'

'Seems to me,' he said, 'McGraw's been around for a long time. I see his name in the papers but I can't remember, is he rated?'

'No.'

'What's his record? Something like nine and one?'

'Eleven and two. He's lost on points the last two outings.'

'And your kid?'

'Four and four. Except the first two were before I got him

and the second two were at the very beginning. If they don't count, I make him four zip.'

A telephone rang somewhere in McBride's office and a fax machine took the call.

'Got anything else besides a left hook?'

'A right hook.'

'It's two more punches than you ever had.' He swung his chair around to face a table behind him, and waited like that for pages to come through. As the machine sliced them off, he handed them to me.

There were seven in all. The most recent was a couple of paragraphs announcing Bickerton's suicide. The others were about the European Research Project and either quoted Bickerton in the article or otherwise mentioned his name. The machine beeped to signal the end of the transmission, then almost immediately answered another call to receive two more pages. One was an article that had been published in the *Guardian* about Government funding that contained a quote from Bickerton. The second was a large black square. It turned out to be a photo that couldn't be transmitted. The caption explained that it was a group photo taken at Bickerton's retirement party.

I showed it to McBride and he shouted out to the newsroom, 'Mr Greystone the Third.'

The young guy reappeared. 'Coffee, sir?'

'Where's my granddaughter?'

He looked around the newsroom, then admitted, 'I don't know, sir. But you can check her planning schedule on the computer. From your menu, just key in Control-Alt F3 . . .'

'Find her,' McBride snapped, waving him away.

Greystone backed off and went to key in Control-Alt F3 himself.

'Nobody has to do anything any more.' McBride shook his head. 'Life on the planet is being reduced to Control-Alt-F3. Her mother begs me to hire her because she decides she wants to be a news photographer. So against my better judgment, I give her a job. Now if I want to see her I've got to make an appointment with some bloody-fucking-computer.'

'It's called progress.'

He pointed to his own computer. 'If I knew how to work this Goddamned thing I could probably do it myself. Otherwise, I'll get the photo sent up from Brighton. They cover Eastbourne and the editor down there is pretty good. But never tell him I said so.'

'Wouldn't dream of it.'

Greystone appeared at McBride's door. 'She's back, sir.'

McBride glared past him to spot her rushing through the room to her desk. 'In here,' he bellowed.

Katherine McBride Docherty – a baby-fat twenty-two-year-old redhead with short hair dyed to make it look more orange than red, torn jeans, a San Francisco 49ers sweatshirt and one of those sleeveless nylon flak jackets with lots of pockets that photographers wear – dropped her camera bag on her desk, grabbed a roll of exposed film and brought it over to show her grandfather. 'What a prize.' She held it above her head. 'It's Blur in their underwear.'

He looked mystified. 'It's what?'

'Blur.'

'Blurred?'

'No, Harold . . . Blur.' She shook her head in disbelief. 'It's Blur.'

He turned to me. 'I'm Harold.'

I smiled and extended my hand. 'And I'm Vincent. We met a long time ago, when you were a little girl . . .'

'That was a long time ago,' she snapped. 'Gotta get these processed.'

'Just a minute.' McBride grabbed the faxed news photo. 'I need a copy of this.'

She studied the page, then pointed to his computer. 'It's right there, Harold. If you'd just learn how to work the bloody thing . . .' Moving past her grandfather, she pounded on his keyboard until an image came up on the screen. ''Bye, Vincent. 'Bye Harold.' And with that she left.

I looked over McBride's shoulder at the photo, but from where I was standing there was too much light reflecting on his screen. 'Is there any way I can get a copy of that?'

Nodding, 'I think so . . .' McBride pushed one button on his keyboard. 'This much I can do.'

A printer, precariously balanced on the ledge of the windowsill, started churning and after a few seconds a page appeared out the top. The photo showed ten people standing in a line behind a round table that was set for dinner. Two of them were shaking hands.

'She calls me Harold,' he said softly.

The caption explained that this was a party for Dr L. Roger Bickerton, retiring head of the European Research Project at Eastbourne but didn't specifically identify anyone.

'It would sound a little silly if she called you Grandpa.' I stared at the two men shaking hands.

He glared at me. 'How about Mr McBride?'

I didn't recognize either of them.

Chapter Nine

'Come look at this,' I said to Henry, as I went straight to my desk to search through the top drawer for my elk-foot-handled magnifying glass.

'What is it?'

'Not the guy I thought he was.'

'What does that mean?'

'Our client.' I found the magnifying glass, put the photo flat on my desk and, with a pencil, carefully circled the faces of the two men shaking hands. 'One of these two.'

'I can't see a thing,' she said, leaning over, nearly pushing me out of my chair. 'How do you know?'

'What do you mean, how do I know? It's Bickerton's retirement party. It says so at the bottom. And one of these guys is saying goodbye to the other one.'

'Or saying hello.'

'Why would he be saying hello to a guy who's leaving?'

'I can't see because you're holding it at the wrong angle.'

I handed the magnifying glass to her. 'Here.'

'This is disgusting,' she said about the elk's foot. 'How can you keep trophies like this?'

'It's not a trophy, it's a magnifying glass . . .' I started to say, then decided I didn't have to make explanations like that. 'Hey, you were the one who was so concerned about our client. So there he is.'

She took the magnifying glass and the photo over to the window and held them both up to the fading afternoon light. 'I still don't know how you know.'

'Read the caption . . .'

Someone knocked at the front door.

I shot a glance at Henry, who looked first at the door, then at me and shrugged. When the person knocked a second time I suggested, 'Maybe you could answer it.'

She went to see who was there. 'Can I help you?'

I heard a man with a thick Yiddish accent ask, 'You got someone here named Vincent Barolo? Maybe he's expecting me.'

Henry wanted to know, 'Do you have an appointment?'

'What appointment? He asked to see me. He's the one who has the appointment.'

I realized immediately who it was. 'Come in, please.'

A squirrelly little guy walked past her, gave her a scowl, gave me the once over, then extended his hand. 'Charlie said you wanted to talk.'

'Please.' I gestured to one of the chairs facing my desk and offered Moe Moses a coffee or tea. He said he'd like tea. But Henry was standing in the doorway, behind his back, shaking her head to tell me we were out of tea. 'Actually, I recommend the coffee.'

'Coffee is fine,' he said. 'Especially if there is no tea. I take it white. With the spoon up.'

That was an expression I first heard in Liverpool. It meant that he wanted plenty of sugar.

Henry went to make his coffee while he and I made small talk, like about how long each of us had known Charlie.

'Thirty years.'

'You got me beat.'

'I'm not surprised.'

'You ever see him fight?'

'He was good.' Moses pointed to his head. 'But no *kopf*. It means head. He couldn't think on his feet. And *kopf* is the difference between a good fighter and a winning fighter.'

When his coffee was ready, I asked him if he'd ever seen Hambone fight.

'Can't say I have. But I've seen him spar.'

'What did you think?'

He nodded. 'A comer.'

'So what does it cost to turn a comer into a winner?'

'For you, a grand.'

I said, 'For me a grand? How much for somebody else?'

'You want to haggle? Or you want me to start work? We're talking two weeks. Right now he loses. A grand later maybe he wins.'

'And for £500?'

'Maybe he half wins.'

'What do you know about Davey McGraw?'

'Pretty boy? Stays pretty because he's a ducker and diver.'

'Can he be hit?'

'Anybody can be hit.'

'Can my guy hit him?'

'Now, no. A grand later, I hope so.'

'He needs to win.'

'So do I.'

'Fair enough,' I said. 'You're hired.'

'It's up front.'

'Do you need any chairs?'

'What kind of a question is that?'

'I've got some chairs . . . I figured maybe we could work something out.'

'What are you, a chair dealer? Well, I'm a cash dealer.'

'I'll give you a cheque on Monday.'

'Cash is better.'

'I'm sure it is,' I said. 'You'll get a cheque on Monday.'

'Okay. No need to ruin a perfect friendship so soon. A cheque on Monday. So on Monday, I start.' He stood up. 'The kid's going to be all right.'

I mumbled, '*Alevai*,' which means, from your mouth to God's ears.

He looked at me with a startled expression. '*Tallenas*?' That means, Italian. 'So where did you learn Yiddish?'

I walked him to the door. 'From a Mick priest.'

'If this was in a newspaper,' Henry said, going over the photo again, 'how come the caption doesn't say who's in the picture?'

'It says what the picture is.' I was trying to figure out how I could come up with a grand by Monday.

'But it doesn't say who the picture is.'

I took the photo and the magnifying glass back from her. 'See the two guys in the middle? One of them is Bickerton.'

'But it doesn't say that, does it?'

Instead of admitting to her that she was right, I looked at each of the other faces. There were three women facing sideways. And three men looking straight into the camera, obviously holding their smile too long, the way people have to do when a photographer calls out, 'Say cheese,' and waits longer than he should to click the shutter.

There was a man, standing fifth from the left, who was looking sideways. And another man, the guy standing second from the right, who was looking down at the table.

Finally there were the two men in the middle shaking hands.

'It might help if you had the proper caption,' Henry insisted.

'Hey, you don't like this caption, you go get a better one.'

'I will. Where's the photo from?'

'Try the Caldwell-Herald newspaper in Brighton.'

She nodded and left me alone to stare again at the two men shaking hands. That's when a fax came in.

'Dear Dad, I thought you'd like to see a copy of my report card. You know what I did? One of my friends from school has a fax machine, well it's not really his, it's his father's, but it's at home, so I went over there and faxed a copy of my report card to myself which went straight into my computer, you know, the fax program that came with the modem you got me, and then all I had to do was type this letter to you and attach the TIF file, which is what the program turns the report card into and fax the two of them to you like this. Pretty cool, huh? And then you want to know what I did? I left my computer on, hooked it up to mom's phone and told it to send this fax to you at exactly twelve o'clock, which is five o'clock your time. I'm not even there. I'm in school. I hope mom doesn't figure it out. I love you, Johnny.'

He got three Bs, one B-minus and two C-pluses. It wasn't the stuff of Harvard but for a kid who'd been traumatized by his parents' divorce, I figured it was good enough that he was passing everything. And his attendance was a lot better than mine when I was his age.

I read his fax a couple of times, and was just about to start reading the articles McBride had given me, when another fax arrived. Henry took it from the machine and handed it to me. 'See, I told you so.'

It was from the photo editor's desk at the *Southcoast Evening Herald*. 'The caption in question should read, "Dr Roger Bickerton, outgoing head of the European Research Project at

Eastbourne, looks on as Dr C. Barry Tyrone, ERP co-ordinator
of research, welcomes Dr Hans–Dieter Mars, overall director
of research, who hosted the dinner honouring Dr Bickerton.
Attending were (l–r) Dr P. Stafford, Dr Rosemary Schlessinger,
Mrs Hannah Mars, Dr Bickerton, Dr Tyrone, Dr Mars, Dr
Ghislain Cesari, Dr Eric Schluter, Mrs Josephine Tyrone and
Professor T.P. Tsung."'

I grabbed the magnifying glass – again Henry crowded in so
that she could see too – and I looked at the fourth man from
the left.

'So I guess they aren't saying goodbye.' Henry had to
rub it in.

The fourth man from the left was standing sideways.

'Don't bother admitting that you were wrong,' she said.
'Don't bother saying, thank you Delia for pointing out that
Dr L. Roger Bickerton, our late client, isn't one of the two
men in the middle shaking hands.'

'The profile,' I said. 'How do you like that. He never once
looked at me. All I saw was his profile. And there it is.'

'You mean, you do know him?'

'Kind of.'

'So who is he?'

'Bickerton.' I pointed. 'Right there. Yeah, that's him.'

'I know his name. So what's his story? How come he sent
you money and then killed himself?'

I told her the truth. 'I have no idea.'

After she left for the evening, I put the faxes and my
magnifying glass in my attaché case and brought all of them
home with me. I read the articles several times and studied
the photo again. Eventually I put the photo and the magnifying
glass on my night table and turned off the light, but even then
I lay on my back with my eyes still open, running the names in
the caption through my head.

I began imagining that something about those names seemed
vaguely familiar.

I was just this side of sleep when it came to me.

Cesari.

I'd seen it in Bickerton's obituary.

Chapter Ten

I stepped into the office just as Henry was saying to someone on the phone, 'No, he's not here yet.'

I mouthed the words, 'Who is it?' in case it wasn't someone I wanted to speak to.

'Oh . . . yes, he is,' she told the person on the other line. 'He just walked in.' She handed it to me, mouthing the word, 'Charlie'.

'What's going on?' I asked.

He answered, 'Your kid's on the canvas.'

'What happened?'

'He was getting a little too smart with a heavyweight named Maury Roscoe. The two of them had words. So Roscoe invited him to strap on a pair of gloves . . .'

'A heavyweight?' I demanded, 'Why would you let them . . .'

'Let them? Who let them? I walked in and found your kid on his back.'

I didn't want to believe that Hambone could be so stupid. 'Two weeks before a fight . . .' I stopped, then wanted to know, 'Since when does this guy Roscoe hang around your place?'

'Believe me, Vince, if I'd been here . . . Maybe you should talk to him . . .'

'If he's still out, don't bother waking him.'

'Wait a minute. He wants to talk to you.' Charlie handed the phone to Hambone.

'Vince, it wasn't my fault. Honest, the bloke taunted me.'

'Are you crazy? What kind of a stupid stunt was that? You're two weeks away from a fight. We're trying to get you to a payday . . .'

'He was like insulting me, Vince. You wouldn't have let him get away with insulting you.'

'You mean, you were just minding your own business and he just walked up to you and just started saying stuff about your mother?'

'I was minding my own business. I was working the big bag and it wasn't about my mother . . .'

'Get dressed and go home. You're finished for the day. Put Charlie on the line.'

'Vince, I've got my workout . . .'

'Do that!'

'Okay,' he said meekly. I heard him tell Charlie, 'He wants to talk to you.'

'I'm back,' Charlie said.

'Shove him in a taxi. Make sure when he leaves that he leaves alone. And I don't want any strangers hanging around when Hambone's training.'

'Come on, Vince, I don't run a private training camp. This is a gym. We got all sorts of guys . . .'

'Charlie, since when has this heavyweight been training there?'

He hesitated, 'I don't know . . . couple of weeks?'

'I never saw him there. I never even heard of him.'

'Well . . . I'm telling you he's been here . . .'

'Who's his manager? Who promotes him?'

'He's one of Fuzzy White's boys.'

'Fuzzy White?' I should have guessed. 'Charlie . . . how on earth could you . . .'

He suddenly figured it out. 'Oh, shit. You're right, Vince . . . okay . . . he's history. I promise . . . I mean, business isn't so great that I can turn down fighters . . . but I should have known . . .'

'Get Hambone out of there.' Fuzzy White's brother-in-law was Mickey O'Reardon, a fight promoter with absolutely no scruples, who just happened to own Davey McGraw.

'I'll keep an eye out from now on,' Charlie promised.

'I hope so.' I hung up, thinking to myself, we're a few weeks away from a fight and O'Reardon tries to set up Hambone. I kept asking myself why. And the only answer I could come up with was, maybe he thinks Hambone can actually beat his boy.

Tossing my attaché case on my desk and myself into my judge's chair, I toyed with the idea of phoning O'Reardon. I wanted to remind him that Hambone might have been born yesterday, but I wasn't. Except, I could hear his end of the conversation. He'd say, I don't know what you're talking about. I'd say, I know that you know and I'm phoning because I want you to know that I know that you know . . . and after playing the scene in my head, after hearing how ridiculous it could get, I decided, the hell with it. There was more to be gained by reminding Hambone every few days how pissed-off I was at him, and reminding Charlie every few days that he screwed up. Hambone would worry because he didn't have anyone else to take care of him. And Charlie would worry because he needed every fighter he could get to keep his place open.

It's called, keep the insecure insecure.

But all of that could wait. 'Get on the phone,' I told Henry. 'I need you to call that newspaper in Brighton. I also want you to find out if there's a newspaper in Guernsey. I want to see whatever they've run on Bickerton.'

She was standing in my doorway staring at me. 'So?'

'So please get on the phone with that newspaper in Brighton and see if they have any other photos of him. I want full face. Ask them to fax one to us.'

'If you know who he is, what do you want with his photo?'

'Because I need to . . .' She had a very annoying habit of asking me to explain things that I couldn't always explain. 'Because I need it.'

'If you don't know why,' she mumbled, returning to her desk, 'you don't have to tell me.'

I didn't tell her because I didn't know. Except, I remembered how Bickerton kept talking about settling old scores. About getting even. And now he was dead. And I do not believe in coincidence.

A few minutes later she was back in my room. 'There's a paper in Guernsey called the *Evening Press and Star*. I asked them to fax whatever they could. As for the paper in Brighton, the photo you've got is the only photo they've got. The fellow there suggested you try the European Project press office in Eastbourne. He gave me a number . . .'

I dialled it myself. A woman answered, 'ERP.' I asked for the press office and she demanded, 'Are you a member of the press?'

'Absolutely.'

'What organization, please?'

I invented, 'The *E–U News.*'

'Just a moment please . . .' There was a click, some elevator music, then another click, after which a young guy with a very docile voice said, 'Press Office.'

'Yeah . . . good morning. Name is . . . Brinkley . . . David Brinkley.' I spoke quickly because that's the way I remembered Pat O'Brien speaking in the original version of *The Front Page*. 'Tell you what I need. That ex-director of yours . . . Bickerton . . . his official bio and a pic.'

'Ah . . . Dr Roger Bickerton?'

'He's the one . . . I'll give you a fax number. We're trying to make a deadline . . .'

'You want me to fax something . . .' there was a nervous edge to his question, ' . . . about Dr Bickerton?'

'Whatever you've got. Canned bio is fine. And a pic. I've got to have a pic.'

'And you are . . . ?'

'Sorry, working on a deadline . . . hold on . . .' I half-cupped the phone so he could hear me shout to Henry, 'Did I just see Alastair? Tell him to get his ass over to Number Ten or he's going to miss that briefing. Sarah? I need that copy right now.'

Henry looked at me like I was crazy. 'Alastair? Sarah?'

'Sorry,' I said, coming back onto the line. 'Yeah, I'll give you my fax number. It comes right in to me. No need to send a cover page. Bio and pic. Unless, you got anything else on him?'

He was hesitant. 'Who . . . did you say this was?'

'Brinkley, *E–U News* . . . hold on a sec . . .' I half-cupped the phone again. 'Who's on line two? Okay.' I came back to the press officer, said, 'Just five seconds, I'll be right back,' and put him on hold.

Henry demanded, 'What are you doing?'

'When I point to you, yell M–O–D on line five.' I took the press officer off hold. 'Sorry about that. It's all happening. Did I give you the fax number?'

'You said this was a newspaper?'

'Agency. You know, AP, Reuters . . .' I pointed to Henry.

'M–O–D on line five,' she called out while making a weird face.

'Hold on again.' I shouted back to her, 'Tell him I'll take the call right away . . .' then gave the press officer my fax number. 'You got it?' Before he could answer, I repeated it. 'Listen, thanks a lot. Can I have it as soon as possible?'

He seemed very confused. 'Ah . . . I mean, this may take a few minutes . . . '

'Ten minutes is good. Five is better. Thanks, big guy, I owe you one. What did you say your name was?'

'Terry . . .'

'Okay, Terry . . . thanks, buddy.' I hung up.

Ten minutes later a four-page fax arrived. There was a two-page biography, an official portrait and a note typed on ERP letterhead. 'Dear Mr Brinkley, attached is the biography and photo you requested of the late Dr Roger Bickerton. Any further enquiries must be directed to the Chief Constable, Guernsey Police, St Peter Port, Guernsey, Channel Islands. Yours sincerely, Terry Dunn, Press and Public Relations Officer.'

The Chief Constable?

It struck me as a strange thing for my new friend Terry to say, so I called information and got the number for the cops in St Peter Port. When a woman answered, I introduced myself as me – being a lawyer when you're talking to cops is better than being a lawyer when you're talking to a press office – and explained that I wanted to speak with the officer handling the Bickerton case. She put me through to a Mr Lascasse.

Immediately, I asked him if he spoke English.

He had a very gruff voice – it made me think that he must be short and fat – and my question clearly didn't please him because he quickly reminded me, 'This is part of the United Kingdom of Great Britain.'

I apologized, then asked if he was the officer handling the Bickerton case.

That didn't please him either because he wanted to know, 'Why are you interested in the matter?'

I explained that I was Dr Bickerton's attorney and needed some information for his estate.

'I'm afraid there is no information to release at the moment. This is an ongoing investigation.'

'I thought it was suicide.'

'Mr Barolo . . . you sound American.'

'I am.'

'And you are representing Dr Bickerton's estate?'

'I'm based in the UK. I've been representing Dr Bickerton in an American matter . . .'

He paused for a moment. 'I'm afraid that there is nothing I am prepared to say to anyone over the phone . . .'

It was obvious from his tone that I'd reached the end of the road. 'I understand. When your investigation is completed, if you might be kind enough to contact me . . .'

'I'll need to have any request of that nature in writing.'

'No problem.' I got him to spell his name, give me his address and fax number. When I hung up, I dictated a letter to Henry which we faxed to Mr Lascasse on my letterhead.

Much to my surprise, within half an hour, the gruff voice was back on the phone. 'I'm certain you can appreciate our position.'

I reassured him, 'Of course.'

'The case is not being treated as suspicious because there was a suicide note that we firmly believe to be in Dr Bickerton's own hand. We have conducted a search for the body, but the currents on that side of the island are very strong and we don't expect to find anything. One of his shoes turned up. So has a coat. They washed ashore. But there's been nothing else. A final determination will have to come from the Coroner's office, and I have no idea when that might be. These things can usually take anywhere from six months to a year.'

'Why?'

'Why? Because whenever there is an apparent death but no body, it's up to the Coroner to determine the disposition of the case.'

'It was his car, right?'

'Yes. A Renault Laguna, registered to his home address in Brighton.'

'Do you know how he got to Guernsey? Or when?'

'We assume that, because he was in his own car, he took the ferry from Weymouth. But traffic from the United Kingdom is not subject to Customs or immigration checks.'

'What is that, a couple of hours' trip?'

'Two and a half.'

'Have you checked with the ferry company to see what boat he was on?'

Lascasse asked, 'Does it make a difference?'

'Just curious,' I answered.

'He was on the boat Tuesday morning.'

'And he died Wednesday morning.'

'That's when his car was found.'

'What did he do all day Tuesday?'

'You seem to have a long list of questions, Mr Barolo. Are you sure this is just curiosity?'

I reminded him, 'The man was my client.'

'We don't know what he did all day Tuesday. But we'd be interested, in case you might know.'

'I don't have the slightest,' I said, without volunteering the fact that Bickerton had phoned my office on Tuesday. 'If anything comes up, will you let me know?'

'Anything of what nature?'

'Anything,' I said, 'of any nature. And thanks for calling me back.'

He said, 'Goodbye, Mr Barolo,' and I said, 'Goodbye, Mr Lascasse,' and we both hung up.

As soon as my line was clear, I phoned the newspaper on Guernsey and asked for the editor-in-chief. A fellow named Mark Maurois said that he was the news editor. I introduced myself, explained that I'd been representing Dr Bickerton in another matter and was curious about his death. Maurois said there wasn't much to report because the police on the island were treating it as suicide. I asked if the paper ran any stories about it and he said he'd be glad to fax them to me.

While I waited for those faxes to come in, I kept thinking the same thing I did when I asked Greta if she knew anything about Guernsey.

It seems like a long way to go just to kill yourself.

Chapter Eleven

For do-gooders, the practice of law is a noble attempt at righting the wrongs that will invariably consume us if those who opt to do wrong are given free rein. For philistines, it's a means to an end, such as a fine house, braces on the kids' teeth, pretences maintained at the local country club. For boxers, it's a lot like being in the ring. But for those of us who years ago abandoned our cross of youthful outrage, and who lost the house as part of the divorce settlement, and who all too quickly grew all too brittle to take a punch, the practice of law becomes a way to charge people money for spending time trying to rationalize truths and falsehoods in an otherwise irrational world.

Lawyers seek the truth.

The truth is the greatest virtue.

Therefore, lawyers are the most virtuous.

It only came to me once I stopped having illusions about myself, when I was finally able to admit that my abilities were limited. We grow too old too soon, too smart too late. It was only after I started wearing the bottoms of my trousers rolled and had to ask myself do I dare to eat a peach, that I began to relax enough to amuse myself with a modest pursuit of sound reasoning in a world that is neither sound nor reasonable.

Truth is absolute. But is the tree trunk on the floor of the living room really a couch or is the couch really a tree trunk?

There are no absolutes. Thirty divided by two equals fifteen. Except, if you have thirty students in a classroom and you sit the boys on one side and the girls on the other, then thirty divided by two can equal sixteen plus fourteen.

Therefore there are no truths. Does that mean it is illogical to assume that logic should always be logical?

Consider the case of the man who feels he is too old to attend law school and so hires a private tutor. The tutor says to the student, I will charge you $1,000 and for that sum I guarantee you will pass the bar exam and be granted a licence to practise law. But the student says to the tutor, it is not enough that I am admitted to the bar, I want to become as good a lawyer as you and win many cases. The student says, therefore to ensure that you will teach me well, I will pay half your fee when I am admitted to the bar and the other half after I win my first case. The tutor agrees and teaches the student all about the law. The student passes the bar exam and duly pays the tutor $500. But then, he announces that he has decided not to practise law. So the tutor sues the student for the remaining $500, claiming that the agreement to divide the fee in two parts was predicated in good faith, and that it is forfeitable only if the student practises law and never wins a case. The student cannot afford to hire a lawyer and appears in court on his own behalf. He argues, if I win my case I don't have to pay because the court says I don't. And if I lose, I don't have to pay because I have fulfilled my good faith part of the bargain by practising law and have not yet won a case. The tutor argues, if I win the student must pay because the court says he must and if I lose, the student must pay because as a practising lawyer he has now won a case.

How should the judge rule? If he favours the student's logic, he refutes as illogical the argument of the tutor. And yet, if the tutor's logic is valid, does that mean the student's is not? In fact, both are logical and so deciding for one or the other becomes illogical. Therefore, the only answer is no answer. But is it logical?

As someone who had to teach himself how to think – and has perhaps, ever since, spent too much time mulling over the hand he was dealt in life – who has grown too weary to still be a do-gooder, too cynical to still be a philistine and can no longer take a punch, what remains is a guy just trying to survive on an excursion between sense and nonsense.

The truth is not necessarily logical.

That which is logical is not necessarily the truth.

The truth is not necessarily the truth.

On Saturday, I got up early, the way I always do, and walked through the market at Portobello Road because when you collect chairs you never know when the great illusive one is going to appear. Like people who play the lottery every week, collectors too live in fear that the one time they don't play, that's when their numbers will come up.

I always start from the bottom.

I walk down to Notting Hill Gate, pick up a couple of newspapers and *Boxing News* – it comes out every Friday and the newsagent there keeps one for me – then meander up Portobello Road. There are half a dozen people I check on regularly and probably twice as many stalls I stop to look at when I feel like it. Sometimes my regular guys have chairs. Most of the time they don't. Sometimes my regular guys ask me if I want to sell a chair to them. Most of the time I don't. The dealer I like best is Holly, whom I met when her husband died and she took over his antiques stall. I not only bought a few chairs from her, but we also wound up having a little fling. I'd known her a year or so. We were talking chairs one Saturday morning and I told her about an eighteenth-century *padouk* I'd just bought and she asked to see it. So she stopped by that afternoon and we wound up in bed. She then started coming over to my place every Saturday after work. But she has a bunch of kids, always had to be home by supper time and could never get out during the week. After maybe two months of Saturday afternoons, she started feeling guilty about stopping by just for that and decided to call it off. She asked me if we could stay friends, and of course I said yes. So now I sometimes drop in to her place, about halfway up Portobello Road, on the left, especially if it's raining. And if she's not busy we have a cup of coffee and talk about chairs as if those Saturday afternoons never happened.

Except, it wasn't raining now and she was busy, so I just waved and kept on walking.

The street was covered with tourists, many of them painstakingly sifting through the stuff on the outside stalls, never realizing that the best stuff was long gone by the time they got there, or hidden away under inside stalls, held by dealers for their regular clients. At least, that's the way it works with the guys selling mugs. I don't always get the cheapest price, but I get first dibs and when you're talking about two or three bucks, how much lower can the guy go? So when a young fellow I know named Stu saw me walking by and signalled for me to come inside the covered market where he sells, I did.

'Mugs?'

'Better,' he said. 'Souvenir plate.'

'Not for me. Thanks. Only mugs.'

'This one you'll like.' From under the stand he pulled out a large blue and white serving platter inscribed around the rim with the words 'Sam and Sophia – Bass River – 1974'.

I started to smile. 'That's kind of funny.'

'Obscure enough?'

'How much?'

'Let me have eight quid.'

'Eight quid?' I looked him in the eyes. 'Since when do I get the tourist price?'

'Seven. I've got to get seven. Come on, no one's seen it yet. I held it just for you.'

I wondered, 'Got any souvenir mugs from Estonia?'

'Where's that?'

I reached into my pocket and pulled out exactly five pounds. 'Seven for the plate is too steep for me.' It was the way we played the game.

'How am I supposed to get my newborn baby into Eton? Call it six.'

I added a pound, although if I'd insisted he probably would have taken five. 'Thanks.' I waited for him to wrap it, then carried it carefully under my arm, to a cheese store at the far end of the market. They have adequate provolone and some decent aged Parmesan. I can't get good salami anywhere in the market, but that's all right because there's a guy in Soho who sells great salami and I always try to pick up enough during the week so that I have some on the weekends.

Except, this week I forgot. So I bought Canadian bacon instead and after I got my cheese, I went home because it was time for my call to Johnny.

I phone every Saturday at exactly one o'clock. He knows that and Louise knows it too, so when the phone rings at eight in the morning their time, she doesn't answer it. Which is why I always keep to the schedule. By nature I'm a creature of habit, at least those habits I like, and in this case calling every week at exactly the same time means I don't have to talk to Louise, which suits me fine. Her too.

'Hiya,' Johnny said, picking up the phone.

'Hey.' I munched on a chunk of provolone. 'What are you up to?'

'You get my fax?'

'Your grades are okay. But they could be better.'

'They'd be better if I was living with you.'

'That's putting the cart before the horse. You get those grades up and, I told you, you come to college here. But you've got to get good grades in order to get into a good school.'

'Can I come for the summer?'

'You know I'd like that.'

'If Mom says okay, can I?'

'Hey, you're asking me? If I had my way you'd be here for dinner tonight.'

'So all I have to do is get her to say okay?'

I didn't want to tell him that his chances were about the same as the State of New Jersey putting a man on the moon. 'It's a deal.'

We talked for another ten minutes – he said he was trying to come out of a batting slump and his average was down to .275, which I reminded him was still pretty good – and that his computer was working great. 'Mom says I can get my own phone line for the computer. I'll have to pay for it myself, but this way I'll be able to leave my modem hooked up all the time and you'll be able to fax me any time you want to. And of course, with e-mail . . .'

'Sounds great.' Actually, I didn't know if it was or wasn't but he was excited about it so I figured I'd go along with him. 'Don't forget to send me your number.'

'Come on Dad, you'll be the first one . . .'

I said, 'I'm counting on it,' and told him I'd phone again next Saturday. 'Same time. Same station.' I said, 'I love you,' and when I hung up I sat there for a while, staring at the phone, thinking to myself, what the hell am I doing stuck in her country when his British mother is living with him in mine and if he did spend the summer with me, I'd be tempted never to send him home.

But then, I knew, that was precisely why Louise would never let him come here.

Hambone rang Saturday afternoon. Except, when I heard it was him I let the machine take the message. Charlie also rang. He got the machine too. I planned on letting them both stew for another couple of days. Then a guy I know named Hal called. He's one of those strange guys who has his fingers in a lot of different pies – I never ask too many questions because I know that I don't want to know – one of which is a sports video business. He's the guy who gets me fight tapes that I could never find anywhere else, so I took his call. He said he'd just come in possession of a bootlegged copy of Roberto Duran's fight in June 1980 when he won the welterweight title from Sugar Ray Leonard and, on the same tape, the rematch when Leonard won the title back again. I told him I already had it. Next, he said, he'd only this morning obtained a copy of the first Marvin Hagler-Roberto Duran championship and on the same tape was the first Marvin Hagler-Tommy Hearns championship. Hagler won them both. I had that one too. He asked, 'What don't you have?' I said I wanted anything he could find with Gene Fullmer. He thought about that for a while, then said he might know where to find Fullmer's 1957 middleweight title bout against Sugar Ray Robinson. I told him, 'You get it I'll take it.' He phoned back about an hour later, all excited, because someone had put together a tape with the first Fullmer-Robinson fight, when Fullmer won the title, the rematch later that spring when Robinson took it back and Robinson's fight that autumn when he lost the title to Carmen Basilio. I asked, 'How much?' He said, 'It's yours for £55.' I told him if he delivered it within two hours I'd give him £20. We settled on £30 cash.

I spent Saturday night eating cheese macaroni in a late-Georgian Windsor wheelback armchair, reliving 1957.

On Sunday, I rolled out of bed early, made scrambled eggs and bacon and watched the tape again. I knew Greta wasn't home – she was never around on weekends – but that didn't stop me from dialling her number and leaving a message on her machine. 'I bought you a present yesterday. If Bogie and Bergman can always have Paris, we can always have Bass River.' That was all.

Then I started feeling bad about Charlie, so I phoned him at home and told him I'd come to the gym on Monday to watch Moe Moses put Hambone through his paces.

He said, 'All is forgiven?'

I said, 'All is forgiven.'

He said, 'Then ring Hambone because he's a mess.'

So I phoned Hambone who started crying that whenever I was angry at him it was like when his own father was angry at him. I told him, 'You did a stupid thing. I hope you learned your lesson.'

He said, 'I left a message for you to say I'm sorry.'

I assured him, 'I got your message. Okay. It's over. Go to Charlie's tomorrow. Moe Moses will meet you there. I'll come by in the afternoon.'

He kept saying, 'Thanks, Vince . . . I love you, man . . . really, you're like my dad to me . . .'

Around noon I walked down to the newsagent's to pick up the papers and on my way back, I bumped into Patel.

'Why, Mr Barolo. May we expect you to dine with us this evening? I will always hold a preferential table for you.'

I demanded, 'What the hell do you put in your lamb vindaloo?'

'Why, Mr Barolo, are you informing me that there was something displeasing? If there was anything that did not rise to your highest expectations, please know that the entire staff and management at the Taj Mahal of the India Gourmet . . .'

I stopped him. 'You ever hear of the story about the lady who spilled hot coffee on her own lap at McDonald's?'

'McDonald's, Mr Barolo?'

'Yeah. She spilled coffee on her lap and sued McDonald's for nine zillion bucks.'

'Why, Mr Barolo, did you spill your lamb vindaloo . . .'

'Yeah. All over the bathroom.'

He seemed genuinely shocked. 'Why, Mr Barolo . . .'

'My preferential table won't be used tonight. Or this month. Or this lifetime.' I left him standing there not knowing what to say.

Back home, I put on some Ella Fitzgerald, grabbed the papers and climbed into bed. I sorted them, with Saturday's first, Sunday's next and *Boxing News* last. Getting the order right is important. It's like eating different flavours of ice cream. You have to save your favourite flavour for last because, that way, the best taste lingers longest.

But I never got to *Boxing News*.

I worked my way through the Saturday papers, switched Ella

for Carmen McRea, and was halfway through the Sundays when I saw a little story in the *Sunday Times*.

'Fire destroyed the Brighton laboratory of the late Dr L. Roger Bickerton in the pre-dawn hours of Saturday. Fire officers were called to the blaze at around 3 a.m. in the small laboratory that the genetic scientist had used since his departure as head of the European Research Laboratory at Eastbourne last November. Dr Bickerton is believed to have committed suicide in Guernsey, Channel Islands, earlier this week. His car and a note were found at a cliffside location near the Point de la Moye. His body has not yet been recovered. East Sussex County Fire Brigade inspectors are treating the blaze as suspicious.'

Chapter Twelve

There wasn't anything I could do about the East Sussex County Fire Brigade on Sunday night, so I headed for the office early on Monday morning, found a number for them in some place called Lewes and told the woman who answered the phone there that I wanted to speak with someone about the Bickerton fire. She said she didn't know what I was referring to, but that was only to be expected because the Brigade had twenty-four stations spread throughout its area of responsibility. 'Do you know which station responded to the fire?'

I said, 'As far as I know, the fire was in Brighton.'

She gave me the number of the East Sussex County Fire Brigade on Preston Circus in Brighton and told me to ask for the case officer handling the specific incident. So now I phoned there and told the woman who answered that I wanted to speak with the case officer on the Bickerton fire. She said she didn't know what I was talking about and put me through to a man who suggested I ring brigade headquarters in Lewes. I explained that I'd just spoken to brigade headquarters in Lewes and they were the ones who gave me this number. He mumbled, 'Oh, you should have said that,' and passed me along to a fellow who wanted me to understand that he didn't handle fire inspection. I asked, 'Who does?' And he said, 'If you'll stay on the line, I'll try to find someone.'

I sat there waiting, reassuring myself that if I was getting the run-around, at least I was getting the run-around by human beings and not by some computer who instructs you to keep pushing buttons on your phone so that at the end of it, if you're patient enough, you can wind up talking to an answering machine.

Hello, this is the John F. Kennedy Memorial Hospital. If you

need emergency medical care, press one. If you need an operation . . .
Beep. You have chosen, need emergency medical care. If you have
been injured in a car accident, press one. If you are the victim of
a knife attack, press two. If you are the victim of gunshot wounds,
press three. Beep. You have chosen, victim of gunshot wounds. If
your wounds have been inflicted by a hand gun, press one. If your
wounds have been inflicted by automatic weapons fired by fewer
than three people, press two . . .

'Senior Divisional Officer Gerry Raymond.' A voice broke
into my thoughts. 'May I help you?'

'Are you a real person?'

'I beg your pardon.'

'Sorry,' I said, 'you caught me daydreaming. My name is
Barolo. I'm an attorney in London and I'm trying to get some
information about the Bickerton fire.'

He told me, 'Doesn't ring any bells.'

'Bickerton.' I spelled it. 'There was a blurb in the papers
yesterday . . .'

'No . . . still doesn't ring any bells. But that doesn't necessarily mean anything. If you saw the pile of paperwork on
my desk you'd understand why. And even if I have it here
somewhere, I can't send you a copy until it's been filed with
the police and they've dealt with the matter.'

Playing up to him I said, 'I know how busy you must be. I
mean, in your job it's like never ending, right? My uncle was a
fire fighter in Brooklyn for thirty years.' In truth, it was closer
to thirty minutes. 'Ended up commanding the one-oh-seventh
in Flatbush.' I have no idea if that's what the NYFD ever called
their Flatbush fire house but if I didn't know, I figured, this guy
wouldn't know either. And, the only thing he commanded was
the polish to keep the pole shiny. 'I'm a firehouse brat. Trust
me, I understand what it's like.'

'Firehouse brat?'

'It's an American expression. It means I grew up there.' Half
a mile was more like it. 'You know, hanging out there after
school and on weekends.'

He chuckled. 'I like that expression.'

'It's a very different business today. In those days, every fire
house in America had a Dalmatian. It was almost obligatory.
Our fire dog was called . . .' I thought fast, 'Brinkley.'

'None of our watches is supposed to keep pets, but a few of

them have adopted stray dogs and cats. We've got one that has two iguanas.'

'No kidding.' I could have cared less. 'Fire breathing lizards. I love it.'

'Fire breathing lizards? That's funny. I'll have to tell them that.'

'How long you been on the job, Mr Raymond?'

'Me? Too long. I just finished twenty-two.'

'Not easy. I guess you get to see a pretty gruesome side of life.'

'We don't get the volume of cases they do in places like London,' he said, 'but there still aren't enough hours in the day, or enough days in the week.'

'Tell me about it,' I said. 'Listen, I don't mean to take up your time, but is there any way I could get a look at your report? We're trying to tie up the loose ends of the estate. It's all routine stuff.'

'Estate? Was there a death involved here? If there was . . .'

'No. He's the guy who died a couple of days ago in the Channel Islands. Guernsey. It was suicide.'

'Oh . . . wait a second. I know what you're talking about. It was a small private laboratory. Early Saturday morning.'

'That's it.'

'Hold on.' He put the phone down and I could hear him rummaging through papers. After a few seconds he started whistling. It was two choruses of 'My Bonnie Lies Over The Ocean' before he grabbed the phone to announce, 'Found it. Yes. Bickerton. But I've got to warn you there's really nothing I can say . . . at least not a lot, except in the most general terms. It's up to the police.'

'I understand. I just need a few facts to clear up my file.'

There was a long silence while I listened to him turning pages. Then he said, 'Well . . . I can say that the fire is being considered suspicious. I wasn't there but . . .' He stopped, obviously to read something . . . 'that's the conclusion of the senior on-scene officer. Yes, we've already acknowledged that the fire has been officially categorized as being of a suspicious origin.'

'In other words, arson.'

He hesitated. 'In some cases, that's what it could mean.'

'In this case?'

'In this case . . .' He finally admitted, 'I think you can safely assume that this is arson.'

Now I wanted to know, 'Who reported the fire?'

He checked the paperwork. 'Fire out at 03:50. That's sixteen minutes from the time the engine arrived. And the call came in at . . . 03:12. It was responded to by . . . it says here . . . by PC Carney and PC Hoving.'

'Are they the investigating officers?'

'No. They simply answered the call.'

'Carney and Hoving.' I jotted down those names. 'Was everything destroyed?'

'Apparently . . . let me check . . . yes, our report says the building and contents were a total write off.'

'What happens now?'

'About what?'

'About the fact that it was arson.'

'That's up to the police. They investigate it.'

'How long should that take?'

'In cases like this, just between you and me, about as long as it takes to do the paperwork.'

'And then what?'

'And then the paperwork sits for years in a file called unsolved arson.'

'How come, unsolved?'

'Statistical reality,' he replied. 'Most cases of arson never get solved.'

Chapter Thirteen

Henry couldn't believe I was already in the office. 'What are you doing here?'

'I work here.'

'It's Monday morning.'

'I work here on Monday mornings too.'

'No, you don't,' she corrected. 'Sometimes you work here on Monday afternoons, but most of the time . . .'

'I promise not to make it a habit.'

'I can tell this is a new experience for you. You see, people who get to the office early usually make coffee.' She pointed to the fax machine. 'And they always check the night faxes.'

I hadn't noticed that the wire basket at the back of the machine was full. 'I'll leave the coffee to you.'

The first fax was a handwritten note from McBride – 'Did you see this?' – with a copy of the *Sunday Times* story on the fire at Bickerton's lab.

Then there were several pages from Sandy Miller, who was chief counsel at Great Lakes Reliance, a small insurance company in Chicago with whom I have a tiny retainer deal. It isn't a lot of money, only $500 a shot, but it adds up over the year. He wanted me to settle a shipping claim on their behalf.

Next was a fax from Hartley saying he was thrilled with the BA settlement.

Finally there was a page from a solicitor in London named Halliwell who represented the Galleria Leonardo-Bellini on Cork Street.

And suddenly I had a problem.

About six months ago, a couple from New York, the Lustigs, had strolled into the gallery – just three doors down from

Greta's place – and struck up a conversation with the owner who called himself Count Gunther von Dürer. According to what the Lustigs told me, he claimed to be a direct descendant of Albrecht Dürer and hence heir to his title. Except, of course, Dürer never had a title. Still, they were impressed enough that when they spotted a little bronze reclining figure by Henry Moore – which he graciously agreed to let them have at thirty per cent off – they wrote him a cheque for $17,750, to cover the selling price of £11,500.

According to the Lustigs they bought the sculpture, one of an edition of eight, on the understanding that the Count would furnish a certificate of authenticity from the Henry Moore Foundation, arrange for their export rebate on the value added tax, refund to them any overpayment – depending on the foreign exchange rate at the Count's bank – and handle all shipping expenses. The sculpture was small enough that they could have stuck it in their suitcase, but they said that he said it had to be cleared by the English Heritage Export Authority – whatever that was – before the Government could permit any of Moore's masterpieces to leave the country.

So they went back to New York happily believing that they'd bought a masterpiece at thirty per cent off. When the little bronze didn't arrive after two weeks, Lustig phoned the Count who explained that the paperwork was going through the bureaucracy at English Heritage. Two weeks later, the Count said he'd been told by English Heritage that the export committee had approved the request and that the paperwork was being passed along to HM Customs and Excise who merely had to rubber-stamp the VAT rebate. Two more weeks passed. The Count now insisted that the VAT people had only just completed the paperwork and that the sculpture was being packed by the shipper. The following week his excuse was that the shipper had presented the certificate to Customs at the airport who'd refused to allow the export because English Heritage had forgotten to enclose a proper authentication from the Henry Moore Foundation.

Lustig finally threatened that unless he received the sculpture within seven days, he'd cancel the deal. So the Count said that because Lustig and his wife had been forced to wait so long, he would make it up to them by sending them a larger, more expensive piece as a substitute. The Lustigs were justifiably suspicious, but the Count faxed them a photograph out of Moore's *catalogue raisonnée* showing a reclining mother and child, part of a numbered edition of six. Lustig said he wanted to see the piece before making any commitment.

Within two days a sculpture arrived in New York. But it wasn't the same size as the one in the catalogue, there was no authentication from the Henry Moore Foundation, there was no paperwork from English Heritage, there was no export approval from Customs and Excise, it wasn't signed, and instead of being an edition of six, the piece was stamped 'AP' – which stands for artist proof – and not otherwise numbered.

Lustig immediately got in touch with his lawyer who, in turn, found me.

The first thing I did was write a stern letter to the Count demanding that he make good on the original deal. Halliwell answered that his client was greatly disturbed by Lustig's continuing harassment, that his client was refuting all of Lustig's allegations, that the transaction between the two parties had been suitably concluded, and that if Mr Lustig chose to pursue this matter, to the detriment of Count von Dürer's professional reputation, the Count would institute libel proceedings against Mr Lustig.

I took that to mean that the gloves were off, so I rang Greta and asked her about the Count. She assured me, 'His title has one too many vowels.'

Because I was way out of my depth here – a shipping claim is one thing, the world of art another – I asked her if she knew anyone I could speak with who knew how the Count did business. So she introduced me to Theo Waddington, whom she described as, 'The world's greatest living authority on phoney art dealers named after Renaissance artists born in Nuremberg.'

A robust fellow in his early fifties with a warm smile and gentle voice, Waddington owned a major contemporary art gallery further up the block on the other side of Cork Street. He said he first ran into the Count back in the mid-1970s when he – Theo – was running a gallery on Sherbrook Street in Montreal. He'd just opened a major Eskimo sculpture show – museum-quality soapstones – every piece of which was on consignment from a friend who'd apparently gotten them directly from some Eskimos in Frobisher Bay in exchange for the equivalent weight in beef and onion flavoured potato chips.

The Count wandered in, saw the sculptures and immediately bought six pieces for £19,000. He paid with a cheque and Waddington gave him a receipt, but was smart enough to keep the sculptures, waiting for the cheque to clear. It didn't. However, a week later papers arrived from an attorney in Toronto seeking claim of the six Eskimo pieces, because the Count had traded them for an Antoni Clave oil painting at a gallery in Chicago. Unfortunately for the dealer in Chicago, he wasn't as smart as Waddington and had permitted the Count to take the painting with him.

Although Theo was well within his rights to keep the sculptures, it cost him several thousand dollars in legal fees to stay clear of the Chicago dealer's battle with the Count. Ever since, Waddington faithfully collected whatever dirt he could on the Count and was happy to share it with anyone who asked.

According to him, the Galleria Leonardo-Bellini was owned by a shell company on the Isle of Man, which was in turn owned by another shell company in Luxembourg. Furthermore, von Dürer wasn't the Count's real name – he'd been born Albert Schmidt in Vaduz, Liechtenstein – and although he'd been operating as von Dürer for at least twenty years, Waddington said, he'd only legally changed his name in Liechtenstein six years ago.

The title was, obviously, invented. But Schmidt had registered his title along with his assumed name as a limited company in the Bahamas five years ago. And that, I must admit, was a clever little trick. It meant he could claim that whenever he introduced himself as Count von Dürer he was using his company name like a professional name, as valid a way to conduct business as Alexander Archibald Leach calling himself Cary Grant or William Sydney Porter using the *nom de plume*, O. Henry.

Because the gallery and the assumed name were both worthless companies, my first stop was the phone booth that my friend Rodney uses as an office.

If he has a last name, I don't know what it is. I've dealt with him for maybe a dozen years but have no idea what he looks like. He has a Cockney accent, he once happened to mention

that he lost a leg in a motorcycle accident, and when he bills me
he always asks that my cheque be made out to a woman whose
address is a hotel in Blackpool. Still, he has to be the most
valuable voice at the end of any payphone anywhere in London
because Rodney, a professional researcher, is cursed with the
fear that there is always one stone yet to be overturned.

I told him about the Count and the Count's companies. The
next morning he sent me a pile of stuff he'd found at Companies
House – that's where the British Department of Trade and
Industry keeps their official records of incorporation – which
detailed several companies owned by the Count, their various
subsidiaries and his various directorships. Of course, the records
at Companies House are public. On the other hand, records held
by credit card companies aren't. Those arrived from Rodney
that afternoon.

The next day I had the Count's records from the Department
of Motor Vehicles – again, not something otherwise available to
the general public – which revealed that one of his three cars was
owned by a company not registered at Companies House.

With Rodney's research skills and Theo Waddington's
tutelage, I was able to navigate my way inside the Count's
world of art. It led me, eventually, to two of his ex-wives and
three of his bank accounts. From there, Rodney was able to find
a Liechtenstein *anstalt*, a secret company owned by Schmidt,
that in turn owned a villa in St Paul de Vence, in the south
of France. And among the *anstalt*'s assets were a number of
watercolours by the French artist Raoul Dufy.

When I mentioned the paintings to Theo, he told me
about an upcoming sale of Dufy's work at Sotheby's. So
I went with him to Sotheby's and together we were able
to ascertain that three watercolours – each estimated to
be worth £8,000–£10,000 – had been put into the sale by
von Dürer, claiming to represent a client who was selling
them on behalf of a company in the Bahamas, cutely named
Intaglio.

One phone call to the Bahamas later, and on behalf of the
Lustigs, I filed suit against Intaglio in Nassau, then against
Albert Schmidt in London, served notice on him at the
gallery, published a notice of proceedings against Schmidt
in the Marxist newspaper the *Morning Star* – just because
no one reads it any more doesn't change the fact that notice

has been published – waited five days and then, as part of our claim against Intaglio, arrested the three Dufys.

No, I didn't get a sheriff to walk into Sotheby's and say to the watercolours, you're under arrest. I attached a lien on them, preventing Sotheby's from either selling them or returning them to Schmidt, von Dürer, his representative or any representative of Intaglio. It's a good gimmick, which I'd first used a couple of years ago to force a guy in the oil business to pay a debt. I'd heard about a cargo he'd just bought and arrested the ship. Well, at least I'd tried to. Unfortunately, I'd fumbled the ball, had failed to get the court order delivered in time and had wound up standing on the dock watching the ship sail into the sunset. My client was less than thrilled. But I'd learned a new trick. And this time I pulled it off.

At least I thought I did.

I delivered a court order to the auction house with plenty of time to spare, instructing them to retain possession of the painting until the dispute was settled. But here was a fax from Halliwell saying that the Dufys were actually owned by a gallery in Los Angeles, the owner of which had purchased the house in France two days before I arrested the paintings. Attached to his fax was a copy of the bill of sale for the *anstalt*. Also attached was a letter from an attorney in Los Angeles instructing Halliwell to sue me personally for the paintings.

Clearly, the bill of sale had been backdated. And I'm sure that with Rodney's help I could have proved that. But I was only in the game for a third of what I could collect for the Lustigs and the sudden appearance of another attorney was about to wipe out my contingency fee. It also put the Lustigs in a position where, to stay in the game, they'd have to come up with some money.

It was too early to ring New York and tell them that von Dürer had pulled a fast one. But Halliwell didn't have to know that. I phoned him and lied that unless he had a settlement in mind my clients were instructing me to go all the way. Luckily he didn't call my bluff. Instead he said, 'I settle best over doughnuts,' and suggested we meet halfway between his office and mine, which turned out to be a doughnut shop off Piccadilly.

'The vanilla ice-rings are the best,' a man called to me

from a seat in the window where he'd taken possession of two chairs by spreading out across them.

He was the only person in there over the age of sixteen, so I knew this was Halliwell.

I nodded hello, told the guy behind the counter that I'd take a coffee and a jelly doughnut, waited there for it, paid for it and then carried it to Halliwell's table, already littered with a Styrofoam cup of coffee, a pile of paper napkins, two ice-ring doughnuts, one prune pastry and a burning cigarette that looked as if it was just about to tumble out of a tiny metal ashtray and onto the floor.

'You look like you must be Vince.'

I wanted to say, and you look like you've had one too many meals here, but wound up with a benign, 'How are you.'

His blue pinstriped suit had seen more winters than his tailor had expected, his vest was unbuttoned because it no longer fit around his bulging middle and his white hair had turned slightly yellow along the side, the way it often seems to happen with chain smokers.

I extended my hand to shake his.

He hacked, picked up his cigarette, puffed on it, put it down, shook my hand and bit off another mouthful of doughnut.

There was no reason to beat around the bush, so after a sip of my coffee – it was too hot and otherwise awful – I took my best shot. 'I'm going to get you and your pal in Los Angeles on conspiracy to defraud and land your phoney Count in a pile of shit with the French authorities for the sale of the house.'

He didn't so much as blink. 'Forget it. You can't win. You're out of your league here.'

'You willing to bet on that?'

He never stopped chewing. 'I am but you're not. Maybe if you'd been able to keep the Dufys . . . but the minute you lost them, you lost us.'

'Who says I lost them?'

'Come on.' He swallowed his first doughnut, washed it down with a swig of coffee and began devouring the Danish. 'We just opened a second front. What are you going to do? Sue us in France and California and here?' He looked at me. 'You're in for what, a third? Half? There's no way that your clients will cough up any more money. If they do they're fools. Either way, you're stuck.'

'So far the only thing I'm stuck with,' I said, toying with my pastry and checking to find the jam inside much too bright-red, 'is terrible coffee and a doughnut filled with artificial colorants.'

He pointed at it. 'You don't want it, I'll eat it.'

I had to know, 'What are you going to do when one of these things becomes a wad of cement in your arteries . . .'

'If it happens now, then maybe you can collect your fee from your clients. If it happens next week, or tomorrow, or even after I make you a deal and you refuse, then it's too late.'

'My clients are in for the duration,' I said. 'But I'll carry the message for you. So what kind of deal are you talking about?'

'They get the mother and child from the catalogue, the one von Dürer was willing to substitute for the original piece they claimed to have bought. But they have to pay the VAT on top of the money they've already paid, which comes to an additional £2,012.50. They also pay shipping. Call it an even twenty-two hundred.'

I tried to recall which sculpture was which. 'This is the mother and child . . .'

'One of an edition of six.'

'The other one was . . .'

'Not the artist proof.' He finished the Danish and moved on to his final doughnut.

I took my pen and wrote it down on my napkin. 'Just between us, whatever happened to the first sculpture? The one they paid for?'

'Got lost somewhere in the translation between English and American.'

'In other words, either your guy never owned it to begin with or sold it for more money out from under my clients.'

He grinned. 'The art world is an amusing place.'

'Sounds boisterously entertaining,' I said.

He looked at me. 'Deal?'

I stood up. 'I'll let you know.'

'Close of business today,' he said, then pointed to my doughnut. 'Not going to eat it?'

'Be my guest.' And with that I walked out, thinking to myself, I hope he makes it until close of business today.

As long as I was in Piccadilly, I strolled over to Cork Street

and poked my head in Greta's place. The sign on the door
said closed – she didn't open on Mondays until one o'clock
– but she was there, so I knocked and when she spotted me
she let me in.

'You up for lunch?'

'Too early,' she said. 'And anyway, what makes you think
I'm available on short notice?'

'Wishful thinking,' I told her, studying some of the paintings
on her walls. 'People pay money for this stuff?'

'Not only do you come in here thinking I'm instantly
available,' she said, 'you also insult my artist.'

'It's just lots of coloured-in squares and rectangles.'

'No. It's more than that. But if you tried doing it, then yes,
it would be just coloured-in squares and rectangles.'

'What's his name?'

'John Hoyland.'

'Never heard of him.'

'He's very famous.'

'How can he be very famous if I never heard of him?'

'Who was that baseball player you once told me about . . .
someone you met?'

'You mean Roy Campanella? Now, he was really famous.'

She grinned. 'How can he be really famous if I never heard
of him?'

I confessed, 'I'm getting nowhere fast.'

She agreed. 'Nowhere at all.'

'Too bad about lunch.'

'I might accept a doughnut and coffee.'

I grimaced and headed for the door. 'I may not be able to
look a doughnut in the face ever again.' Then I stopped to stare
again at the paintings. 'Rectangles, squares and green paint.'

She said, 'Men in their pyjamas swinging bats at baseballs.'

'But Roy Campanella was really famous.' I waved goodbye
and left.

I went up Cork Street, saw that the Count's place was closed
on Mondays – looking through his window I saw a whole room
full of stuff by more famous people I'd never heard of – then
moved along the block only to discover that Theo Waddington
was closed Mondays too. So I walked back to the office thinking
about how I was going to convince the Lustigs that the only

way they could win was by putting another couple of grand into the game.

It wasn't until I was in front of One Hung's that I wondered how come Greta never asked me about my Bass River message.

'Well, I'm afraid that's the way the purchasing department here operates,' Henry was saying on the phone as I stepped inside. 'If you want, I'll let you speak directly to the purchasing manager. Just a minute please . . .' She cupped the receiver and said to me, 'We're now out of toner for the laser printer and if you ever want to print anything again, you'll have to tell the cretin on line two your name is Robert Hawke and that you're the purchasing manager.'

'Robert Hawke . . . as in the former prime minister of Australia?'

She grinned one of those 'see for yourself' grins. 'Tell them it's for an HP-3.'

I walked into my own office and grabbed the phone. 'Hawke,' I announced, 'Purchasing.'

A woman on the other end said, 'This is Inninout Office Supplies.'

'Inninout?' I didn't understand. 'You mean, like in and out?'

'Inninout. Yes. Do you want something?'

'Yes. We're trying to order some toner for a laser printer.'

'Certainly, sir. As I was trying to determine from your boss, have you got a laser printer?'

'From my boss? Ah . . . yes, and I want to order some toner.'

'Of course, sir, what sort of toner?'

'Don't you mean, what sort of printer?'

'No, sir, first I need to know what sort of toner.'

Henry appeared at my door. I shot a glance at her and raised my eyebrows. 'What are my choices?'

'We sell toner for printers and photocopiers.'

'This is for a printer.'

'All right, sir, what sort of printer?'

'An HP-3.'

'No sir, not the brand, the type.'

I asked, 'Okay, what are my choices?'

'Laser, bubble jet or wheel.'

'Ah . . . laser.'

'Fine, sir. And what is the make of the laser printer?'

I repeated, 'HP-3.'

'No sir, I just need the make. Is that HP? As in hotel papa?'

'Yes. Hotel. Papa.'

'And the model number?'

'Ah . . . could it be three? As in the trilogy?'

'I wouldn't have any idea what model number you have, sir.'

I confirmed, 'Three.'

'Fine, sir, is the toner going to be used?'

That stopped me. 'I beg your pardon?'

'Are you going to use the toner?'

I had to find out, 'What are my choices?'

'Sir, I have no way of knowing what you intend on doing with it. That's strictly up to you.'

'Why would you ask if I'm going to use it?'

'I presume you are an American, sir. I can tell that from your accent. So you might not be *au fait* with all our various Customs and Excise rules. You see, sir, if you are going to use it, the price is £32, plus VAT. If you are not going to use it, the price is only £28 plus VAT.'

'That makes it very clear,' I said, shaking my head, then assured her, 'No, I'm not going to use it.'

'That's fine, sir, may I take your account number if you've dealt with us before, or if you are a new customer I will need your credit card number and address and will at the end of this order furnish you with your account number, then arrange to have you invoiced and at the same time arrange a delivery. Will someone be in your office tomorrow between nine am and five pm?'

'Yes. Thank you,' I said. 'Just a moment please . . . my boss has all that information.' I handed the phone to Henry. 'It's the cultural difference between the old world and the new.'

She made a face at me and took the phone.

The morning mail brought confirmation from a lawyer in Minnesota to whom I'd subcontracted a negligence suit that the settlement had been finalized. There was a letter from a shipping company in Miami about an insurance claim, a note from a lawyer in LA asking me to help him with the conveyancing of a yacht his client was buying in Spain and, best of all, last week's copy of *Boxing Week*.

I shouted to Henry, 'Hey, boss, you want lunch?'

She wanted to know, 'Why?'

I answered, 'Why not?'

On the way to Giovanni's, Henry and I stopped at the bank to deposit the British Airways cheque. As long as I was there, I asked the cashier if the cheque we'd deposited the other day had cleared yet. She punched a few buttons on her computer, said it had, but reminded me that the funds wouldn't be available until Tuesday. I said no problem and made a mental note to hold on to Moe's cheque until later that afternoon when the banks were closed.

Giovanni asked Henry what she wanted for lunch and after insisting that he call her Anna-Maria – 'I think I'll be Italian for a while' – she reminded him that she was on a diet. He was too polite to say she needed to be on a diet, but I could tell he was thinking that. Anyway, she proceeded to order spaghetti carbonara, which considering the cream content is hardly what people on diets should eat. I was about to tell him that I'd have the veal, when he decided that I'd have spaghetti carbonara too. So we both had that and then she had some of Giovanni's home made gellati for dessert. I nursed a coffee. Giovanni waited for her to go back to the office before he pulled out the bottle of grappa and sat down with me.

'What's new with the dead guy who sent you the cheque?'

'I just spent it all on a trainer named Moe Moses. He's taking on Hambone for a few weeks.'

'I'm coming to the fight with you,' he promised. 'You're saving me a seat, right? I really want to be there. When is it?'

'A week from Friday night.'

He wrote himself a note on a paper napkin and shoved it into his pocket. 'What kind of money can I get on the kid?'

'I don't know if anybody's making book on it yet. It's too small a fight. They probably won't bother. But on the night you can put some money down with those Maltese guys, Scarface and his friend. You know who I mean?'

'Never again with those guys. They were happy to take my

money last time but weren't so happy when it came time to paying out.'

'So why do you think one of them is called Scarface?'

'Forget it. I'll go over to the Cypriot's place and talk him into giving me a price.'

I felt obliged to tell him, 'You don't have to bet on Hambone if you don't want to.'

'Sure I do.'

'I figure he's probably the 7–4 underdog. Don't tell him I said that, but the kid he's fighting is supposed to be fast. And right now, I'm not sure that Hambone thinks he can win. Anything better than 9–4 I reckon is a good bet.'

'Who's going to give us that?'

I pointed in the direction of the Cypriot's place. 'Why don't I go in there and see what kind of numbers he'll give me on McGraw.'

Giovanni was shocked. 'You're going to bet against your own fighter?'

'If the Cypriot thinks I am, he might be willing to stretch a few points for you on Hambone.'

He started to grin. 'You mean, you're going to make him think Hambone's taking a dive . . .'

I held up both hands to proclaim my innocence. 'I never said anything of the kind. I just want to know what sort of numbers he's willing to offer someone who wants to put a couple of hundred pounds on McGraw.'

'How much do we go with Hambone?'

'If the numbers are right, what would you say to splitting five hundred?'

'You're on,' he said.

If I could goose up Hambone's odds, the Cypriot could wind up paying for most of Moe's fee.

Giovanni leaned forward and whispered, 'This legal?'

'What kind of a question is that?'

'A straight question. How about a straight answer?'

'Hey. I'm a lawyer.'

'Oh, yeah, I sometimes forget.' He sat back and poured two more glasses of grappa. 'Tell me something, Mr Lawyer, this dead guy who sent you money, they find his body yet?'

'Nope.'

'His cheque clear?'

'Yeah.'

'So how come his next of kin hasn't bothered to close his bank account?'

Chapter Fourteen

I'd planned to spend the afternoon sorting through all of last week's paperwork – the way I do every Monday afternoon – before going to Charlie's to meet Moe Moses, but I couldn't get the conversation with Giovanni out of my head. I wound up, instead, moving gradually from obvious answers like, his next of kin forgot, to obvious questions like, how come a man I meet once mutters something about getting even and turns up dead?

So I phoned the Brighton police and asked for PC Carney. He wasn't in. Neither was PC Hoving. I didn't leave a message.

Then I rang Gerry Raymond. His office said he was out for the rest of the day. I didn't leave a message for him either.

Because I didn't have anybody else to talk to, I dialled information and asked if they had a listing for L. Roger Bickerton in Brighton. The woman gave me a number. I let it ring for a long time, but there was no answer. I reasoned that if the phone had been shut off, there would have been some sort of recorded message saying as much. I decided that whoever forgot to close his bank account had also forgotten to cancel his phone.

Now I started to wonder, who is that person?

I got Henry to call the European Research Project, on the pretext of being the wife of an old friend of Bickerton's, to ask if there was going to be a memorial service for him. I listened on my extension while she was put through to that same guy in the press office, who told her that he knew of no plans to do anything of the sort. He said very firmly, 'A memorial service would be a private family affair and the ERP would not be involved.'

'What about his widow?' She explained, 'I would so much like to send her a card.'

'His widow?' There was a long pause. 'He wasn't married.'

'He wasn't? Isn't that odd . . .' She ad-libbed . . . 'Because I'd recently heard that he was with someone. Of course, it could have been his ex-wife. Yes. I'm positive that's who it was. Have you got an address for her?'

Now the fellow was openly suspicious. 'Who did you say you were?'

'My name is Helen Porter Mitchell.'

'Miss Mitchell . . .'

'Mrs Mitchell,' Henry said, overacting.

'Mrs Mitchell . . . I ah . . . and you're the wife of an old friend . . . I'm sorry, but I really can't give out too much information. I mean, I wouldn't know where to get in touch with his ex-wife.'

'Is she no longer in Eastbourne?'

'I don't know anything about her,' he said.

'No, of course not.' She tried again, 'But if you had some sort of address for her . . .'

'I'm afraid I don't. And it won't do any good to ring back here because no one else will give you any information either. Now if you will please excuse me, I must take another call . . .' And with that he hung up.

'Do you like the way I handled that?' She stepped into my office. 'Pretty good, eh?'

'How come he's so nervous?'

'Do you like the way I came up with the name Helen Porter Mitchell?'

'He didn't want to talk about Bickerton.'

'Of course, you recognize the name Helen Porter Mitchell.'

'I wonder where his ex-wife lives?' There was a library not too far away on St Martin's Street. 'Sure I recognize the name.' I stood up. 'If I'm not back by five, go ahead and close up. See you tomorrow.'

She challenged me. 'So who is she?'

I took a wild stab – 'How many famous Australians do you think there are in the world?' – and left her standing in my office believing that I did know.

Hambone spotted me as soon as I walked into Charlie's. He ran over, threw his arms around me and gave me big sweaty bear hug. 'I won't let you down.'

I stood there for a few moments, then hugged him back. 'I know you won't, Derek.'

Now Charlie came up to me. 'It won't happen again. I gave you my word. I called Fuzzy first thing this morning and told him his guys weren't welcome here.'

'Thanks, Charlie.' What else could I say? 'Where's Moe?'

'He's in the office making a call.'

I nodded to reassure him that all was forgiven, told Hambone to start hitting a bag and went into the office. A two-by-four cubbyhole in the corner next to the door that leads into the showers, Charlie's desk was piled high with boxing magazines and his walls were totally covered in fading fight posters. A bare bulb hung from the ceiling.

Moe was comfortably ensconced in Charlie's oak hall chair, trying to convince someone on the other end of the line, 'He's not getting a motorcycle.' When he spotted me he said to whoever he was speaking with, 'I've got to go,' paused, then added into the phone, 'It doesn't matter why I have to go, he's still not getting a motorcycle.' With that he hung up, made a face and asked me, 'You got a sixteen-year-old grandson?'

'I've got a fifteen-year-old son.'

'He got a motorcycle?'

'No.'

'Good.' He nodded. 'Now I can assure my grandson that he isn't the only teenager on the planet without a motorcycle.'

'This is for you.' I handed him his cheque. 'Did Charlie tell you that some heavyweight was in here last week and taunted Hambone to get in the ring with him?'

'Why would he get into the ring with a heavyweight?'

I wanted to say, because sometimes Hambone does dumb things. Instead I answered, 'One of Fuzzy White's fighters.'

'That still doesn't answer the question why your guy would get into the ring with him. I presume you know who Fuzzy's ex-brother-in-law is?'

'I know who he is but I didn't know he was an ex.'

'Sure. They were married to sisters. Fuzzy dumped his wife first and when O'Reardon saw what fun Fuzzy was having, he got rid of his wife too.' He started to cackle, which seemed to be his way of laughing. 'It's good to know that divorce doesn't wreck friendships.'

'It's good to know that Mickey O'Reardon might be worried about my kid.'

'Hah.' Moe nodded several times. 'It may not be true. But if it is true, it's good to know.'

'You don't think it's true?'

'Let me put it this way, if Mickey O'Reardon is worried, I wouldn't put it past him to try something like that.'

'Why else would he do it?'

'Why wouldn't he?'

I stared at this little guy for a long time and even though I sensed I didn't have to remind him that Hambone needed to get to a payday, I wanted him to know, 'I'm counting on you to look after him.'

He reached for the cheque, folded it and put it in his pocket. 'Normally anything that has to do with ham is a problem for me. In this case, I'm making an exception.'

St Martin's Street Library is also known as the Central Reference Library, which means they have dozens of directories that tell you everything you want to know about anybody who is, or ever was, anybody. And because I particularly hate it when Henry manages to get one up on me, I started with *Who's Who* and Helen Porter Mitchell. She wasn't listed there, but I did find her in *Who Was Who*. 'The Australian opera singer known professionally as Dame Nellie Melba, she gave her name to a dry, brittle piece of toast in addition to an ice cream and peach dessert.' I had to laugh. Henry never heard of Puccini but she did know ice cream.

Back at *Who's Who*, I found the listing for Roger Bickerton.

'Bickerton, L. (Louis) Roger. CBE 1988. Director, European Research Project, Eastbourne Laboratories since 1984. *b*. 17 November 1938; *s* of late John Howard Bickerton and late Josephine Bickerton (*née* Peltier); *m* 1972 Ghislain Cesari (*marr. diss*. 1980), *d* of late Prof. Etienne Cesari; *Educ*: Cambridge, 1st cl. Hons BSc Biology 1959, MSc Biology 1961, Haute Ecole des Etudes Scientifiques, Paris, PhD Biology 1965. Fellow, King's College, Cambridge; FRAS; Director, Nestlé-Needham Laboratory, Cambridge, 1981; Director, European Research Project, Eastbourne Laboratories, 1984.'

There was his life, reduced to fewer than a hundred words.

And there was the former Mrs Bickerton . . . the boss's daughter.

I photocopied the entry, then went in search of any other references to him. He was in the *International Who's Who*, *Current Biography* and the *Biographical Dictionary of Science*. I photocopied all of them even though the entries were similar.

As long as I had the *Biographical Dictionary of Science* open, I checked the entry for Etienne Cesari – it took up nearly one full page – but the most interesting thing about it was a cross-reference to his daughter. And she was the next listing.

'Cesari, Ghislain: Assistant Director of the Centre National de Recherches Scientifiques, Marseilles (France). Born Paris (France), 21 April 1942. Daughter of Professor Etienne Cesari (dec.) and Véronique Masseyeff. Married 1972 Paris (France) L. Roger Bickerton (divorced 1980). Education: La Faculté de Médecine de Paris, L'Institut National Supérieur d'Etudes de Recherches Médicales. Upon completion of her studies, Dr Cesari spent three years as an associate at the Institut Pasteur, one at the British Institute at Carshalton, then joined her father at the Haute Ecole des Etudes Scientifiques. Following his death in 1984, she assumed the post she presently holds at the CNRS.'

There was a short list of abbreviations which I took to be various honours, including the French Légion d'Honneur, and then there was a long list of her publications, all of the titles in French, none of which made any sense to me.

After reading all my photocopies again, I walked back to the office – Henry was already gone – picked up the phone, asked international directory inquiries for the number of the CNRS in Marseilles, flicked on my tape recorder and dialled it. A couple of seconds later a woman answered, 'CNRS. J'écoute.'

'Ah . . . good afternoon . . . do you speak English?'

'Yes, please,' she said. 'May I help you?'

'Dr Ghislain Cesari, please.' I pronounced it like Gillen.

'What is the name please?'

'Ghislain . . . ah, Cesari, Dr Cesari.'

'Ah. Ghislain Cesari.' Except she pronounced it like Jiz-len. 'Just one moment please.'

I listened as an extension rang four times, then heard an answering machine with the voice of a woman speaking in rapid French. The only thing she said that I could understand was, 'Projet Européen de Recherche.'

Chapter Fifteen

Monkeys lie.

I know that for a fact because I read it in an inflight magazine.

People stuck on planes thumb through those glossy publications shoved into the pouch in front of their seat because they can't think of anything else to do between take-off and the honey-roasted peanuts. But very few people ever seem to read them. I've noticed men flick the pages and stop at the ad for the *Sports Illustrated* swimsuit edition. I've noticed women flick the pages and stop at the ad for Chanel shoes. And although I've never spotted anyone actually doing the crossword puzzle at the back – six across, three letters for type of aeroplane, beginning with 'j' – there's obviously at least one person on the planet whose mission in life is to ink in only half the puzzle in every copy of the magazine.

Except, I read inflights cover to cover, much the same way I devour back issues of *Reader's Digest* when I go to the dentist, because I learn a lot of stuff from them that I would never learn otherwise. Where else could I expect to find out about wooden shoes in Kinderdike, the annual spaghetti-tree hoax in Pescara, the stamps of Tierra del Fuego, *bonang* gong-chime musicians in Java, and primate mendacity.

One man's pabulum journalism is another man's passkey to the world.

In fact, I duly credit inflight magazines for my entire knowledge of zoology. *National Geographic* notwithstanding – we used to sneak copies into Fat's room, not to learn about the stalking techniques of the snow leopard but to gawk at photos of native girls attending rites of passage ceremonies along the banks of the Upper Sepik River – my only other contact with the animal kingdom was in 1959 when Fat, Guido and I cut school for a week to hang out at the Bronx Zoo after the *Daily*

News published a picture of an eighteen-year-old Austrian beauty who'd just been hired as the youngest lion trainer in the world. It saddened us that we never got to meet her. It was too painful for words that the zoo was packed with other guys cutting school who'd also fallen in love with her photo.

Be that as it may, according to that inflight article, all animals perfect stealth techniques – a form of lying – whether it be to protect themselves and their young from predators, to safeguard their food supply or to comply with the demands nature places on them to procreate. Birds change colours. Rabbits hide their carrots. And there is a type of male lizard that pretends to be a female so he can sneak into a neighbouring harem and have his way with some other lizards' wives. But monkeys are unique because they lie just for the sport of it. That's especially evident when you drive around one of those open zoos where monkeys run loose and think it's particularly funny to pee on your car. What's more, they develop the lying knack at an early age, learning to taunt their elders, to tease their peers and to con gaping children out of ice cream.

In those respects, we're a lot like monkeys.

Most of us probably lie more often than we are willing to admit, which is, in and of itself, a lie. We even make up words for our untruths – we call them fibs or little white lies – specifically so that we don't have to confront ourselves with guilt. And while academia is probably sinking under the weight of postgraduate theses on why we do it, how often we do it and the types of lies we tell, I suspect that most prevarication takes place because it is, quite simply, convenient. 'I'm not hungry' has saved countless children from vegetables. 'My parents are still awake' has saved generations of teenage girls from overenthusiastic teenage boys. 'The cheque's in the mail' has saved many of us, at some time or another, from foreclosure, bankruptcy or just a punch in the nose.

Yet it is the lie we tell to protect ourselves and our young from predators that is, for my money, the most revealing because it so clearly reflects our fears. Lies such as, 'I wouldn't know where to get in touch with his ex-wife.' And, 'I don't know anything about her.'

At least monkeys have enough common sense to run away when they steal your ice cream.

*   *   *

I went back to the caption under the photo of Bickerton's retirement party. Left to right were Stafford, Schlessinger, Mrs Mars, Bickerton, Tyrone, Dr Mars, Cesari, Schluter, Mrs Tyrone and Tsung. I counted ten people, took a sheet of paper, drew a line and listed their names like a seating chart.

As it was Bickerton's going away bash, making him the guest of honour, proper etiquette should put him to the immediate right of whoever was hosting the evening. In this case, that would be Tyrone. The next most important person would therefore be Mars because he was seated on Tyrone's left. That explained why Mrs Mars was on Bickerton's right. That also explained why the person on Dr Mars's left was Dr Cesari, the former Mrs Bickerton.

Life is often about pecking order.

But was she there in her capacity as an ex-wife or was she there because she worked for the ERP? If it was because of her job, why was she put in the seat that would normally go to the guest of honour's wife?

I argued the case out loud.

Bickerton doesn't have a wife so the place that normally goes to her should go to Tyrone's wife. Except, Mrs Tyrone doesn't rank as high as Dr Cesari because she's two seats further down the table. So if Dr Cesari is there in her role as Bickerton's ex-wife, just how ex- is ex-? Except, she works for the ERP. So if Dr Cesari is there because she's so senior, how come the guy in the press office lies that he doesn't know where to find her?

I answered those questions with another question. How come the guy in the press office doesn't want to talk about Dr Bickerton or his ex-wife?

I answered that question by phoning the police in Brighton again. This time I left a message for the two cops, Hoving and Carney. It was late and I didn't really expect to hear from them that evening, but about an hour later Hoving returned my call. I explained who I was and asked about the fire at Bickerton's lab. He said he didn't have any more information than he'd included in his original report and referred me to Gerry Raymond at the fire brigade.

'I spoke to him this morning.'

'He's really your best contact. We responded to the call but it's the fire brigade you need to speak to. And, I guess, maybe the SOCO.'

'The who?'

'The Scene-of-Crime Officer. If you hold on for a second, please, I'll see if he's still around.' I waited for several minutes before Hoving came back on the line to say that the man I needed to speak with was David Chorley.

I was about to say, 'Thanks,' when he clicked me off, and someone else clicked me on. 'My name is Chorley.'

After introducing myself, I asked if he was the Scene of Crime Officer at the Bickerton fire. He responded, 'We refer to it differently,' and rattled off some official sounding numbers. But he spoke too quickly and I didn't get a chance to write them down. Instead, I decided to humour him. 'You know, my uncle was a cop in Brooklyn for thirty years. Ended up commanding the one-oh-seventh in Flatbush.'

'How nice for your uncle,' he mumbled. 'But I'm not a police officer. I'm a civilian employee.'

'Oh . . . I see . . .' So much for Brownie points. 'That's tough work. Do you specialize in arson?'

'Not at all. We take charge of a crime scene so that forensic evidence can be gathered.'

'And this fire the other night . . . the one I refer to as the Bickerton fire . . . you consider it a crime?'

'Yes, we consider it a crime.'

'Can I ask why?'

He hesitated. 'In the case of fire, it's the fire brigade officer-in-charge, or a qualified fire investigator who makes the initial determination. He's the one who decides if a fire is of a suspicious origin. If it is, then we get called in.'

'And the fact that you've been called in to this one means there is something suspicious.'

'That's right.'

'Does suspicious mean criminal?'

'Not always.'

'In this case?'

He thought about his answer before conceding, 'This is arson.'

I wanted to know more. 'There's a fellow I've already spoken to at the fire brigade . . . SDO Raymond . . . and if it's all right with him, and it's all right with you, and if I just happened to be in Brighton one of these days, do you think we could all get together for a cup of coffee?'

'For a cup of coffee, perhaps. For a discussion of specifics about this case, that depends. After all, this is an ongoing investigation . . . we believe a crime has been committed . . .'

'I accept that. But I'd like to get some things straight in my own mind about my client and this fire . . .'

'The decision is not mine to take.'

'Well, then, who's got the authority to okay a meeting?'

'I would have to clear this with my superiors and, I suspect, SDO Raymond would have to clear it with his.'

'When can I expect to hear from you.'

He said flatly, 'I will get back to you as soon as I can.'

'I'd be grateful.' I gave him my office number and then, as an afterthought, gave him my home number too.

I left the office that night thinking to myself that if I didn't hear from him by tomorrow afternoon, I'd start with Raymond, then call Chorley's boss, then call Raymond's boss and just work my way up the ladder. But it wasn't necessary. As I was walking in my front door the phone rang. It was Chorley saying that he and Raymond would meet me tomorrow morning at ten at fire brigade headquarters.

I went to bed that night having totally forgotten to tell the Lustigs about my meeting with Halliwell.

Chapter Sixteen

The 8:08 train from London's Victoria station pulled in at exactly 9:00, and with an hour to spare I headed for the beach.

They have a boardwalk in Brighton, England, although it's not made of wood like the boardwalk in Brighton Beach, Brooklyn. It doesn't smell of hotdogs, knishes and cotton candy. And they never heard of skeeball. The English Channel isn't the Atlantic Ocean and the beach is covered in stones. There are two piers jutting out into the sea. One of them is Palace Pier, a noisy, neon-lit amusement park – perhaps ladies and gentlemen of another age took their mid-morning tea there, or danced there on summer nights – and the other has long since decayed beyond the point where it's safe. So they chopped the second pier off at the boardwalk and left the rest of it sitting on rotting stilts in a few feet of water, looking something like a half-sunken ship that is too heavy now to be properly buried further out to sea.

Leaning against the railings, I tried to pretend it was the way I really wanted it to be, and breathed deeply, hoping to find that point at the bottom of my lungs that used to ache just a bit whenever I took in too much salty air.

An old man walked his dog.

A couple strolled along the water's edge.

Two small children threw stones into the sea.

Two little old ladies unfolded chairs on the stones, then lowered themselves carefully into them.

Two girls came by on bicycles.

I shut my eyes and somewhere in the back of my head I could hear the tyres of my second-hand English racer as they skimmed along the narrow groove in between the wooden slats of the boardwalk in my Brighton. The air was rushing into my face

as I pedalled as hard as I could because I wanted to beat Nina
Bartelotti who was pedalling as hard as she could. Suddenly, my
front tyre was trapped in that groove and I couldn't steer out of
it and when I braked my bike flew away from me. I crashed onto
my side. My arm scraped along the wood, filling with splinters.
It hurt real bad, but I refused to cry. Nina hurried off her bike
to help me stand up. Then she pulled some of the splinters out
of my arm. And when she was finished she told me I was very
brave. I pretended that she was right. As a reward, she told me
I could kiss her. I said okay, all the time thinking she'd chicken
out at the last minute. We took our bikes onto the beach and
found a place under the boardwalk, at the back where nobody
could see us, then lay down in the sand. I awkwardly put my
arm around her shoulders. She easily moved close to me. I
waited. She said, you can do it now. So I leaned over and put
my mouth on hers but that's as far as I got. She kept her eyes
open and when I didn't close mine she said, you don't know
how to do it, do you. I said, sure I do and she said, no you don't
so I'll teach you. And she did. And later, when I told Fat and
Guido that Nina and I had been making out they didn't believe
me. Even when I showed them how badly I'd scraped my arm,
they still didn't believe me.

When I opened my eyes the old man with the dog was
gone.

The couple at the water's edge were getting wet.

The two small children were being yanked away by their
mother.

The two little old ladies were pulling sun hats over their
heads even though there wasn't a lot of sun.

The girls on their bicycles were nowhere to be seen.

I went down to the beach, where the stones clicked loudly
under my shoes as if the Rockettes were rehearsing but all of
them were out of step. From cubbyholes under the boardwalk,
a girl with pink hair sold painted starfish, an old lady with blue
rinse sold small paper cups of cockles, mussels and whelks, and
an old man with a pot belly sold bad ice cream and slightly
suggestive postcards.

I wondered whatever happened to Nina Bartelotti.

I took off my jacket and rolled up my sleeve and looked at
my arm, to see if there were still any scratches left from that
day, but of course there weren't.

I wondered whatever happened to my bike.

I took another deep breath but the air wasn't salty enough and no matter how hard I held it in my lungs, I couldn't find that feeling.

I wondered whatever happened to me.

Children screamed with glee as the roller-coaster on Palace Pier spun them through loops, and tossed them upside down. It made me think of my two weeks at the Jersey shore with Johnny.

I wondered why that seemed so long ago.

I made my way slowly up the ramp from the beach to the boardwalk, and thought to myself, this isn't Brooklyn. No, it's a poor man's version of Atlantic City, back in the days before gambling, back in the days when people still cared about the Miss America Pageant and salt water taffy, back in the days when the place needed a lot of fresh paint.

I took one last look at the beach.

It's better than nothing, I tried to convince myself.

If only it wasn't made of rocks.

I have lived my life needing sand in my shoes.

The fire station on Preston Circus took up an entire corner, wrapping itself around the block in an oval, with huge dark, double doors ready to lunge open, and shiny fire engines poised behind them, ready to race away. It was a three-storey brick building, with the date 1938 inscribed on the front of it and just inside one of those big doors I could see a fire pole. That made me smile because it reminded me of Mrs Alterac's fifth-grade class when we took a trip to a fire station and they showed us how to slide down the pole. They even let us try it. Guido dared me and I did it. Then I dared Guido and he did it. But Fat was too scared and Guido and I teased him until he started to cry. Because he was crying we teased him even more and he got so mad that he took a swing at me. But I didn't hit him back because I knew if I did I'd hurt him and I loved Fat and after he got killed in Vietnam, Guido and I sat around getting very drunk, telling each other how sorry we were for making him cry like that, all because of the fire pole.

'You must be Mr Barolo.' David Chorley was waiting for me at the side door, just around the corner into Viaduct Street.

I was fifteen minutes late. 'It wasn't as close as I thought.'

He was in his early fifties, a squat, heavy-set fellow with short-cropped brown hair who wore his too-narrow tie pulled just off centre and his collar unbuttoned. His grey tweed jacket was thrown over his shoulders, making me think that he'd gained weight since he'd bought it because even as a cape it seemed half a size too small.

'Nice to meet you.' I shook his hand, then pulled one of my business cards out of my pocket just so that he could see the words Attorney at Law. 'I hope you haven't been waiting too long.'

His expression didn't hide the fact that he had been waiting, and that it was too long. 'We're expected.' I followed him up two flights of stairs, then along a dark hallway with half a dozen closed doors until we got to the end of it. SDO Raymond's office was in the rear of the building, a tiny room with a metal desk, two straight-backed metal chairs and two green metal filing cabinets. There was a large East Sussex County Fire Brigade emblem framed on the wall.

'Good morning.' Raymond took my hand and pumped it, then pumped Chorley's hand as well. 'This your first visit to Brighton?'

'I've been here before,' I said, but couldn't remember the last time, so I didn't go into details.

'How do you like it?'

I sort of told him the truth. 'It makes me think of Atlantic City,' then apologized to him for being late. 'It's my fault. I got a little lost.'

A lanky man in his early forties, he had dark hair just beginning to go grey and wore a perfectly pressed uniform. 'Can I get you some coffee?'

'Thanks.' I took a seat at the side of his desk, Chorley sat facing it, and as Raymond went to fetch the coffee I noticed that he walked with a very obvious limp.

Stopping in the doorway, he turned to ask, 'White or black?'

That was one of the strange things about the British. They only knew two ways of drinking coffee. Black meant black, which was fine, but white meant white, which was like drinking half a glass of milk with a little coffee in it. They drank tea that way too. Anything in between was called khaki but you couldn't have it that way unless you knew the word for it. And God forbid you should ask for sugar because they piled that in by the shovelful. Spoon straight up, as Moe Moses would say. 'Black. Thanks.' I thought of trying to impress them by saying, spoon lying down, but didn't. 'No sugar.'

Chorley said, 'White.'

Raymond nodded and left the office.

There was a long silence. To fill it, I thought small talk might help. 'Been in forensics long?'

'I've been a scene-of-crime officer for fifteen years. It's not quite the same thing as forensics.' He crossed his legs and folded his arms across his chest, showing me with his body language that he wasn't much for small talk.

So I nodded and smiled and settled for no talk, waiting for Raymond to come back.

He returned a few minutes later balancing three Styrofoam cups, a bunch of napkins and a paper plate with store-bought pastries. Chorley took something horrible looking with chocolate icing, Raymond took a round thing with cream inside. I thought of Halliwell – that's when I remembered that I hadn't phoned the Lustigs – and begged off. 'Not for me, thanks.' I toasted them with the coffee. 'To your health.'

Raymond sat down and sipped his carefully.

Chorley just munched.

There was another extended silence. So this time I decided to give Raymond a try at small talk. I pointed to his leg. 'That happen in the line of duty?'

He nodded. 'It will be nine years in July.'

'What happened?'

'A bit of foolishness.'

I dared, 'Foolishness or bravery?'

He shook his head. 'Foolishness. You spend your life worrying about all the big stuff and it's the little ones that sneak up on you.'

I presumed, 'A fire?'

'Electrical. Small office block around the rear of the station.' He made a face. 'Started in the basement but was already moving through the ground floor by the time we got there. I wasn't supposed to be inside but there was a problem getting people out because the doors at the rear of the building had been blocked off. People just don't think when they do stupid things like that.'

'No,' I agreed, 'they don't.'

He shrugged. 'Someone took a bad decision. Instead of trying to knock out the rear doors, we headed back through the smoke to the front. A partition caved in and brought a ceiling beam down with it. Took them almost half an hour to reach me.' He shrugged again, 'It got me this job.'

Staring at the medals on his chest, I gambled with one on the top row. 'Got you that one too.'

'You recognize it?' He grinned proudly. 'Of course you do. Your uncle.'

I changed the subject before Chorley could wonder if my fireman uncle was the same as my policeman uncle. 'Kind of like the Purple Heart. You know, the one they give you in the Army for getting shot.'

'You get that?'

'Not me,' I said. 'I'm a full-time coward. Unlike you.' I hated myself whenever I got smarmy but he seemed to appreciate it. 'Takes a special type of person.'

'It's not all that bad,' he said.

'Eating smoke?' I shook my head. 'Thanks anyway.'

'It's not the smoke, it's what happens after the flames are out and after the smoke clears.' He sorted through one of the folders on his desk, pulled out a large colour photo and warned, 'You don't have to look if you don't want to.'

I reached for it, glanced at it only long enough to notice several well-charred pieces like sides of beef all huddled together in a corner, and handed it straight back to him. 'Thanks anyway.'

'A husband, a wife and four of their children,' he explained. 'They were lucky because we could still identify the remains. Sometimes you investigate a fire and there's nothing left. He reached into his desk drawer and took out more photos. 'You may not want to see these . . .'

I forced myself to look at what was left of someone's face staring at me.

'That was once a teenage girl.'

'On second thought . . .' I quickly handed them back.

'She was in a car. Hit head on. The two fellows in the other car walked away without a scratch. Her petrol tank ignited. It's not supposed to happen and it doesn't happen most of the time. Some cars are better built than others. The petrol tank is protected. But sometimes petrol spills and gets ignited by a spark from the electrical system. Or metal scrapes against metal, like Boy Scouts lighting a fire with two sticks of wood. The car explodes. Tyres burn. Glass melts. Metal warps. The air is highly toxic. People don't live through that.' He paused, found another folder on his desk, extracted three photos from it and assured me, 'These aren't as rough.'

I studied each one but didn't see anything more than a char-blackened room.

'It's your client's laboratory.'

Now I studied them more closely. But even then I eventually had to admit, 'I can't tell a lot from this.'

'If you were a trained fire investigator you could,' Raymond said. 'Just about everything you want to know is in those photos.'

'Such as?'

Raymond glanced at Chorley.

The Scene-of-Crime Officer thought for a moment, then nodded.

So now Raymond told me, 'Such as proof of arson. The place was torched.'

'You're sure?'

'It's fairly obvious arson,' Raymond said. 'We can't be sure from this whether or not there was a break-in. But the other signs . . . it's easy to spot when you know what to look for. The neon lights gave it away.'

'Gave what away?'

'The seat of the fire. The heat gets very intense, it rises, the glass on a neon strip-light melts closest to the source of the heat, and the neon gas shoots out, reshaping the melted glass into a finger pointing towards the source of the heat.' He leaned across his desk and showed me the area of the ceiling he was referring to. 'That indicated one of the two seats of fire.'

Except, I couldn't see anything that looked like neon bulbs. 'I presume that by seat of fire, you mean where the fire actually started?'

'That's right.' He handed me another photo, which didn't mean anything to me, either. 'See here, how the concrete on the wall is spalled? This is the other side of the room. This is the second seat. The flames travelled up the wall.'

I shook my head. 'Looks totally burned out to me.'

'Accidental fires start in one place. A chip pan. A gas heater.

A fuse box. A blocked chimney flue. But when you have two separate seats of fire, that means arson.'

'You can tell that from these?' I was mystified.

Raymond explained, 'Anyone can learn to read a fire just like anyone can learn to read a book. Once you know how, it's easy to see where it started. Once you know where it started, you can begin to figure out how it started.' He returned the pictures to his folder. 'Last night, after David said you were coming to see us, I spoke to the watch commander who responded to the fire. He told me exactly what he'd put in his report, that he could smell accelerants as soon as he got inside. David agrees.'

'I smelled it too,' Chorley confessed. 'It was diesel fuel. That's now confirmed by our forensic people.'

'Diesel fuel?' I asked. 'Like the kind you can buy at any gas station? There was something left? I would have thought anything like fuel would all burn off.'

'Amateurs always think that,' Chorley smirked. 'But the odour of accelerants is frequently very obvious.'

Raymond continued. 'Accelerant was poured on a pile of old rags. And it looks as if someone might have set a timing device to start the fire. That's so that whoever started it could be long gone when the fire happened.'

'A timing device?' I had to know. 'You mean like a bomb?'

'Nowhere near as complicated,' he said. 'If you know how, you can start a fire with a telephone.'

'You can?'

'You rig the phone so that on a certain number of rings it sets off an electrical spark. The spark lights a fuse. The fuse burns down and lights the propellant. All the arsonist has to do is dial the number from ten thousand miles away.'

'That sounds pretty professional.'

Chorley cut in. 'No fire fighter would be this sloppy.'

'Fire fighter?'

Raymond nodded. 'Professionals are almost always ex-fire fighters. Think about it, who knows fire better? When I walk into a fire scene, I know exactly what to look for. So when a professional sets a fire, knowing what I'm looking for, he doesn't leave tell-tale signs like neon bulbs.'

'You get a lot of fires started by firemen?'

'Thank God, no.'

I joked, 'What about scene-of-crime officers?'

Chorley didn't find that amusing. 'In my opinion . . . this was probably a first timer. One of the things you do when you sift through a fire site is look for items that are either not where they should be or don't belong there in the first place. When you find the remains of an alarm clock in a bedroom fire, that's one thing. When you find the remains of an alarm clock on the floor, next to rags that had been doused in accelerant, you have to ask yourself, why are they there?'

'An alarm clock,' I mused.

'Let me show you something.' Raymond took a blank sheet of white paper and drew a rectangle. 'The room was like this . . . door here, windows here . . . there seemed to have been a laboratory table running along this wall, and a desk here. The filing cabinet next to the desk was disturbed and the computer, which would probably have been on the desk, had been moved onto the chair which was here, at the second seat of fire. The alarm clock was found in the rubble, at the first seat of fire, here.'

'Door . . . windows . . .' I studied his diagram. '. . . chair and computer here . . .' I asked, 'How can you tell that someone put the computer on the chair?'

'Because not everything gets destroyed in a fire.'

'Was the computer destroyed?'

'It was completely melted,' Chorley said. 'The chair was badly burned but not destroyed. What remained of the computer was still sitting on top of it.'

'The filing cabinet,' I asked Raymond. 'What do you mean by, it had been disturbed?'

'Pulled away from the wall,' Chorley went on. 'Drawers opened. Most of the contents destroyed.'

'And no sign of break in,' I said more as a statement than a question.

'And no sign of break in,' Chorley confirmed.

I sat back, saw that there was still some coffee left in my cup and swallowed it. 'Pretty strange, I'd say.' The coffee had gone cold.

'I'd say, pretty common,' Chorley volunteered. 'All the earmarks of an insurance fire.'

'Insurance?' That didn't make any sense to me. 'Insurance companies don't pay out when the police say it's arson. Anyway, the guy's dead.'

Chorley suggested, 'Maybe his next of kin just aren't very good at starting fires.'

Raymond apologized that it wasn't up to him to let me have a copy of the official report and passed the buck to Chorley who refused to let me have a copy because this was an ongoing police investigation. But then, I wasn't sure I needed one. So I shook both their hands, thanked them for their time and got directions back to the train station.

I went downstairs alone but once I was outside, Chorley caught up to me. 'I've got a car. It's on my way.'

The station was only a five minute-walk, however he insisted, so I said okay, followed him to his car and climbed in. He started the engine, said, 'Don't ever tell anyone I did this,' and drove me to Bickerton's lab.

It was at the rear of a small industrial park, kind of a large garage in a row of large garages that had all been converted into little warehouses. There was yellow Police tape across the front and a notice tagged onto the badly charred door forbidding anyone from entering. Obviously, that didn't mean us. Chorley brought me inside – the stench of the fire was still very strong – and I looked around, trying to recall how everything fit into the diagram Raymond had drawn.

'Fire one,' he pointed. 'And fire two.' He motioned to the neon light that had once run the length of the ceiling. 'See how it indicates the seat of the first fire.' He showed me the wall. 'This is where the cement spalled.'

The neon bulb was broken and the wall was badly charred. Then I studied the deformed heap of melted plastic on the chair. I saw how the filing cabinet had been pushed away from the wall and into the middle of the room so that it would burn easier. The drawers were open and the papers inside were now just ashes.

'Now you know what arson looks like, Mr Barolo.'

I agreed. 'Now I know what arson looks like, Mr Chorley.'

He drove me back to the railroad station, told me there would be a London train in – he checked his watch – another nine minutes, and wished me good luck. I thanked him, got out, went inside and waited for him to pull away. Once he was gone, I phoned Henry.

'Call the bank. That cheque we deposited from Bickerton.

Find out what branch it was drawn on and if they keep a record of the account number. I need it.'

She asked, 'You want to hold on?'

'No. I'll call back in a little while. Oh, and get me a number for the Lustigs in New York. Actually, get me their attorney's number. I'll handle it with him. And Halliwell's number too.'

'Is that all?'

'For the time being.'

'That's what you think. You'll be delighted to know that the jerk's been ringing all morning. It's about his new kit.'

I didn't understand. 'What kit?'

'The Equalizer.'

'What are you talking about?'

'The jerk's new wardrobe. He's decided to call himself The Equalizer.'

'Hambone is calling himself what?' I couldn't deal with this now. 'If he phones again tell him I'll speak with him tomorrow. Just, please, get me the information on that bank and those phone numbers.' She said she would.

Hanging up with her, I went in search of a phone book. There wasn't one in the booth and the lady at the newsstand didn't know what I meant when I said phone book until she figured out that I was asking about a directory and then she announced that they don't sell such things. I said I just wanted to borrow one. She told me customers had to use the phones in the station, that her phone was for business use only and therefore her phone directory was for business use only too. I shook my head and went to the ticket office, where the clerk said he didn't have a phone directory. Then his supervisor came by and said yes they did. I asked if I could please borrow it to look up a number. He suggested I should try directory enquiries first. I said I'd be grateful if he would just loan me the book for a second. He thought about it, told me again about directory enquiries, then gave in. But only after making me promise that I would not run away with it.

I copied down Bickerton's address, returned the phone book and jumped into a cab.

He'd lived in a small modern high-rise, one block from the beach, at the west end of Brighton, almost on the border with the next town, which is Hove. From the cars parked along the street, it was obviously a respectable neighbourhood. Bickerton's name was on the bell at the entrance – there were a couple of marble steps and the doors were tinted glass – so I rang it. No one answered. I rang it again. Still no one. It didn't matter to me who helped me get inside, so I pushed three other buttons and when I heard a woman's voice ask, 'Who's there?' I answered, 'It's Harold for Maude.' She said, 'Who?' Just then another voice came over the intercom. 'Yes?' I saw that one of the bells had the name 'Feldman' next to it, so I said, 'Harold for Maude . . . Is that the Feldman residence?' Someone said, 'Sorry, it's just upstairs.' Then the first voice asked again, 'Who is it?' I said, 'I just locked myself out,' and by that time the people on the intercom were so confused that someone buzzed me in.

I turned on the light in the small marble lobby, found the mail boxes on the side wall and tried to peek into Bickerton's. I couldn't tell if it was empty, but it clearly wasn't full.

The elevator was just there, a small cage with a sliding door. Because Bickerton's outside bell was second from the top, I took it to mean that his apartment was on whatever floor was second from the top and when I saw that the elevator had six buttons, I pushed the one marked five. I rode up, it stopped, I got out and the bell on the door facing me read 'Dr L. R. Bickerton'.

Not exactly sure what I would do if he opened the door, I pushed the bell, heard it ring inside and waited. I put my ear to the door, pushed again, and listened for a moment. There was no noise inside, except the ringing bell, which sounded slightly hollow.

It was the same sound I would have expected to hear in an empty apartment.

Now I went down one flight, read the name on the bell – Mrs Gladys Leonard – rang it and when a woman inside asked, 'Who's there?' I told her, 'I'm terribly sorry to bother you. It's about Dr Bickerton, upstairs.'

'Oh. Yes. Just a moment please.' She unlocked the door and looked at me. 'Are you a friend of poor Dr Bickerton?'

Slightly shrunken, she was way up in her seventies with very thin white hair. I couldn't have gotten any luckier because little old ladies and I speak the same language. 'Mrs Leonard? I'm terribly sorry to bother you. I'm a very old friend of Dr Bickerton's . . .' I extended my hand. 'Isn't it awful. I mean, you must have heard what happened . . .'

'Oh yes,' she said, nodding her head several times. 'He was

such a quiet man. There was never any noise with him. He played his telly very softly and never had loud parties. In fact, I don't think he ever had any parties at all. Of course, if he did have parties, and he would have been perfectly within his right's to have a party from time to time, I never heard a peep.'

'That's very comforting,' I assured her, 'to know that he was a good neighbour.'

'Isn't it awful, when such a terrible thing happens to such a quiet neighbour.'

'Absolutely.' On a hunch I tried, 'I don't know if he ever mentioned me to you, but I just came over from the States . . . I'm American as you can tell . . . and I was wondering if he might have left a spare key with you . . .'

'No, no, no.' She shook her head several times. 'Nothing like that. He always kept to himself. I hardly ever even saw him taking out the rubbish. We have to put the rubbish out at night, you see, and I don't go out at night any more . . .'

'I don't blame you. Especially at night.'

'My friend Ruthie had her building society savings passbook stolen. A young boy on a motorcycle. Just rode up to her and reached into her handbag.'

'You must be very careful,' I warned.

'That's what the other gentleman said to me, too. Just after I learned the news about Ruthie's savings passbook . . . what a shock that was . . . well, just after I learned that news, a policeman came here to look inside Dr Bickerton's flat. I heard the lift going up to his floor and then, about half an hour later I heard noise, like furniture being moved, which is something I never heard before . . .'

'You mean, someone went inside Dr Bickerton's apartment?'

'It wasn't just someone, it was a police officer. I know, because he told me that's who he was.'

'He told you he was a police officer? Was he wearing a uniform?'

She shook her head. 'He was such a nice young man. He didn't know I'd heard him go upstairs, but you see here . . .' She wanted me to see the spyhole on her door, '. . . I can watch everyone coming and going and I saw him in the lift.'

'And then he knocked on your door?'

'No. I saw him in the lift. After he left Dr Bickerton's flat,

I wanted to see exactly who he was, so I opened my door and stood right here until he started down in the lift and I looked at him. A woman alone can't be too cautious.'

I nodded. 'So . . . when did he tell you he was a police officer?'

'When he saw me. He stopped the lift . . . there's a little button in there you can push that stops it right away . . . he'd just gone past my floor . . . and then he stopped the lift and came back up and smiled at me. He told me not to be alarmed, that he was a police officer and had been to Dr Bickerton's flat because there'd been an accident. He was the man who told me Dr Bickerton had . . . that he was . . . gone.'

I smiled reassuringly. 'Did he show you his badge or any sort of identification?'

'No.' She seemed a bit startled. 'Should I have asked to see something like that?'

'When was this?'

'Just before the news. I always watch the news on television at one o'clock. I boil an egg and make some tea and toast . . . that's what I have for lunch . . . and then I sit down to watch the news on television.'

'I mean, do you remember what day it was?'

'Last week.' She thought about it, then confessed, 'When you reach my age every day looks alike. Except Sunday, of course, because I go to church. And Saturdays, because that's when I go to Marks and Spencer.'

'Of course.' I wondered, 'Perhaps you can remember one or two of the stories that you saw on the news that day.' That would pin it down. 'You know, what happened on the news that day.'

'But I never got to see the news,' she said, as if that should have been obvious. 'I was watching for the lift and then speaking to the police officer. And I over boiled my egg.'

'Ah.' I shrugged. 'What did this young man look like?'

'Wednesday,' she said. 'Yes. That's right. I buy six eggs every Saturday and I never eat one on Sunday. That way I have one every day. And Saturday I didn't have one and it surprised me and I stood in my kitchen wondering why I didn't have an egg and that's when I recalled that I had to boil a second egg on Wednesday.'

That would have been the day the news of Bickerton's suicide was announced. 'What did this police officer look like?'

'It was Wednesday. That's what I told myself on Saturday.'
She kept nodding. 'He looked just like that Kinsella fellow.'

'Who?'

'The fellow with the baseball.'

'The baseball?'

'Baseball. Yes. You're an American, so you must know all
about baseball. I saw it on television. I watched the whole
thing. It was very late. And that's what I remember thinking
when I saw the young police officer. That he looked just like
that Kinsella fellow.'

'Baseball? You watch baseball?'

'It was a film.'

'Oh.' I smiled again, then dared, 'You wouldn't know if Dr
Bickerton's wife . . .'

'But Dr Bickerton didn't have a wife.' She leaned forward
to whisper, 'I never even knew that he had a lady friend. Of
course, he was very discreet and he was perfectly entitled to
have a lady friend. But I hardly ever saw him and never, or
hardly ever, heard him moving about. You can then imagine
my surprise when that woman arrived with a key. Perhaps if
you ask her. I mean, obviously, she has one.'

'What woman?'

'The woman with the key. She was here just three days
ago.'

'In Dr Bickerton's apartment?'

'You must understand . . .' she cautioned me, 'I mind
my own business and Dr Bickerton always minded his own
business, which I believe makes for very good neighbours. But
on Saturday afternoons, well I already told you that I always go
to Marks and Spencer on Saturday afternoons. That's where I
do most of my shopping, because they have such well prepared
meals and I don't care to cook much any more. Well, I was just
coming back and she got into the lift with me. She was very
polite. I said hello and she said hello and then she asked me
what floor I wanted. I told her four and she said she was going
to five. I said, oh then, you must have known Dr Bickerton
and she said yes, she'd known him for a very long time. She
was a very pleasant woman. She helped me bring my packages
inside. I had two packages. They weren't very heavy. But she
still helped me with them even though she had her own small
overnight bag. You know, one of those expensive bags that's

covered with initials. She left it in the lift to block the door, while she brought my shopping inside for me. I thought to myself, I hope the door doesn't crush her bag. She was very sweet. Most people wouldn't bother. And she had the loveliest French accent.'

Chapter Seventeen

Gladys never saw the woman with the French accent before. And never saw her again. That didn't surprise me. But the police officer's visit bothered me. It struck me that a real cop would have done more to identify himself than simply say he was a police officer, especially with a little old lady. And then I wondered why anybody, cop or otherwise, would be moving furniture?

Downstairs, on the street, I looked around for a phone booth, couldn't see one and headed for the Grand Hotel.

One thing you learn when you travel through Europe is that if you dress the part – you know, wear a tie and jacket, look like you belong and walk with an air of confidence – no one would dare challenge you when you stroll into the best hotel in town. It means you always have a place to go if you need to make a call, if you want directions or if you just have to pee.

The doorman at the Grand was even happy to see me.

First, I called Henry. She gave me the number of Bickerton's account and the address of his bank, a number for the Lustigs' attorney in New York and a number for Halliwell. It was much too early to phone the States, so I called PC Hoving instead. He wasn't in. I left a message, asking him to please ring me at the office at the end of the afternoon.

The concierge gave me directions and a map to get me to the bank. And finally, just to make my pit stop complete, I visited the men's room.

By the time I arrived at Barclay's bank, the manager had already left for lunch. No one else could help me or, for that matter, seemed willing to. All I wanted to know was whether or not Bickerton's account had been closed. I was sure it had been. But the woman at the desk in the front near the door said she had no authority to discuss another client's business with anyone. And her boss, who turned out to be the personal loans manager, claimed British banking regulations strictly prohibited him from revealing that kind of information. I tried telling him that my uncle had been with Barclays for twenty years, but he couldn't have cared less.

Knowing a dead-end street when I was at the end of one, I stared at the long line of people waiting for a teller, said, 'Oh well, thanks anyway,' then mumbled, 'I just need to get some money,' and went to the end of the line.

At the little stand with the various blank forms, I took a deposit slip and filled it out. When my turn finally came, I reached into my pocket, brought out a handful of change, dropped it into the little metal tray under the cashier's thick, bullet-proof window, slid in the deposit slip and said, 'If you'd be kind enough to put this in my account.'

She gave me a strange look, took the coins, counted them and announced, with mild disdain, 'Three pounds and twenty-two pence.'

I smiled broadly. 'A penny saved is a penny earned.'

Stamping the slip, she passed it back to me.

I looked at it, nodded, said, 'Oh,' put on my best slightly confused expression and asked, 'Is it seven or four?'

'Seven or four what?'

'My account number.'

She signalled for me to return the slip. I did. She looked at it, turned to the keyboard of her small computer terminal, punched a few numbers, waited until something came up and said, 'Bickerton?'

I nodded.

She handed the deposit slip back to me. 'The account number is correct.'

I thanked her and walked away.

For £3.22 I felt entitled to wonder why the woman with the French accent had cleaned out his apartment but not bothered to close his bank account.

As long as I'd gone this far, I figured what the hell, found a taxi and asked the driver to take me to Eastbourne. 'I want to go to the offices of the European Research Project.'

He didn't know where those offices were, so he called

his dispatcher on the radio who looked it up in the phone directory. When he had it, he announced, 'Okay, get in,' and off we went.

Eastbourne was only twenty-three miles down the beach, but there was traffic and it took us more than forty minutes to get there. The driver wanted to talk. I didn't because I was trying to recall the names of the people in the photograph from Bickerton's retirement party. So I pretended to take a nap. He kept talking anyway. By the time we pulled up to the front gate, I'd only come up with Cesari, Mars and Tyrone.

The ERP was a large, modern, glass-front building, set back in a field with trees, separated from the road that led up to it by a good-sized parking lot and a fairly serious-looking high chain fence.

The guard at the gate was an old man in a blue serge uniform with a lot of braid trim, a sleepy left eyelid – it was half closed – and a tooth missing from the bottom row in the front of his mouth.

He gave me a mistrustful nod and asked who it was I'd come to see.

'Wow, all that traffic.' I glanced at my watch. 'Well, I'm not all that late. Dr Mars and Dr Tyrone. I can find my way in. No problem.' I started past him.

But he summoned me back. 'Just a minute. You said, Dr Mars?'

'You know how angry those two can get.' I pointed to my watch.

'I haven't seen Dr Mars . . .'

'But you have seen Tyrone's temper. The instant he starts tapping his toe, you know you're in trouble.'

'What did you say your name is?'

'I'm so jetlagged . . .' I forced a yawn. 'You know what time it is in my life?' I started rummaging through my pockets. 'Just a second . . . Don't tell me I left my pass in my luggage at the hotel?'

'Your pass?'

'Yeah . . . no need for Mars to have left any visitor's name at the gate . . .' I chuckled . . . 'Hardly a visitor.' Then I asked him, 'You're not Al, are you?'

'Al?'

'Yeah . . . the guy who was here last time . . .'

'Al?'

'Yeah . . . tall guy . . . about your age . . . ex-Army.'

'Al? Ex-Army?' He was genuinely confused. 'I've been here seven years and I never heard of a bloke called Al . . .'

'I could have sworn he told me he was ex-Army . . . how about Albert? Or Bert?'

He shrugged. 'There used to be a fellow who worked in security named Benny and . . . well, I think he was ex-military . . .'

'That's it.' I tapped him gently on the shoulder several times. 'Not Bert. My memory isn't what it used to be. Ben. That's right. Benny. What ever happened to him?'

'He died.'

'Such a healthy guy, he died?'

The old guard nodded. 'About six, maybe five years ago.'

'Gee, has it been that long already?' I tapped his shoulder again. 'He was a nice guy, Benny. Too bad. But I guess, hey, you never know when your time is up. Imagine that, Benny died. Couldn't have been that old.'

He thought about it. 'Maybe my age. I don't know. Late sixties.'

'Listen to me.' I leaned closer. 'You've got to take care of yourself. Watch your diet. Get some exercise.' I spotted a package of cigarettes on the desk just inside the shack door. 'And you've got to give those up. Believe me, trade those in for girls. They'll keep you younger.'

'Girls?' He started to laugh, as if he was remembering the good old days. 'Fags are cheaper.'

I didn't say that only the British call cigarettes fags and that where I come from if you were trading girls for fags you wouldn't be doing it just to save money. 'Hey, it's good to see you.' I moved past him again. 'I'll check in with reception. Tyrone must have left instructions there . . .'

He hesitated. 'What did you say your name is, sir?'

I called back, 'Barolo . . . It's okay, I know my way . . .' waved and walked onto the property.

But my gate-crashing was short-lived. A very fat woman sitting behind the large reception desk just inside the front door stopped me with a snarl. 'May I help you?'

'Dr Mars and Dr Tyrone, please.'

'Dr Mars?'

'Or Dr Tyrone.'

'Do you have an appointment with Dr Mars?'

I tried a flirtatious smile. 'He's not exactly expecting me . . . it's kind of a little surprise . . . you understand . . . I'm just in the country . . .'

But she was immune to my charm. 'Do you actually know Dr Mars?'

I gestured, 'Do I know Dr Mars?'

She wasn't having any of this. 'Then you know that Dr Mars is in Brussels. He doesn't even . . .'

'Of course, I know that.' If only I'd had the other names in the photo. 'I faxed him that I was coming and he faxed back that he might be able to meet us . . . well, I guess he couldn't make it . . . but Dr Tyrone . . .'

This game was definitely lost. 'I'm terribly sorry, sir. It's our policy that if you don't have an appointment . . .'

'Policy? Yes, of course.' The famous British fallback position which translates to mean, sorry but no one pays me to think. 'Could I trouble you, please, for a piece of paper?'

She pondered that one and, because she couldn't come up with any policy why not, reluctantly handed me a small pad.

'Thanks.' I took my pen and wrote, 'I have something you might want.' I hoped that would be intriguing enough. 'I'm downstairs.' And at the last second I added, 'Dr Bickerton was an interesting man.' I asked her if she had an envelope and she did. So I folded the paper, slipped one of my cards into it, stuffed them both into the envelope, sealed it and wrote on the front, 'Dr Tyrone. Personal.' Then I asked her, 'Can you please send this up to him? I'll wait.'

After staring at me – probably trying to find an excuse to save her own butt in case someone accused her of not following policy – she finally agreed. 'Please wait there,' and motioned towards a leather couch next to a potted plant on the other side of the lobby. I sat down. Once I was out of hearing range, she took her phone and dialled a number. She spoke softly for a few seconds and hung up.

I had no idea who she phoned although I could tell the call was about me because she kept looking at me, as if she wanted to be certain I couldn't hear anything. A couple of minutes later, a young boy in a loose-fitting grey suit appeared through a door just behind her. She handed him the envelope and motioned towards me. He glanced over, gave me a good long stare, then backed away, disappearing through the same door.

I crossed my legs and looked around. There wasn't a picture on the wall. No company logo. Not even a magazine on the small coffee table in front of the couch.

And the plant turned out to be plastic.

She caught me inspecting the leaves and when our eyes met, I smiled, but she quickly turned away and went back to whatever it was she was doing just out of my gaze, under the reception counter.

Several more minutes passed until a woman walked through that same door. She was wearing a dark blue suit and had eyeglasses on a silver chain dangling around her neck. She looked at me anxiously and the woman at reception nodded.

I stood up.

In her very early sixties, with short dark hair, she had a soft jowly face that, I imagined, thirty years ago had been very pretty. 'Mr Barolo?' She walked across the lobby towards me and when she was close enough, I extended my hand to shake hers. 'Sorry, I didn't mean to disturb anyone . . . your name is?'

'My name is Clare Prout.' Her grip was firm. When she let go she started toying nervously with my envelope. 'I'm Dr Tyrone's administrative assistant.'

'Mrs Prout . . . I was just hoping to have a word with him . . .'

'I'm afraid that isn't possible, at the moment. Perhaps if you would tell me what it is you have that he might want . . .'

'Gee . . .' I shrugged. 'I'd really prefer to discuss this directly with him.'

On the surface she seemed very businesslike, but her eyes gave her away. 'I'm afraid it simply isn't possible . . .'

On the spur of the moment I decided to try, 'It's about Dr Bickerton.'

'Your note mentioned his name. Is . . . there something I can do . . . after all, he left here some months ago . . .' Flicking the edge of the envelope under her thumbnail, she insisted, 'Under the circumstances . . . perhaps it would be prudent to put any matters regarding Dr Bickerton in writing . . .'

I forced a smile to show her that I meant no harm. 'My card is in there. Perhaps someday if he feels like talking . . .'

'But you mentioned something you have that he might want . . .'

I confessed, 'Just my way of attracting his attention.'

'I see.' She stared at me as if she wasn't convinced. 'I'll see that he gets your note.'

'Thank you, Mrs Prout.' I extended my hand.

She shook it again. 'Goodbye, Mr Barolo.'

And I walked out.

Of course, the moment I got outside I realized I was in the middle of nowhere and didn't have any way to get back to Brighton. So I told my new pal at the guard shack, 'The taxi didn't wait.'

'No problem,' he said. 'Reception can ring for another one.'

'You mean I have to go back there and deal with that old battle-axe?'

He knew who I meant. 'She takes some getting used to.'

I saw that there was a phone on the desk in front of him. 'Could you do me a favour please and call for a taxi? I'd rather wait here with you than face her again.'

He nodded several times, searched through a small notebook on his desk, assured me, 'I've got the numbers here . . . where are you going?' And started to dial.

'Brighton,' I said.

He got someone on the line, ordered a cab and when he hung up, told me, 'Ten to fifteen minutes.'

'No problem.' I leaned against the side of the shack and mumbled sadly, 'So Benny died.'

'I didn't know him too good. He kind of kept to himself a lot.'

I suggested, 'Sort of like Dr Bickerton.'

He looked at me. 'Dr Bickerton?'

'Quiet type. Kept to himself. Actually, I liked him.'

'He left here . . . retired . . .' Then, as if he wasn't sure I knew, he wondered, 'Did you hear that he died?'

'Terrible. Just last week. I was very upset. And they say it was suicide. Of all things. Why would a guy like that take his own life?'

He said in a very quiet voice, 'Just between you and me . . . I think this place got to him.'

'Oh yeah?' I asked in an equally quiet voice, 'You really think so?'

He held up both hands to show me that he didn't want to go into too much detail. 'I only work the front gate. I don't know a lot about what goes on inside. I don't . . . I probably shouldn't talk about anything.'

I tapped his shoulder again. 'He was a good guy, Roger. Probably always waved hello to you, every morning.' That was a safe bet because most people wave hello and goodbye to the guard at the gate. 'You really think this place had something to do with it?'

'I don't know anything. It's just what I hear. I mean, well, he didn't exactly retire. They fired him. It got pretty nasty. I was sorry to see him go. Not everybody here is as nice as he was.'

'Getting fired like that . . . he was very bitter.' I spoke about Bickerton as if I'd known him all my life. 'Never stopped talking about how they shafted him. But you don't think . . .' I moved closer and asked quietly, 'I mean, you don't think they had anything to do with his death?'

'Like I said, I just work at the front gate.'

'Except, he did say hello to you every morning, didn't he?'

He thought about it and conceded, 'Well, sure he did. Look . . . I shouldn't say anything . . . I mean, I don't think they killed him or anything like that . . .'

A car came up the road and slowed at the front entrance.

'I only hear what I hear.' He glanced at the car, then motioned to show me that it was my taxi. 'But, maybe they drove him to it.'

'You think so?'

'It's not me. There are other people who think that way too.'

'Like who?'

'Like . . . well, I heard his secretary said that to someone. Maybe she did. Maybe she didn't. I wasn't there. It's only, you know, a rumour. And I wouldn't want anybody to think I said that. You'd have to ask her. You'd have to speak to Mrs Prout.'

When I told the taxi driver that I wanted to go to the railroad station in Brighton to catch a train to London, he convinced me that trains from Eastbourne were just as good.

So I went to the station in Eastbourne and got the next train home.

For the entire ride, I sat there wondering what Mrs Prout knew about Roger Bickerton's death.

Chapter Eighteen

My office was teeming with people.

Okay, so it's a tiny office and five people is a teem. But they were all hovering around Henry's desk, all talking at the same time, which not only made it difficult to open the door and step in but the moment they spotted me, they started talking to me all at once. The only person I recognized was Hal, the fellow who sells me those boxing videos. 'I'll get to you as soon as I can,' I promised, fighting my way through the crowd. 'If everyone would be kind enough, please, to wait just a minute.' I extricated Henry from behind her desk, which wasn't easy because for some reason there were a dozen cardboard boxes in the way.

Dragging her into my room, I shut the door, then demanded, 'What the hell is going on?'

'First of all, your friend the jerk. He's responsible for the very tall bloke out there who says you owe him £385 for the kit. He says if you don't pay him right away, he's not going to finish the work.'

'What work?'

'The Equalizer. I told you on the phone,' she insisted. 'The jerk thinks he's Mike Tyson. He ordered shorts and a silk robe and shoes and, God only knows, probably a monogrammed jockstrap too, all embroidered with his new name on it, and he promised to pay the bill two days ago, which, surprise, surprise, he didn't. So the tall bloke out there started the work and when the jerk didn't pay or couldn't pay, he promised you'd pay. So now the man wants to be paid . . .'

I held up both hands. 'Okay. Who are the other people out there?'

'That bloke Hal . . . he's with the fellow with the moustache . . .'

'Where did all those cardboard boxes come from?'

'The fellow with the moustache,' she said, as if I hadn't been paying attention. 'The other two are from Valparaiso Pacific something or other. One is a solicitor and the bloke with him is their local insurance agent . . .'

'What's Valparaiso Pacific?'

'If you'd come to the office once in a while and read your faxes . . .' She pointed to my desk. 'It's been sitting right there since I found it at ten o'clock this morning.' Now she handed me a bunch of phone messages. 'The usual suspects. The jerk about four times. Charlie only once. Giovanni wanted to know about the Cypriot . . .'

I went to look at the fax, but before I could get there, someone knocked on my door. Henry opened it. A head poked in – it was the very tall guy – to announce, 'There's someone else here. Someone new.' So I motioned for Henry to find out who it was while I read the fax.

It was from Sandy Miller at Great Lakes Reliance. A cargo of ball bearings had been lost somewhere between Bremerhaven, Germany and Duluth, Minnesota. It ultimately turned up in the Colon Free Zone, which is a huge industrial trading centre along the banks of the Panama Canal. It's also one of the first places anyone ever looks for stolen cargoes. Valparaiso Pacific was offering to return the cargo with a minor payment for inconvenience, but Great Lakes Reliance had already paid out on the claim to the company in Duluth. In the meantime, the price of ball bearings had fallen and where Great Lakes Reliance might have otherwise sold the cargo on the open market, accepting title to it now would mean taking a loss which, according to the fax, amounted to nearly $83,000. And because insurance companies are not charities, they don't give away $83,000 without a fight. Miller wanted me to see how much I could get out of Valparaiso Pacific's own insurance company before they would make a decision to sue.

Henry came back in to ask, 'Fuzzy White?'

'What Fuzzy White?'

'You want to see him?'

'Why?'

'He's here.'

'Son of a bitch.' I couldn't imagine how he had the nerve to show his face. 'Let him wait.' I intended to deal with these other people first. 'We go days without seeing anyone . . .'

But Henry had no sympathy. 'And at five o'clock I'm going to my aerobics class.'

'Okay. Before that room turns into a scene from a Marx Brothers movie . . .'

'Wow, I saw that one,' she said gleefully. 'They're all crammed into a ship's cabin and the waiter arrives . . .'

'. . . Send in the guys from Valparaiso Pacific.' This was about earning a living. 'I'll get to the others as quickly as I can. Give them all a cup of tea, or have One Hung send up *dim sum*. I don't know. Just keep everybody busy.'

The two fellows representing Valparaiso Pacific walked in – a very young solicitor and a very weary-looking, middle-aged insurance broker – introduced themselves and I purposely left them standing in the middle of my office. 'Most people make appointments.'

'We rang your secretary,' the solicitor said. 'She suggested it might be all right . . .'

'To show up like this you must be pretty damned worried about what Great Lakes Reliance is going to do to your client's reputation and his pocketbook. But then, rightfully so. This is called, protecting your client's interest. You'll remember it from law school.'

He gave me a very nasty look.

'I presume law school wasn't all that long ago that you've forgotten anything.'

'There's no need to be rude.'

He didn't know it, but there was. This was good cop, bad cop, where I played both roles. It was another way of separating a client from his counsel in order to create that very valuable situation where the client thinks he's smarter than his lawyer.

'I'll save us all a lot of time.' I looked to the insurance broker and addressed him in a more civil tone. 'You tell me what your best offer is and I'll say yes or no. We're not negotiating this. Great Lakes Reliance is ready to sue you guys not only for the loss of the cargo but also for the damages incurred by the shipping line's gross negligence.' Now I added for good measure, 'We're planning to ask law enforcement in the States, the UK, Germany and Panama to look into the theft of the cargo and the possibility that one or more employees or agents of the company might be implicated.'

'Theft?' The solicitor blanched.

The agent explained, 'We represent the shipping line's insurers. We don't know anything about . . .'

'You insured them. The cargo gets stolen, that's not our problem, it's yours. So we come after you . . .'

'Fair enough,' the solicitor said. 'But theft is hardly the way . . .'

'Best offer, guys. One shot. No haggling.'

The lawyer stammered, 'This is most unprofessional . . .'

'No, this is called, either come up with enough money to make us go away or we separate you from your gonads.'

They looked at each other as if I was a crazy.

'This is not the way I care to proceed.' The young lawyer tried to hide his discomfort with aggression. 'I say we take this up with your head office . . .'

'I'm the only game in town.'

'Let's just step back a moment.' The insurance agent was old enough to know there was an easier way out. 'Perhaps we should take a deep breath and ask you how much is enough?'

'You choose the numbers and I'll choose where to put the decimal point.'

The young solicitor snapped, 'This is not the way I do business and not the way I would advise any of my clients to do business.'

I turned away from him and put on a sympathetic face for the insurance man. 'Talk to me.'

He tried, 'How about full title to the cargo, plus half the $83,000 differential.'

I shook my head. 'No soap.'

'Or . . . you can assume half title to the cargo and one quarter of the $83,000 differential. In fact, I think that's more than fair and totally in keeping with our desire to . . .'

'Good luck.' I extended my hand to him. 'Thanks anyway. See you in court. Oh, and when the story breaks in the shipping press that you guys were party to the cover up of maritime theft . . .'

'Why do you keep talking about theft?' the solicitor demanded. 'Who ever said anything . . .'

'What do you know about the Colon Free Zone?'

'Nothing,' he confessed. 'But that doesn't indicate . . .'

I turned to the insurance broker. 'Someone needs to tell Rumpole Junior here the facts of life. Such as, how lost cargoes aren't supposed to turn up for sale in nationalized pawn shops like the Free Zone.'

'How much do you want?' the insurance broker asked.

'This is blackmail,' the solicitor objected.

The older guy held up his hand. 'This is business,' he said, then asked me again, 'How much?'

I stood my ground. 'You offer, I say yes or no.'

'Okay. Full payment for the cargo upon sale, plus the differential.'

I shook my head. 'We're not in the business of supporting your cash flow.'

'All right. Full payment for the cargo.'

'Plus interest. Plus costs.'

'No way,' the solicitor cried.

'It's a deal,' the insurance broker agreed. 'Costs must be itemized and may not exceed ten per cent of the claim.'

'You're on.' But then I warned, 'Subject, of course, to approval of Great Lakes Reliance.' I extended my hand.

The insurance broker shook it. But because oral agreements, in the words of the great Sam Goldwyn, aren't worth the paper they're printed on, I grabbed two sheets of my letterhead, wrote out the terms on each, initialled one and handed it to the insurance broker. Then I got the solicitor to initial my copy. I took their cards and promised that, subject to my clients' agreement, I would forward final copies to them within a few days.

As they walked out the solicitor glared at me and said snottily, 'You've got a pretty good bark.'

I couldn't stop myself. 'It's not the bark that counts. It's the bite.'

I quickly put in a call to the States to tell Miller what the deal was. He couldn't get over it. 'We would have settled for the differential.'

'I'll remind you of that next time we negotiate my retainer.' Hanging up with him, I buzzed Henry. 'Next victim. How about the guy who's looking for money.'

An extremely tall and very thin man stepped in, nodded nervously and demanded, 'A cheque please for £385. VAT is included.'

'Nice to meet you,' I said, offering my hand. 'Your name is . . .'

He refused to shake. 'Croxford. I'm with Croxford and Croxford, and you, sir, owe us £385, which includes VAT.'

He must have been six foot six at the very least and didn't look as if he'd eaten in months. 'Why?'

'Because VAT is always included in our prices.'

'No, I mean, why do I owe you anything?'

'Because someone calling himself Derek the Equalizer placed an order from us for two pairs of monogrammed shorts, two pairs of designer boxing boots and a large silk robe, plus sweatshirts for his corner men, all of them in day-glo silver, red and blue and all of them inscribed. Now, normally, we would have asked for a deposit of say fifty per cent . . .'

'Listen, Mr Croxford . . .' I needed to get rid of him. 'I'll have to speak with Derek about . . .'

'Here.' He forced an invoice into my hands. 'People who don't pay their bills get taken to court.'

I reminded him, 'I'm a lawyer.'

'From the look of the people assembled in your outer office,' he stared at me down his nose, 'I would have thought you were in show business.'

I asked, 'Will you give me a couple of days please to straighten this out? You will get your money . . .'

'I'll take a postdated cheque,' he said flatly.

The easy way out was to write him a cheque for £385, but I took him up on his offer, and I postdated it for Monday. That reassured him, and still gave me plenty of time either to settle the matter with Hambone or stop the cheque before it cleared.

He left and Hal came in, struggling with the cartons, followed by the other fellow, who was also carrying cartons.

'What the hell . . .'

'I can explain.' Hal urged the other guy, 'Come on, hurry up, Mr Barolo is a busy man,' then walked up to me and whispered, 'That's Fuzzy White out there.'

'So it seems,' I said.

'He was supposed to have been pretty good in his day. I wonder if he wants to buy some videos . . .'

'Hal, I'm busy. What the hell is going on?'

'I got a little problem,' he confided as the boxes kept coming in. 'I didn't know who else to turn to. We're talking a week, two at the most.'

'Two at the most, what?'

'You must have a closet or something . . .' He looked around. 'Or just here in the corner.'

There were fourteen cartons in all, and when Hal's friend announced, 'That's them,' Hal told him to wait in the other room. Then he shut the door. 'Here, look at this.' He ripped open one of the cartons and showed me that they were filled with video tapes. 'A mate of mine had some temporary financial difficulties and he couldn't exactly come up with the dosh he owed me. Then I heard that he owed a lot of people a lot of money and that certain creditors were about to visit him and help themselves to whatever he had. So I sort of, well you understand, you're a solicitor, I sort of helped myself first. Here.' He started to hand one to me, but held on to it long enough to read from the label, 'Behind the Green Door'.

I screamed, 'This is a hard-core porn tape.'

'Sorry,' he quickly pulled it back. 'Sorry, wrong carton. Wait a minute.' He lifted the open carton and dropped it on the floor. 'There's some boxing stuff in here. I mean, you can help yourself. Take whatever you want. Five quid a tape. Special price. That's like ninety off. It's the least I can do for my solicitor.'

'I am not your solicitor and I want this garbage out of my office.'

He ripped into the second carton, checked the label on one of the tapes, mumbled, 'Whoops,' and opened the third box. 'Here. I knew I'd find it. Look. Kid Gavilan. The championship fights. Right up your alley. Remember him? The bolo punch?'

'Yeah, I remember him.'

'A fiver. Where you going to find stuff like this for a fiver?'

'Son of a bitch, you already sold that one to me for £30.'

'Here.' He forced the tape into my hand. 'Now you got two. There's also a lot of NBA basketball in here. You like basketball? You got to rummage through it. American football? Whole bunch of Super Bowl stuff. Take your pick.'

I had to know, 'Is this garbage hot?'

'Hot?' He shrugged. 'No. It's not hot. Like I said, it's just, well, not mine. Not officially. The guy promised to pay me, so this is, like collateral. Give me a week. I promise. It's gone in a week.'

'Monday,' I said. 'Either you get it out of here first thing Monday morning, or it gets left on the street.'

'How's Wednesday?'

'Monday,' I said, then pointed to my door. 'First thing.'

'Okay,' he conceded. 'Hey, thanks. And take whatever you want. If you don't have the fiver, you can owe it to me. Anything.'

'Out,' I ordered.

Hal promised he'd never forget me for this, opened the door and started to leave. That's when One Hung walked in with a huge order of *dim sum*.

'Hey,' Hal started to applaud. 'Is this for everyone? Do you mind?'

I shot a glance at Henry. 'Help yourself.'

Henry shrugged. 'You were the one who . . .'

'Okay.' I waved to One Hung, looked at Fuzzy White – 'I've got a bone to pick with you' – and told him to come in. But before he did he also helped himself to some food. Henry brought in a plate for me, then announced, 'I'm out of here.'

'See that my new clients leave with you,' I said, pointing to her office.

'They're eating.'

'Tell them it's takeaway.'

She lifted a bun off the plate, bit into it, mumbled, 'So good,' and left.

I turned to Fuzzy. 'What kind of shithead stunt was that, sending some heavyweight into Charlie's place to set up Hambone?'

He was a wiry little guy, with short grey hair, a boxer's nose – it had probably been broken a dozen times – and rectangular sunshades that snapped onto the frame of his eyeglasses, which he always wore up on the crown of his head. 'I didn't know anything about it until Charlie called me . . .'

'Don't give me that bullshit.'

'I'm telling you, Charlie was the first I heard of it.'

The phone rang. 'You're full of crap, Fuzzy.'

'Hey, I'm here to make peace.'

It rang a second time, then a third time . . . 'O'Reardon send you?' Realizing that Henry was gone, I grabbed it. 'Hello?'

'Mr Barolo? PC Hoving, returning your call.'

'Hi. Listen, I was curious about something. That matter we'd discussed . . . the gentleman in question . . .' I didn't want to go into detail with Fuzzy sitting there, hanging on my every word. 'I'd like to get the name of the officer who visited his flat last Wednesday. Can you find out for me, please, who it was?'

'One of our officers went to Dr Bickerton's flat?'

'Seems so. Can you get me his name?'

'Last Wednesday?'

'That's what I was told.'

'I'll try. If I find anything out, I'll ring you back. But it may not be today.'

'Thanks very much.' I hung up and looked at Fuzzy chewing on a dumpling. 'So O'Reardon did send you.'

'What are you talking about?' His mouth was full. 'I'm not Mickey's bumboy.'

I forced a laugh.

'Hey . . . I'm here to offer your kid a shot at one of our kids, and you sit there insulting me.'

'You must think I'm a total idiot.' I realized immediately that was the wrong thing to say, so before he could come up with something like, 'Not total,' I asked, 'Who is he and how much?'

'First things first.' He swallowed. 'You got something to drink?' I shook my head. 'You gotta drink with this stuff. You know, tea or something.'

'I've got other things to do than feed your face. Who's the kid?'

He wanted me to understand, 'This is only supposing that your kid can get past Davey McGraw. I'm not sure he can . . .'

'Which is why you decided to do your brother-in-law a favour by dispatching a heavyweight to soften him up.'

'Ex-brother-in-law, and I'm telling you I didn't know anything about that. But you believe what you want to believe. Name is Miller Toole. You know, The Hammer.'

He was a rated fighter. 'Since when have you got Toole?'

'Picked him up two weeks ago and this morning I put him on a card in Birmingham. There's a purse. Two months from now. So I'm sitting around thinking who I could stick into the ring with him when I remember my old pal Vince.

This will give your kid six weeks between fights. He up for it?'

I'd just seen Toole's name on the *Boxing Monthly* list. 'It's hard to believe you could have a guilty conscience.' I couldn't remember if Toole was listed eighteenth or nineteenth, but beating him would put Hambone on the list. Except, that didn't explain why Fuzzy would risk his guy's place against an unlisted fighter, rather than go for one several places higher up. 'Why Hambone?'

'Why not Hambone? But it's conditional on him getting past McGraw.'

'How much is in it for us?'

'Two grand.'

'What terms did you offer McGraw?'

'Hey, I don't discuss somebody else's terms with no one else.'

That meant he was giving McGraw better terms. 'You see, Fuzzy, the thing is, when Hambone gets past McGraw, he can probably get the guy on the list who already refused to fight Toole, the one you hoped to get before you thought about your old pal Vince.'

'Who says anybody's refusing to fight Toole?' He popped another bun into his mouth. 'You want the fight or not?'

I did, except I wasn't going to let Fuzzy know that just yet because I needed to find a way to get more money out of him. And anyway, I wasn't convinced that Hambone was ready for it. Trying to get a fighter into the top twenty too soon was short-term thinking. If he won a ranking, he probably wouldn't be able to hold on to it. If he lost on his first attempt, he'd be hard pressed to find anyone willing to pay him for a second. 'I'll sleep on it.'

'What's there to sleep about?'

I stood up. 'I've got an appointment.'

He glanced at the tape on my desk. 'Kid Gavilan? The bolo punch?' He pretended to throw one, winding his arm in a circle, then bringing his clenched fist up, like a wind-mill throwing an uppercut. 'I remember him. You ever see him fight?'

'Before my time,' I said. 'Only on tape.'

'This stuff is pretty hard to come by.' He looked at the stack of cartons. 'You in the business?'

'Something like that.' I pointed to the tape. 'But you're right that this is hard to come by.'

'How much?'

'Gavilan normally sells for £50, that is, if you can even find it. Yours for £40.'

He took the tape, looked at it, then wondered, 'How about £30 for a friend?'

'If I had to price the tape based on our friendship, you couldn't afford it.'

'Come on.' He reached into his pocket and pulled out three tens. 'Do it for Fuzzy.'

'To Fuzzy,' I corrected.

He even shook my hand to thank me.

I moved all of the cartons against the wall, returned Charlie's call – except he was already gone for the evening – decided Hambone could wait, and started to lock up.

That's when I remembered the Lustigs.

The first thing I needed to do was stall Halliwell. So I phoned him. He reminded me, 'The deal closed twenty-four hours ago.'

I lied, 'My clients want your head in the stocks. Same goes for your Count and your pal in LA.'

'Too bad,' Halliwell said, 'you should have taken it when I offered it to you.'

'Not me, sport. I'm only the bus driver.'

'So . . .' he said, then asked, 'that's it?'

It struck me as an odd thing for someone to say if a deal was really closed. I took a punt. 'That's it.'

'Well . . . too bad, really. We should have worked it out.'

'But the deal closed twenty-four hours ago and the best I could get out of my clients was a desire to see your head on a platter.'

'Just like you, I'm only the bus driver.'

I hoped this might be my opening. 'So maybe the deal didn't expire twenty-four hours ago. Maybe you and the Count have had second thoughts. Maybe there's a way we can still work it out.'

He said, 'Maybe.'

I said, 'What will it take?'

'Your people pay the VAT, we pay the shipping.'

That reassured me. 'We pay the shipping, you pay the VAT.'

'Sorry.'

'Me too,' I said.

'I suppose then, the bus is leaving.' He hung up.

And in the pit of my stomach I knew I'd missed it.

'Here's the deal.' I explained it all to the Lustigs' attorney in New York when I finally got him on the phone.

'It's out of my hands,' he said. 'Strictly between you and them. But I can tell you now they'll never go for it.'

So I phoned the Lustigs and their lawyer was right. 'No way.'

I tried to make them understand that the Count and his sleazebag lawyer had pulled a fast one. But the Lustigs didn't want to know. All they cared about was getting their money back. I assured them it was retrievable, but advised that the costs would outweigh the gain. They accused me of having fumbled the ball, and promptly fired me. I told them I would send my entire file to their lawyer in New York and wished them good luck.

Lustig ended the call by telling me that as far as he was concerned, no money was due me.

I hung up, not only having missed the bus, but also having lost a decent fee.

I made photocopies of everything in the Lustig file, typed a letter to their lawyer, put it all in a FedEx envelope and jotted a note to Henry, asking her to send it first thing tomorrow morning.

It had been an expensive day.

Win some, lose some, I told myself.

But it wasn't a very comforting thought.

What the hell, I said out loud, winning isn't everything. I snapped off the lights, locked up and reminded myself, breathing is.

My first stop was the Cypriot's place to ask about the numbers. It was a dingy basement betting shop that permanently smelled of bad plumbing and cigarette smoke. But there was always a lot of action, not just horses and dogs but football games and boxing. I spotted him behind the counter – a young wiseguy with plenty of gold chains and shiny black

hair who called himself Homer – motioned to him that I
wanted to talk and he came out to see me. I pulled him over
to the corner and asked what the numbers looked like on the
McGraw-Hannover fight.

'Small potatoes,' Homer said. 'That's your guy, right? We'll
work out something. But I'd probably lay it off somewhere.
You'd get better numbers in the room on the night. But you
already know that.'

'Pick a figure.'

'What do I know?' He motioned, 'What a minute,' and left
me standing there while he made a few calls. When he came
back he said, 'Best I can do is 7–4 against.'

'And if I wanted to put some money on McGraw?'

He understood right away. 'In that case, even money is the
best I'll give you. Hey, I'm no fool. But I'll keep my mouth
shut. How much are we talking about?'

'A couple of grand. Maybe more.' I promised, 'I'll let
you know.'

Homer winked. 'It's always a pleasure.'

The seed planted, I headed for Giovanni's. He was in the
kitchen getting everything organized for dinner. 'Wander in
tomorrow like you don't know anything. He was offering 7–4
on Hambone. Until I told him I might want to go the other
way. Suddenly McGraw is even. Look innocent. And don't
play it unless the numbers are right.'

'You said what, anything over 9–4?'

It was hot and smoky in there, and the cooks kept hurrying
past us, not hiding the fact that we were in the way. 'As high
as he'll go.'

'We split £500?'

'Yeah. But you'll have to put it all down when you bet it.
If you tell him you'll come back later and he doesn't see me
in there first, he won't fall for it.'

'No problem.' Giovanni was too nice a guy to ask for
my half.

Except, I could read his mind. 'I'll give it to you tomorrow.'

'No hurry,' he said, then wondered, 'you want to stay for
some food?'

I begged off, 'Too tired,' waved and got out of there. I didn't
want to think about the Lustig loss so, with Fuzzy's cash, I
treated myself to a cab home.

The mail was bills and junk, none of which I wanted to bother with. There were no messages on my machine. And because I hadn't gone shopping since Greta was there, the fridge was pretty empty. I settled on a small bowl of spaghetti with butter and garlic.

While I went through the motions of eating it – I was really too wiped out to care – I started thinking about Clare Prout.

The little voice in the back of my head told me I'd pushed some sort of button by showing up in Eastbourne like that.

And now I wanted to know what that button was.

My mother always used to say, the squeakiest wheels get the oil, so when I was done with dinner, I flopped down on my bed, grabbed the phone and asked information if they had a listing for Clare Prout in Eastbourne. They didn't. I said, how about Brighton? Nothing there either. Then I wondered, anything at all in the Eastbourne region?

Normally, when you ring information, British Telecom only allows you a couple of tries because that way they can charge you a second time when you have to phone back for more. It's a corporate philosophy that encourages inefficiency, reinforced by the fact that, in London at least, they only give you a telephone book for your general area. I live in west London, so they supply me with the west London directory. If I want a number in south London, I've got to ask for it. Which means, I've got to pay for it. Because they know you can't get numbers any other way, the less helpful the operator is, the more you have to dial Directory Enquiries, which means the more they can charge you.

Except, this time the woman on the other end was obviously new at her job because she was helpful. To begin with, she didn't insist on having an address before she checked the Eastbourne area. Normally they say, without the address they can't come up with the number, which is slightly ludicrous because if you don't have the number of someone you don't know, chances are you won't have their address either. It's the same argument I used to have with my mother when I was a kid doing my homework and I'd ask how to spell a word. She'd always answer, look it up in the dictionary. Except, in order to look up a word in the dictionary, you have to know how to spell it.

Anyway, the woman on the other end of the line said she
would see what she could find in the Eastbourne area and
after a few minutes she reported back that there were three
Prouts in East Sussex. There was an F.D. in Bexhill, which
was down the beach from Eastbourne, a G. in Polegate, to the
north of Eastbourne, and a second G. in Berwick, to the west
of Polegate. I asked if I could have all three and she gave them
to me. I started with F.D., a man answered, I asked for Mrs
Clare Prout and he told me there was no one there with that
name. I then tried the first G. There was no answer. So I tried
the second G and a woman answered with the words, 'Clare
Prout.'

Smiling, I licked my index finger then marked one point in
thin air. 'I'm sorry if my visit this morning upset you. It's
Vincent Barolo.'

There was a long silence.

'I hope this isn't an inconvenient moment.' I imagined, she
was trying to hide her surprise.

But I was wrong. 'My instincts told me you would get back
in touch. I'm glad you didn't ring the office.'

I probably would have had I not found her at home.
'And my instincts are telling me there is something very
wrong about Dr Bickerton . . . his suicide, the fire at his
place . . .'

'You said in your note to Dr Tyrone that Dr Bickerton was
your client.'

'I was retained by him some weeks ago.'

'To do what?'

The easiest thing was to hide behind attorney-client privilege.
'I'm sorry, but I'm sure you can appreciate that I can't
discuss that.'

There was another long pause. 'When you mentioned that
you had something Dr Tyrone might want and then said to
me that was just your way of attracting some attention, was
that the truth?'

I told her, 'Yes.' But wondered what it was she thought I
might have.

'Perhaps you should know . . . perhaps you already know . . .
Dr Bickerton did not leave the European Research Project on
the best of terms.'

'You were his secretary.'

'I was his administrative assistant for nearly five years.'

'Can you tell me why he left?'

'Suffice it to say that there are some people who are very angry with him.'

'What for?'

Now she confessed, 'I did not give your note to Dr Tyrone. Under the circumstances, I didn't think it appropriate.'

'Is Dr Tyrone one of those angry people?'

She took a deep breath. 'I don't know how much I can say . . .'

I didn't want to spook her, so I asked carefully, 'What is it that you thought I had when I came to see Dr Tyrone this afternoon?'

'Really . . . please understand . . . I just don't know how much I should say.'

That sounded to me like someone who had a lot to say and might even want to say it all. 'Perhaps we could meet. Perhaps that would be easier than speaking on the phone like this.'

'I don't know . . .'

'You liked him as a boss, didn't you?'

'Mr Barolo . . . I liked Roger Bickerton as a human being . . . as a person.'

'And you think he got a raw deal.'

She didn't say anything.

I suggested, 'He was your associate . . . your friend . . . he was my client . . . there might be a way to right the wrong.' I had no idea what I was talking about but it sounded good. 'There might be a way to do one last thing for him.'

Obviously I touched another button. 'Not at the office. And this would have to be just between us. No one must ever know. This must be in the strictest of confidence.'

I assured her, 'No one will know. The confidence, of course, will be respected.'

'I can't come to London. Perhaps . . .' She blurted out, 'The airport. I can get there. Tomorrow. During my lunch break.'

'The airport?'

'Yes. Gatwick Airport. Can you meet me there? Trains run regularly from London. I'll look for you at one o'clock.

Where the trains come into the terminal. Just there. Is that all right?'

I said I'd be there, hung up and lay back on my bed, replaying the conversation in my head. I kept hearing her say, there are some people who are very angry with him.

Chapter Nineteen

I had only enough time to tell Henry I'd be out for the rest of the morning, to remind her about the FedEx envelope, to pick up my pocket recorder and to hook up the little sleeve mike I use when I don't want anyone to know they're being taped.

'There are bills to pay,' Henry said, dropping a small pile of them on my desk. 'And the jerk already called twice this morning.'

'Did you mention to him that I'm not happy about his costume bill?'

'He knows and he wants to apologize.'

'See?' I said to Henry. 'He's not so bad, after all.'

She didn't want to know. 'Where are you going?'

'The airport?'

'What for?'

'Good question.'

'How about a good answer?'

'Curiosity.'

'Not good enough.'

'If I ever think of a better one, I'll let you know.'

There are special trains direct to Gatwick from Victoria station every fifteen minutes, so getting out there was no problem and I was at the airport with half an hour to spare.

A monument to the architect of the package tour, the main terminal was filled with people stuck on a treadmill that extended from Britain to the Costa Brava, with a shopping centre at one end where you can stock up on duty-free booze and diarrhoea pills, and a shopping centre at the other end where you can get stupid drunk on cheap beer, throw up and buy a silly hat. In between, you burn in the sun, eat bad food

and sleep with people you might not otherwise even talk to. Mr
Cook, we who queue salute you.

I poked around the newsstand for a few minutes – there
was nothing at all on boxing, so I bought a copy of the
International Herald Tribune and checked the sports pages –
and wound up reading the entire paper, standing just inside
the terminal, where she told me to meet her.

She arrived ten minutes late. But that was okay. At least
she showed up. Except, she wasn't any more relaxed now than
she had been yesterday and clung nervously to her Burberry
raincoat. I suggested coffee. We wound up in a crowded
cafeteria. She insisted that we take a table at the rear, in the
far corner, where we were less likely to be seen together. I sat
down to her right because the microphone was hidden in my
left sleeve. 'Who shouldn't see us together?'

'Anyone from work.'

As she reached for the sugar, I casually put my hand inside
my jacket and snapped on the recorder. 'Was Dr Bickerton in
some sort of trouble?'

'It wasn't good when he left.'

With all the background noise I didn't know if the mike
would pick her up, so I let my left hand dangle on the table.
'Why was he fired?'

'It wasn't that he was fired.' She stirred her coffee much
too quickly for someone who was simply trying to cool it down
and dissolve the sugar. 'They used the term, redundant. But it
was strictly office-political. He couldn't have cared less about
politics. That was his problem. He never played office politics.
So they got him.'

'Who got him?'

'Brussels. But especially the French. It was mainly the
French because they wanted to control as much of the work
as possible.'

'What was the work?'

'Dr Bickerton is . . .' She stopped, then corrected herself,
'was a geneticist. He was working in the field of the human
genome project.'

I confessed that I didn't know what that was.

'It has to do with characteristics of genes.'

'This project . . . the French wanted to take it over . . .'

'No.' She shook her head several times. 'The human genome

project has become a field of science. There are lots of people working independently . . . I didn't mean to imply that it was one organized thing. But that's not the problem. It's what happened after he was forced to retire. A lot of his work . . . a lot of very technical data went missing.' She stared at me. 'They think he stole it.'

Now I understood why my note with the words, 'I have something you want,' attracted her attention. 'He stole files?'

'I think . . . they think that he permanently erased them from the computer. He knew how to do that. The back-ups have been tampered with as well. They're now, all, unretrievable.'

'Getting even,' I muttered, recalling his speech on the plane. 'What sort of files were they?'

'They think . . . no one is sure exactly what was on them . . . but his work had to do with a gene in human chromosome 5 and something about another gene in human chromosome 13.'

I made a face. 'That explains everything.'

Forcing a smile, she admitted, 'I'm not a scientist, I'm an administrator. But I've seen a report.' She stopped and looked at me for a long time.

'And?'

She didn't answer.

I asked, 'His laboratory fire . . . did you know that it was arson?'

'I heard it had burned down.'

Now I dared, 'Do you think he committed suicide?'

She took a deep breath. 'No.'

I waited a moment before I said quietly, 'I'd very much like to see a copy of that report.'

There was another few seconds pause before she reached into the pocket of her raincoat and brought out a manila envelope folded in two. 'Please . . . I could probably be arrested if anyone ever found out . . .'

I nodded. 'I understand.'

She shoved the coffee away, pulled her coat around her again and stood up. 'There are several pages of his notes in there too. Most of them are doodles but . . . well, I found them when he left. I meant to give them back but they didn't seem too terribly important . . . then.' She looked at me. 'He was a kind man who got a rotten deal.' And just like that, she walked away.

An airport cafeteria didn't strike me as the most private place to read whatever was inside the envelope, so I stuffed it into my pocket, turned off my tape recorder, finished my coffee and got on the next train back to London. I found a seat alone and waited until we were on the way before I opened the envelope.

The report was a one-page memo to Dr Tyrone from someone called Carl Denton, whose title was head of security, outlining his suspicions that Bickerton had helped himself to ERP data about those two human chromosomes. While Denton wrote that the data had been deliberately removed from the computer and effectively erased from the back-up system, his recommendation was that no official action be taken against Bickerton.

I stared at the word 'official'. I wondered if that implied unofficial action would be taken.

Or had been taken.

Also enclosed were eight pages on lined paper, obviously ripped from a small notebook. There were lots of doodles – orderly arrangements of circles within squares within triangles within circles — and on another page were three sets of numbers. One set had letters at the beginning and the end. The second was eight numbers, with every two separated by a period. The third was locked inside a doodled rectangle, with the numbers 707 on top and a not-too-bad rendering of a jet plane next to that. It was easy to assume they were each some sort of scientific formula. Then there was a tiny sketch in ink that looked as if it spelled the word 'monachus'. Other scribbling was not quite as apparent, although I could clearly make out four names – Alberik, Mendel, Pincer and DesRocher.

I had no idea what any of this meant.

When we pulled into Victoria station, I phoned Henry to say that I wouldn't be back at the office for a while. She said Hambone rang several times, was at Charlie's and sounded desperate. There was also a call from PC Hoving in Brighton.

I dialled Charlie's first. Hambone started whining to me about Moe Moses and apologized about the problem with

Croxford's. He was very down. I told him I was busy for another few hours. He insisted that he needed to see me. I told him to meet me at my place at seven. He asked if I was inviting him for dinner. So I said, 'Yeah.'

That's all it took to cheer him up.

Next, I phoned Brighton.

It took a while before Hoving came on the line but when he did, he wanted to know, 'Are you sure one of our fellows was at Bickerton's flat last Wednesday?'

'That's what I was told. Wednesday, at around one pm. That would have been within a few hours of the news of his death.'

'No record here of anyone doing that.'

'Plainclothes?' I said. 'A detective or something?'

'It would have been logged somewhere. Or should have been logged somewhere. I've asked around and no one knows anything about it.'

'Thanks.' I hung up, thinking to myself, how come that doesn't surprise me?

I grabbed a taxi at the station and went straight to the British Museum in Bloomsbury. Housed in the middle of the museum is the British Library Reading Room and one of the best things I've ever done is gotten a pass to use it. When you first call, they tell you that the Reading Room is not for use by the general public. But if you know how, it's not difficult to talk your way in. So they gave me an admission card valid for five years, and once I had that, renewing it every five years was easy.

Haunted by the ghosts of the century's great thinkers – Freud worked here, Marx too – the room is magnificent, with tens of thousands of books packed onto shelves, and thousands of shelves balanced on old wooden balconies that stretch from floor to ceiling. Work benches go around the floor, in ever decreasing circles, with the librarians' counters in the middle. Because it is the copyright library, every book published in Great Britain over the past several hundred years is there. That means everything I could ever want to know is there. All I had to do was find it.

I started with the *Oxford English Dictionary* and checked the word 'monachus'. It wasn't listed. The word which appeared immediately before the place where monachus should have

been was monacholite. The word which appeared immediately after the place where monachus should have been was
monacid. The first was a spelling variation of the word
monothelite, being an adherent of the heretical sect which
maintains that Christ has only one will. The second meant
having the power of saturating one molecule of a monobasic
acid. I didn't personally know any monacholites and didn't
have the slightest notion how to saturate monobasic acid
molecules. But I was struck by the fact that there were so
many words I'd never heard before. I decided that monachus
probably had something to do with monacid, if for no other
reason than because Bickerton must have known a lot about
molecules.

From there, I wrote the four names on a slip of paper and
showed it to one of the research clerks, who directed me to
the computers and card index files. Mendel was the easiest of
the four. There were several very extensive entries for him, but
the one in a book called *Tennant's Historical Science* seemed the
simplest to understand.

'Mendel, Gregor Johann, 1822–84. Austrian monk noted for
experimental work in the field of heredity. From the age of
21 and for the next 25 years (1843–68), while living at the
Augustinian monastery in Brno, Mendel conducted numerous
experiments on basic garden-variety peas. Using what was in
those days considered a sophisticated controlled pollination
technique, he was able to combine physical evidence with
statistical analysis, thus enabling him to produce the first
scientifically accurate explanation for hybridization. Although
his findings were published in 1866, they were otherwise
ignored for the next 34 years, until being rediscovered by
three separate botanists (Hugo De Vries, Karl Erich Correns
and Erich Tschermak von Seysenegg) in 1900–1902. Since then
Mendel's conclusions, among them that inherited characteristics are determined by the combination of two hereditary
units, known as genes, coming one from each of the parental
reproductive cells, known as gametes, have been credited as the
basic tenets of genetics.'

I mumbled to myself, 'Okay,' and picked up another reference
to him, in a volume called *Beressmen's Science*. It said, basically,
much the same thing, although what caught my eye was a quote
accredited to Mendel. 'Medical research took a giant step in the

year 1080. Constantine the African was a physician who studied both medicine and magic at Babylon. Disguised as a monk and in hiding at the Benedictine monastery at Monte Cassino, he had by this point translated into Latin the works of several scholars, among them Arabian, Jewish, Greek and Roman. This included the writings of Galen and Avicenna, through which, medicine was delivered out of the religious bonds that had until now held it. Much of those works were later translated by Alberik and formed the basis for the plenitude of his contribution to my work.'

So there was another name from the list. Except, I couldn't find anything in any of those volumes specifically about Alberik.

I asked again if the research assistant could help and she eventually located an English translation of a book written in Latin called *Lives of the Benedicts*. His entry there read: 'Alberik: (1622–1684), French Benedictine monk falsely credited with having formed the basic tenets of genetics.'

I photocopied that, plus what I'd found on Mendel, and began looking for the other two names. Using the library computer, I was able to search Pincer and DesRocher singularly and then, on the research clerk's advice, I searched for any references to all four names combined. Nothing came up under the foursome, but there were several references to Pincer and DesRocher together. One of them was in a small article in the Journal of the Albert Einstein College of Medicine at Yeshiva University in New York. Again with the research clerk's help, we found the text in an on-line service that the library subscribed to called Aesculapius.

According to the article, Dr Thomas Alexander Pincer and Dr Raoul DesRocher were two very eminent genetic scientists. They were also bitter enemies who'd been immersed in a professional feud for the past several years. Pincer ran a company in Washington called Taptech. DesRocher ran the Centre National de Recherches Scientifiques in Marseilles.

Hambone was standing on my doorstep. 'I don't want you to think I'm, like, ungrateful or anything . . .'

'Hiya, Derek.' I unlocked the door and we went inside. 'I'd offer you a drink, but you're in training.'

'That's what I mean . . . honest, I'm not being ungrateful . . .

but it's all this stuff he says I have to do and all this stuff he
says I can't do . . .'

'Who?' The mail was a phone bill.

'This Moe Moses bloke.' Derek followed me into my
bedroom.

'He's making you work hard and you're complaining?' I put
all the stuff I got at the library on my night table, took off my
tie and hung it up along with my jacket.

'You know that he's a Jew?'

I went back into the living room to check my answering
machine. 'So what?'

'So he's killing me.'

There were no messages. 'What does that have to do with
anything?'

Hambone thought about it for a moment. 'Well, I don't
know . . . my momma says Jewish people don't get along with
black people.'

I told him, 'Sammy Davis Junior was Jewish.'

That stopped him. 'He was?'

'Tell your momma I said so.'

'He's still killing me.'

'You ever hear of Maxie Rosenbloom?'

'No.'

'He was one of America's greatest boxers. Came out of
Brooklyn.' Actually, I was only guessing that he was from
Brooklyn. 'We're talking Hall of Fame here.' I wasn't sure
of that either. 'Light heavyweight champion of the world from
1930 to 1934.' I knew that much. 'Now you ever hear of a guy
named Mickey Walker?' He hadn't. 'Well, Mickey Walker held
the world welterweight belt for a bunch of years in the 1920s
and then he won the world middleweight championship and
held on to it for about five years. He was one of the greatest
champions in boxing history. And you know who beat him?
Maxie Rosenbloom.' I didn't explain that Walker was nuts
to get in the ring with Rosenbloom. 'So when you talk about
Jews and boxing in the same breath, those guys know what
they're doing.'

He looked at me with a schoolboy expression of awe. 'You
sure know a lot about boxing.'

Now I made one up. 'Ever hear about a guy named Hank
Greenberg?' He was a famous Jewish baseball player but that

didn't matter because Hambone didn't know anything about baseball. 'Who do you think was in Rocky Marciano's corner when he knocked out Joe Louis in 1951?'

He shuffled his feet for a few seconds. 'I didn't mean to insult anybody . . .'

'How much road work has he got you doing?'

'Ten miles.'

'Hey.' I put my arm over his shoulder. 'I'd complain too.'

He hugged me back. 'Thanks, Vince.'

'Now what's all this about boxing shorts and The Equalizer?'

'I was . . .' He shuffled his feet and started to blush. 'I was going to pay for it, really I was, but then my mother . . . we had to send some money to her sister in Jamaica . . .'

'So you put it on my tab?' He stared back at me with those huge dark eyes of his and I realized there was nothing to be gained by rubbing it in. 'It's only a loan. You can pay me back when . . .' I wondered if I should tell him about my conversation with Fuzzy White, then decided not to. 'You can pay me back when you've got it.'

He hugged me again. 'I don't know what I'd do without you, man.'

I changed the subject. 'What do you want to eat?'

'How about a burger?'

'What's second choice?'

'How about that Indian place down the street?'

'Burgers it is.'

I nursed a regular, with a bottle of beer and a side of potato chips, which the British call crisps even when they're soggy, the way these were. Hambone gobbled an extra-cheese with extra fries, swigged a large Coke, burped, asked if he could have seconds and when I said sure, he ordered everything again.

'You ever go into the ring,' he chewed, 'knowing you were going to get beat?'

'Nope.'

'Honest?'

'Honest.' I finished my beer as he washed his meal down with a slice of apple crumble, which is apple pie aptly named because none of it sticks together.

'Moe's trying to tell me to stay off the ropes with this guy.'

'You can't win a fight when you're backed onto the ropes.'

'But I keep telling Moe that I can wear him out like that.'

'Except, you're the one who's getting hit.'

There was a time when I could eat the way he does and never had to give my weight a second thought. I remember one Christmas dinner at my uncle Sal's place. I'd already gone through two helpings of white meat when I arm wrestled my cousin Little Sal for both drumsticks. But those days were long gone. So is my welterweight status. Sometimes I stand in front of the mirror after I take a shower, you know, look at myself naked, and wonder whatever happened to that rock hard flat stomach. Unfortunately, it's gone too. But then, so is a good five-cent cigar. Flat tummies and nickel stogies. The sort of stuff you tell your grandchildren about when you're trying to convince yourself that the good old days were a lot better than they really were.

'I'm not going to let him beat me,' Derek said, as if he was trying to convince himself.

'No good,' I lectured, 'you've got to say, I am going to beat him.'

'What's the difference?'

'It's the difference between winning and losing.'

I paid the bill and walked him to the tube station at Notting Hill Gate.

'I guess I won't really know if I can beat him till the first bell sounds.'

'Tell Moe I said to teach you how to win before the bell sounds.'

He didn't understand. 'You mean before the fight even starts?'

'Yeah.' I put my hands on his shoulder. 'That's the best way to win. Before the fight even starts.'

He hugged me – 'Vince, I love you, man' – and hurried down the steps. I waited until he was out of sight, then turned and went back to my place to settle in for a night of reading all that stuff from the library.

The first paragraph began, 'Pierre de Maupertuis challenged the pre-existence theory of genetics as advanced in 1699 by

Jan Swammerdam whose ovist theories, at least according to Maupertuis, were insufficient to explain either congenital freaks or the creation of hybrids, or for that matter, the simple fact that offspring customarily possess characteristics of both parents.'

I read it three times and still didn't understand it.

'Furthermore, de Maupertuis also challenges the theory of spontaneous generation as postulated by John Needham in 1748. His own thesis of "monsters by default" and "monsters by excess" anticipates the eventual discovery of supernumerary or missing chromosomes. Having observed that offspring reveal characteristics present in both parents, he made a sufficient case to show that ovist theories simply do not explain the occasional six-fingered hand or albinism in blacks.'

That didn't register either.

'Mendel recognized that dominant or recessive characteristics depend on basic units, which today we call genes, and that proper engineering of those basic units can create improved varieties of plant and animal life. His law therefore states, the first generation of progeny produced by mixed parents will be hybrids. However, he goes on, in the second generation only half will be hybrids; one quarter will bear the traits of one parent; and one quarter will bear the traits of the second parent.'

I said out loud, 'So if your mother has big feet and your father has a big nose . . .' then tossed those pages onto the empty half of my bed and picked up the next bunch.

I was still at it by one am, trying to figure out how, or even if, any of this tied Bickerton to the four names on the hand-scrawled pages. The obvious link was genetics. But then what? I kept going back to the article from that on-line service that mentioned the Pincer and DesRocher feud. Then I started to think about how I'd found it in cyberspace. And the more I thought about that, the more I asked myself, what else is out there?

So I reached for the phone and dialled New Jersey.

Louise answered. 'Hello?'

'Yeah . . . hiya . . . it's Vince. How are you?'

All she wanted to know was, 'Is it Saturday morning already?'

'I'm glad to hear that you're well.' What was I going to do, get into an argument with her? 'Is Johnny there?'

'He's just finishing his homework and he's still got to have dinner.'

'I'm glad to hear that too. You think I could have a word with him for a couple of minutes?'

She mumbled, 'It's your dime . . .'

I started to remind her, 'He's also my son . . .' but she didn't hear that, which was just as well.

She called, 'Johnny? It's your father.'

And right away he picked up. 'Hi.'

'Hey. How you doing?'

'It's not Saturday.'

'So? I can't call my own kid except on Saturday?'

'I went two for three this afternoon. We played down in Passaic. They got some hot shot southpaw who caught me looking the first time up but then I doubled to left, scored two, then got a single to right. Let me tell you, the guy could really throw a slider. That's how he caught me the first time. Infuriating. But he didn't catch me twice.'

'That's great,' I said. 'How's school? Baseball's not getting in the way or anything, is it?'

'No, it's okay.'

'And your computer?'

He whispered, 'I think I've got the phone line all set up for next week. You know, for my modem.'

'What does your old lady say about that?'

'Well . . . I guess she doesn't exactly know yet. But what can she say, it's my money.'

I suggested, 'How about if she says it's her house?'

'Except it isn't,' he snapped.

Instead of getting into that, I said, 'Listen, I was thinking about your computer and your modem, you know, and how you told me you can get onto the Internet and all that stuff. You got a pencil and a piece of paper handy? I've got five names I want you to check.'

'Where do you want me to look?'

'On the Internet.'

'Dad, the Internet . . . it's kinda like the New Jersey Turnpike. You can get anywhere you want but you've got to know what exit to take.'

'Take whichever exit they buried Jimmy Hoffa under.'

'Who?'

'Look him up, too. You got that pencil and paper? Here are the names.' I told him, 'Alberik. He was a monk. Next is Gregor Johann Mendel. I guess he was also a monk. Then there's Dr Thomas Alexander Pincer, Dr Raoul DesRocher, and Dr L. Roger Bickerton.' I went through the list again, this time spelling each name for him. 'You got that? They all have something to do with genetics so you might look under science. And don't worry about phone bills or anything, I'll take care of whatever it costs. Just let me know and I'll send you some money before your mother starts complaining.'

'Dad, the Internet doesn't work that way.'

'You're telling me it's like the Turnpike. Okay. So I'm paying for the ride. You're driving. If the Turnpike doesn't work, get off and take Garden State. Oh, this Pincer guy runs a company in Washington called Taptech. That may help.'

'What do you want me to find out?'

'Whatever there is to find out.'

'And what do I do once I find out?'

'Does your mother know that you can send faxes with your modem?'

'No.'

'So fax me.'

Chapter Twenty

Henry was holding the little wire basket that normally sits at the back of the fax machine. 'There must be . . . like, thirty pages.' She challenged me, 'Do you know how much fax paper costs? I mean, what is all this?'

'What does it say?'

'Who knows? There's only one handwritten page.' She read, 'Jimmy Hoffa is buried all over the NJ Turnpike.'

My first thought was, what will Johnny's mother say when she sees the phone bill?

'Here.' Henry poured the tray's worth of faxes into my arms and walked away.

I took them to my desk, dumped them in the middle, sat down and started rummaging through them.

There were several articles copyrighted by the Associated Press which Johnny had obviously pulled out of some computerized newspaper archives. The first was headlined, 'Protein Makes Fat Mice Thin' and datelined Washington DC.

'Hopes that dieters' fantasies will someday come true were raised by the Taptech Corporation when they announced today that they have isolated a gene in mice that causes obesity. According to Taptech chairman, Dr Thomas Alexander Pincer, he and his team of genetic scientists have successfully triggered weight loss in mice through manipulation of a gene in mice chromosomes that they believe may be duplicated in human chromosome 5.'

A second AP article went into great detail about how, until this point, much of the research into human obesity had centred around experiments with something called leptin, which was a protein normally produced by the OB gene in mice. OB turned out to stand for obesity. It said that when the gene is flawed and leptin is not manufactured in suitable quantities, mice become obese. Many of the mice used in the various laboratory experiments with the OB gene then developed diabetes and other fatal conditions. However, after two weeks of leptin injections, some of those mice lost up to one-third of their body weight.

'Yet, such is the excitement generated by Pincer's discovery,' the article concluded, 'that research in this field could be abruptly rerouted away from leptin and the OB gene to a further, more detailed mapping of human chromosome 5. "I am firmly convinced," Pincer said, "that the discovery and the isolation of the FAT gene in mice will produce applications that should make human obesity almost unknown within ten to twenty years."'

I flipped past several similar articles until I came to a lengthy and much footnoted article in the *International Journal of Obesity*.

'Corpulence had already been recognized as a menace to health by the Greek physician Hippocrates, more than four centuries before Christ. Overeating was, in those days, looked on as a moral weakness. However, it wasn't until the nineteenth century that specific types of obesity were catalogued. Based on the belief that the cell was the basic building block of life, it was generally accepted that obesity was due to too many fat cells. Then researchers began to theorize that the presence of too many fat cells might represent some sort of metabolic disorder and have, at its origins, inherited factors. This set the scene for genetic scientists to come along almost three-quarters of a century later and view obesity as a symptom of some malfunctioning gene.'

Next came an article published in the *Journal of the National Institute of Health*. 'A Summary of Obesity Research – Fitting the Pieces Together' looked as if it was an overview of the work being done in the field. But I could tell from the first sentence that this was anything but an instant road map. 'The B3–adrenergic receptor, whose presence in adipose tissue is clearly noted, turns out to consist of seven transmembrane domains.' I merely skimmed through the rest of it, stopping only at two short paragraphs.

One of them quoted Pincer, speaking from his Taptech laboratory in Washington DC. 'I would suggest that while other researchers over the past seven years have claimed to describe no fewer than five genes that might be involved in overeating and its consequential obesity, the results of my work to clone the single FAT gene in human chromosome 5 represent the most significant breakthrough in this field.'

In the other, a little further down, DesRocher did not mince words in his opinion of Pincer's findings. 'While these results have indeed generated genuine interest, and rightfully so as it is our obligation as scientists to consider all new ideas so that we may test them and sort the valuable from the worthless, it is both unsupported by the facts and at the same time highly unlikely, that any cloning of the gene in mouse chromosome 8 suitably translates to the genetic make-up of human chromosome 5, especially in respect to the encoding of carboxypeptidase E.'

I didn't understand the specifics of what DesRocher was saying, but it was obvious that he was telling the world that Pincer was full of crap.

Then there was a *Wall Street Journal* article which illustrated a three-pronged attack on obesity. The giant pharmaceutical companies had, for years, centred their attention on drugs that could suppress appetite, that burned off excess fat or that prevented the absorption of fat in the intestine. Next, researchers began to theorize that if obesity is caused by a lack of certain proteins, then by giving the person the missing protein, the body could regulate itself. So drugs poured onto the market which tried to tell the brain to stop eating and also to speed up metabolism. The third step was to say, if the body itself did not produce the necessary protein to control overeating – as a result of a defective gene – then isolate that gene and replace it.

Enter here Pincer and DesRocher.

A second article in the *Journal of the NIH* clarified the significance of Pincer's discovery. 'Considered by some to be the single most important health problem in the United States, obesity directly relates to heart disease, cancer and diabetes. In an attempt to control body weight, Americans spend $30 billion a year, in spite of the fact that most techniques fail and most dieters regain lost fat within a few years. If reports from Taptech are substantiated through further laboratory tests, this represents a potentially momentous breakthrough for dieters.'

But all that glittered was not Slimfast.

A story in the *Washington Post* warned, 'Controversy, which has dogged the career of Dr Thomas Alexander Pincer, founder and chairman of Taptech Corporation, showed no signs of abating now that the scientific community has had time to study his recent claims that the key to eradicating human obesity lies in some as yet non-demonstrable similarities between a mouse gene and the uncharted faculties of human chromosome 5. According to Dr Raoul DesRocher, director of the National Centre for Scientific Research in Marseilles, France, Pincer's discovery is nothing more than a plagiarized version of studies published by DesRocher's laboratory on human chromosome 13, for which DesRocher earned the prestigious Prix Mendel from the French Academy of Science last year. "Overwhelming evidence in the quest for the so-called 'FAT gene'," DesRocher insisted, "points to its existence in the genetic structure of human chromosome 13," adding that his own work in that area had recently been licensed by Berghaun Arzneikundlich GmbH in Fulda, Germany. Pincer refused to comment on the charges, but it is believed that Taptech is negotiating a licensing agreement with the giant Swiss conglomerate Kaducee-Pharmacopeia.'

That was followed by 'FAT Gene Quest Promises Obese Profits' which appeared in *Genetic Engineering News*. Noting that a person was medically considered obese if they were twenty per cent or more above their normal ideal weight . . . and that, perhaps, as many as thirty-five million Americans were caught in that definition . . . obesity in the western world was dramatically on the rise. In 1960, nearly one quarter of all American adults in the twenty-four to seventy-year-old age range were considered overweight. Today that figure has passed the one-third mark. In Europe, over the same period, obesity had doubled.

With so much at stake, the article continued, it was no surprise that all the big companies were trying to get in on the game. Until now, scientific licensing fees, on average, had hovered around the $25,000 mark. But Glaxo-Wellcome and Hoffmann-La Roche had pushed licensing fees into the strato-sphere, and even those deals quickly paled by comparison with Amgen's record up-front payment to Rockefeller University of $20 million for the right to exploit its work with a protein called leptin. And $20 million was only for openers. Additional but undisclosed sums were to be paid for clinical milestones – verifiable discoveries that were made along the way – which, *Genetic Engineering News* estimated, could be worth several times $20 million, and those would then be followed by royalties on the sale of any drugs that were developed as a result of the research.

Even then, Amgen's record didn't stand for very long.

Word around the industry was that Berghaun Arzneikundlich, which was Germany's largest pharmaceutical company, was paying DesRocher $29 million up front and that Pincer had asked Kaducee-Pharmacopeia for $32 million.

At the end of the article, there was a series of footnotes, referencing several dozen other articles about making fat mice thin, and calculating that sales of an over-the-counter fat-reducing drug might be expected to bring in $10–$15 billion to the company who first gets it onto the market.

Then there was a story from the *New York Times* headlined, 'Biotech Is Thieves' Hottest Target'.

'That the US biotech industry is a plum begging to be picked is hardly a surprise. That the world's biotech thieves have only just figured that out, is amazing. However, in recent months they have more than made up for lost time, fleecing the sector for tens of millions of dollars.'

I skimmed the page looking for Pincer, DesRocher, Taptech or the CNRS. But the only reference I could spot that would have induced Johnny to include this with the others was a lengthy description of how Amgen had been the victim of two attempted thefts.

Pushing it aside, I went back to the article from *Genetic Engineering News*, stared at those numbers for a very long time, picked up the *Washington Post* story again, took a red pen, circled the word 'plagiarism' and, in the margin, doodled a very large dollar sign.

Chapter Twenty-One

The most valuable lesson I ever learned about being a lawyer was not something anyone taught me in school, it was more like a rash I caught while wading neck deep through society's refuse as a journeyman in the public defender's office.

It was, how to practise law on a shoestring.

The only requirements are a phone book, a phone, a finger to dial, some place safe to park your ego and a pretty good gullet so that you don't choke when you start to swallow what's left of your pride.

Begging for hand-outs is not a sport for the haughty.

I was duty-bound to produce the best possible defence that money could buy, except there was no money to buy anything. So I had to ferret out sources by myself, beseech people to help, connive to get whatever I needed for free.

It took a long time before I figured it out. And I know that I lost cases in the meantime. My boss – an old drunk named Al Testaverdi who couldn't make a living in the real world and wound up spending his entire career as a public defender – often chided me that I was wasting too much time on each of my cases. This is about volume, he used to say. This is about shuffling people through the system in the most efficient, least painful way for those of us who were assigned to be their escorts on the tour. At the same time, some of the other lawyers in the office, the ones who weren't yet as jaded as Al, accused me of being a loner who was only looking for that one big grandstand play so that he could make a name for himself. But that wasn't it at all. I was looking for anything I could grab on to in order to even the odds in a game where the prosecution held all the cards and the poor bastard sitting next to me at the defence table was permanently out of luck.

I paid my dues with every case, and I might well have been destined to play in the minors – for ever Shoestring Joe – until an eighteen-year-old black kid named Thurlow Adams was arrested on a murder charge. This was the one I'd been waiting for. And by the time I walked into Room 201 of the New York City Criminal Court building up on Schermerhorn Street, there was no doubt in my mind but that I did have the knack.

A couple of young kids had robbed a gas station over on Bedford, not far from where Ebbets Field used to be. They got $45 out of the till and that might have been the end of that, except when they started to run away, the owner – an old white guy who'd lived in the neighbourhood all his life – began screaming for help. A middle-aged couple sitting in a car waiting for gas reported that one of the kids had a baseball bat and before running away, to stop the old man from shouting, the kid clubbed him to death. Thurlow got picked up later that night two blocks away with a baseball bat in his hand and $75 in his pocket. The couple in the car made a positive ID. But Thurlow swore he was innocent. His alibi was that, at the time of the murder, he was at the opera.

I said, 'Of course. Singing Verdi.'

'No,' he insisted, 'it was Puccini.'

I reminded him, 'You're no longer a juvenile. If they find you guilty, and there are two solid witnesses to say it was you, the best you can hope for is life. And right now, even that's pretty remote.'

'The opera . . . that's where I was.'

'Yeah, you and your baseball bat.'

'No. I found it after.'

The problem with the baseball bat was that the police lab had retrieved blood and hair fibres from it which matched the victim's. When you added forensics into the equation with two reliable eye witnesses and no believable alibi, the case against Thurlow was just about airtight. In fact, the evidence was so strong that the Assistant DA assigned to it – a guy named Danny Kuhn who'd been a couple of years ahead of me at Brooklyn Law – refused to do anything more than trade a guilty plea on murder one for life without parole. 'This is non-negotiable,' he declared. 'No other deal is possible.'

The alternative if Thurlow were to lose in court was the

electric chair. Still, force of habit, I told Danny, 'No soap. We go to the jury.'

Thurlow's alibi was so off-the-wall, so totally implausible, that I had to wonder, maybe it's true. Talking the case through with Testaverdi, I explained that the witnesses who identified Thurlow were sitting in their car, at night, fifteen yards away from the office with their view partially blocked by a gas pump. The lighting wasn't good. And because the old man hadn't yet filled up their tank, he hadn't yet cleaned their windshield. That's how long ago this was, every time you got gas, someone wiped your window. The couple couldn't ID the other kid but claimed to have gotten a good look at Thurlow's face as he ran past them.

That's exactly what they both said, 'As he ran past us.'

Except, Thurlow had been born with a club foot and couldn't have run even if he'd wanted to.

Danny quickly dismissed that by saying his witnesses really meant that he walked fast.

Testaverdi tried to make me believe that my whole case rested on my ability to convince a jury that running and walking fast weren't the same thing. I told Testaverdi it would never work. He reminded me I had a stack of other cases waiting on my desk.

Instead, I went back to Thurlow to talk about Puccini.

He claimed he was hanging out that afternoon over on Flatbush Avenue when a white guy – middle-aged, crew cut and glasses – came up to him and asked, out of the blue, do you want to go to the opera? Thurlow answered, yeah okay. So the guy handed him a $12 ticket and started to walk away. When Thurlow asked where the opera was and how he was supposed to get there, the guy answered, 'Lincoln Centre,' reached into his pocket, pulled out a $100 bill and told him, 'Here, take a taxi.'

I needed Thurlow to understand, 'You have as much chance of making a jury believe that as you do telling them you're Mario Lanza.'

He insisted, 'It's the truth.'

I asked, 'Where is Lincoln Centre?'

He answered, 'I don't know. I took a taxi.'

'What was the number of the taxi?'

'I don't know.'

'What did the driver look like?'

'I don't know.'

'How much did it cost?'

'I gave him ten bucks.'

'Where did you sit?'

'Upstairs.'

'Where's the ticket stub?'

'I lost it.'

'What was the name of the opera?'

'*Madame Butterfly*.'

'What happens?'

'It was all in some foreign language.'

'Which one?'

'Italian.'

'Yeah, so, what happens?'

That's when he proceeded to give me the basic storyline. He also told me about the woman who sang the lead – he said she was so very beautiful and remembered that her first name was Leontyne – and how he liked a big painting of flowers in the lobby. Of course, the storyline was in every library and Leontyne Price's name was in every newspaper ad. There'd also been a photo in the papers of that painting in the lobby – it was an Andy Warhol silk-screen – when the Metropolitan Opera moved into Lincoln Centre a few years before. None of this was enough to convince anyone that he'd actually been there.

Then he mentioned the sneeze.

'She was standing there,' he said, 'right in the middle of the stage, getting ready to sing this song, and nothing happened for like ten seconds. And she looked down at the conductor, like she was waiting for him to start, and all of a sudden he sneezed. The conductor sneezed and everybody laughed. Even her.'

'The conductor . . .' I started it as a question but finished it as a statement, ' . . . sneezed.'

Thurlow nodded. 'Yeah. Like . . . hah-choo.'

There was no way I could explain to anyone in the office how I was going to base my defence on a sneeze, so I didn't say anything to anyone. I simply went about my business, and spent the next three days ferreting, beseeching and conniving.

Then we went to trial.

Danny Kuhn made his case in an intelligent and ordered way. The cops who arrested Thurlow positively identified him

and positively identified the bat and described in vivid terms
what the dead man looked like. They horrified the jury, which
was precisely what Danny intended. He reinforced that horror
with the couple from the car, who described the beating – now,
suddenly, they claimed to have heard the old man's screams –
and positively identified Thurlow as the kid they'd seen 'walking
fast' away from the scene.

I put them through as tough a cross-examination as I could,
eventually extracting from the husband that he was supposed
to wear his glasses when he drove but wasn't wearing them
that night. He couldn't explain how he heard someone fifteen
yards away through a shut window. Nor could he explain why
he'd never mentioned the screaming before. I also got the wife
to admit that their windshield hadn't yet been washed, hoping
to bring home the point that their visibility wasn't as good as
Danny had made it out to be. However, we had a white jury and
this was a black kid being accused of battering to death an old
white man, and I knew the two things they'd remember were
the description of the corpse and the positive ID of Thurlow
hurrying away.

My first witness was Dr Jerry Epstein, whom I easily established as one of New York's foremost orthopaedic surgeons. He
testified that he'd examined Thurlow and that with the severity
of his condition, it would have been impossible for him to run,
or even walk very fast. Danny tried to pin him down on how
fast was very fast, and although he didn't win any points with
the jury, I knew I was still way behind.

Next I called Thurlow's mother, who swore he was a good boy
and had never been in trouble before. Then I called his minister
who testified that Thurlow was a member of the church choir,
although on cross, Danny got the minister to say that Thurlow's
attendance at choir practice was pretty poor.

Then I put Thurlow on the stand.

My first question was, 'Have you ever seen *Madame Butterfly*?'

Danny objected. I promised the judge that my line of
questioning would soon prove relevant and he ruled that I
could proceed.

Now I asked Thurlow all about *Madame Butterfly* and
Lincoln Centre, deliberately keeping the scope of my direct
examination extremely narrow, so that under cross Danny

couldn't ask about anything except the opera. I got Thurlow to say he especially liked the famous love duet, and he ended his testimony with the story of the sneeze.

Danny tried to get Thurlow to explain how he'd gotten to the opera, to put on the record the story of a stranger giving him a ticket and $100 for a taxi. But I objected that it was outside the scope of my direct examination and the judge reluctantly sustained it. Then Danny tried to get Thurlow to talk about the taxi ride to and from Manhattan – which would have been a back door into how he paid for the ride and therefore how he got the ticket – and again I objected and again the judge sustained it. Frustrated by the limited range I'd allowed him, Danny's cross didn't last very long.

Stepping up for re-cross, I asked Thurlow if there was anybody in the courtroom he recognized from his night at the opera. To the utter shock of the jury – and from the dumbstruck expression on Danny's face, I knew I'd caught him square on the chin – he pointed to a handsome black woman sitting in the second row. 'That's her,' he said, 'that's Madame Butterfly.'

So my next witness was Mary Leontyne Violet Price.

Despite Danny's strenuous objections – which the judge overruled because it wasn't every day he had a major opera star in his courtroom — she took the stand and in that wonderfully smoky voice of hers, confirmed the story of the sneeze.

The jury was, to say the least, seriously impressed.

When I asked her about the love duet, she not only described it precisely as Thurlow had, but stood up, faced the jury and sang several bars from it.

I thought Danny was going to have a conniption fit.

Having kidnapped his jury, I immediately asked for a forty-eight-hour recess.

Now Danny was almost out of control with rage and objected to the break. The judge wanted to know why I needed it. I said we were waiting for another witness. Danny demanded to know who it was. I answered truthfully, 'I don't know.' The judge asked us both to step up to the bench and out of earshot of the jury castigated me for wasting court time. I apologized that I didn't know the witness's name but insisted that he was pivotal to the case. Danny complained, correctly, that this was totally out of order. I willingly conceded it was odd, but begged the judge to consider the fact that a young man's life was on the line and that two days of the court's indulgence should not be too much to ask. He warned me, 'Forty-eight hours and not one minute more.'

The sheriffs took Thurlow back to his cell and I escorted Ms Price outside where Guido had arranged with a cousin of his who worked at Channel 5 to have a TV crew ready. There was also a reporter from the *Daily News*. I made sure they got the story of the mysterious stranger who'd given Thurlow the ticket and the money. We not only got Channel 5 and the *Daily News* the next morning, we also got a mention on the *Today* show the morning after that.

As a result, three people came forward, all of them claiming to be Thurlow's mysterious benefactor. Unfortunately, none of them checked out. But I happily provided Danny with their names and addresses and led him to believe that I might call any one or all three. He wanted to interview them first, so when my forty-eight hours were up and we came back into court, it was his turn to ask for a recess. The judge gave us another two days. I got a story into *Newsday*, just in case the mystery man lived on Long Island, and then did an interview with WCBS, which ran on the evening news the night before we were due back.

My bet was that the mystery man who gave Thurlow the ticket would show up. Same for the two cab drivers whom Thurlow had over-tipped that night. In fact, two more people stepped out of the woodwork. One claimed to be the driver who took him into Manhattan– except he didn't have any of the facts right – and another claimed to have seen Thurlow that night at Lincoln Centre.

I put him on the stand.

He didn't recall enough to be convincing – couldn't remember what Thurlow was wearing or where he was sitting – but he did say that he'd seen Thurlow limping on his way out of the theatre.

Danny tore large holes through most of that guy's testimony. He didn't have his ticket stub or a programme or a receipt for his ticket nor could he give the name of anyone who'd confirm that he'd been to the opera that night. Danny wanted the jury to believe that the fellow read in the papers or heard on the news that Thurlow had a club foot and therefore reasonably concluded that he would limp. But the fellow stuck to his story, and looked pretty good on re-cross when I got him to stroll in front of the jury, imitating Thurlow's walk.

Next I called a young woman who worked in the Metropolitan Opera's press office – it took a lot of pleading on the phone to get her to show up – and introduced into evidence the entire press file on that production of *Madame Butterfly*. My point was, not one single clipping mentioned the sneeze.

When she stepped down, I turned to the judge, and said, 'There is one more witness, your honour, who is here at the last minute.' And without giving Danny a chance to object, I called, 'Leonard Bernstein.'

Frankly, I didn't know until the last minute whether or not he'd appear. I can't recall ever imploring anyone as much for help. But there he was in the back of the courtroom and when I gave Danny a gloating grin, Danny gave me the meanest glance I have ever gotten from any human being outside a boxing ring.

Bernstein answered my first question by turning towards the jury, sweeping his hair out of his eyes, giving them an embarrassed smile, making a huge shrugging gesture and admitting, 'Yes, I was the one who sneezed.'

I asked him if sneezing in the middle of an opera was a regular habit of his. In his own inimitable rambling style, he told the jury that once, as a young conductor, sometime around 1950 or so, he was watching Arturo Toscanini rehearse the NBC Symphony Orchestra in Beethoven's Fifth. After the famous four opening notes, in that brief second's silence, Bernstein let rip with a massive sneeze. Toscanini took the next four notes, and in that brief second's silence before the entire orchestra came back into the piece, Toscanini shouted at the top of his lungs, 'Gezundheit.'

The jury was mesmerized.

Danny went wild with objections.

But the judge was loving it too.

Now I asked Bernstein, 'Were there any repercussions to this now famous sneeze on the night of the murder?'

He wondered, 'What do you mean?'

I said, 'We've just heard from one of the Metropolitan Opera's press officers that your sneeze was not reported in the papers.'

Danny objected. 'Leading the witness.'

The judge allowed the question.

Bernstein answered, 'Until this trial, no one who wasn't there would have known about it.'

Jumping off his feet, Danny was livid. 'Your honour, this is sheer conjecture and has gone way beyond the point of farce . . .'

The judge agreed and ordered the jury to disregard Mr Bernstein's speculation.

But I had every intention of making certain they could never forget Mr Bernstein's speculation. 'It is your contention that anyone who knew about the sneeze must have been in the audience that night . . .'

Again Danny objected.

I apologized, 'Sorry, your honour,' bowed towards Bernstein and said, 'Thank you very much, maestro. And, belatedly, gezundheit.'

The jury laughed.

For the price of a few dozen phone calls, plus one helluva lot of bowing and scraping, I'd successfully changed the mood of the trial. In doing so, hopefully, I'd nullified the picture the cops had painted of an old man with his head bashed in lying in a pool of blood on the floor of his poorly lit gas station.

Danny was experienced enough to understand that there was nothing he could do with Bernstein that would get his case back on track, and smart enough not to try. He said, 'No questions, your honour.'

And I responded, 'The defence rests.'

Leonard Bernstein stepped out of the witness box and headed for the door. Every eye in the courtroom watched him make his exit. True to form, just before he left, he turned to the judge, smiled, looked at the jury and took a small bow. It was a majestic stunt. And before Danny could do anything about it, Bernstein was gone.

In his closing statement, Danny argued the evidence. When my turn came, I reminded the jury that Thurlow couldn't have run away from the scene because of his handicap; that neither one of the prosecution's eye witnesses had seen the perpetrator up close or under suitable conditions and could easily have been mistaken in their identification of Thurlow; and that a witness had indeed seen Thurlow at the opera. I concluded by further developing the seeds that Leontyne Price and Leonard Bernstein had planted, that a poor black kid from Brooklyn who had no previous interest in opera would almost certainly never have known about the sneeze had he not been there that night to hear it. I argued, that Thurlow did know about the sneeze was, in and of itself, more than enough reasonable doubt to find him not guilty of murder.

It took the jury forty-five minutes to acquit.

The man who'd given Thurlow the ticket and the $100 never came forward. Nor did either of the taxi drivers. Danny Kuhn stayed furious at me for ever and nothing I could say about practising law on a shoestring would change his mind.

Six months later, I managed to convince Dr Epstein to operate for free on Thurlow's foot. Two years after that, now able to walk almost normally, Thurlow Adams was killed by the police in Brooklyn Heights when a gas station hold-up went wrong.

These days, practising law on a shoestring is second nature.

It is all part of a day's work.

It is also the only way I can afford to get by.

I grabbed the phone book and started hunting. I checked under the Royal Society for Genetic Scientists, the Royal Association for Genetic Research, the Genetic Society, the Council on Genetic Medicine, and every combination I could think of for those words. When I couldn't spot anything official with genetics in it, I found the number for the British Medical Association, dialled it and asked the operator who answered if they had a committee on genetics. Before she'd tell me, she had to know, 'Are you a doctor?'

I announced, 'Dr Barolo calling.'

And she immediately put me through to the press office.

I asked the woman who answered there, 'How can I get in touch with the chairman of the BMA's genetics committee?'

She said, 'You can't because we don't have one.'

'Well . . . would you know where I might get in touch with the Royal Society of Genetic Scientists? Or some sort of Association for Genetic Research?'

She checked her files and came back with two numbers. 'I've got one for the Clinical Genetics Society in Newcastle. And one for the Genetical Society in the Department of Biology at the University of York.'

'Which one do you recommend?'

'It's a coin toss.'

I took her advice – York won – called that number and asked to be put through to the director's office.

A young woman wanted to know, 'Who are you and what is this call about?'

I told her, 'I'm an attorney doing some research into genetics.'

She said, 'Unfortunately, the Department of Biology cannot advise anyone working on a research project. After all, if we had to give advice to every researcher who phoned, that's all we would do all day. You see, the stated purpose of the Genetical Society is to provide general information to the general public about the general field of genetics and also to answer specific questions. So do you want general information or have you got a specific question?'

'Yes.'

'What is it?'

I came up with, 'I'm trying to establish the relevant frequency of frannaporsonnon in . . .' I grabbed one of Johnny's faxes, '. . . the B3–adrenergic receptor when its presence in adipose tissue turns out to consist of seven transmembrane domains?'

She huffed, 'Just a minute please,' and put me through to the director.

I could only sigh and shake my head.

He introduced himself – 'Dr Lawrence Westerberg here' – and asked how he could help me. I introduced myself, said I was an attorney, and explained that I was trying to get some background information on genetics. He asked if I was ringing from the States. I told him no, that I was in London. He suggested, in that case, I might find it easier to speak with one of his colleagues in London, and gave me the number for a Dr Sherman Straw at the Hammersmith Hospital. Thanking him, I got right through to Straw without having to double-talk my way past any operators or secretaries.

'I'm calling on the advice of Dr Westerberg at the University of York.' I told him who I was and said, 'I'm hoping I might be able to take a few minutes of your time, now or later, whenever it's convenient, to get the entry level lecture on genetics?'

He said, 'Any time,' and gave me his address.

I said, 'How about in twenty minutes,' and jumped into a taxi.

His office at Hammersmith Hospital was on the top floor of a wing that overlooked a lower floor of another wing. The room was half the size of mine, and twice as cluttered. A nurse showed me in and suggested if I could find somewhere to sit I should and that Dr Straw would be with me as soon as she could locate him.

I looked around, managed to find a chair buried under a huge stack of papers, thought about putting them on the floor and sitting down, but decided maybe I should wait. After all, I was here to beg a favour and beggars should never pretend to be at home before the favour gets delivered.

'Hello . . .' A tall, well-built, light-haired fellow in a rumpled suit with a goatee and pale eyes stepped into the room. 'I'm Sherman.'

'I'm Vince.' I shook his hand. 'I appreciate this.'

'No problem.' He might have been forty but his build and hair made him look much younger. 'I'd offer you a place to sit, but real estate is not one of the benefits of research science. If you want, we can go somewhere for coffee . . .'

'I'm fine if you are.'

'Well then . . .' It took him a couple of minutes to move all the papers from on top of the chair to under the chair and then to make room for half a buttock on the edge of his desk so he had someplace to sit. 'What do you want to know? Overall basics?'

'Actually, I was curious about one gene in particular.'

He opened his arms. 'Welcome to Genes "R" Us. Which one?'

'How about the FAT gene?'

'One of the Holy Grails.'

'What do you mean?'

'What I mean is, it may or may not exist. There have been all sorts of studies recently suggesting that it does exist in mice, but that doesn't necessarily mean it exists in humans. However, if it does . . . finding it would be like finding pots at the end of the rainbow. Both ends.'

I wondered, 'If it does exist, how would it work?'

'Think of genes as switches,' he said, 'that turn things on and off. Now, if you're speaking about the humane genome, which is the entire collection of switches that makes up each of us, at least the ones that are active, they number around a hundred thousand and are spread over twenty-three pairs of chromosomes. Maybe you should think of chromosomes as banks of switches. So you've got something like one hundred thousand active switches crammed onto twenty-three pairs of panels. But now you should know that very few of these switches have yet been labelled. To turn on one specific lamp, you need to somehow find the right switch, and that usually means trial and error. Even then, the lamp you're hoping to turn on might not be hooked up to a switch. Or it might be hooked up to more than one switch that can be turned on in any order. Or it might be hooked up to several switches that have to be turned on in an exact order. Or there might be a slew of switches and a slew of combinations, and in each combination every switch has to be turned on in a very specific order. Follow me, so far?'

I made a face. 'I think so.'

'All right.' He leaned forward. 'Now let's go back to consider one single lamp called optimal body weight. To put it in simple terms, if your optimal body weight, based on your height, your metabolism, your age and other factors is, say, one hundred and seventy-five pounds, then fifty pounds too much is fat and fifty pounds too little is skinny. Still with me?'

'I guess.'

'Then let's suppose that by lighting that one lamp, regardless of how many switches it takes, you could return someone to optimal body weight. The person who is fifty pounds too light will naturally gain enough to weigh one hundred and seventy-five, and the person who is fifty pounds overweight will naturally lose enough to weigh one hundred and seventy-five. And once they get there, they will stay there without any conscious effort on their part.'

I interrupted. 'You mean, if this switch exists, the entire diet industry goes out of business.'

'Not only the diet industry but a lot of pharmaceutical companies. The only one left in business will be the one who knows where the switch or switches are and owns the key . . . call it a drug . . . to turn the switch on and off at will. But the FAT gene is not only about obesity. It's also about all the illnesses associated with obesity. Conceivably, the sky's the limit. Heart attacks. Strokes. Anorexia. Cancer.'

'Wow.' I sat back and thought about that for a moment. 'We're talking big money.'

'As I said, both ends of the rainbow.'

Now I asked, 'What is leptin?'

'Ah.' He raised his index finger to make a point. 'Not a lot of people know this, but it's named after the Greek word for thin.'

I chuckled. 'So how does leptin fit into this?'

'In simple terms . . .' he thought about that for a few seconds, '. . . it's a hormone that the body produces to tell the brain that you've eaten enough. There have been studies which show that daily shots of leptin, injected into OB-defective mice . . . let's say those are mice who are believed to be genetically obese . . . well, given leptin, they tend to lose a great deal of their body fat.'

'Are you saying that leptin turns on and off the switch?'

'No . . . it's the switch which turns on and off the production of leptin.' He made a face. 'I'm afraid that this can get pretty complicated.'

'Tell me slow,' I said.

'Okay . . . leptin fools the brain into thinking that the cells which produce leptin are already fat enough and therefore it's time to stop eating. The work with leptin is based on the belief that defects in the protein account for obesity. In other words, there is something wrong with the cells which naturally produce leptin in the body, or the natural leptin itself, causing the message which those cells send to the brain to arrive garbled.' He stopped and stared at me.

I nodded.

He went on. 'The brain doesn't know the cells are already fat enough, so the brain says, keep eating. At least that's the way it apparently works in mice. Leptin tests with humans haven't necessarily produced the same results and therefore don't automatically support the theory. One offshoot of the work with leptin has been to approach the problem from the other side. That is, to suppose the message arrives ungarbled and that it's the receptors in the brain that have misinterpreted them.'

'Wow.'

'I warned you.'

'Then what?'

'Then . . . that's it.'

'That's all?' I was relieved.

'That's the entire course.'

'Well . . . how about if I throw some names at you.'

'Try me.'

'Pincer?'

'Taptech,' he answered right away.

'DesRocher?'

He started to laugh. 'Dr Pincer's best friend.'

'Really? I thought they were . . .'

'Just joking. DesRocher runs an outpost of the CNRS in France. It's another big laboratory. He and Pincer are about as close as Mother Teresa and Saddam Hussein.'

'Which one is Saddam Hussein?'

'Ah . . .' He contemplated that. 'It might be more accurate to say that neither of them is Mother Teresa. But these fellows haven't been working with leptin. They've been trying to find the switch itself, to isolate the gene that controls weight. You see, until Pincer and DesRocher came along, conventional wisdom had it that no single gene could be responsible for obesity. They claim they can prove conventional wisdom wrong. And the betting line is that one of them will. They're each looking for the same thing but they're looking in two different chromosomes. You know, totally different banks of switches. Whoever finds it first, wins. No prize for coming in second.'

'Are they just going up to banks of switches and flicking them all to see what happens?'

'That's basically what the human genome project is. People flicking switches, hoping something wonderful will happen.'

'Win some, lose some, huh?' I tried not to think of the Lustig case.

'Mostly lose some,' he said.

I mumbled, 'Sounds familiar.'

He said, 'Don't forget, we're speaking of a hundred thousand switches. If I remember right, Pincer is working on human chromosome 5. Or maybe he's the one who's working on human chromosome 13 and DesRocher is working on human chromosome 5. Whichever, both of them are still a long way from harnessing what would perhaps one day be called the FAT gene. If there even is such a thing. There may not be.'

I thanked him for his help. 'You've been great. I really appreciate it.'

'Any time,' he said. 'If you need any more information, let me know.'

'And if you ever need an American lawyer who does

insurance work . . .' I stood up and handed him one of my cards.

'Your fax number on here?' He saw that it was. 'Let me see what I can find on our database about all this.'

'My main interest is Pincer and DesRocher.' Then I wondered, 'Ever hear of a guy named Bickerton?'

'L. Roger?'

'That's him.'

'Committed suicide. He worked at the ERP. They're on the south coast. Eastbourne.'

'How important was he?'

'Not in the Pincer or DesRocher league. A rung or two down. But solid. I never met him but Westerberg must know him. Same generation. Anyway, genetics is a relatively small industry and everybody usually knows everybody else, or at least everybody knows someone who knows everybody else. Bickerton ran the ERP work on the human genome project until he retired.'

I took a punt. 'Could he have been somehow involved with either of those human chromosomes? You know, 5 or 13?'

'Possible,' he said. 'There's a lot of stuff around in the professional press, you know, in scientific journals. Let me check our database and I'll fax you whatever I can.'

I thanked him again and found my own way out.

An hour later, nineteen pages poured through my fax machine. One of them – a two-line reference with a bunch of numbers at the top and the bottom – had a handwritten note on it from my new friend Sherman. 'Is this any help?'

It was a print-out of a patent pending in the name of L. R. Bickerton.

Chapter Twenty-Two

Lawyers and doctors share a common affliction. It's called, where did you go to school and do I know anyone you went to school with? I'm not sure why it should matter, but it does.

The first time I saw it up close was when Louise and I were told we couldn't have a baby. Fat was dead by then but I stayed in touch with his mother and she had a distant uncle named Gene Snyder who was a big deal specialist at Mount Sinai Hospital in New York. Our own doctor had recommended we see a lady gynaecologist named Ellen Ray. But Fat's mom begged us to see Uncle Gene instead. Except, he was an ear, nose and throat guy. No matter what I said, I couldn't make her understand that he was working the wrong end of the problem. So to appease her, I phoned him and explained the situation. He was not only very understanding, he insisted on looking up Ellen Ray's background in something called the *American Medical Directory*. Published by the American Medical Association, it tells you where every physician in the country went to school. When he found her, he announced, 'She trained here at Mount Sinai,' and based on that, duly proclaimed, 'It's okay to see her.'

The legal equivalent of the *American Medical Directory* is a huge volume called *Martindale-Hubbell*. For shoestringers like me, it is an invaluable catalogue of names to drop. Although I recognized the names of some American attorneys in the UK, I'd never been one to socialize with other lawyers and I didn't personally know anyone who specialized in patents. So I dug into *Martindale-Hubbell*, nosed around for an East Coast patent firm with offices in London, checked the backgrounds of the partners stationed here, noted where they went to law school and then went in search of someone I knew who might have gone to school with one of them.

The guy who came up trumps was Lyle Benedict Junior whose father ran a New York operation called Crown-Benedict-Higham. The reason I settled on Junior was because he'd graduated from Princeton Law ten years ago, the same time that a school buddy of mine was on the faculty. I got him on the line, introduced myself, said that I'd heard he'd gone to Princeton and was wondering, 'Whatever happened to Bobby Baldero?'

'Professor Baldero? How do you know him? He taught me contracts. He also taught a class in estate planning and probate.'

'No kidding.'

'Freshman year, he was the guy they got to do the standard lecture in torts.' Junior was hooked. 'Gee, I haven't thought about Professor Baldero in a long time. I'll tell you something about him. His lecture on prenuptial agreements was the funniest routine I have ever heard. I mean, Jay Leno couldn't compete. He did it once a year and the place was always packed . . .'

This was kid's play. 'Small world, huh? Whatever happened to him?'

'He died. A couple of years after I left school. Heart attack. Walking down Nassau Street in the middle of the day. Got his picture into the *New York Times*. How did you know him?'

'He's my age . . . was my age . . . Jeez.' I always hate hearing stories about people my age winding up dead. 'We went to Brooklyn Law together. He was a great guy.' Actually, if I remembered right, Bobby was a schmuck but there was no reason to bring that up. 'Your old man does patent law, doesn't he?'

'You know my dad? Yes, we're a patent and trademark firm.'

'Of course, I know . . . you know . . . of him.' A little flattery never hurt. 'He's the best.'

'I'd like to think so.'

'No contest,' I said. 'It's good clean work, patent work. How long have you been over here?'

'Seven months,' he said. 'My dad figures I should do two

years, you know, to get European patent experience. What about you?'

'Me? Ever since Christ was a corporal.' I changed gears. 'Hey . . . what does your diary looked like for lunch? Let's break bread for Bobby Baldero's sake.'

'Yeah . . . sure. When?'

I tried, 'Ah . . . I don't know . . . what are you doing today?'

'Today?'

'Yeah. For Bobby.'

'Ah . . . yeah . . . sure . . . okay.'

He'd just committed the cardinal sin of making himself too available – no lawyer should ever be that easy about anything but he'd have to learn his own lessons – so I told him, 'Terrific,' said I'd reshuffle my schedule and arranged to meet him at Giovanni's at one.

As soon as we hung up, I photocopied the patent reference Straw had faxed me, whited-out Bickerton's name, re-photocopied it, ripped it into a small slip and stuck it in my wallet.

Patents are a by-product of man's eternal quest to get rich quick by building a better mousetrap.

The definition they made us memorize in law school goes, 'A patent is a grant bestowed by a government which confers upon the creator of an invention the sole right to make, use and sell that invention for a particular period of time.'

What that means is, a patent is a monopoly through which inventors protect their intellectual property. It's a deal that you, as the owner of an invention, strike with the country where you want to exploit that invention. As long as you're willing to tell the country everything you know about the invention, the country will legally exclude everyone else from making, selling or using your invention. It doesn't mean that your better mousetrap will sell, it merely guarantees that no one can do anything with it unless he obtains your permission, which generally translates into some sort of payment for the privilege.

The first step in obtaining a patent is a novelty search. The burden is on you to prove that your mousetrap is new, useful and non-obvious. And those three words are critical.

'New' means different. As long as nothing exactly like it exists, that's easy.

'Useful' means useful. Frankly, it's tough to find an invention that isn't in some way useful with the obvious exception, perhaps, of perpetual-motion machines.

The tough one is 'non-obvious'. This refers to both the invention's elements and the results it produces. If, for instance, you discover that an old drug can suddenly be used in the same dosage to cure a totally unrelated ailment for which it had never been used before – say, rubbing an aspirin on your head to cure baldness – you'd be unlikely to get a patent for hair-growing aspirin because it fails the non-obvious test.

Once you've made your way through the novelty search, the next step is to file for your patent. To do that, you must submit a definition of the invention, drawings to explain it, technical data and anything else you have which proves that the invention is indeed new, useful and non-obvious. If the patent-granting authority then agrees, you've got your monopoly. If they disagree, you can appeal. If they aren't sure, they can ask for models, which is what they do with perpetual-motion machines. Or they can demand that you produce verifiable experimental documentation, which is what they do with magic mushroom cures for cancer.

That's as much as I knew about patents. Lunch was intended to be an investment into my further education.

Junior turned out to be a good-looking, athletic, stereotyped Princeton WASP, the kind of kid who had, quite plainly, relied on his looks and daddy's connections to get through life so far. He never needed to become street smart. And that made him a shoestringer's dream.

We paid homage to Bobby Baldero over linguini and by the time Giovanni delivered two plates of veal piccate, I'd easily manoeuvred the conversation around to patents.

'Most of our work is pretty routine,' he said. 'Filing here for clients in the States merely requires a talent for photocopying. You can get a patent here automatically if you've got one in America, although you must file for it and you only have a year. The majority of our clients show up with just a month to go, which is great because they're in a panic and we can calculate our fees accordingly. The rest of my time is spent digging up clients here who need to file in the States, which not only requires my photocopying skills but also means I have to play a lot of squash.'

'It beats standing in line at the Patent Office.'

'I'm proud to say that I've never been there. It's in Wales somewhere. Luckily, the British Library has just about everything I need. Everything else is faxes, phones and dog sleds.'

'The British Library at the British Museum?'

'No . . .' He wasn't sure what that was. 'I think they call it the Science Reference Library. It's part of the British Library but it's nowhere near the British Museum. Do you know where Chancery Lane is? They're in a dirty old building on a dead-end street with a stupid name. From the outside it doesn't even look like they have electricity. But I have to give them credit because despite the building they're pretty advanced. Almost everything is on-line.'

'You mean, it's all computerized?'

'I was surprised too. You expect it in the States but not here. In fact, it's so advanced here that, if you know how, you can find anything you want with your own laptop on the dining-room table.'

'No kidding.' I thought about that for a moment and wondered if that applied to someone whose dining room was in New Jersey. 'Except, it's pretty technical stuff.'

'Sure. But that's why most patent attorneys in the States have a technical background.' His own law degree was supplemented with one in electrical engineering. His dad was also a part-time electrical engineer.

Now I wanted to know, 'How often do you deal with the little guy?'

'You mean, the garret inventor?' He shook his head. 'Nah. It's almost always the professional. That means corporate. The system just isn't geared to help the Rube Goldberg types who come up with anti-snoring devices. It costs too much.'

'How about a guy who works for a company? I guess anything he patents has to be put in the company's name, right?'

'The fate of the professional inventor is a hot issue,' he said, 'especially on the international level. We see that all the time. Professionals working for a company invent something of great importance, the company makes a fortune and the inventor gets nothing. There's a general trend in Europe now that an inventor in a corporate situation should have a piece of the action. In the United States, however, it's still the exception for a corporate inventor to get anything, except from occasional award systems.'

'Yeah, but what about the guy who works for a corporation and then has a little something on the side that he patents in his own name?'

'It's expensive. It's also risky. Companies usually claim rights to all, or at least some, of that kind of intellectual property. I suppose, in the end, it depends on the man's employment contract. But we don't see that all too often. Like I said, the little guy doesn't stand much of a chance.'

'But the little guys exist.'

'Sure they do. The world is filled with weekend inventors screwing around with nutty ideas. The majority of them, however, never get any further than a widget to show their neighbours. The only way you know they're out there is because inventions magically appear when their time has arrived. Remember when New York had that massive "Clean Up After Your Dog" campaign? My dad got hundreds of people banging on the door with various kinds of pooper-scoopers.'

'Good one.'

'Better than that, he once had some whacko show up who was worried about premature burial and had invented a coffin with an escape hatch.'

'Did your dad take him on?'

'Absolutely. Got him a patent, too.'

'Sell a lot of coffins?'

'Would you buy one with an escape hatch?'

I conceded, 'I'm not that much of an optimist.'

'How about the guy who came to my dad with a device that was supposed to eliminate head-on collisions between trains? It was a system where a track ran up the front of the locomotive, across the top of all the cars and down the back of the caboose. The idea was that any oncoming train would simply go up and over.'

'He get a patent for it?'

'Yeah he did.'

'How many did he sell?'

'About as many as the guy with the coffin.'

I laughed, motioned to Giovanni to bring the bill and some grappa, and after he served two glasses, I reached for my wallet.

That's when the photocopy I'd prepared landed on the table. 'Talk about patents . . . you like this one?'

'Let me have a peek.' He didn't seem to catch on because the food had dulled his senses. 'Bibliographic data . . . publication number . . . application number . . .' He sipped and read at the same time. 'This is all standard stuff. International classification . . . dates . . . dates . . . number . . . states designated . . . see, this is what I mean.' He pointed towards the bottom and the letters AB. 'Look at that abstract. It tells you everything you have to know without saying anything.' He handed the paper back to me and finished his grappa. 'I mean, how does anyone expect anyone else to figure out anything from that?'

'Gee, I don't know.'

'Hey,' he grinned proudly. 'That's great patent lawyering.'

'It is?'

'Sure. It says nothing. That's what my clients pay for. The more double-talk I can get onto a patent application, the less chance anyone can steal it. Believe me, I wish I could charge by the double-talk. You know, the better the double-talk the higher the fee.'

'The old adage is true,' I said. 'You only get what you pay for.' He seemed to think that was a compliment. I didn't tell him I was referring to his free advice.

Chapter Twenty-Three

Back at the office there was a message from Greta that I didn't understand. 'Massachusetts or New Jersey?' And a message from Moe Moses that I did understand. 'I quit.'

There was a message from Hal. 'Maybe next week was optimistic. Is a month okay?'

There was a four-page fax from Straw and more clippings from Johnny.

'So the old guy couldn't put up with the jerk either,' Henry smirked. 'By the way, I'm calling myself Schaunne.'

I nodded, 'How do you do, Schaunne,' and dialled Greta.

'He said he'd be at Charlie's until he heard from you.'

It rang several times. 'Who?'

Greta came on the line. 'Rose-Morrow.'

'The jerk,' Henry said.

I asked Greta, 'Massachusetts or New Jersey, what?'

Henry added, 'Don't count on him giving you your money back.'

'You tell me,' Greta said.

'Don't count on who?' I asked Henry.

'On who, what?' Greta wanted to know.

'Moses,' Henry said.

Greta overheard. 'What about Moses?'

I told her, 'He doesn't live in Massachusetts or in New Jersey,' then said to Henry, 'Find him and get him on the phone.'

'Who are you talking to?' Greta wondered.

'Henry,' I said.

'Schaunne,' Henry corrected.

'Okay, Schaunne.'

'Who's Schaunne,' Greta asked.

'She used to date Moses before Ruth,' I answered. 'What about Massachusetts and New Jersey?'

'You sound slightly confused.'

'Ruth who?' Henry cut in.

'I am,' I confessed to Greta, then told Henry, 'Babe Ruth.'

Greta enquired, 'Too confused for dinner tonight?'

'Babe Ruth?' Henry nodded. 'That was the movie with John Goodman. You know, the guy from *Roseanne*?'

I wasn't thinking straight. 'I'll phone you later.'

'Next time you're in port, sailor?'

'Dinner tonight is fine.'

'Don't sound so enthused.'

I put on my best enthused voice. 'Dinner tonight is wonderful.'

'How about Indian?'

'How about Italian?'

'Massachusetts or New Jersey?'

'London is closer,' I reminded her. 'I'll pick you up at six.'

The other line rang. Henry grabbed it, then announced, 'Babe Ruth's friend Moses.'

So I kept the phone to my ear, punched Greta off – I wondered again how come she didn't get the message on Sunday night and asked myself, how come she's only calling me about it today – and punched him on. 'What does that mean, I quit?'

'It's only two words and they're both very short.'

'You can't quit. He's got a fight next week.'

'Believe me, I can quit whether he has a fight next week or not.'

'Where are you now?' I needed to get him back in Hambone's corner. 'Can you come here?'

'No, you can come here.'

'Where?'

'Charlie's.'

'I'll be there in fifteen minutes,' I promised. When he hung up, I asked Henry, 'What is this message from Hal?'

'He's the guy who left the porn videos here.'

'I know who he is. But what does this mean?'

'Just what it says. He had to go out of town.'

'Go out of town or get out of town?'

'He used the word go.'

'Did he leave a number?'

'No.'

'Try the number that I've got for him. It's in my book. See if you can find him. I've got to run out.' I stood up and headed for the door. 'I'll be back.'

She asked, 'When are you going to get smart?'

'About what?'

'About the jerk?'

'What about him?'

She shook her head as if it was obvious. 'He's using you.'

And I said, as if it was equally obvious, 'He doesn't have anybody else to use.'

Hambone was sitting on one side of the bleachers, brooding, with his arms folded across his chest and a towel wrapped around his neck, then tucked into the top of his sweatsuit. Moe Moses was sitting on the other end, brooding, with his black raincoat buttoned all the way up and his hands shoved into the pockets. He was closest so I started with him.

I pretended to listen intently while he told me that Hambone complained all the time about everything and had finally complained his last complaint. Then I moved over to where Hambone was sitting, and pretended to listen intently while he complained that Moe Moses was a tyrant and that he couldn't stand tyrannical people. Eventually I convinced them both to take a short walk with me, steered them into Barney and Bernie's deli, sat them down so they had to look at each other and ordered three bowls of kreplach soup.

In no time I had Hambone admitting that maybe Moe was right when he screamed during sparring sessions. And even if I couldn't get Moe to admit that maybe Hambone was right about anything, I still persuaded Hambone that Moe had apologized.

Textbook perfect negotiating skills.

They both walked away thinking they'd won.

I even complimented myself on the way back to the office.

Maybe someday, if I ever retire, I can get myself a part-time job teaching in Law School. I'll call the course, 'Dr Barolo's Foolproof Method for Successful Negotiation: A Basic Philosophy of Dialogue and Soup'.

*   *   *

I found the office door wide open and that made me wary about the rather large guy in a blue baseball jacket who was waiting for me.

Henry introduced him. 'This is Mr He-wouldn't-give-me-his-name. Apparently, he's a friend of your friend Hal.'

I looked at him. 'Can I help you?'

'Yeah.' He stood up. 'You're Mr Barolo, right? Well, Hal sent me to pick up some boxes.'

'What boxes would those be?'

'You know, some cartons.'

'And you are Mr . . . ?' I pulled myself up to my full height – which wasn't as tall as him – and waited for him to give me his name. When he didn't say anything, I repeated, 'And you are Mr . . . ?'

'A friend of Hal's.'

'You got a name?'

'Yeah,' he said. 'Hal's mate. That's my name.'

I shrugged. 'Sorry, Hal's mate, but I don't know anything about any cartons.'

'Yeah, well, he said I had to collect them.'

'Yeah, well, have him phone me and I'll discuss it with him.'

The guy glared at me for several seconds. I stared him back. And he blinked first. 'Yeah, okay,' he said, turned and left. I shut the door behind him.

Looking at Henry and raising my eyebrows, I suggested, 'If you leave the door open, you never know who's going to walk in.'

She snapped at me, 'The door was shut when he got here. I kept it open because I wasn't going to stay here alone with him.'

'Monday those tapes go,' I said. 'Hal or no Hal, they get taken away.'

'Where to?'

'I don't know. The sidewalk. The garbage. But they go.' I went into my room. 'Anybody call?'

'No.'

I mumbled, 'Good,' and finally had some time to read those faxes.

Straw's was on the top, so I looked at that one first. It was a 1992 recapitulation of the much publicized squabble between

Dr Luc Montagnier of the Institut Pasteur in Paris and Dr
Robert Gallo of the National Cancer Institute's Laboratory
of Tumour Cell Biology in Bethesda, Maryland. The headline
read, 'The Most Indecorous Dispute in Modern Research
Science'.

The story began in 1983 when the Pasteur Institute filed
patent applications in both the United States and Europe for
a blood test developed by Montagnier which revealed the
presence of HIV. The following year, Gallo and the National
Institutes of Health also filed a patent application for an HIV
test. When the US Patent Office granted Gallo's request while
still not having ruled on Montagnier's, the French cried foul. As
their application had been filed first, they felt they should have
had priority. The Patent Office refused to revise their decision
and so the French filed suit.

The two sides faced off and spent nearly six months trying
to negotiate a way out of this mess. At one point, the Americans
agreed to recognize Montagnier as a co-discoverer of the AIDS
virus, alongside Gallo. But Montagnier wanted more than just
fame. Egos were taking a backseat to money. The Pasteur
Institute had licensed the fruits of its research to a company
in Seattle. Gallo's group had licensed the fruits of its research to
five different American biotechnology companies. Montagnier
firmly believed the US Government was in breach of contract
when it granted a patent to Gallo based on research done in
Paris and felt entitled to all future royalties on AIDS diagnostic
kits in addition to damages in excess of $1 million.

Gallo stood fast, denying the charges.

The ensuing publicity corresponded with growing public
awareness of the AIDS epidemic. A solution was finally imposed
by the two governments but only after direct intervention
by President Reagan and French Prime Minister Chirac.
Montagnier and Gallo were awarded equal credit for the
discovery and both governments agreed to share the ensuing
royalties.

There the matter lay for two years, until DNA sequencing of
Gallo's HIV samples revealed that the virus he worked on was
indeed the same as the one discovered and supplied to him by
Montagnier. Gallo noted that those results were nothing new,
that the information was known before the 1987 agreement and
anyway, that his patent application was based on original work.

But claims to the contrary poured fuel onto the fire. Pulitzer Prize-winning reporter John Crewdson published two huge exposés of the affair in the *Chicago Tribune*. In the first part he asserted that Gallo had made deliberately misleading statements in reference to his claim to the HIV discovery. In the second, he charged that a 1985 top-secret NIH investigation revealed that Gallo had, in fact, no rightful claim to the discovery. The report apparently alleged fraud in the American lab and recommended that a named Gallo associate be found guilty of scientific misconduct. It also supposedly criticized Gallo but did not censure him. Furthermore, Crewdson went on, the information in that report was suppressed by the US Government while attorneys acting on its behalf negotiated a settlement with the French.

Now the Pasteur Institute demanded that the agreement dividing royalties be scrapped because Gallo had merely 'rediscovered' Montagnier's virus. In a nineteen-page memorandum, attorneys representing the Pasteur Institute stated that both the American and French versions of the test were based on a strain of HIV isolated in France, therefore altering the premise on which royalties had been based.

Handwritten in the margins on the last page, Straw had added, 'Science = Money'.

Johnny's fax consisted of two very lengthy articles and several smaller blurbs. The little ones were mostly mentions of Pincer and DesRocher in newspapers and on wire services. They didn't tell me anything I didn't already know. The first of the long articles was titled, 'Interferongamma Expressing Transduced Autologous Tumour Cells – Combination Therapy', by T. P. Tsung.

I let my eyes run over the text, couldn't spot anything of interest, asked myself why Johnny sent this to me, and then scanned it again. This time I spotted a reference to Pincer and Taptech, but it was all very technical and I couldn't figure out what any of it meant.

The second big article was from *Genome Research* and titled, 'Application to the mapping of human chromosome 7, plus integration of physical, genetic and cytogenetic maps: Construction, characterization and screening'. I didn't understand that either. Although, again, there were references to Pincer and DesRocher. The thing that amused me, however, was the fact that the by-line was shared by no fewer than eleven different people. By coincidence, T. P. Tsung was one of them.

Pushing them aside, I saw that it was already after four. But that was only the end of the morning in the States, so I picked up the phone, asked information for Taptech in Washington DC, got the number and dialled it. I told the operator who answered that I wanted to speak with Dr Pincer and she put me through to a woman who answered the phone, 'This is Jean Burke.'

'Miss Burke, good morning, my name . . .'

'Mrs Burke,' she corrected. 'May I help you?'

'Mrs Burke.' I began again, 'Good morning, my name is . . .' I couldn't use one of my usual aliases because she'd recognize an American name, so I came up with, 'Dr Fuzzy White. I'm looking for Dr Pincer.'

'May I ask what this is concerning, please?'

'It's a personal matter.'

'Does he know you?'

'It is a personal matter and therefore I would prefer to discuss it directly with him.'

'I'm terribly sorry, Dr White, but I'll have to know more about the nature of this call if you expect me to put you through.'

I could tell I wasn't going to get past her without giving up something, so I suggested, 'Perhaps you would tell him I'm calling about the death of Dr Bickerton.'

'Just a moment please.' She put me on hold where I waited for several minutes, before she came back on the line to say, 'I'm terribly sorry, Dr White, but Dr Pincer informs me that he's never heard of Dr Bickerton, and suggests that if there is anything further you might care to discuss that you put it in writing.'

'Never heard of Dr L. Roger Bickerton . . .'

'That's correct, sir. If you need our address for any further communication, I will be happy to give it to you.'

'No,' I said, 'I don't need your address.'

'Well then, thank you very much for calling and I'm sorry that we are not able to be of assistance to you.' Just like that, she hung up.

I believed that she was telling the truth when she said that Pincer claimed he'd never heard of Dr Bickerton. Except I think she knew that Pincer was lying because she was much too curt on the phone. This was a woman who didn't want to speak with me. And I could only conclude that was because her boss didn't want her to speak with me.

Suddenly I was curious to see what DesRocher's reaction would be.

I already had the number of the CNRS in Marseilles, so I phoned there, asked for Dr DesRocher's office and was put through to a woman who was decidedly less efficient than Mrs Burke. I asked for Dr DesRocher, and she wanted to know, in faltering English, 'Please, can you repeat that for me but please . . . slowly . . .' So I did. Now she wanted to know, 'Please . . . can you tell me where you are from?'

'America,' I lied. 'The name is . . . Cronkite. Dr Walter Cronkite.'

'Please . . . may I inform him what this is going to be all about?'

'Sure,' I decided. 'Tell him I'm calling about Dr Bickerton.'

'Please . . . just a few minutes, please.' But she didn't keep me on the line for more than thirty seconds. 'Please . . . I am informed to tell you that Dr DesRocher has nothing further to say about Dr Bickerton.'

'Perhaps if I could speak with him directly and . . .'

'I am sorry. No. Goodbye.' And she hung up on me.

I said out loud, 'Zero for two,' redialled the number and this time asked for Dr Cesari. All I got was her answering machine again.

That's when Hal rang. 'Listen, this may take a little longer than I'd originally planned . . .'

'Where the hell are you?'

'I'm sort of . . . let's just say, I'm otherwise occupied. But you've got to do me a favour.'

'No,' I said firmly. 'I already told you the deadline was Monday. And who was this guy who showed up here this morning?'

'What guy?'

'Big guy in a blue baseball jacket. He said you sent him.'

'Holy Christ,' he screamed. 'You didn't give him the tapes, did you?'

'No, I did not give him the tapes.'

'How the hell did they know to go to you?'

'Who is they?'

'It doesn't matter. But . . . listen . . . do me a favour and
get rid of that stuff for me. I figure it's worth fifteen hundred
quid. I'll take half. Seven hundred and fifty for the lot.'

'What the hell are you talking about? I'm not buying it from
you and I'm not selling it for you. I'm throwing it out.'

'Five hundred, Vince. Get me five hundred and we're
square.'

'What square?' I warned him, 'Either you collect it Monday
morning or the garbage men get it Monday noon.'

'Hey. Please. Don't turn your back on me like this.' He
sounded desperate. 'Let me make a few calls. Give me an
hour. I'll find somebody to take them off your hands. Either
I'll call you back or someone will on my behalf. I'll make all
the arrangements. Just hold on to the money for me.'

'What money?'

'I've got to go. I'll ring back in an hour. Goodbye.'

He hung up and I sat there like a stooge for the next hour,
waiting for him to call back.

Henry left at five.

I reread those faxes from Johnny.

By five thirty, Hal still hadn't called back. So I phoned
Charlie to make sure that Hambone and Moe were still friends
– they were – turned on the answering machine, locked up and
went home.

I completely forgot about dinner with Greta.

Chapter Twenty-Four

I tossed and turned all night.

There was something bouncing around inside my brain trying to get free, but it wouldn't come out.

The best cerebral laxative I know is late-night black-and-white films on cable TV – especially Jimmy Cagney films – except, I don't have cable, so it kept me awake until I fell asleep through sheer exhaustion.

When my alarm went off, I was too tired to worry about it. I woke up again sometime around ten, phoned Henry to say I'd be there later, and filled the tub. I soaked for the longest time, nursing a cup of coffee, until the water started to cool off and the coffee was cold. But I didn't know the coffee was cold until I tasted it, and when I did, that's when a conversation came back into my mind. A conversation that took place over another cup of cold coffee.

'Pretty strange,' I'd said and David Chorley had answered, 'Pretty common. All the earmarks of an insurance fire.' I'd said, 'The guy's dead,' and Chorley had answered, 'Maybe his next of kin just aren't very good at starting fires.'

Wrapping myself in an old blue terry cloth robe that Louise gave me for a birthday when we were still in Liverpool, I fumbled through the address book I keep in my night table until I found Dom Powers's card.

He answered the phone with, 'Speak.'

I told him, 'It's been a long time.'

'Who the hell is this?'

'Brother Barolo.'

'You buying lunch or just looking for a free one?'

'Neither,' I admitted. 'Just begging a favour.'

'Nothing changes,' he said. 'I'm here.'

'I'll be there,' I said, hung up and hurried into some clothes.

Powers was an Old Etonian, Oxford double honours shyster solicitor who finally got disbarred a couple of years ago, after almost twenty years of committing just about every conflict of interest imaginable. The reason it took the Law Society so long to toss him out was because, for much of those twenty years, he was one of the best connected people in Britain. A one-man rumour archive who kept files on everyone – it's not who you know, he'd growl, it's what you know about them – he was not the sort of man you ever wanted to irritate.

I liked him, not because he was an appalling scoundrel, but because he knew more about the law than I'd ever know and, at least every time I was with him, he was very jovial. I also appreciated the fact that whatever you needed, he knew someone who could get it for you. Although I never accepted any of his offers for illegal wire tap equipment or information he could obtain straight off Scotland Yard's central records computer, I recognized his talent for being able to do stuff I'd never want to get caught doing. It was Dom, for example, who taught me how to get credit card information on anybody in the country.

At the same time, I recognized that he had the soul of Fagin. I never saw it first hand, but I'd heard how, when he felt threatened, he went straight for the jugular. While it took a five-man committee to ambush him and strip him of his licence, it was no coincidence that within six months of his disbarment, all five of the men on that Law Society committee had met with some sort of personal crisis. Two of them were sued for divorce when their wives somehow came into possession of graphic evidence of their husband's infidelities. One of them was made redundant by his senior partners and couldn't get another job. The fourth lawyer wound up with a very mysterious broken leg. The last guy became the object of a suspect paternity suit which consequently ruined for ever his chances of a knighthood and a seat on the bench.

Dom had lost his office at upmarket Lincoln's Inn and now occupied a room with one big desk and several phone lines just off the very downmarket Tottenham Court Road.

I banged on his door, he bellowed, 'You're late,' and I opened it to find him scowling behind his desk, looking tanned and healthy. 'How much is this going to cost me?'

He'd gained some weight since I'd last seen him, and he could have used a haircut. But then, there is something very fit looking about a shaggy sixty-eight-year-old who outfits himself like a man half his age and can move like one too. 'Where did you get the sunburn?'

'You never call. You never write. Just like the gorilla joke.'

I knew the joke and laughed. 'So where did you get the sunburn?' I closed the door behind me, came into the room and shook his hand. 'I don't think I've ever seen you looking better.'

'Spain,' he said. 'But you never get any better looking.'

'What were you doing in Spain?'

'Take a look around you . . .' He gestured to the four walls of his office. 'You think just anybody can be lucky enough to deserve all this?'

It was pretty stark, although one wall was covered in little brass plaques with company names. 'Flogging offshore smoke and mirrors?'

'Got to earn a living,' he said, motioned for me to sit in the room's only other chair, fell into his chair and said, '*Diga-me.*'

'You've even gone native.'

'Spain's a great place to be as long as you aren't Spanish. I play golf. I get to spend time with the wife. I make paella. So what have you got against that?'

'You cook?'

He snapped, 'You eat?'

'You must be doing something right.'

'With six grandchildren running around? What I'm doing right is keeping out of the way. So what do you need? And what's it going to cost me?'

'Insurance information.'

'Give me the w's.'

I told him who, what, when, where and why. 'Two policies. One life. One fire.'

He jotted it down. 'Either I'll get back to you or someone else will. It depends on who finds who first. You still in the same office?'

'Yeah, I am.'

'Next time, lunch is on you, mate.'

'Just say when.'

'No. I'll say where. How about Spain?'

'Any time,' I said. 'Any place. Thanks.'

He walked me to the door and gave me a wallop on the back. 'Don't be such a stranger.'

Every shoestringer needs a friend like Dom Powers.

From Tottenham Court Road tube station it was only two stops east on the Central Line to Chancery Lane, so I figured, why not, and headed for Lyle Benedict's dirty old building on a dead-end street with a stupid name. It turned out to be a wonderful Victorian structure that looked to me as if it had been built by Hollywood for a Vincent Price film about a paupers' hospital with a torture chamber.

The Science Reference and Information Service of the British Library is housed in Southampton Buildings, which also happens to be the name of the street. And there I have to agree with Junior. It's one thing to name an edifice after a street but doing it the other way around is like calling 34th Street, Empire State Building, which if you had an office there, would make your address Empire State Building, Empire State Building. That's much too confounding for New Yorkers but obviously not too confusing for Londoners.

I had to sign in to get past a couple of overweight, sleepy Asian security guards, but once I stepped into the three-storey vaulted chamber that is the main reading room, I couldn't get over how striking the place was. Two levels of balconies were covered with bookshelves and a domed skylight ran the length of the vault.

At the help desk, in the centre of the room, I buttonholed a middle-aged, dark-haired woman with half-glasses falling off the end of her nose, not just because she seemed to know her way around but mainly because the other people behind the help desk were displaying obvious reverence. My philosophy is always to go for the person who appears to be in charge. I told her, 'I need to check on some patents and don't have a clue how to go about it.' So she escorted me to a series of computers, sat me down and gave me the crash course.

'We have on record,' she explained, 'nearly forty million patents. And while there are several different programs available to help us search the archives, those programs still have to work their way through forty million. Because this can take a long time otherwise, I suggest we begin by deciding precisely what it is you want to know.'

I explained, 'I'm looking for patents held by three specific people.'

'Together, separately or in groups of two?'

I wasn't sure how to answer that. 'Is it possible to look at each one separately and then see if they share something?'

'Of course. The next step, after we search by name, is getting hold of that information, which we can do.'

'Sounds good to me.'

'Is that all you want? Because there's a further step. We can add to that information.'

'To get what?'

'To find out, for instance, exactly what it is that they've patented. The first search will produce an abstract. More detailed searches can and should produce the full description.'

'That sounds like what I want.'

She leaned over to the keyboard, typed a few letters, checked to see that the screen was ready and asked, 'First surname?'

'Bickerton.' I spelled it, she typed it and a couple of seconds later, a patent application appeared that was a duplicate of the one Straw had faxed me. I thought that was all, but then she went to the next page and there were three others.

She pulled some sort of plastic card out of her pocket, put it into a machine which read it, then hit another key and almost instantly, a nearby printer started typing the information on the screen.

'Next surname?'

'Pincer.'

She typed, the screen flickered, a list with several hundred references appeared and she printed that out.

'And DesRocher,' I said.

An equally long list rattled through the printer.

'Now, to see any combinations of those three names . . .' She typed 'Bickerton OR Pincer OR DesRocher', explained, 'That will bring up all three separately again, plus the various permutations of two,' and hit one of the keys. The screen flickered and more lists scrolled by. She printed them out too. 'That's it,' she announced, much like a high school English teacher proclaiming time had run out on some test.

I said thank you.

She nodded. 'If you have any problems understanding the use of the search engine as described here on these printed directions, anyone at the enquiries desk can help you.' She walked away. Class dismissed.

The information supplied by the computer was skeletal. There was the application number and the date of application, the publication number and the date of the publication, the international classification and whether or not there were patents pending or held in other European countries. There was the name of the patent application and the name of the inventor. In Bickerton's case, the two were the same, although I noticed that with Pincer and DesRocher the names didn't always match, meaning that while Pincer and DesRocher might have owned the patent, they weren't always the inventor. And there was the abstract.

Following the letters AB in Bickerton's first application were two words: 'Genetic ligature'. The other three applications were more detailed – I thought about Lyle Benedict's little discourse on double-talk – none of which I understood. Except the words 'genetic ligature' appeared in all of them. I wasn't intending to read through all of Pincer's and DesRocher's print-outs, although the abstracts on theirs seemed to be more detailed and, in general, somewhat easier to understand.

Sitting back, I looked at the computer for a few minutes, then reached for the printed directions. I had no idea what a search engine was, but the directions seemed very straightforward.

To clear the screen, press X.

With some trepidation, I pressed X and the screen went back to something called Main Menu. It gave me several choices and one of them was a new search. I selected that. Under that heading, the computer asked me to specify what field I wanted to search, and when I realized that field meant category, I looked for AB. It was there so I pressed the key to designate that I was doing an abstract search. Now the screen asked me for key words. I wondered if I had to put OR between them the way the librarian had. That's when I saw on the printed directions that for key word searches, if you want two or more words to appear in a certain order, you had to use the word AND. So under key words I typed 'Genetic AND Ligature'. Then I pressed ENTER.

I was all set for the computer to do what it promised it would, except it didn't. Which is why I am tenaciously suspicious of computers. It suddenly asked me for limitors. And I didn't have a clue what limitors were.

Back at the printed directions, I couldn't find anything that even looked like the word 'limitors'. And I was about to give up when I spotted the lady who'd helped me. 'Excuse me, do you have any limitors handy?'

Without so much as a minor smile, she peered over my back, studied the screen and explained, 'A limitor in this case might be the date or the names of patent holders or the names of inventors or the countries where such patents have been registered . . .'

'Got it,' I announced, and typed 'Pincer OR DesRocher'. She walked away, I hit ENTER and two references appeared. All the various numbers were different and the abstracts made no sense to me, except the words 'genetic ligature' appeared in both. What caught my eye, however, were the dates that these applications were made. Both of them were within a few days of each other. And when I thought back, I realized that both were also within ten days of my flight from New York to London with Bickerton.

After printing that out, I went to the enquiries desk to say thank you to the lady with the half-glasses. Instead I found a young man with patchy blond stubble that made him look like a Swedish version of Yasser Arafat. 'Mrs Belevedere? A woman with spectacles? I'm afraid she doesn't deal with the general public.'

He was easily bluffed. 'She's expecting me.'

'Oh . . . ah . . .' He shrugged, 'In that case . . .' and told me how to get to her top-floor office.

I found Mrs Belevedere sitting behind a small desk, staring at a computer screen which occupied most of it. Piles of pale green folders took up the rest. 'Hello?' I knocked gently on the open door. 'I appreciate your help and just wanted to say thank you.'

She typed as she spoke . . . 'You're welcome . . .' and never took her eyes off the screen. 'Did you locate what you need?'

'Yes. Although I'm not sure I understand it.'

'Come in and take a chair.' She continued typing. 'Unfortunately, feeding a database is like feeding a growing bear. The more you give it to eat the more it grows and therefore the hungrier it gets.' A few key strokes further, she stopped. 'One sincerely hopes Charles Babbage is amused.'

'That's a pretty good trick,' I said.

'What's that?' She finally turned around to look at me.

'Simultaneous typing and talking.'

'It takes practice. But not terribly much, especially if you have a mind that naturally functions in halves. It's the typing equivalent of rubbing your stomach clockwise with one hand and rubbing your head anti-clockwise with the other.'

'What's your title here?' I had to know. 'I mean, do you own the place?'

'I'm curator of the patent collection,' she said as if I'd somehow insulted her.

But I knew how to get past her. 'That would be sort of like Head Librarian, wouldn't it? My uncle . . . well, his wife, my aunt, was Head Librarian at our local library in Brooklyn. Library Science is a very interesting field. Kind of runs in the family. I grew up in that library . . .'

'Isn't that interesting,' she said, making it plain that my story held no interest at all for her. 'But my field of expertise is patents not Library Science.'

I beat a fast retreat. 'Then would you mind if I begged a little more free advice?'

She didn't answer.

'How about one fast question? I find patents very confusing.'

'Most people do,' she said, 'because they are.'

'If you don't mind?' I handed her the four Bickerton pages. 'Does this mean he actually owns patents on all of these?'

She thumbed through them quickly. 'Pending on these two . . . and these . . . actually they aren't two.' She hummed while she read. 'This is all the same.'

'All the same?'

'Yes. This is really only one patent.' She flipped through the pages again. 'Yes. It's one patent pending made purposely to look like four.'

Now I showed her the Pincer and DesRocher print-outs with the words 'genetic ligature' in the abstracts. 'Are these the same as well?'

'That I can't tell without a full search. It can take up to eighteen months before an application is published and these . . .' she checked the dates, '. . . no, these won't be published for some time. That makes it more difficult. Of course, once an application is published there is usually a way of tracking it down. But until then . . .' She handed the print-outs back to me. 'We offer several services which may be of use, including on-line literature surveys, subject overviews, regular current awareness updates and document supply. And although we would endeavour to work within the limitations of your budget, I'm afraid there are charges for these facilities and, because of demand, there is also a backlog which means a slight delay.'

'I see.' Actually, I didn't. But I felt that was the correct thing to say. 'Thank you. I'll have to think about that.' Except, I'd already thought about it and I wasn't interested in spending money for information that I could get for free. 'Is it usual practice to make several applications for the same invention?'

'It is not usual practice,' she said. 'It is fraud.'

'Fraud?' That startled me.

'You seem surprised? Did you expect scientists should always be trusted to tell the truth?'

I shrugged. 'Aren't scientists supposed to be disinterested seekers of truth and wisdom?'

She asked me, 'Do you know any solicitors?'

I simply answered, 'I see your point.'

'Fraud, deception and malpractice in the scientific community are on the increase. Scientists, after all, are only human and the pressures put on them, especially economic pressures, can become unbearable. Outright fraud is still rare, but misconduct isn't. Data is suppressed. Plagiarism is on the rise. Computer theft and industrial espionage are genuine concerns. Do you know of the case of Doctors Gallo and Montagnier?'

'As a matter of fact, I do.'

'And of Dr Gallo's associate, Mr Salahuddin?'

'No . . . that name doesn't ring a bell.'

She scribbled some notes on a piece of paper. 'There have been several articles on the matter. If you show this to anyone at the enquiries desk . . . anyone there will help you locate the references.'

I took the paper from her. 'Thanks.'

'Patent fraud takes many different forms.' She pointed to my print-outs. 'What you have there is not the most common way to do it, but it is, unfortunately, one of several. In your case, each patent is either sold separately or they're all sold as a package, and by the time the buyer sorts it out, the seller is long gone.'

'Long gone, huh?' I wondered, 'But if you spotted it so easily, wouldn't anybody who knows anything about patents also recognize it? I mean, wouldn't the buyer cotton on to the fact that . . .'

'Greed makes people myopic.'

'Greed?'

'Again, you seem surprised. Greed, after all, is the basis of the patent market. It is the undercurrent of all markets, perhaps, as people buy and sell for the sake of the purchase and the sale. But where patents are concerned, it is even more pronounced, because all too often, patents are bought and sold with nothing more in mind than profit.'

'You mean someone buys a patent simply to sell on?'

'Often that is the case. Other times, people sell patents that don't necessarily exist, much like faked paintings. It's known as the Corot syndrome.'

'Corot?'

'Jean-Baptiste Camille Corot was a nineteenth-century French landscape painter. There are those who even believe that he might have been one of the most influential. He is best known, perhaps, for his Italianate drawings and paintings. If memory serves, there are approximately ten thousand works in his *catalogue raisonné*. However, there are said to be nearly twenty-five thousand Corot works that have come onto the market.'

'Fake patents.' I mulled that over carefully.

'Do you know the name Dr Christopher Frederick Donald Bearde?'

I admitted that I didn't.

'He is the man who patented the never-ending light bulb.'

'Good idea.'

'Evidently, also a very lucrative idea.' She explained, 'In the early 1960s, Dr Bearde was working as an electrical engineer for a small aeronautical design firm in Toronto, Canada. Those were heady days, what with the space race heating up. New ideas were pouring into patent offices around the world. Among them were several in Dr Bearde's name for this type of light bulb. It was based on exotic alloys and rare gases. In each of his many applications he claimed that his new bulb produced three times as much light as any on the market, but only consumed a quarter of the electricity. What's more, he boasted they would never burn out.'

'Pretty impressive.'

'All the more so because Dr Bearde's credentials and his supporting paperwork were sound.'

'But was it real?'

For the first time, she actually smiled. 'It hardly mattered, as long as the world's light bulb manufacturers believed it could be real.'

I understood. 'They did and they panicked.'

'They were deeply concerned and, perhaps, rightfully so. After all, if Dr Bearde's never-ending light bulb received a patent and went into production, the world's light bulb manufacturers would go out of business.'

I reminded her, 'Except, they didn't.'

'Perhaps that's because Dr Bearde's patent application disappeared. They bought him out. And in so doing, they buried his never-ending light bulb.'

I waited for her to go on. When she didn't, I asked, 'And whatever happened to Dr Bearde?'

'Apparently, a reporter tracked him down in the mid-1970s. He was living somewhere in California. Although he never admitted that he'd perpetrated a hoax, and would have been unwise in the extreme to do so, he could be confident that none of the light bulb manufacturers to whom he sold his patents would ever acknowledge having buried the patent. So it turned out to be something of a perfect crime.'

'Wow.' I raised my eyebrows. 'What a good story. Is he still alive?'

She shrugged. 'I'm told there was a book written about him once upon a time. Or it might be his autobiography. But I've never seen it.'

'I presume you've checked.'

'I did bother to see if we had a copy in our holdings and we don't. At least there's nothing under his name, or under the headings "light bulb", "patent" or "fraud". However, that doesn't necessarily mean anything more than it probably wasn't published in Great Britain. I have never bothered trying to find it through the Library of Congress catalogue.'

I wondered, 'Does the name Alberik mean anything to you?'

She shook her head. 'Not at all.'

'You've been a very big help. Thank you.' I shook her hand, reclaimed my photocopies and returned to the enquiries desk. I told the young man with the blond stubble what I was looking for and he led me to a computer at the back of the room where he brought up several references. They all contained the name Salahuddin. I almost chose one at random, but as I paged down through the list, under the heading 'Named References' I spotted the words Pincer and Taptech Corporation.

'How do I get this one?' I asked.

The fellow leaned across, punched a few keys, the screen flickered and up came an August 1990 article from *Business Week* magazine.

'When the US Attorney in Baltimore, Maryland announced the indictment last month of Syed Zaki Salahuddin, a top scientist who was, until recently, at the forefront of the war on AIDS, he was unlocking yet again the jar of worms that is otherwise known as scientific deception.'

Noting that Salahuddin – a forty-nine-year-old native of Bangladesh who referred to himself as 'Doctor' despite the fact that he reportedly never earned such a degree – was charged with two counts of felony for conflict of interest and accepting illegal kick-backs, *Business Week* explained that the charges stemmed from a financial relationship to Pan Data Systems, a Maryland-based biotechnology firm that he helped to found six years ago.

Hand in hand with the indictment, they said, came a second probe, this by a congressional watchdog committee seeking to find out if others at the National Cancer Institute's Laboratory of Tumour Cell Biology in Bethesda – which they described as the cornerstone in the nation's efforts in the fight to find a cure for the AIDS virus – had financially benefited from illicit relationships with other biotech companies. At the heart of that was whether or not the Salahuddin case was an isolated one, or if it was part of a more intricate pattern of conflict of interest abuse throughout the scientific community.

In the wake of those questions, they cited a third investigation, noting that it was, potentially, the most damaging. Quoting reliable sources at the National Institutes of Health, they wrote that an enquiry was underway, with the assistance of the National Academy of Sciences, into French claims that Dr Robert Gallo had illegally obtained the AIDS virus from a French research group in the early 1980s and subsequently laid false claim to having independently discovered the disease.

These charges had been levied on the heels of an investigation into financial irregularities at Taptech Corporation.

Business Week went on, 'Dr Raoul Pincer, a Gallo contemporary, with contractual links to the US Government, left the NIH in 1981 to form Taptech. Within six years, the paper start-up company he'd created in rented premises on a small farm outside Vienna, Virginia had grown to a thriving entity, and boasted $6 million annual sales.'

It was at this point, the article noted, that Pincer went public with a small over-the-counter offering. But he quickly grew dissatisfied with requirements to publish financial data, claiming at the time that because the biomedical world had become so highly competitive, a small firm like Taptech could not afford to give away any access to information. And that, by its very nature, a public company was jeopardizing its own security by publishing accounts. So he took the company private again, paying what he deemed to be at the time a fair market price for the shares. Taptech's annual turnover for 1989, which was then the most recent set of audited accounts, valued the company at $9.43 million. Six months later, Taptech announced a co-operative development agreement with the NIH and sub-licensing pacts with Glaxo and Bayer.

The article concluded, 'Amid charges that he knowingly undervalued the company for the sake of the share buy-back, Government auditors were called in and although they established that Taptech could be worth as much as $32 million, the Justice Department announced that there was insufficient evidence that Pincer knew of the true worth of the pending deals. Nor could it be proven that he in any way had tampered with the share price or violated SEC insider-dealing regulations and charges were never lodged.'

I printed that out and on my way back to the office, made a note to ask Johnny to see what he could find about any relationship between Pincer and Gallo. For good measure, I threw in Montagnier and DesRocher. I also wanted him to see if he could locate anything on that book about the never-ending light bulb and, using that CD-Rom phone directory I'd bought him, see if there was a listing somewhere in California for Dr Christopher Frederick Donald Bearde. If there was, I figured I'd just pick up the phone, dial that number and see what happened when I announced to whoever answered that I was phoning on the advice of Dr L. Roger Bickerton.

Chapter Twenty-Five

Maybe my investment in feeding Lyle Benedict Junior hadn't been a washout after all.

I kept staring at the words 'genetic ligature'.

Look at that abstract, he'd advised. It tells you everything you have to know without saying anything.

I grabbed my dictionary.

'Ligature (lig'-a-choor) n. 1. A cord, cable, wire, or bandage used for tying or binding. 2. A thread, tie, cord or wire used to close vessels or to tie ducts. 3. A bond, bridge or link, something that unites. 4. A character or type combining two or more letters. 5. Music. a. A group of notes to be played as one phrase. b. A curved line indicating such a phrase. [From Latin *ligatus*, past participle of *ligare*, to bind.]'

I reread the full entry and settled on number three – a bond, bridge or link, something that unites.

All sorts of questions came to mind. Had Bickerton found a connection that would, or could, bond, bridge or link human chromosomes 5 and 13? If so, was it the solution that DesRocher and Pincer were both looking for? If so, had Bickerton put DesRocher and Pincer in a situation where one of them might become desperate enough to do whatever was necessary to keep the other from getting to Bickerton first?

And then I had to wonder, if so, did that include arson and murder?

Someone knocked on the door. Henry answered it. A young man with a very meek voice asked for me, adding, 'I'm here on the advice of Mr Powers.'

I told him to come in.

Pencil thin, wearing a suit that was one size too big and hardly old enough to shave, he approached cautiously, gripping a manila envelope. 'Mr Powers wanted me to get in touch with you.'

I thought to myself, that was quick. 'And you are?'

'My name? Yes . . . my name is Duncan Littler.'

I asked, 'What can I do for you, Mr Littler?'

He was very ill at ease. 'Please . . . if anyone knew that I'd been here . . . you see, I'm a records clerk at Warminster Providential St George, you know, the insurance company. Mr Powers said to give you some information. Two policies. One life. One fire.'

I wondered, 'Did he mention any names?'

'Bickerton, L. Roger.' He handed me the envelope. 'The policies aren't underwritten by us but I managed to locate them nevertheless. Both policies are with one of our competitors.'

I didn't ask how. Nor did I make any comment about the sanctity of corporate confidentiality. 'This is them?'

He nodded several times. 'Both of them.'

Opening the envelope, I pulled out the fire policy. It had been written two years ago and was never amended. The sole benefactor was Bickerton, L. Roger. Then I pulled out the life policy. Originally written in 1981, it had been amended just four months ago. Apparently, Bickerton had elected to change the sole benefactor from Cesari, Ghislain with an address at 13 rue d'Italie to someone called Peltier, Joelle at 12 rue Mesnil, Paris 75016.

I looked at Littler. 'Do you know if claims have been filed against either policy?'

'Yes,' he said, 'this week and on both. It's in there.'

I checked the envelope and found two more sheets of paper. Both were dated Tuesday and stamped received by Warminster Providential St George on Wednesday. They were filed by a lawyer in Paris named Jean-Pierre Rosso whose address was 109 place d'Italie, 75013 Paris.

How interesting, I thought. Madame Cesari and Mr Rosso seem to be neighbours, of sorts.

After giving the envelope one final check – there was nothing else – I thanked Littler and asked him if there was anything I could do for him.

He said, 'No, no, not at all. Except please never tell anyone.' And with that he left.

Now I grabbed the phone, got international information and asked for the number of Ghislain Cesari in Paris.

I said out loud, 'I thought she lived in Marseilles.'

It rang a dozen times before I gave up.

I'd gone through the mail and paid what bills I could and sent a few faxes to clients in the States who had not yet settled their bills with me, and had just spoken to both Hambone and Charlie when someone knocked on the door.

Getting to be like Grand Central station, I mumbled out loud and heard Henry say, 'Come in.'

I heard a man ask for me.

I heard Henry ask, 'Do you have an appointment?'

I heard the man say no.

I heard Henry ask, 'What is your name and what shall I tell Mr Barolo this is in reference to?'

I heard the man say, 'Tell him I'm a friend of David Brinkley.'

Getting up from my chair, I walked to my door, opened it and saw a fellow standing there . . . late thirties-early forties, fairly well built, dark hair, wearing a black double-breasted blazer, a white button-down shirt, a dark red tie and grey slacks. He was carrying an attaché case and looked vaguely familiar.

'I'm Barolo,' I said.

He nodded. 'I think we need to talk.'

I tried to place him but if I'd met him before, I couldn't recall where. 'Who are you and what's it about?'

'The name is Denton.'

I waited.

He stared.

I said, 'Okay. That's who. Now, what?'

'Where do you think I might be able to get in touch with your friend Mr Brinkley?'

'What's that supposed to mean?'

He suggested, 'Perhaps we should talk in private?'

I nodded okay, he stepped past me, I glanced at Henry, she shrugged, and I shut the door. Denton sat down and put his attaché case on the floor in between his feet.

That's when I noticed his shoes. Standard-issue black brogans. The kind cops wear with their uniform, and ex-cops

wear with theirs. 'Okay, we're in private.' I took my place behind
my desk.

'Your fax number was given to the European Research
Project press officer by a Mr Brinkley who requested some
information about Dr Bickerton.'

Now I realized who he was. The ERP security guy that Clare
Prout had spoken about. I was sure I'd never met him before . . .
at least not with the name Denton . . . but it bothered me that
his face was familiar. 'You'll have to do better than that.'

'What's your interest in Dr Bickerton?'

'Who says I have any interest? And why do you want
to know?'

He reached into his pocket, took out one of his business cards
and handed it to me. 'This will explain why.'

I glanced at it, then put it aside. 'So what?'

'So I'm investigating a possible security leak.'

'What does that have to do with me?'

'It seems you have recently been expressing quite a bit of
interest in Dr Bickerton.'

'And why is that any of your business?'

'Because if there has been an offence committed, it might
become your business.'

I put on my best angry-lawyer face. 'Are you making an
accusation, Mr Denton?'

He held up his hands as if to say not yet, then leaned back
and linked his fingers behind his head. 'Maybe we can help
each other.'

'How's that?'

'You show me yours and I'll show you mine.'

'Who says I've got anything to show? Or that I particularly
want to see yours?'

'Calls to the press office with a phoney name . . . a visit to
Eastbourne . . . talking your way into reception . . . dropping
names like Mars and Tyrone . . . the guard at the gate is a nice
enough old bloke, but he works for me.' Now he reached into
his jacket pocket, took out a small envelope and tossed it onto
my desk.

I didn't touch it.

'Go ahead,' he said. 'They're small. But if you want a few
souvenir eight by tens I'll let you place an order.'

Curious, I opened the envelope and poured out a dozen

proof-sheet size colour pictures obviously taken by security cameras. It was me at the guard shack and me at reception and me sitting alone on the couch and then, worryingly, me talking to Clare Prout.

I pushed them aside. 'I always photograph heavy.'

'It's not necessarily your weight that you should be watching.'

'What does that mean?'

'What were you doing there?'

'Slumming.'

'Was Bickerton your client or are you working for someone else?'

I answered by pointing to my law school diploma. 'See that?'

'All right. If that's the way you want to play it.' He stood up and grabbed his attaché case. 'I'm sure we'll meet again one of these days . . .'

The phone rang. I saw that it was the line we use for the intercom, so I picked it up. 'Yes?'

'There's someone here for you,' Henry said.

I wondered if Denton's attaché case had a secret tape recorder in it. 'Who?'

She answered, 'A Mrs Prout?'

Jeezus. 'No kidding.' I shot a glance at Denton.

He nodded. 'Thanks for your time,' and turned to leave.

I blurted out to him, 'I've got one question for you . . .'

He stopped.

I told Henry, 'Listen, I'm glad you rang. Why don't you think about One Hung . . .'

'Think about what?'

'I'll catch up to you.'

'When?'

'Yeah, that's right, One Hung,' I said, hoping Denton didn't realize that I was trying to keep him from understanding. 'So . . . we can discuss it there . . .'

Henry didn't always get it the first time. 'What are you babbling about?'

'You arrange it . . . go on . . . and I'll catch up to you.'

Denton moved over to inspect the shelf with my boxing trophies and nearly tripped over one of Hal's cartons.

'Oh, you want me to . . .'

'That's right. I certainly do.'

'Got ya,' she said. 'We're outta here.'

'Have a good trip,' I said, 'Bye-bye,' and put down the phone.

Denton asked, 'What is it you want to know?'

I glanced at his shoes. Brogans. 'It's not what I want to know.' I came up with, 'It's what you should know. It's about what's wrong with being an ex-cop?'

'Who says I am?'

'Aren't you?' I stood up.

'So what if I am?'

'It's those two letters, E-X. Ex-cop. As in, no real authority.'

He pointed to the cartons. 'Leaving town, are we?' Then he motioned towards the trophies. 'You know what's wrong with boxing?' He headed for the door. 'In boxing, you have to keep the other guy in front of you. In real life,' he looked at me, 'you have to worry about the guy coming up behind you.'

I got to the door first, opened it, and was relieved to see that Henry and Clare Prout were gone. Turning to him I asked, 'But do you know what's right with boxing?'

'What's that?'

'The smarter guy wins.'

He grinned, mumbled, 'Only sometimes,' and left.

I waited until I was sure he was down the stairs and out of the building, all the time asking myself, where have I seen him before?

Clare Prout was nervously toying with the handle of the white china teapot at that big round table on the far side of One Hung's kitchen. Henry was just finishing a spare-rib.

'Sorry to have kept you,' I said sitting down.

We were the only people there.

'Denton knows,' she said.

One Hung came over and asked if I wanted anything. 'Tea is fine,' I said, so he poured a cup for me.

'What do you mean, he knows? About what?'

'He knows that I've spoken to you. He will probably be coming to see you.'

I didn't tell her how close they'd come to bumping into each other. 'There's nothing to worry about.'

'He can be very nasty . . . he was very nasty, not to me, but to that young press officer, Terry.'

'What about?'

'About your call to the press office. And all your enquiries . . . you know, asking about Dr Bickerton.'

'He doesn't know we met at Gatwick.' I said it as a statement but meant it as a question.

'Are you sure?'

'What I mean is, he hasn't asked you about it?'

'No. But he did ask me about our conversation in the lobby. And the note you sent.'

'The note?'

'He saw me holding it. There are security cameras every-where. He saw it on the tape.'

'What did you tell him?'

'I told him it was a note asking for an appointment with Dr Tyrone. That's all. I destroyed the note so he had to take my word for it.' She looked at me anxiously. 'If he ever found out about those papers . . .'

'He won't,' I reassured her. Then I asked, 'What was Dr Bickerton working on when he was made redundant?'

'He was head of the laboratory.'

'Is that the job Dr Tyrone has now?'

'No. It's an odd system. Very bureaucratic. Roger . . . Dr Bickerton reported to Dr Tyrone. Dr Bickerton ran the laboratory but he didn't run the entire Eastbourne centre. Dr Tyrone was, is, director of the European Research Project in Britain. He's the one who reports to Brussels.'

'You mean, Tyrone is the administrator and Bickerton was the scientist?'

'Yes . . . and no.' She tried to make me understand, 'Nothing happens there without Dr Tyrone's approval. Even scien-tific work.'

'How can I find out exactly what he was working on at the end?'

'Without Dr Tyrone knowing? And Mr Denton?' She shook her head. 'It would be almost impossible. They're security fanatics. There are cameras in the laboratories and in the offices too.'

'You told me papers were stolen and computer files erased . . .'

'That's what Mr Denton says.'

'Can you find out what they were?'

'I . . . it would be very dangerous. I'm not sure I can.'

I took that to mean, she wasn't sure she wanted to. 'Don't do it for me. Do it for Roger.'

She wasn't convinced.

'Did you know anything about his personal life?'

'Such as?'

'His ex-wife.'

First she shook her head to suggest she didn't, then she hesitated, then she confessed, 'They stayed very friendly.'

'When did he set up his own private lab?'

She thought about that. 'Maybe two years ago. Maybe three.'

'Why?'

'He said he wanted to do some of his own work. It's not uncommon, you know. He once explained to me that an employee owes the fruits of his intellectual labours to his employer. He said he wanted to do some things for his own benefit.'

'Do you know what it was he was doing in his own time? What he was working on?'

'No.'

I wondered, 'What about the name Joelle Peltier? Does that ring any bells?'

She thought for a moment. 'No.'

'All right.' I smiled slightly, then reached over and gently touched her hand. 'I don't want you to worry about anything. No one will ever know that you're trying to help him.'

She looked at me. 'If . . . I don't know . . . but if I can find something . . .'

'Here.' I took a napkin and wrote out a series of numbers. 'Office phone. Office fax. My home phone. If you need me, call me.'

Nodding slightly she said, 'I'll try to help.'

I got Henry to walk her outside and find a taxi. In the meantime, I went upstairs, and rifled through papers looking for Bickerton's listing in *Who's Who*.

But it wasn't there. I'd left it at home.

'She's scared,' Henry said, returning to the office.

'The guy who was just here . . . you didn't happen to spot him in the street, did you?'

'No. Why? You mean the guy who was in your office when she showed up? The one who looks like Kevin Costner?'

'Who?'

'Kevin Costner. You know. The guy in *Field of Dreams*. It was on television the other night. The baseball flick.'

Chapter Twenty-Six

I started thinking about movies.

I saw that one with Kevin Costner and the thing that struck me about it was how, at the end, while the credits were still rolling, the women in the audience stood up to leave while the men sat there with red eyes.

I decided, crying over a great ending is a very satisfying thing to do.

Then I tried to recall films that made me cry.

The first one that popped into my head was *Old Yeller*. What a hoaky movie that was. A boy. His dog. The love and friendship they shared. And at the end the boy has to kill the dog. Leave it to Walt Disney to push all the right buttons.

A fax arrived, breaking into my thoughts. It was the Lustigs' lawyer saying that his clients were extremely annoyed at my having loused up whatever chances they had for a settlement with the Count. I thought about the fee I'd lost and mumbled, 'Me too.'

I tried to remember who was in *Old Yeller*. That was a long time ago. I closed my eyes and saw *Davey Crockett*. Oh yeah. Fess Parker. I wonder whatever happened to him. Davey Crockett, king of the wild frontier. I used to watch that every week on television. Buddy Ebsen was his faithful sidekick. *The Beverly Hillbillies*. That's where Buddy Ebsen ended up. But whatever happened to Fess Parker? And what were his parents thinking about when they named him Fess?

A second fax broke into my thoughts.

It was from Sandy Miller at Great Lakes Reliance. He wrote that Valparaiso Pacific had contacted him trying to renege on the settlement I'd negotiated. He said, 'Their attorney claims you bullied them into an arrangement and they want to talk directly with me. A: Did you bully them? B: Have you got it on paper? C: Have we got a leg to stand on? D: Did we get the best settlement? Comments please.'

I took the phone and dialled his number, but his secretary said he was at lunch and that he had appointments out of the office for the rest of the afternoon.

I went back to thinking about the movies.

Fess Parker ... *The Alamo* ... *Old Yeller* ... Kevin Costner ...

I tried to remember the last time I'd been to the movies. It was with Johnny in Atlantic City. And before that? It must have been in London ... I guess when I dragged Greta to see that reshowing of *Gunfight at the OK Corral*. She hated it. But I loved it, even though the colour had badly faded so that Kirk Douglas and Burt Lancaster both looked pretty strange – it suddenly dawned on me that Burt Lancaster was in *Field of Dreams* too – but Rhonda Fleming always looked terrific, even if the colour wasn't true. I liked her. She was one of those women I sort of fantasized about when I was a kid. Fat liked Jayne Mansfield and Guido had the hots for Marilyn Monroe but all Rhonda Fleming had to do was ask and I would have been hers. It was that red hair ... kind of like Louise.

I hadn't thought about that before.

Rhonda Fleming and Louise.

Funny I didn't think of Louise when I saw the picture with Greta ...

Oh, Christ. Greta. Dinner.

I looked at my watch and guessed she'd still be at the gallery. So I grabbed a piece of paper, hand-wrote a fax to Sandy – 'The answer to all your questions is yes' – sent it, closed up the office and made a dash for the florist's. I got there just as she was closing, bought a really nice bouquet and hurried to Cork Street.

She'll like this, I told myself. She'll understand. She'll give me a tough time for about five minutes and then she'll tell me how beautiful the flowers are and afterwards she'll say, please don't ever do that to me again. And I'll say, I'm really sorry. I'll tell her the truth, that I got caught up in something else, and I'll promise that it won't ever happen again. And she'll say, okay. And that will be that.

I got to Cork Street, turned the corner and spotted a crowd in front of the gallery.

I stopped.

Men and women were milling around on the sidewalk, many of them holding glasses, and inside there were even more people standing around holding drinks. Some of them were holding small booklets too, catalogues, that they balanced in one hand, trying to read from a page while also looking at a work of art and also not spilling their drink.

From where I stood, on the other side of the street, I spotted Greta inside, standing in front of some sculptures – cellos and violins that all seemed to be sliced up, and on the walls there were huge canvases with paintbrushes stuck to them and colours dripping down – and the name on the front window of the gallery said ARMAN.

What happened to the rectangles and squares coloured green?

I stood there, watching Greta work the room, kissing some people hello, shaking hands with other people, leading a man with a stubby white beard around to greet her guests.

Sliced up cellos and violins. Paintbrushes stuck to canvases. I didn't understand any of this. It was another world. It was a part of Greta's life where I would always be a foreigner.

After a few minutes, I simply turned and walked away.

Rhonda Fleming and Louise.

I should have stuck with Rhonda Fleming.

When I got home I put the flowers into a vase, put the vase on the table in front of the door and spent the rest of the evening watching George Foreman beat Joe Frazier and then Muhammad Ali beat George Foreman.

And all the time I kept thinking to myself, oh well, at least tomorrow I can live in my own world, one that I understand, my usual Saturday morning.

Chapter Twenty-Seven

Except, my usual Saturday morning got hijacked by a woman in a suit and a man in a dress.

I'd just gotten up when someone rang my bell. I opened the door as far as I could with the chain still in place and spotted a guy with a moustache wearing a bright red dress.

'Hi,' he waved. 'I'm Doris.'

It's Halloween, I told myself, and they're collecting for UNICEF. 'Can I help you?'

The person standing next to Doris announced, 'My name is Sam Masters.' Except, he was a she, wearing a smartly tailored business suit, with a white shirt and tie, and a rather handsome pair of Gucci's. 'The embassy sent us. It's about our friend who's been arrested.'

They both had American accents, so I unhooked the chain and opened the door all the way. 'The embassy sent you?'

'Yes. Are you Mr Barolo? The lawyer? We need a lawyer. Sorry about the time. It's . . .' Sam checked her large Oyster Rolex . . . 'seven-eleven, then extended her hand. 'Hi.'

'Like the store,' Doris volunteered. 'Don't you just love to go to 7–Eleven on a Saturday night to get the Sunday papers and ice cream?'

I shook Sam's hand.

'The embassy gave us your name and address,' she said. 'It's about our friend Crosby. She got arrested last night in Selfridges, you know, the department store. Well, it's taken us until about an hour ago to find out that she's got to appear before a magistrate at ten thirty and we need a lawyer.'

Doris made a face. 'The police keep you standing around waiting and never tell you anything. Can you imagine?'

'Look ah . . . Mr Masters . . .' I wasn't sure that was the

correct form of address but she didn't mind. Mr Masters, I'm not a criminal lawyer. I don't do work like that. I do insurance work. What's more, I'm not licensed to practise law in Britain . . .'

'We'll never be able to find a British lawyer at this hour . . . and anyway, we know Crosby will feel more comfortable with an American attorney.'

'I'm sure he would, but . . .' I didn't know what else to say. 'If it's just something like shoplifting, I'm sure there's a public defender . . .'

'I'm afraid Crosby got caught soliciting in the men's room.' Sam made a face. 'It was probably not the smartest thing Crosby has ever done before. But that's not the point. The British Government wants to deport us all. Please . . . we have no one else to turn to for help . . .'

I couldn't leave them standing at the front, and anyway, they looked harmless enough, so I brought them in.

Doris remarked immediately, 'Pretty flowers. It acknowledges your feminine side. This is good.'

'Ah . . .' The best I could come up with was, 'Have a seat. I'll make coffee.'

'Love your chairs,' Doris called to me. 'I have an Eames.'

I answered. 'Milk and sugar?'

'Black for both of us,' Doris said. 'Unless you can do cappuccino?'

'Sorry.' I brought out three mugs.

'We've been up all night,' he pointed out.

They both downed their coffee in a few gulps, and even though I couldn't be bothered to make ham and eggs for them, I figured the least I could do was be hospitable, so I went back into the kitchen, refilled their mugs and also brought out some tea biscuits.

While Doris ate most of them, Sam told me they were from Ohio – as if that was supposed to explain their gender confusion – and that they were in Europe on some sort of last fling grand tour before she got married to another lady. I was curious to know if the bride planned to dress like a man too, but I couldn't bring myself to ask. She said they tried to get the embassy to intervene but no one there wanted to know. The best they could get out of officialdom was my name and address.

Doris kept interrupting to let me know that he was 'dreadfully upset' about Crosby's arrest, and then to coo over my chair collection. 'I just adore Shaker furniture. Do you have any Shaker chairs?'

'Ah . . . no . . . sorry, I don't.'

'We need to stop the instant deportation,' Sam said. 'The three of us had hoped to spend the rest of the weekend in Britain before leaving for Paris on Tuesday.'

I reiterated that I did insurance work, that I wasn't licensed to practise in Britain and that the best thing I could do for their friend was phone a few solicitors I knew and try to find someone who'd help. But she insisted Crosby needed me and urged me to accept the case by reaching into her back pocket, taking out a wallet and handing me five one hundred bills. 'Perhaps you can plea bargain for us.'

Thinking to myself, this covers the cheque I wrote to Croxford's for Hambone, I asked what the charges were.

'Solicitation,' she answered.

'When did he get arrested?'

'She,' Sam corrected.

'She?'

Doris assured me, 'Stella Crosby. Well, Stuart to his mother. Stella to people who don't know her. Crosby to her friends. She's a she even if, well, you know . . .'

'Okay . . .' It was too early in the morning for the grittier details. 'When did she get arrested?'

'Last night, just before the store closed. We were there, in the shoe department, and Crosby went to the bathroom. Normally, she goes to the ladies, but, well . . . she spotted someone walking into the men's room and . . . after all . . . how was she supposed to know he was an off-duty detective?'

'She propositioned a cop?'

'It wasn't her fault.'

'Where is she being held?'

'It's a police station on someplace called Seymour Street. And she's supposed to appear in court . . .' Sam took a slip of paper out of her shirt pocket and handed it to me. 'It says, Magistrates' Court on the Marylebone Road. Ten thirty.'

'I'll see what I can do. No promises,' I told them. 'You wait for me at the police station. I'll be there in half an hour. I just need to shower and shave . . .'

'We can wait for you while you shower,' Doris volunteered.

I guess my face must have given me away because Sam said right away, 'I don't think so, dear. Let's meet him at the police station.' They got up, shook my hand and left. I finished my coffee, staring at the $500.

In the good old days, cops looked like grown-ups. But the good old days were obviously long gone because the kid at the front desk at the Seymour Street police station seemed only barely old enough to drive. 'Barolo,' I handed him my card. 'You've got my client in a holding cell. Name is Crosby. Like Bing.'

'Who?'

'Crosby. Like Bing.'

'Who's that?'

On second thoughts, I decided, maybe he wasn't old enough to drive. 'A fellow who calls himself Stella Crosby.' I took a punt. 'Possibly wearing a dress?'

'Oh yeah,' he smiled. 'Her.' Then he looked at me. 'But you're American?'

'So?'

He hesitated. 'I think I can only allow a solicitor in to see someone.'

'See what it says on the card? Attorney-at-law. That's American for solicitor and barrister all rolled into one.'

He wasn't sure, so he called for the custody sergeant and the two of them went off to a corner to talk about it. The older guy – a large man with a double chin and a stomach just peering over the top of his belt – came to ask me, 'Are you representing Mr Crosby?'

I replied, 'Yes.'

He asked, 'Are you allowed to?'

Even if I wasn't under the strictest terms of British law, in my mind Crosby had the right to be represented by anyone he wanted, so I confidently answered, 'Yes.'

He shrugged, 'Okay, this way.' He escorted me to a tiny, windowless cubicle, then went to get Stella, née Stuart, who arrived after a few minutes in a pale green and yellow dress. I introduced myself, sat him down and asked him to tell me what happened. He gave me his version of the story, which had it that when he walked into the lavatory, the off-duty detective told him what a beautiful dress he had on. 'It was love at first sight.'

I couldn't help chuckling.

But that must have offended him. 'You don't like me, do you?'

'What's not to like?'

'Do I make you nervous?'

'No. Do I make you nervous?'

'You've hurt my feelings by laughing at me.' He crossed his arms. 'I didn't do anything wrong. This is all about gay bashing.'

'No,' I corrected him, 'this is about soliciting which happens to be a criminal offence. And also being stupid enough to have solicited a cop.'

'It would be different if I were, you know, more of a woman.'

I suggested, 'You mean less of a man.'

'I am a woman,' he insisted. 'The only reason you think of me as a man is because of an accident of birth.'

I wanted him to know, 'Which is the same reason you don't think of me as Paul Newman.'

That drew a smile. 'You're so butch.'

'Yeah. First let me get you out of here and do something about the charges against you, and then I'll think about buying a Village People CD.'

He started to sing, 'In the Navy . . . da da, da da da da . . .'

'Let me tell you what we used to say in the Navy about . . .'

'About fags?' He made a face. 'Frankly, I never minded the word fag. But they ruined such a good word, didn't they, when they started calling us gays. We all used to be able to brag about having a gay old time. Now straight people have to settle for mildly amused.' He leaned forward. 'Do tell, what did they say in the Navy?'

'They have gang showers . . . you know, one big shower for a lot of guys.'

His eyes lit up. 'Heaven.'

'Well . . . what they used to say in the Navy is, never pick up the soap.'

He rubbed the side of his face. 'Who knows, had you not followed that advice you might even have re-enlisted.'

I grinned. 'For a fruitcake, you're amusing.'

'You mean, quite gay?'

'I guess that's what I mean.' I stood up and walked to the door. 'Wait here.'

I asked the custody sergeant if there was any chance I could speak to the arresting officer and maybe get the charges dropped.

'Won't work,' he said. 'I already tried. Between you and me, this is a bit over the top. But it was DI Cary Yeats. Gays get up his nose. Anyway, he's normally off today. Although, he will be in court.'

'His friends told me that someone threatened Mr Crosby with instant deportation?'

'Yeats, again.' He shook his head. 'He told Mr Crosby . . . this is before his friends said they wanted him to have a solicitor . . . he told him that usually, if a foreigner pleads guilty to an offence like this, the magistrate bundles him out of the country on the next train.'

'If you're going to get rid of him anyway, why hold him in a cell all night?'

'Foreigner. Yeats insisted he'd jump.'

'You take his passport?'

He nodded.

'So, tell me something, where do you think he can go without his passport?' I didn't give him a chance to answer. 'Why don't we just settle this thing with a police caution. Save you the paperwork.'

'I can't.' He seemed genuine. 'It's not up to me. Your Mr Crosby had the bad luck of propositioning Mr Yeats.'

I wasn't going to get anywhere with him, so I asked, 'What's the procedure?'

'We chauffeur him to the magistrates' court. If you can talk Yeats out of making a hullabaloo, which you might be able to do if Mr Crosby enters a guilty plea, maybe he's looking at a hundred quid fine.' He shrugged. 'Offer fifty and see what happens.'

'And if Yeats decides to raise a stink?'

'He's been known to.'

'All right. How far is it from here?'

He said I could walk it in under ten minutes, so I went back to Crosby and promised him I'd see him there, then picked up Sam and Doris and followed the custody sergeant's directions to the magistrates' court.

We got there early. As soon as I walked in with these two, a short, sour-faced woman carrying some folders challenged us. 'Yes?' There were two civilian guards at the entrance, but they seemed more amused by my companions than she did. 'Can I help you?'

I smiled. 'Which court is in session please?'

She scowled. 'Are you appearing?'

I wanted to know, 'Does that change the answer to my question?'

She glared at Sam and Doris. 'Are you an attorney and are these . . . persons . . . your clients?'

'And who,' I wondered, 'are you?'

'I'm in charge here,' she sneered, 'and this is not a fancy-dress ball.'

'But this is a magistrates' court and courts in this country are open to the public, is that true?'

She moved towards a door where a glass window looked in on an office – 'If you have any complaints you are perfectly free to write to the Lord Chancellor's office' – and went inside.

I looked at Sam and Doris. 'What was that all about?'

Sam shook his head. 'Permanent PMS.'

'It's an omen,' Doris said. 'Crosby is doomed.'

'Gay bashing,' Sam pointed out, 'is not a particularly good sign.'

'Don't be silly,' I waved him off. 'She was just jealous because Doris has a better dress.' Then I asked the civilian guards, 'Which court did she say was in session?'

One of them pointed, 'Down the hall. Courtroom two.'

We walked along a narrow corridor where red metal chairs were lined up against one wall, and at the end of it was a large waiting room, complete with a coin-operated soda machine. Around the corner, a couple of steps down led to two doors. One was marked public gallery. The other was the entrance into the courtroom. I motioned for Sam and Doris to wait in the gallery – a tiny room with two rows of chairs and a slatted-glass window so they could see and hear what was going on.

The courtroom itself was small, with a raised bench for the magistrate, a desk facing sideways across the front of that bench for the clerk, a witness stand to the magistrate's left, a long table in front of him for the lawyers, a few rows of seats behind that and the defendant's dock at the rear. There was also, nicely

enough, a balcony that ran along the far wall and the back of
the room where, I presumed, they could also put spectators.

No sooner had I stepped into the courtroom itself than
a woman carrying a clipboard came over to me. 'Are you
appearing, sir?'

'I'm here representing Mr Stuart Crosby.'

She checked the list of cases on her clipboard. 'Yes, sir,
please have a seat, sir.' So I sat down.

It had been years since I'd had to plea bargain with a judge,
and thinking about it now took me back to some very good times.
The twelve-year-old kid who'd robbed his grandmother's TV
set to buy himself a second-hand bike that his cousin had
stolen. The old lady who knifed the local butcher when he
trapped her in the meat freezer and tried to molest her. The
fourteen-year-old girl who blinded her gym teacher by throwing
acid in his face after he raped her in the locker room. The wife
who pushed her husband, his lover and the lover's German
shepherd out the sixth-floor window when she caught them
in bed together.

A very deep voice brought me back to the moment – it was
the clerk announcing the arrival of the magistrate – and as I
stood up, along with everyone else in the room, I was amazed
to see that most of the seats in the public gallery were now
taken, as were most of the seats in the courtroom.

Sam and Doris were leaning forward in the front row, their
noses almost pressed against the glass window. Sam caught
my eye, smiled and poked Doris who showed me that he was
keeping his fingers crossed.

Now there were also two very young lawyers sitting at the
front desk, facing the magistrate. There was a pencil-thin
woman with short dark hair in a black dress and an almost
equally thin, pasty-faced fellow in a dark suit. One of them
would be the on-duty attorney for the Crown Prosecution
Service. The other would be the public defender. Neither of
them looked old enough to be out of high school. And the last
thing I wanted was to have some young, gung-ho kid getting
in my way.

The magistrate was a roly-poly fellow in his mid-fifties, with
a thin moustache and what appeared to be a permanent scowl. I
thought back to the sour-faced woman who'd claimed to be in
charge and decided her good humour must be contagious. His

name was Rhodes and when he was ready, he nodded to the clerk who nodded to the woman with the clipboard who called the first case.

A Pakistani gentleman was accused of fraud. He was escorted into the dock by a custodial officer and told to remain standing. The young woman turned out to be the prosecutor because she was the one who read out the charge.

The clerk then explained to the defendant that he had the right to plead not guilty and have the case heard here or in the high court, or that he could plead guilty and have the magistrate either decide sentencing now or, if he so wished, refer the case to the high court for sentencing. The fellow was then asked how he wished to plead. He answered by trying to make a speech. 'Your worship, may I begin this morning's proceedings by saying that . . .'

Rhodes shut him up right away. 'All I want to know is how do you plead?'

'But, your worship, it is not that simple . . .'

The public defender stood up and asked the magistrate, 'Sir, if I may . . .' Rhodes nodded, so he went to the rear of the courtroom to speak to his client. A few seconds later he returned to his desk and announced, 'We are entering a plea of not guilty and asking for the case to be heard at the high court.'

The young woman stood up. 'Sir, we ask that bail be set at £10,000.'

The young man remained standing. 'Sir, the accused is in steady employment, earning £375 per week. He has a home and a family and I would ask, sir, that the court not consider him a risk for flight.'

Rhodes cut him off. 'Bail is set at £10,000.' He nodded to the clerk who filled in the proper forms. Then the magistrate announced, 'Next case.'

Two black guys were brought in and charged with auto theft. They were bound over without bail. Another black guy was led in, charged with carrying a knife, pleaded guilty and was sent away for two months.

The parade of people continued for another hour. Most of them were black or Asian. Although there were two well-dressed white couples charged with making a public nuisance of themselves – they'd been caught copulating, leaning against the same tree in Regent's Park – and two white men, not so well dressed, one of whom had been nabbed for drunk driving. His friend was booked for assaulting the arresting officer.

Then the list caller said, 'Sister Mary Agnes,' and a nun stepped into the dock.

Rhodes showed no surprise at seeing her there.

The charge was read out. 'Sister Mary Agnes O'Mally of the Jesus, Mary and Joseph Convent, is charged with illegal removal of a wheel clamp, wasting police time, abusive behaviour and destruction of property.'

'You did all this?' Rhodes asked.

'I did,' she said in an especially defiant Irish brogue. 'The man in the wheel clamp vehicle was parked just down the block, illegally, I might add, eating his lunch. There was a police officer with him. I gave them both a piece of my mind. Then I called the police and asked that they be arrested for illegal parking.'

He said, 'You tried to have them arrested for illegal parking?'

'I didn't just try, I insisted. They were illegally parked. What right do they have to disobey the law?'

'But you were illegally parked. Otherwise, your car wouldn't have been clamped.'

'Does two wrongs make a right?'

'That's not what this is about,' he snapped.

'No,' she snapped back, 'this is about an ongoing battle for territory. But you might not understand that because you probably have your own reserved parking space here.' The woman was fearless. 'Well, there's no parking outside the convent. I'd been on a hospital call and came back only to be told there was another. I needed to go inside to get the address and the only place to put the car while I was doing that was in a no parking zone. But the clampers were illegally parked when they clamped me so why shouldn't someone clamp them?'

He put his head in his hands and looked back at the charge sheet. After several minutes he asked the prosecutor, 'Why is this case here?'

The prosecutor jumped up. 'Not because of the parking violation, sir. But because of the subsequent arrest. It was then decided that the four charges could be more cost efficiently handled if they were presented at the same time.'

'Is the arresting officer present?'

A young patrolman came forward. 'PC Snelling, sir.'

The magistrate nodded. 'PC Snelling, the charge of destruction of property relates to what?'

'The wheel clamp, sir.'

'The wheel clamp?'

'Yes, sir,' Snelling responded. 'When the lady removed it from her car, some of the large bolts that hold it together went missing.'

The magistrate raised his eyes to stare at her. 'You know how to remove a wheel clamp?'

'I do indeed. And would be glad to give you a lesson.'

He nodded. 'I assume that the charges of wasting police time and abusive behaviour relate to the Sister's reaction to you when you arrived on the scene.'

'Yes, sir. She was . . . how shall I put it, sir . . . she didn't exactly use language befitting a nun.'

'That's no crime.'

'I understand, sir. But . . .'

'Will you withdraw the charges of wasting police time and abusive behaviour?' He stared first at the cop, then at the prosecutor.

She jumped up quickly to answer, 'Sir, I agree that they are probably unnecessary.'

It began to dawn on me that maybe Mr Rhodes wasn't so bad, after all.

'Good.' He took a deep breath, then turned to the nun. 'Sister Mary Agnes, there are two remaining charges against you. Illegal removal of a wheel clamp and destruction of property. There is also the matter of the parking fine, which I see from PC Snelling's report you said you would refuse to pay. How do you plead?'

'I have certainly done everything he says that I have.'

'A guilty plea is entered. The parking violation carries with it a £65 fine. Illegal removal of the wheel clamp is £275. Destruction of property . . . I am inclined to assess that at £25. The total comes to . . . £365 . . . or five days in jail. Next case.'

Jeezus. I couldn't believe that this guy just threatened to send a nun to jail. And where did he expect her to come up with £365?

The list caller said, 'Stuart Crosby.'

I quickly reassessed the situation. An appeal to his generosity was clearly not going to work. Our only chance, I reckoned, was to blindside him with confusion.

As my client was led into the dock, Rhodes's facial expression changed. 'What are you disguised as?'

I stood up. 'Vincent Barolo, your honour, for Mr Crosby.'

'Mr Barolo?' He glared at me. 'Are you a solicitor, Mr Barolo?'

'I am an attorney-at-law, yes, sir. I've been asked to intervene in this matter, introduced to the defendant by the US Embassy.' That wasn't exactly the way it happened, but it was close enough and he'd never find out any different. 'I would be grateful for a few moments of your time. May I approach?'

He thought about it, then motioned, 'All right.' But when I got to the bench, before I could say anything, he warned me, 'Make it brief.'

'I'm here, your honour, hopefully as a friend of the court.'

'This isn't the OJ Simpson trial, Mr Barolo. If you want to represent someone . . .' He looked again at Crosby, '. . . under the circumstances, which seem to be a bit unique, you are welcome.'

'I don't think there's any chance of this being turned into the Simpson case. I'm not nearly as dramatic as Johnny Cochran.'

'So how come your client is dressed like Marcia Clark?'

I shrugged. 'I know how difficult your job is. My uncle . . . he was a night-court judge back in Brooklyn. Played to the same crowd. First instance stuff. The backbone of the court system. I spent a lot of time with him when I was growing up. Because of him I'm a lawyer. So I understand the pressures you've got. He spent his life overworked, underpaid and unloved.'

Rhodes wasn't in the least impressed. 'What's your point, Mr Barolo?'

'I was an assistant district attorney for many years in Brooklyn, New York. One of the things we were pretty good at was working out plea bargains. Now, I know that you don't have the same system here . . .'

'Miss Harrington?' He cut me off, looked at the prosecutor and asked her, 'What are the charges?'

She stood up – 'Solicitation, sir' – and read the arresting officer's version of the events. She finished her little speech with, 'Mr Crosby is an American and his passport is in our possession.'

Now the public defender came to his feet. 'Sir, I had not been advised that Mr Crosby is being represented.'

I grinned at him and extended my hand. 'Your honour, if the young man might be invited to join me . . .'

Rhodes shrugged. 'Would counsel like anyone else on the defence team?'

I motioned for the public defender to come forward to the bench. 'What is your name?'

He approached so slowly I thought he was afraid.

I extended my hand. 'Vincent Barolo.'

'Arnold Middlebrook,' he said, with a dead-fish handshake.

'With the court's indulgence,' I turned to Rhodes, 'and without impinging on my learned friend's previously prepared defence of our client, would your honour consider either letting this matter drop or simply settling it by sending it back to the police to issue a caution?'

Rhodes demanded, 'Why should I?'

'Your honour . . .' I grabbed Arnold Middlebrook's arm and moved him closer to the bench, then whispered to the magistrate, 'Take a good look at the defendant. Mr Crosby isn't exactly playing with a full deck.'

'That's no excuse. This isn't Brooklyn. I'm not your uncle.'

I wanted to say, my uncle wouldn't fine a nun, but I wasn't going to push my luck. 'Your honour, our client's a fruitcake. Perhaps the prosecutor . . .' I turned and motioned for her to come forward.

Now the clerk objected, 'Sir, this is not in keeping . . .'

'Of course it's not,' I said to him. 'But I'm hoping that his honour will consider a few salient points.' I moved Miss Harrington closer to the bench as well, purposely trying to crowd the judge. 'Your honour, no act took place, no money changed hands. Under normal circumstances . . .'

'Is it normal that he walks around wearing a dress and solicits another man?' Rhodes shook his head.

'Wearing a dress is certainly not a crime,' I pointed out. 'Miss Harrington, for instance is wearing a dress.'

That was just enough to bait her. 'Sir, are you allowing an American attorney to represent the defendant in this court?'

'Yes,' he said curtly.

She wanted him to understand, 'Sir, I must object. I agree with the clerk that this is not in keeping . . . sir, that this is highly irregular . . .'

I needed to get more people around the bench, so I put on my most sympathetic face. 'I understand Miss Harrington's objections, your honour, but perhaps if the arresting officer . . . I believe he is in court . . . could he please be invited to approach? I'm certain there is a simple way to work this out without taking too much court time . . .'

Rhodes stared at me, I nodded gently, and he asked in a loud voice, 'Is the arresting officer here?'

Miss Harrington pointed to a stocky, short-haired man with large ears and a very prominent scar running down the side of his face, from his left ear to his chin. 'Detective Inspector Yeats,' he announced, standing up.

I signalled for him to come forward, then turned to Rhodes. 'If your honour doesn't mind that he becomes party to this sidebar.'

Rhodes mumbled, 'Party seems to be a suitable word.'

Now I leaned over and whispered in the public defender's ear, 'You take care of the prosecutor, I'll take care of the judge.'

He gave me a look of sheer horror.

'What is this all about?' Rhodes demanded of Yeats.

'I arrested Mr Crosby for solicitation last evening in the gent's at Selfridges . . . you know, sir, on Oxford Street . . .'

'I know where Selfridges is,' he snapped. 'What happened?'

'What happened is . . . well, he propositioned me.'

I cut in with, 'Your honour, that is debatable. No matter what DI Yeats claims was said, no money changed hands. In fact, my client will testify that money was never mentioned.'

Rhodes asked Yeats, 'Did he offer you any money?'

'Ah . . . well, sir . . . no.'

'Did any money change hands?'

'No . . .'

'Nor did any act take place,' I added.

Rhodes asked Yeats, 'Did any act take place?'

'Ah . . . no, sir . . .'

There was a long pause, at which time I jumped in with, 'Then perhaps there was no solicitation. Shame on the police and, frankly, shame on the prosecutor's office for bringing this before you.'

Yeats snarled, 'I understand very well what he offered to do . . .'

Miss Harrington protested, 'Sir, this is totally out of order . . .'

I reminded Rhodes, 'Your honour, even if it wasn't Mr Crosby's word against Detective Yeats's, perhaps you might consider the fact that Mr Crosby doesn't have any money so he can't afford to pay a fine. He's an honest person, and honestly feels he is not guilty. If you hold him over he'll stay in England until his trial comes up. But he'll have to stay in jail because he can't post bail. And then what? We both know what happens. DI Yeats isn't available to testify. Some flashy silk takes the case because the press has complained about the way homosexuals are treated by the courts. The gay movement hears about it, they campaign on his behalf, you personally get criticized in the papers for being homophobic, Crosby becomes a celebrity and questions are asked in Parliament why any of this ever happened.'

He stared at me as if I was certifiably nuts.

Miss Harrington reiterated, 'This is highly irregular, sir . . .'

I nudged my new friend Arnold.

He joined in with, 'Perhaps, sir, in this case . . .'

I moved out from between him and her so they were now standing side by side. 'Your honour, if Detective Yeats and Miss Harrington will drop the charges, and if you will allow Mr Crosby's passport to be returned to him, I'll see that he's out of the country by . . . how about, Tuesday?'

Rhodes said, 'He was probably leaving on Tuesday anyway.'

Miss Harrington cut in with, 'Sir, in all my years . . .'

He glared at her. 'In all your years?'

I nudged Arnold again. 'Sir . . .' He didn't know what to say . . . 'Sir . . . may I have a word with Miss Harrington?'

'What about?' Rhodes asked.

'Ah . . . I . . . just a word, sir . . .'

Rhodes looked at his clerk. 'What was that expression you used the other day?'

The clerk bellowed with contempt, 'My son, sir, calls it Looney Toons.'

'Looney Toons, indeed,' Rhodes said.

I was hoping that Miss Harrington was one rile away from

exploding. 'She's young, your honour, and with experience she will come to understand that what seems to be in the State's best interest is not always in the court's best interest.'

'I object most strenuously to this,' she blurted out. 'Sir, I find this proceeding . . .'

Now I poured salt into the wound. 'It's youth, your honour.'

'How dare you . . .' she snapped. 'Sir, you have no right to allow this man . . .'

'No right?' Rhodes took careful aim at her. 'Miss Harrington . . . I will not permit another comment like that . . .'

I gave Arnold a very sharp nudge. 'Sir . . . perhaps if I may just have one word with Miss Harrington . . .' He whispered something in her ear. She whispered something back. Then he whispered something to her. I looked at Rhodes and mouthed the words, 'It's youth.'

He just stared at me.

Now Miss Harrington offered, 'Sir, I apologize for my previous comment and would like to suggest that in lieu of prosecution, perhaps if Mr Crosby were to leave today . . .'

'Your honour, with all due respect, that is tantamount to deportation.' I turned to her. 'But at least it's good to see that the State is willing to be reasonable about this. How about, Monday night?'

Yeats cut in with, 'I don't want to drop the charges.'

With clenched teeth, Miss Harrington suggested, 'Sir . . . Sunday night.'

I agreed. 'Deal.'

Rhodes muttered, 'You really do think this is Brooklyn.'

I reached over and shook his hand. 'Judge, my uncle would have liked you.' I shook Miss Harrington's hand – 'You've been very reasonable' – and nodded towards DI Yeats. Then I put my arm around Arnold's shoulder, leaned over and whispered in his ear, 'Never be afraid to create confusion in a courtroom if, by doing so, you can take control of the case away from the judge and, at the same time, annoy the prosecutor into becoming a pain in the ass. The judge is then more likely to grant your most off-the-wall motion because that's the easiest way to regain control, to get even with the prosecutor and to save face.' I patted him on the back. 'Thanks, counsellor,' and left him standing there.

Outside on the steps, Sam, Doris and Crosby were jubilant. I explained that they had to be on their way to Paris by tomorrow night, and they agreed.

'At least the French understand love at first sight,' Crosby said. 'How can I ever thank you?'

'No problem,' I said.

Sam wondered, 'Do we owe you anything more?'

'It's okay.'

'May we recommend you to our friends?'

'I don't think my routine in there will play quite as well the next time.'

The three of them shook my hand. Then Crosby came up and kissed me on the side of the face. 'Thank you again,' he said. 'And . . . just between us, if you ever need anyone to pick up the soap . . .'

By the time I got home, I didn't feel like doing Portobello. And I was late calling Johnny.

His mother answered, 'He's not here.'

'Okay . . . what's he doing, playing ball?'

'Who knows?'

'Hey . . . I just asked.'

'And, hey, I just answered.'

'Look, Louise, I'm sorry, I was busy.'

'Don't apologize to me. You can apologize to your son. And maybe then he'll apologize to me.'

I checked my watch. 'So I'm an hour or so late. So he's gone out . . . What's the big deal, Louise?'

'The big deal is that when you didn't call on time he and I had a fight and he stormed out of here swearing that he wasn't coming back.'

'What are you talking about?'

'I'm talking about your son. He waited here for your call. You didn't ring on time. He left. He's gone. He's run away from home.'

Chapter Twenty-Eight

I phoned Louise at five my time, noon hers, then again before I got into bed at around eleven thirty. Johnny was still not home. 'Have you called any of his friends? Who does he hang out with? Where does he hang out? Maybe if you checked with the school . . .'

Instead of thinking of him, she lashed out at me. 'Maybe if you'd have paid more attention . . .'

'What does this have to do with me?'

'Everything.'

'Come on, Louise, why the hell . . .' I stopped short, thinking to myself that, in the end, there was nothing to be gained by arguing with her. 'How about if we save the recriminations for the locker-room show. The thing to do now is find him.' Then I asked, because I had to, 'Have you notified the police?'

'No.'

I couldn't bring myself to ask if she'd tried any of the local hospitals. 'What are you waiting for?'

'What am I waiting for? That's right, pass the buck. Blame me. Always put the blame on someone else.'

'I'm not blaming anyone. I just think you should call the police . . .'

She screamed, 'You always have such good suggestions,' and slammed down the phone.

I tossed and turned for most of the night.

Somewhere in the middle of it, a name crept into my head.

Joelle Peltier.

I lay there in the dark, flipping through the Rolodex that is sometimes my brain, trying to figure out who that was. I went up one side of the alphabet and down the other, looking for a letter that would click, that would associate something else I recognized with this name.

When I stopped at P for the fourth time, I thought of Paris. And then I had it.

I turned on the lamp next to my bed, found the envelope I'd stuffed in my night table drawer with those photocopies about Bickerton, spilled it out, located his *Who's Who* entry and went straight to his mother's maiden name.

Peltier.

I didn't know who Joelle was, and it probably didn't matter, but not being able to place the name was like having had a craving for chocolate. This was intellectual Milky Way. Now, with the taste of it lingering in my mouth, I could fight my way back to sleep.

I must have finally conked out just before dawn because I stayed that way until nearly noon. But when I got up I felt just as tired as I had when I went to bed. I couldn't decide if I should call Louise and ask about Johnny, or wait a few hours. Knowing her, if he was home she'd get angry with me for phoning this early, and if he wasn't, she'd get angry with me for not phoning sooner. Instead, I took the coward's way out and made breakfast.

When I was a kid, like maybe twelve, I invented Eggs à la Vincent, and made them all the time. I'd take two slices of bread and, with a shot glass, cut a hole in the middle of each. Then I'd fry some bacon in a pan, drop the bread into the bacon grease and break the yolk of an egg dead centre into each hole. The trick is to time it just right so that when you flip the bread to fry the other side, the white spreads all over the toast and the yolk doesn't break.

I hadn't made eggs that way in years but I suddenly felt like having them now. And when I took my spatula to flip them, I gave a little hoot that I still had the touch.

Spilling the eggs from the frying pan onto my plate, I added the bacon, poured a cup of coffee and sat down. The yolks were perfect. Except, by that time I'd lost my appetite.

I dialled Louise. 'Did he come home last night?'

'No.'

'Has he called?'

'No.'

'Do you have any idea where he is?'

'No.'

'Hey . . . Louise . . . I'm just trying to help . . .'

'You're a big help.'

'Tell me what you want me to do. Should I climb on a plane? If you want me to, I'll come back and spend the rest of my life walking the streets of New Jersey . . .'

'Do what you want to. He's only your son.'

'Why don't we start by calling police?'

'We? Don't worry about it, I called them last night.'

'And what did they say?'

'They said call back tomorrow.'

I sighed. 'Well . . . okay . . . I'll phone you later.' There wasn't much else I could say.

Back in the kitchen, I told myself I was going to eat breakfast even if I wasn't hungry. But by now, my Eggs à la Vincent were stone cold.

I didn't care about the Sunday papers.

So I shuffled into the living room and sorted through some boxing tapes.

But none of them held any interest.

Instead, I plopped myself down into a Victorian mahogany cabriole-leg grandfather chair, and asked myself what I could do for my son. I was still sitting there an hour later when the phone rang.

Hoping it was Louise with good news, or maybe even Johnny himself, I made a dash for it and pretty solidly banged my knee into the walnut Abbotsford chair I keep next to the phone table.

Damn. 'Hello?'

It turned out to be Sherman Straw. 'Good morning. I hope it's not too early. I know it's Sunday . . .'

'No, it's fine. I'm up. Hi. How are you?'

'I'm on duty at the hospital today and it's pretty quiet so I've been looking through stuff and I found something I thought you should see. Do you have a fax at home?'

'No.' I didn't want to sound ungrateful but I had other things on my mind. 'No, I'm sorry I don't.'

'It's an article in *Genome Research*. It's called, "Application to the mapping of human chromosome 7, plus integration of physical, genetic and cytogenetic maps: Construction, characterization and screening."'

'It was a page turner,' I mumbled 'I've already seen it, except I couldn't even understand the title.'

'You don't have to. It's the by-line that matters. There are eleven names listed.'

I suggested, 'A camel is a horse designed by a committee.'

He made a polite attempt to chuckle. 'I was reading the article and looked at the names because I wanted to know who they were. In the scientific community, like in academia, you get judged by the number of articles you publish. When you hear that someone is on to a good subject, you do whatever you have to in order to get your name on his paper. You strike up a deal so that you get credit for the contribution. If you don't, someone else will. It doesn't matter if you have a real contribution to make or not. You do whatever you have to do. You beg your way on. Or, short of that, there's always blackmail.'

I still didn't understand. 'You make it sound like the Mafia.'

'It is. And my candidate for Don Corleone is right there.'

'Who?'

'Tsung.'

'Who he?'

'The power behind the putsch that forced Bickerton out of the ERP.'

'How do you know that?'

'Westerberg told me.'

'Ah.' I didn't like the fact that other people were starting to talk about my interest in Bickerton. The fewer who knew, the better. 'Listen ...' I needed to say this gently. '... I'm very grateful for your help, but I'd be equally grateful if you and I could handle this on a discreet basis. I mean ... what I'm trying to say is that your world seems to be very small and I'm worried that too many people might suddenly ...'

'I understand,' he said. 'But I've only spoken to Westerberg and never mentioned this in context with you.'

'Can Westerberg be trusted? I'd really be very grateful if you didn't mention my interest to anyone ...'

'I trust him. But if you're that concerned, I'll ring him to say that if he doesn't keep his mouth shut, I'll tell his daughter.'

'Why his daughter?'

'I sleep with her.'

'Ah . . . the current Mrs Straw.'

'She's currently the current Miss Westerberg. But someday she might be the current Mrs Straw.'

'You mean, if she plays her cards right.'

'No, unfortunately, it's only if I play my cards right. She's supposed to marry a nice Jewish boy.'

'Hey, at least you're a doctor.'

'Tell her father that.'

'He was the one who recommended you.'

'Professionally, there's no problem. But I'm not necessarily held in the same regard when it comes to breeding grandchildren.'

'Okay,' I said, 'so tell me about Tsung.'

'I don't know him. But Westerberg said that Tsung used to work with DesRocher. He also has professional ties to Pincer at Taptech.'

'What does he do at the ERP?'

'He's a non-executive director. Brought onto the board by Tyrone.'

'Why?'

'Big name.'

'And where do I find Mr Tsung?'

'Dr Tsung,' he corrected. 'He lives somewhere in London. I don't know him, but he shouldn't be too hard to find.'

'What does he do now?'

'Besides collect non-executive directorships? Apparently he's got a bunch of them. There was a minor brouhaha about it in the professional press when Tyrone appointed him. I know that he's Chairman Emeritus of the Nestlé-Needham Laboratory in Cambridge, and also that he's somehow associated with a small research laboratory called Deoxydev.'

'Deoxydev? What does that mean?'

'I guess it's some sort of combination of the word deoxyribonucleic . . . you know, as in DNA . . . and the word development.'

I wrote it down, spelling it exactly the way it sounded. 'And you say he's honorary chairman of the Nestlé-Needham Laboratory? Wasn't that once Bickerton's lab?'

'It was.'

'Sounds like everybody in your business used to work with everybody else.'

'Science,' he said, 'is seriously incestuous.'

'And for some people, it seems, seriously dangerous.'

'You mean Bickerton?' He didn't wait for an answer. 'Westerberg told me there's a pretty good rumour running around about Tsung and Bickerton. It seems that immediately before being made redundant, Bickerton stumbled onto a gene in a fragment of cloned DNA from a mouse chromosome which he realized was involved in sugar metabolism. But his findings were owned by the ERP. He knew that, before long, someone would get to the next step, would discover that when this gene and the adjacent gene – both from the mouse – were added to the mouse genome in transgenic experiments, the linked gene would make the mouse lose weight.'

I tried to make sense of that. 'Isn't this what DesRocher and Pincer are working on?'

'It relates. Apparently DesRocher and Pincer are both telling people, independent of the other, that they think Bickerton took some of his work home with him and somehow managed to destroy any record of having done these studies on ERP time.'

I suggested, 'Hence his patent for a genetic ligature.'

'If it works,' Straw went on, 'it could be the key to Pincer's and DesRocher's puzzle. If there is a FAT gene in mice, at least in theory, it would be almost identical to the human counterpart.'

I thought out loud. 'So if he linked the two mouse chromosomes, he should be able to link the two human chromosomes.'

'In theory.'

'And in fact?'

'Who knows?'

'What do you think?'

'I think that DesRocher and Pincer are both very worried men.'

I asked myself, how worried? 'Thanks again for this. One of these days, we've got to meet up. How about if I buy you and the current Miss Westerberg dinner some night?'

'We'd like that.' He gave me his home number. 'If she answers, tell her I'd make a good father.'

I promised I would, hung up and reached for the phone

book. There was only one Tsung, T.P. listed – his address was
Onslow Gardens in South Kensington – and I copied it down.
I then found a listing for Deoxydev – on Pelham Street, also in
South Kensington – and copied that down too. Then I fell back
into my mahogany grandfather chair and tried to replay in my
head my conversation with Straw.

I heard myself say, if he linked the two mouse chromosomes,
he should be able to link the two human chromosomes.

I heard him answer, in theory.

Now I began to wonder, if Bickerton could convince someone
that the theory was sound, maybe it didn't matter if it
worked or not.

By five o'clock that afternoon, when there was still no news
from Louise, I got her on the phone and asked for the name
and number of the police officer she'd spoken with. She gave
it to me, cynically adding, 'What good do you think that
will do?'

I didn't say, if nothing else it will make me feel like I'm doing
something. Instead I said, 'I'll talk to you later,' hung up and
rang Sergeant Hector DeAngelis. But he was out of the office.
Someone said, he's probably having lunch. I said I'd call back. I
missed him a second time at five thirty. However, I caught him
just before six and after I introduced myself, and after I told
him where I was calling from, I asked if there was anything I
could do to help him find my son.

He surprised me by saying, 'Your ex-wife said you'd phone.
I spoke to her a couple of times yesterday and a couple
of times already today. She reported him gone less than
twenty-four hours ago, so there isn't yet a missing persons
report.'

'What's the procedure?'

'Officially, we can't do anything until the twenty-four hours
is up. It's our experience that, in most cases, kids eventually
wander on home within that time limit. However, unofficially,
I've already checked with the local hospitals and there's nothing.
I've also checked with his high school principal and we're trying
to put together a list of his friends. As soon as your ex-wife files
a report, we'll get his name, description and a photo on the wires
and see what turns up.'

I wanted him to know, 'He had a fight with his mother. I

think that's what probably triggered this. It's the most likely scenario.'

'She told me he had a fight with her current husband.'

'How convenient. She tried to convince me it was my fault.'

'Listen, Mr Barolo . . . I'm sure this is an expensive phone call and there really isn't much else I can say, except to reassure you that in most cases like this, the kids are hiding out at a friend's house waiting until things cool off. And also to say that I'm a parent, so I understand what you and your ex-wife are thinking.'

'I appreciate that. I just feel . . . you know, helpless being this far away.'

'There's nothing anybody can do just yet. If you want to check in later this afternoon, I'm here until four. That's my time here in the US. I don't know what it would be in England. I'm on days this week so I'm back again tomorrow at eight. But even if I'm not here, just ask for me and they'll put you through to whoever is manning the desk.'

'Thanks,' I said, then told him, 'I'll give you my number. If anything . . . you know, if you need me, call me in London. And you can call collect. It's all right.'

'Okay. I'll do that.'

I gave him the number, then asked, 'Are you sure there's nothing I can do from here?'

'Mr Barolo, it's Sunday. My gut feeling is that everything's going to be all right. But, you know, if you want to say a prayer or something, it can't hurt.'

I put down the phone with him, and without hesitation, reached for the Yellow Pages. The nearest Catholic church was St Francis of Assisi, a ten- or fifteen-minute walk from my place. Their answering machine listed the hours of Mass. There was one at six thirty. So I threw on some clothes, flicked on my answering machine, and hurried out the door.

The church was nearly empty.

Still, I sat in the back because I didn't know anyone, didn't know the priest, and anyway, I just wanted to be alone. After a few minutes, I knelt down and clasped my hands together and closed my eyes and said very softly, 'You may not remember me, but I'm an old pal of John MacNamee, and I know he's up there with you somewhere, and if you don't mind, can you call him over, please, because I need him . . . and I need you too . . . to help find my son.'

When the service was over I went straight home.

There were no messages on my machine.

I waited until nearly midnight before calling Louise.

There was still no news about Johnny.

Chapter Twenty-Nine

Sunday night was worse than Saturday night. I didn't sleep three hours total. I kept waking up. My mind refused to stop thinking the worst.

The first time I woke up, I padded around the apartment until I got so angry at myself for doing nothing that I called Louise. She'd just come back from the police station where she filed a formal missing persons report. I could detect a healthy dose of false bravado as she told me, 'There's nothing to worry about because they already checked the morgue and he's not there.'

The second and third time I woke up I thought about calling her again but I talked myself out of it.

I almost phoned her the fourth time I woke up, but by then my nerves were shot and I was bordering on exhaustion. So I popped a sleeping pill.

Within ten minutes, my system began to shut down.

I remember telling myself, it's okay because you almost never take sleeping pills so this one time won't hurt you.

I remember telling myself, all the pill is going to do is help you get some rest so that in the morning you can wake up with a clear head and make whatever decisions you have to.

I remember telling myself, you can get on a plane tomorrow morning and be in New Jersey by the middle of the afternoon and when you get there Johnny is going to be home.

I remember telling myself, you'll drive up to Louise's house and ring the bell . . .

Ring. Ring. Ring.

You'll ring the bell . . .

Ring. Ring. Ring.

I remember telling myself, it's all right, you're just dreaming, so go back to sleep, don't fight it, let the pill carry you until morning . . .

Ring. Ring. Ring. Ring.

I heard myself ringing the doorbell at Louise's house. Then I opened my eyes. My mouth was bone dry and my eyes wouldn't focus.

Ring. Ring. Ring.

I was confused and slightly disoriented and kept imagining myself ringing the bell at Louise's front door, until I suddenly realized that someone was ringing my bell.

I struggled to get out of bed and into a robe. The ringing continued. I could see from my alarm clock that it was five after nine. I thought to myself it's five after nine at night. But then I realized it couldn't be, that it was five after nine in the morning and that I'd somehow made it through the night.

The bell wouldn't stop ringing.

I remembered the woman in the suit and the man in the dress and I couldn't understand why they were at my door again.

I got to it and flung it open.

A girl was standing there. 'Hi. Mr Barolo?'

She was maybe eighteen, kind of tough-looking, with bright red hair and an American accent. 'Yeah . . .' I told myself, the embassy must have sent her. Redheads run in threes . . . Louise . . . Rhonda Fleming . . . now her. I told myself I really had to phone the embassy and say, if you're going to send clients, can you please hold onto them until I wake up. 'Sorry . . . I'm not feeling too good today . . .'

'I'm Megan.'

'You're what?'

'Not what,' came a voice behind her, 'who.'

I didn't understand. 'What can I do for you?'

'I've come to visit,' she announced.

'Me too,' the voice behind her said.

And suddenly Johnny was standing right there. 'Hi, Dad.'

It took a couple of seconds before I could believe it really was him. 'Jesus Christ.' I grabbed him and hugged him and wouldn't let go. 'What the hell are you doing here?' I kept hugging him so he kept hugging me, until he suggested, 'Hey, can we come inside?'

I brought them both in. Johnny carried a bright blue nylon backpack and whoever this Megan was carried a dirty old green canvas backpack. He kept saying, 'I'm so happy to be here,' and Megan kept saying, 'Oh wow, look at all these chairs.' I sat them down – except, she wouldn't stay in one chair and kept bouncing up and down, trying out a dozen of them – and then they both started telling me how they'd been up all night. I took a few deep breaths to clear my head, and told them, 'I've been up all night too.'

I made coffee for me, Johnny wanted a root beer and Megan asked if there were any vegetables. 'I'm a vegetarian,' she announced. He had to settle for a Diet-Pepsi and when I said to her, go ahead and take whatever you can find, she went through the fridge and found a couple of tomatoes I didn't know I had. So the three of us sat down and had breakfast while Johnny told me all about the fight he'd had with Louise. I said I'd heard it had been with the idiot trumpet player but he insisted, 'No. He was too drunk to care. It was her.' Then he told me how Megan had suggested they might as well run away together.

'My old man is a drunk too,' she confessed. 'It was my idea to pool our money and buy cheap tickets to London.'

'We're going to live with you,' he announced.

'If that's all right,' Megan added.

I asked, 'What do you mean we, Tonto?'

'It's okay,' he reassured me, all the time smiling at Megan. 'We ah . . . you know. I mean . . . well, you know.'

'You mean, I know . . . what?'

Megan volunteered, 'We've been lovers for nearly two months.'

He wasn't yet sixteen. 'How old are you?'

She rubbed his shoulder in a reassuring way. 'I'll be nineteen.'

'You'll be nineteen . . . which means you're only eighteen . . . and Johnny will be sixteen, which means he's only . . .'

'I know what you're thinking, Mr Barolo. And, frankly, I've never had a lover this young. But he's very grown up for his age,' she said.

'And Megan is . . .' He reached out for her hand, 'very grown down for hers.'

They both laughed.

'Yeah . . . well . . .' I suddenly felt very old. And also very out of my depth. 'You gave us all a scare, kiddo. Your mother is upset and I've been worried sick. Do you know that she filed a missing persons report with the police?'

He shrugged. 'I'm sorry, Dad. I just couldn't handle it any more. And Megan . . . she's kinda got the same situation at home . . .'

She cut in, 'Johnny thought it would be terrific if we came and lived with you for a while.'

I tried to think of something intelligent to say, some Solomonic utterance that would make so much sense they'd both see the light. The best I could manage was, 'You guys must be pretty tired, you know, flying all night.'

'Exhausted. And grungy.' She wanted to know, 'Can we take a bath?'

I told myself, it's not as if I can just put them in a taxi and send them home. 'Well . . . you're here, so you can stay for a while . . . I guess, a few days anyway . . . but eventually we'll have to work things out . . .'

Megan stood up. 'Come on,' she extended her hand to Johnny, 'let's take a bath.'

'Hold on,' I said. 'If you want to take a bath . . . I think, maybe it should be one at a time. I mean . . . not together. I mean . . . this is my house so I set the rules . . .' I suddenly hated myself for sounding like my own mother. 'What I really mean is . . . listen, guys . . . you've taken me by surprise here. You're going to have to humour me for a while. Give me some time to figure this out.'

The phone rang.

I pointed to Johnny. 'I've had a rough couple of nights worrying about you . . .' Then I turned to her, '. . . And I'm not quite sure how I'm supposed to be, you know, what I'm supposed to do about you . . .' The more I talked, the more I wished I'd just shut up. 'I don't mean you personally . . . but the two of you are only kids . . .'

The phone kept ringing.

She smiled. 'You're about to miss your call.'

I grabbed it. 'Hello?'

Henry announced, 'We've been robbed.'

'What?'

'We've been robbed,' she repeated. 'Someone broke into the office over the weekend.'

'Shit.'

'I don't know yet what's missing. The computer is still here. But there are files on the floor.'

'I'll be right there.' I warned, 'Don't touch anything,' and hung up.

Johnny asked, 'Something wrong?'

'Yeah. I've got to go.' I hurried inside to get washed and dressed. When I came out, Johnny and Megan were doing the dishes. 'Look, guys . . .' I didn't know how to say this any other way and I didn't have time to think it out. 'There's a spare bedroom.' I pointed to Megan. 'That's yours. You'll find sheets in the closet there.' Then I pointed to Johnny. 'You take my bed.'

They both stared at me in a very strange way.

'I just . . .' I pointed again to Johnny. 'You've got my number at the office, don't you?' He said he did. 'I'll be back as soon as I can . . .' Except, I decided, under the circumstances, maybe just walking into my own apartment might not be such a good idea. So I made a minor concession. 'I'll call before I leave the office . . .'

They kept staring.

I gave up. 'There are towels in the bathroom under the sink.' I headed for the door. 'Have a good bath.'

Chapter Thirty

The office was a mess. There were files on the floor. My desk drawers were open. The top drawer of Henry's desk was spilled out.

I felt violated.

But there was no sign of forcible entry. And no obvious sign that anything had been taken. The computer was still there. So was the printer. So was the fax machine.

My anger quickly turned to worry.

I walked around the office, looking at everything, trying to remember what the cops back in Brooklyn used to tell me when I was in the DA's office. Lesson one: Look closely at the obvious. Lesson two: Look closely at the unobvious. Lesson three: Look even closer at everything else.

'They're bastards,' Henry said. 'Why couldn't they have just stolen whatever they wanted to and not done all this?'

I tried to explain that seeing files on the floor was like hearing static on the radio. 'Don't listen to the noise, try to hear the music.'

'What is that supposed to mean?'

'It means confusion is not the point.'

She shook her head. 'So, what is the point?'

'I don't know yet.' I kept looking. 'Maybe it's just misplaced social protest.'

'Good one.' She put her hands on her hips. 'And just who is supposed to clean up this misplaced social protest?'

The more I walked around the more I told myself that this wasn't a normal break-in. 'No one,' I said. 'Not until we decide what the protest is all about.'

'Save the whales,' she mumbled snidely.

'Can you think of anything that's missing?'

She shrugged.

'Kids steal whatever they find,' I explained. 'Professionals steal something specific, you know, something they know is there.'

'So?'

'So this wasn't done by a thief,' I said. 'This was done by someone who was hoping to find something.'

'Such as?' She stared at me while I walked around for the fourth and fifth times.

'I don't know.' I shoved the obvious into one side of my brain and shoved the unobvious into the other side of my brain.

After a while Henry asked, 'When do we notify the police?'

That's when I saw what was left – a porno tape sitting upright on one of Hal's cartons.

'We must tell them to send over a fingerprint expert,' she decided. 'They can dust the place and unless the thieves wore gloves, which of course they might have . . .'

I stared at the tape, knowing very well that I hadn't left it there. 'The first thing we do is call Giovanni.'

'Huh?'

I checked my watch. 'I hope he's there. He should be, by now. Go on.'

'Why Giovanni?'

'I need a favour. Go on.' She got him on the line and I took the phone from her. 'Have you got any spare storage space? I've got a dozen cartons I have to get rid of fast.'

He responded, 'I'll send over a couple of waiters right now.'

I shoved that single tape back inside the carton, made certain all of the top flaps were double-folded so they'd stay shut, then started sorting through the files on the floor.

When Giovanni's guys arrived, I pointed. 'These go. All of them.'

Henry whispered out of the side of her mouth, 'What are you doing?'

'Making them disappear.'

It took the two waiters three trips to get them out of the office and down the stairs. I then asked Henry to go back to Giovanni's with them, to be certain that everything got stored away, and to say thank you. 'Tell him I'll call him later. And reassure him it's only temporary.'

Once she was gone, I phoned the police to report the break-in.

While I waited for them, I dug into our closet to get my old Polaroid camera and a package of film, then photographed the office as it was, for my own records, and any possible insurance claims.

Two uniformed officers – a young guy and an older woman – eventually showed up to inspect the damage. They'd just begun asking questions for their report, when Henry returned to say that Giovanni needed to speak with me. I let them take a statement from her while I phoned him.

He sounded panicky. 'What are you trying to do to me?' He'd obviously inspected the cartons. 'Is this stuff hot or something?'

'It's all clean,' I said, thinking that might not be the case. 'It's just for a couple of days,' I added, knowing that might not be true either.

'What happens if someone finds this stuff here?'

I tried to reassure him. 'Believe me, it's all right.'

'Maybe if it was only one carton, but a dozen of them? This stuff is hard-core porn.'

With two cops standing ten feet away, I couldn't exactly explain that only some of it was hard-core porn. 'I'll deal with it as soon as I can ...'

'You know who would love this stuff?' He didn't wait for an answer. 'The Cypriot's brother.'

'Wait.' I looked at the phone in my hands and another thought jumped into my head. 'I'll phone you back later.' Slamming it down, I stared at the receiver, cursed under my breath and told the cops, 'We'll go through everything this morning, take as much of an inventory as we can and get you a list of anything that is missing.'

The woman launched into a well practised speech. 'They usually go for the computer. There has been a wave of burglaries over the past several years that specially targets computers because of their memory chips. Although yours doesn't appear to have been tampered with, you probably should turn it on to see if it is still functioning properly. Then you should start to account for any other electronics in the office. Is your fax machine still here?' I pointed to it. 'Answering machine?' I pointed to that too. 'You will need to give us a full list of anything missing or damaged, so that it is on record with us during our investigation. You should keep a copy for your own records, and also one for your insurance company, that is should you wish to make a claim. In most cases insurance companies will ask if the list you submit is an exact copy of the list filed with us.'

'I understand.'

'Maybe,' her young partner suggested, 'they didn't have time to take anything. Do you know when the break-in might have happened? If it was this morning . . .'

'No idea.'

The woman checked the window behind my desk and took a long look at the front door. 'There's no sign of forced entry. Does anyone else have the key?'

I didn't bother saying, he didn't need a key. 'No. But we'll have the locks changed first thing this morning.'

The two officers asked a few more questions, scribbled stuff in their little notebooks, gave me their names and a number where I could find them, and promised that they would get back to me in writing with a case file number.

As soon as they left, I told Henry to find a locksmith who could change the front-door lock right away. I also wanted her to start calling around to see what it would cost to get an alarm system installed. 'When more cops show up, tell them to wait.'

'What, more cops?'

'Just a hunch.'

'About what?'

'About more cops.' I searched for a phone number in my personal directory, then went downstairs to One Hung's to make the call. The guy I needed to speak with was Antony Signorelli. The number listed on his business card was nothing more than a message centre, but I had his mobile number, so I dialled that and when he answered I told him what the problem was. He promised to get to me before the end of the morning.

I also rang Giovanni from there, to apologize for cutting him off but didn't bother to explain why. 'If you're at all uncomfortable with those cartons, call the Cypriot's brother and see if he can take them off my hands. I can't do it from the office. Trust me. I'll explain everything when I can.' He said he'd handle it. Then I warned him not to call me. 'I'll phone you or stop by.'

The rest of the morning was spent picking up files and

helping Henry put them away. It didn't take as long as I thought it would and we had most of it cleared up by noon, when the locksmith arrived. I had him install a new, heavy-duty dead bolt on the front door.

A security systems guy showed up just after the locksmith left, walked around, took some notes and promised to fax me an estimate for a standard alarm system within the next few hours.

I decided, 'Don't fax it. Phone it in.'

'You don't want it in writing?'

'No. Call me.' I didn't want to explain that this wasn't for my benefit.

No sooner had he gone than two fellows appeared, introduced themselves as Detective Sergeants Kerridge and Arnott and produced proper identification.

'You're late,' Henry said. 'They've already taken a statement.'

Kerridge, the taller of the two wanted to know, 'What would that be in reference to, ma'am?'

'The break-in,' she said.

'Break-in?' He looked at me.

I hadn't expected them so soon, but their appearance confirmed my hunch. 'What can we do for you officers?'

'Mr Barolo?'

'I'm him.'

Kerridge said, 'We have been advised, sir, that you are in possession of a large quantity of pornographic materials, including video tapes. That they are being stored on these premises. While you may well be within your rights to possess such materials . . .'

Henry shot a glance at me and from her expression I could see that she'd just figured it out.

I held up my hands to stop him. 'You have been advised wrong, detective.'

'Have we, sir?'

'Yes, you have. Because there's nothing of the kind here. And frankly, I would consider any such allegations made against me as being injurious to my reputation and good standing.' I reminded him, 'I'm an attorney-at-law. Under normal circumstances, any inspection of premises requires a search warrant. But as this is a law office, and as communication with my clients is privileged, any inspection here requires a great deal more. I presume you do not have a search warrant.'

Kerridge asked, 'Do we need one, sir?'

Arnott must have taken that as his cue because he started to make a casual move towards my room.

I said to Kerridge, 'Perhaps you don't think you do,' and motioned to Arnott, 'Your invitation onto these premises extends to this spot.' I pointed. 'Right there. With both feet on it.'

He looked at Kerridge who nodded, then backed away from my door.

'However,' I went on, 'because I am certain that you have been misinformed, and because that misinformation might have been given to you for malicious reasons, I will consent to allowing you a cursory look. Although you must not construe this, in any way, to be a waiver of my statutory rights . . .' I made it up as I went along, hoping that as long as it sounded legal it would put them off. 'Nor is it in any way a waiver of any attorney-client privilege. Even if you believe there is due cause, which is clearly lacking, you will not be permitted to view any files, messages or communication, in written or in electronic form, or any other data in any form whatsoever on the grounds that it is otherwise protected by professional privilege. If you will agree to my terms, I will dictate a letter for my secretary to type which you will be required to sign before making an inspection of the premises.'

That was not what Kerridge had in mind. 'I'm sorry, sir, but I don't think that I am in any position to sign anything of the kind, or agree to any such offer.'

'Well then . . . let me tell you a little story.'

Kerridge asked, 'Would that be a fairy-tale, sir?'

'Consider it a bedtime story.' I gave him a malicious grin. 'Once upon a time, my uncle . . . he was detective with the 107th in Brooklyn. Well, once upon a time he needed to get some information out of a lawyer. The lawyer insisted on a search warrant. That's the little piece of paper you guys seem to have forgotten about,' I glared, 'for whatever reason,' before continuing. 'Well, my uncle actually bothered to obtain one, but the search turned up nothing. The next thing the police department knew, there was a whopping lawsuit filed for malicious intent. And you know who wound up behind the

eight ball?' I stared at Kerridge. 'Not my uncle. After all, he
was only doing his job. Just like you're only doing your job.'
I waited one beat. 'It was the informant.'

'The informant, sir?'

'That's right, detective. The lawyer went after the informant.
And when push came to shove, my uncle had to give him up.
You see, he'd been had. The lawyer was legit. It was the
informant who stank.' Then I added for good measure, 'And
really stank, 'cause he was an ex-cop.'

A nervous twitch in Kerridge's eyes gave him away. 'We will
file a report, sir. And if there is anything further to discuss, we
will get back to you.'

'You'll have to govern yourselves accordingly,' I said, 'and
strictly by the book. If not, I'll have both of your asses in court.
That said, you might want to get a copy of the break-in report
that we gave to the two officers who were just here. I trust
that whatever investigation is pursued by you, or by them,
and independently by me, will eventually reveal the culprit.
I'd really hate to think that anyone would interfere with the
swift pursuit of justice. All the more so if it turns out that a
former police officer is somehow involved.' I grinned again.
'Have a nice day.'

'If you are referring to your break-in and you have any
suspects, sir . . .'

'Pick up enough rocks and it's amazing what you find hiding
under them.'

Without saying anything else, the two of them turned
and left.

Henry demanded, 'What was that all about?'

'One-upmanship,' I muttered, then bent down and continued
picking up the last few files on the floor.

We'd gotten everything put away by the time Signorelli arrived
carrying two large black pilot cases, the kind that the airlines issue
pilots for their maps and charts. 'Ciao, Vingie . . .'

'Hey.' I went to shake his hand but first he had to put the
cases down. 'How are you.'

A chubby, red-faced guy, he was another Dom Powers
connection. I'd met him about ten years ago because I needed
help with a divorce case. He'd just demobbed from the British
Army and had set himself up as a freelancer. Powers claimed
Signorelli was the best. And that proved true. My client was

a wealthy American who'd been working in the City and had
a fling with a congenital Sloane Ranger. She was one of those
flash, bulimic, ersatz society types who showed up at all the
right places, wore all the right clothes, borrowed all the right
jewels and knew all the right people, except she didn't have
ten cents to her name. She hooked the poor bastard good. He
was on a huge contract, one clause of which required him to
return to Wall Street after his three years in London and to
stay with the firm another three years. Well, when it came
time for them to head for New York, she balked. He had no
choice, so he went home alone and she sued for divorce on the
grounds of abandonment. Under normal circumstances, in the
British courts, she might have had a case. But when I got called
in, and Powers put me on to Signorelli, it was no longer normal
circumstances. Thanks to him I learned that she'd worked this
routine once before – husband number one had gone home and
paid up, but she'd exhausted that money – and had even bragged
to friends about possibly working the scam again. We also got
her admitting to extra-marital affairs. So, armed with the tapes
that Signorelli had managed to collect for me, I approached her
to explain, very quietly, that my client was about to sue her for
divorce on the grounds of adultery and ask for half her assets.
To prove that I wasn't going to fool around, I played some of the
tapes for her. She ran to her solicitors who cried foul – illegal
wire taps – but they couldn't prove it and she wouldn't dare
risk proceedings. Her solicitors huffed and puffed but in the
end she agreed to a no-fault, no-money-changes-hands, quickie
US divorce. My client got away scot-free and the last I read
in *Tatler*, Little Miss Muffet had moved in with a friend of
Prince Charles and, once again, could afford new hats for the
Royal Enclosure at Ascot.

'Papers were scattered around,' I briefed Signorelli, 'but
nothing else was touched. At least we haven't found anything
yet. The whole thing was set up to look like a shot fired across
the bow.'

'If there's anything else,' he said, 'I'll find it.'

I pointed to my phones.

He nodded, carried the two black bags to my desk, unpacked
them, set up some gauges and connected some wires. After
checking the phones, he hooked his wires up to the fax machine.
Then he took a strange black metal thing that looked like a cattle

prod and swept through the room. When he was done with
mine, he moved to Henry's room and repeated the procedure.
Then he asked where the phone connections were – we found
them downstairs, in the hallway around the corner from One
Hung's kitchen door – and he checked there too. Next, he went
up to the roof to take a look down at my window, then into the
alley behind the building to take a look up at my window. 'If
anything had been installed outside,' he said, 'no one would
have needed to break in. And if they broke in to plant a device,
they didn't get very far. The place is clean.'

'Are you sure?' I'd have been willing to bet there was
something somewhere.

'I'm absolutely positive.'

'No taps on the phones? Nothing at all?'

'Listen, Vingie, if there's a bug in your office, it's better than
the latest CIA-issue stuff.'

'How do you know?'

'Because I can find the latest CIA-issue stuff.' He started to
pack up. 'I did a job recently for the Saudis. They wanted me
to look for stuff that might have been planted by the Iranians.
You know, the Ayatollahs. Their own guys swept the embassy
and found nothing. So I swept it and the joint was infested with
CIA stuff. None of it was put there by the Iranians. It probably
wasn't put there by your guys, either. I suspect it was put there
by my guys.'

'So what did you do?'

'Hey.' He looked at me. 'Some of my guys are friends.
Anyway, they were only paying me to unplug the Ayatollahs.'

'I would have been willing to put money on it . . .' I looked
around both rooms and shrugged. 'One shot across the bow and
I get paranoid. Oh well . . .' I asked, 'What's the damage?'

'No sweat. Give me fifty quid.'

I had those five $100 bills, so I handed him one. 'Includes
the tip.'

He patted me on the back. 'Stop worrying, the place is clean.'

I told myself, so the warning wasn't just a diversion, it was
the message.

'You really think they tried to bug our phones?' Henry
patently enjoyed such intrigue. 'What are they looking for?'

The phone rang. 'Not they,' I said to her. It was Hambone.
'Hey, how's it going?'

'I'm getting ready. My main man Moe is the best.'

'Your main man Moe?'

Henry asked, 'What do you mean, not they?'

Hambone said, 'He's turning me into a lean, mean boxing machine . . .'

'And teaching you poetry,' I said. 'What's your training schedule tomorrow? I'll stop by. I want you to meet somebody.'

Henry asked again, 'What do you mean, not they?'

'Who?' Hambone wanted to know.

'Him,' I told Henry.

'Him, who?' she asked.

'Him?' Hambone didn't understand.

I asked Hambone again, 'What's your schedule?'

Henry insisted, 'Tell me him, who?'

'We do the road work at seven. We're up to two hours. Back here by nine and we stay until noon.'

'See you tomorrow,' I said.

'Him, who?' she repeated for the third time.

I hung up. 'The guy who broke in here.'

The phone rang again.

'You know who broke in?'

I said, 'Yeah,' pointed to the ringing line, and dialled Greta on the other line.

Henry answered the phone.

The gallery phone rang several times.

Henry said, 'It's your son.'

Greta finally answered it. 'Rose-Morrow.'

Henry said, 'It's an emergency.'

I dropped Greta, without saying anything to her, and took Johnny's call. 'What's going on?'

He sounded out of breath. 'Someone just tried to break in.'

Chapter Thirty-One

I raced home to find Johnny and Megan both dressed – I was grateful for small victories – but very upset.

'He didn't actually get inside,' Johnny said.

'We heard someone . . .' Megan tried to explain at the same time. 'He was trying to fiddle with the door and we thought it was you . . .'

He said, 'So we . . . I mean, I . . . you said you'd call first . . .'

She said, 'Johnny opened the door but by that time the guy was already running away . . . and . . . well, he couldn't exactly chase him down the block . . .'

He added, 'I mean, I would have . . .'

I reassured them, 'It's just as well you didn't.'

'He was trying to pick the lock,' Johnny said. 'I could tell from the noise. You know, like working a bobby pin in there, or something.'

'He almost got inside,' she said.

I asked, 'When did this happen?'

He answered, 'Like three minutes before I called you.'

Megan wanted me to know, 'Johnny says he was white . . .'

'Yeah . . .' He nodded several times. 'I mean, I didn't get a very good look at him because by the time I got the door open he was already making tracks.'

I asked, 'How old?'

'Gee . . .' He shrugged. 'Maybe . . . in his thirties?'

'Hair?'

'Brown.'

'Long? Short?'

'Shorter than long.'

'Slim? Heavy?'

'Medium.'

'What was he wearing?'

'Ah . . . you know, a suit.'

'Did he say anything? Did he have a British accent?'

'No.'

I wondered, 'Did he look like anybody you might recognize?'

'What do you mean?'

'Maybe a singer or an athlete?' I paused. 'Or, maybe a movie star?'

He shook his head. 'Gee. I don't know . . .'

I tried, 'Did he look like Kevin Costner?'

'Who?'

Megan told him, 'You know . . . *Waterworld?*'

'Oh . . . him . . .' Johnny thought about that . . . 'I don't really know . . . maybe . . . I mean . . .' Then he confessed, 'I didn't get a very good look at him because . . . well, I was kinda frightened . . .'

'Okay.' I patted him on the shoulder. 'You did the right thing by not chasing him.' I gave her a pat on the shoulder too. 'You done good, the two of you.'

'How come,' Megan wanted to know, 'Kevin Costner?'

I purposely changed the subject. 'First things first.' I told him, 'We've got to call your mother.' And then I told her, 'We've got to call yours too.'

They said, almost simultaneously, 'Do we have to?'

I said, 'Yes, you have to,' and dialled Louise. The moment she answered, I announced, 'He's here with me. Johnny is here. In London.'

'Damn you.' She was furious. 'You put him up to this. You knew all the time. You send him home right away . . .'

'He and a friend got on a plane Sunday and arrived here this morning. No, I did not put him up to it. And, yes, I will send him home.'

'When?'

'Here.' I decided the best thing to do was to pass the phone to him. 'Say hello to your son.'

Johnny's half of the conversation consisted of, 'No, Dad didn't put me up to this . . . he didn't know . . . no . . . no . . . no, it didn't happen like that . . . no . . .' He handed the phone to me.

'He's pretty tired,' I told her, 'give him a few days . . .'

'You get him back to me.'

' . . . and yes, Louise, I will get him back to you.'

She snapped, 'You'd better,' and slammed down the phone.

Megan didn't fare much better with her parents. They were pretty angry and every time she insisted, 'I'm old enough to do what I want . . .' I could hear them screaming at her, 'The hell you are.' Eventually I took the phone from her, introduced myself and tried to explain to them, calmly, that she was here with my son, that they were both all right, that I would take care of them while they were here and that they would be coming home in a few days. Her father said that if I didn't send her home right away, he'd call the police. I wondered why he hadn't bothered calling the police until now.

'And let me make myself perfectly clear about this,' he warned, 'if she gets pregnant, you're looking at a lawsuit.'

I repeated, 'They will be coming home in a few days,' and passed the phone back to Megan, but by that time, they'd hung up.

'Do we really have to go home in a few days?' Johnny asked.

I told him the truth. 'Yes.'

'Why can't we stay?' She said, 'I could get a job and Johnny could finish the school year here . . .'

'Ah . . . school. Good thinking.' I asked Johnny, 'What's your principal's name? I'll explain the situation to him and try to keep you from getting thrown out.'

'Thrown out?' It was clearly the first time he'd thought of that possibility. 'What do you mean, thrown out?'

'It's also called expulsion,' I said. 'What's his name?'

'Wilson.'

Johnny didn't know the school's phone number, but information did. I dialled it and, after going through who I was and what I wanted at least three times, Mr Wilson finally came on the line. I explained the situation, expecting that he'd make it as tough for Johnny as possible. At least, that's what would have happened – what used to happen – when I was in high school. But I guess times have changed and high school principals have become human beings. He said he knew Johnny had some family problems and that he hoped a few days with his father, even if it was in a foreign country, might help him get his head straight. He asked if I had a fax number and wondered if he could fax the week's school work to Johnny. I said sure. Then Wilson asked to speak to Johnny, told him that as long as he was in London, he had to do a paper on the British parliamentary system and Johnny reluctantly agreed.

Megan was already out of school, so there wasn't anybody else to call on her behalf. Although when I got Sergeant DeAngelis on the line and told him that Johnny had turned up here, I told him about Megan being here too, and gave him her parents' number.

He asked, 'When do you expect them to be coming home?'

I said, 'Give them until the weekend. I'm sure I can straighten everything out by then.'

He said, 'Fine,' then added, 'I'm glad your boy is safe.'

So that was that. Megan's parents didn't seem to care all that much, as long as they weren't going to become grandparents. Louise displayed more anger at me than she did concern for Johnny. The police had one less missing person to worry about. And Mr Wilson was willing to write the whole thing off to growing pains. There seemed nothing left for the time being than to ask, 'You guys hungry?'

Megan nodded. 'How about Indian food? You see, I'm a vegetarian . . .'

I proposed, 'How about Chinese? You can still be a vegetarian.'

Johnny wondered, 'How about the guy? What happens if he comes back?'

'He won't be back,' I assured him. But then, just in case I'd misjudged the situation, I took everything I had about Bickerton with us to One Hung's.

Even though it was now nearly three, the backroom table at One Hung's was full so we had to settle for eating in the restaurant. Still, Johnny and Megan were both impressed that I knew my way around the kitchen.

After lunch I brought them upstairs to introduce them to Henry.

'Blanche,' she corrected. 'My name is Blanche. Like Vivien Leigh in *A Streetcar Named Desire*. It was on the telly last night.'

'You like Vivien Leigh?' Megan applauded. 'I once spent six months calling myself Scarlett.'

Henry wanted to know, 'How do you get your hair so red?'

I left the three of them there to discuss it, moved into my office, tossed the Bickerton papers on my desk and fell into my judge's chair.

There were some faxes in from the States and several phone messages. Hambone wanted to know if I was going to hang out with him in his dressing room before the fight. 'Moe says I shouldn't see anyone but I figure you'll bring me good luck.' Giovanni wanted me to know that the Cypriot's brother was on his way over. 'He wants to inspect the goods.' Sam Masters wanted me to know that she, or he, and Doris and Crosby were at the George V. 'We've taken a big suite and have decided to stay in Paris for at least two weeks and if you happen to find yourself here, you have a place to stay.' Fuzzy White wanted me to know that I had to decide on the Birmingham fight by Wednesday. 'Three grand to your kid, win, lose or draw, take it or leave it.' The alarm systems guy wanted me to know he could make the office unassailable for only two grand. 'Guarantees your safety and protects you from everyone, up to and including Indiana Jones.'

I pushed all the messages aside, except the one from the alarm systems guy, which I threw out. I was no longer worried about becoming unassailable. I was more interested in finding a way to ruin Mr Denton's day.

'How come you don't have a modem?' Johnny asked just as the fax machine sounded. 'I need to check my e-mail.'

''Cause I don't need to check my e-mail.' I pointed to the machine. 'You want to get me whatever that is?'

'I could also look up more of that stuff you wanted me to.'

The phone rang, Henry took it, then shouted in to me, 'Some guy named Ooly.'

'Who?'

'I'm telling you what he told me.' She repeated, 'Ooly.'

'Who's Ooly?'

'He says he's Homer's brother.'

'Ah . . . Ulysses.' The Cypriot's brother. 'Not Ooly. It's Uly.'
I grabbed the line. 'Hiya. Giovanni speak to you?'

Henry muttered, 'Ooly, Uly, oily. Same thing'

'Yeah . . . I'm at his place right now,' Uly said. 'Gee, Mr
Barolo, I'd like to help you out but some of this stuff is pretty
untouchable.'

I asked, 'You mean, too . . .' I shot a glance at Johnny because
I didn't want him guessing what this was about, '. . .you know,
too raw?'

'Nah . . . the hard-core stuff is fine. It's all this basketball junk.'

'Well . . . what about the rest of it?'

'What, the football stuff? There's even boxing stuff . . . I
mean, not even Homer would take it off your hands.'

'No, I meant, the other stuff . . . you know . . . the stuff
that's fine.'

'The hard-core? Yeah, I can do something with it . . . you
know, as a personal favour to you. Most of it is unrated. There's
no X certificate on it and the law says it has to be rated or I
can't sell it legally. So that means I have to sell it under the
counter . . .'

'How many are there?'

'My count? Total? Maybe four hundred. Give or take say,
fifty. Let's call it three fifty.'

Normally I would have said, let's call it four fifty but this
wasn't exactly a seller's market. 'How many of them will work
for you?'

'Couple of hundred. Call it one fifty.'

'Okay. Pay for one hundred and fifty and you get the best
of the National Basketball Association for free.'

'Ahh . . . gee, Mr Barolo . . . it doesn't exactly work like
that.'

'Sure it does,' I said. 'It's called business. I give you
something to sell, you give me money.'

'You mean, you expect me to pay for this stuff?'

'Yeah. With cash. You know, lots of little pieces of paper
with the Queen's picture on it.'

'Up front? Look . . . I figure I'm doing you a favour so . . .
the best I can do is take it on spec . . .'

'Six for the lot. That's four quid a tape.'

'On spec, okay, maybe three.'

'And for money?'

'Money . . . there you go again . . .' He gave it one last try. 'I'm doing you a favour here, Mr Barolo . . .'

'How much?'

'Okay . . . okay . . . but we're not even talking two.'

'Tell you what . . . put all the boxing tapes in a carton and leave them with Giovanni. I'll keep them. The rest is yours for £300.'

'You keep the boxing, I take the rest for £250.'

I had to ask myself, what the hell are you doing negotiating with this guy? 'Deal. Give the boxing tapes and £250 cash to Giovanni.'

'Okay, Mr Barolo . . . any time I can do you a favour . . .'

'Friends like you are hard to find.' He put Giovanni on the line. I explained the deal, told Giovanni to take any of the boxing tapes he wanted and that I'd pick up the rest later. 'Make sure he gives you the cash right away. It's yours, my share of the bet on Hambone.'

That done, I turned to hear Johnny whine, 'Oh no . . .' as he juggled half a dozen pages that had just come off the fax machine. 'What are they doing to me?'

'Who?'

'Look at this . . . homework.'

That reminded me, 'Your term paper.' I asked Henry, 'Who do we know who can get Johnny and Megan tickets for Prime Minister's Question Time?'

She answered right away, 'What's his name, the tyrant.'

'Good thinking.' I picked up the phone and called Harold McBride. 'My son showed up unexpectedly . . .'

McBride understood. 'He finally ran away.'

'Kind of. His school says he's got to do a term paper about Parliament.'

'I don't knowingly publish term papers.'

'How about tickets to Prime Minister's Question Time?'

'Tuesdays and Thursdays. No problem.'

I said, 'Thanks,' then remembered Megan. 'He's here with his girlfriend.'

'Now you want two.'

'You'll like her,' I said, thinking of his granddaughter. 'She and Katy have the same colour hair.'

'My sympathies,' he growled. 'She threatened that if I

didn't give her more expenses money, next week it could be blue.'

I advised, 'Pay up,' mumbled, 'Thanks for this,' and was about to hang up when suddenly I thought of something else. 'Those computers of yours . . . do they all have modems?'

'You're asking me? Hold on.' He shouted for Greystone. I could hear him demand, 'Have all our computers got modems?' And I could hear Greystone answer, 'Yes, of course they do. And all of our modems are v.32–bis, with v.42 and v.42–bis error control . . .' McBride cut him off. 'I asked you what time it is, not how to build a watch,' then came back on the line. 'The answer is yes.'

'Got a spare one that a fifteen-year-old could use?'

'I got an office full of fifteen-year-olds.'

'I'll send him over.'

'Tell him to bring a couple of tickets for the fight. This Friday night?'

'I'd love it if you come along.'

'I'll see you there.'

I said thanks, hung up and told Johnny, 'I got you a modem.'

'For here?' He grinned. 'I can install it. You probably don't have plug and play . . .'

'Not so fast. It comes with an office to do your term paper. And tickets to Parliament.'

He suddenly didn't seem quite so pleased. 'What about . . .' He nodded towards Megan. 'I can't just go somewhere to do my homework and leave her alone . . .'

'She's going to Parliament with you.'

That made him happy.

Because they started to get hungry around five, I invited Henry along for an early dinner and we all went to Giovanni's. He wasn't open yet, but because it was me, he cooked. That made all of us happy.

By the time dinner was over, Johnny and Megan were dragging their heels with jetlag. I was pretty wiped out as well, so I grabbed the boxing tapes and the three of us went home. I told Megan the spare bedroom was hers. I told Johnny the couch was his. That didn't make either of them happy.

But just before I finally crawled into bed, at around nine, I said goodnight to them, went into my room, hesitated and

then figured, what the hell, and shut my door. I fell asleep
pretty soon. I think that made the two of them happy. The
next morning, I got up and found him sleeping on the couch.
Fooling myself made me happy too.

Chapter Thirty-Two

Tuesday morning I took Johnny and Megan to meet Hambone, Charlie and Moe. We spread out along the top row of the bleachers and watched Hambone go through a full-blown six-round sparring session. He was giving away ten pounds to a strapping black guy from Trinidad named Rufus Winger, because Moe wanted Hambone to get used to bigger punches than he'd have to face from Davey McGraw. Granted, poor Rufus was over the hill and forever doomed to day work as a punching bag. But he could still throw a hook, his arms were long enough to make his jabs effective, he caught Hambone looking the wrong way twice and the second time he did, Rufus rolled him on his heels. In the next round Hambone came back and threw a few combinations and one of them landed on the side of Rufus's face with enough force to put him on the canvas.

I'd never seen him in better shape.

Afterwards, when he came over to say hello, he sounded very up. But then Moe went to make a phone call and Hambone started complaining that Moe was a slave-driver and Megan decided Hambone was trying to tell us that Moe had it in for black guys. She said she wanted to confront him about his prejudices. I decided we'd stayed long enough.

Next stop was McBride's to pick up those tickets for Parliament. The newsroom was quiet. But Katy was there with her red hair and when she spotted Megan it was as if they were long-lost sorority sisters – Alpha Epsilon Day-glo. McBride shook Johnny's hand and told him he hoped he would grow up to be something, anything, more respectable than a lawyer. Johnny confessed that he liked journalism – that was a surprise to me – so McBride summoned Greystone and announced that Johnny had just been hired as a senior correspondent. Greystone believed it long enough to turn pale. McBride told him to give Johnny a spare computer, 'With a modem that stretches to every war zone on the globe.' Greystone escorted Johnny to a vacant computer and when Megan saw them huddling over a keyboard, she asked me if she could go with Katy who was going to try to take a photograph of Sting walking into or leaving a building in Soho where, rumour had it, he was posing naked for some music charity's rock star calendar. So I gave Johnny £20, and gave Megan £20 too, made them both promise they'd get to Parliament in time, made Greystone promise he'd give Johnny a map so he could find his way there and back, thanked McBride, and headed to the office to figure out how I was going to pay next month's bills.

There was a letter from a lawyer I knew in Miami who had a client who'd bought a new Mercedes from the factory in Germany, driven it around Europe for a month, shipped it to the States, had nothing but problems with it since and wanted to know if I could help him get some financial satisfaction out of the Germans. I had no idea if I could or not, or why he didn't try to settle the matter with Mercedes in the States. Except, it's tough for a lawyer to secure a retainer if the client doesn't have faith in a successful result, so I dictated a letter back to the lawyer in Miami saying, 'Sure I can help.'

There was a commercial lease to look at for a solicitor I knew whose client was trying to set up offices in Salt Lake City. It was pretty standard stuff and from the little I knew about real estate law I didn't think any changes were necessary. Except, you can't keep a straight face when you bill another lawyer for a consultation fee if you're not even going to pretend it's more than basic stuff, so I rang him to say that these things are never standard and promised to get back to him next week.

There was a receipt from Croxford's acknowledging that payment in full had been made on Hambone's new gear, a message from the Cypriot asking if I was still interested 'in the matter we previously discussed' – which meant he was getting desperate to cover himself on the odds he'd given Giovanni – and a bill from Inninout Office Supplies for six laser printer toner cartridges.

'What's this?' I shouted to Henry. 'Why are they billing us for six of these printer things?'

'Pay it,' she shouted back. 'They made a mistake and sent us a dozen. We've doubled our money.'

'I thought we only ordered one.'

'We did,' she answered, as if that was supposed to explain everything.

There was a message from the guy who was promoting the fights Friday night, asking how many tickets I needed. I told Henry to get a dozen, just in case.

There was a letter from an insurance salesman asking me if I had sufficient cover on my life policy, which I promptly rolled into a tiny ball and tossed into the wastepaper basket. 'Two points.' And another letter from something called the American Overseas Business Directory, telling me I'd been specially selected from a list of distinguished American businessmen to take advantage of their one-time-only fifty per cent reduction in advertising rates. That also got turned into a basketball. 'Four points.'

Finally, at the bottom of the stack, I found last week's copy of *Boxing Weekly*. That made me especially happy because I hadn't realized it was this late.

It was now well past lunchtime and I thought about sending down for *dim sum*, but for some strange reason seeing the magazine reminded me that I still hadn't apologized to Greta. So I rang her. I thought about saying, I stopped by the other night but you were busy, and wondered whether or not I should ask, how come it took a couple of days before you got that message I left on your machine.

Except, someone else answered.

I didn't want to leave a message that went all the way, such as, Vince called to say he's sorry. Nor did I want to leave a message that didn't go far enough, such as, Vince called, goodbye. So I compromised and left no message at all. Except, I still felt bad about having stood her up, so I rang the florist and sent Greta a dozen roses with a note that simply said, 'Sorry, but my son ran away from home.'

I knew it was only half the story and that one thing didn't really have anything to do with anything else. But I also knew it would get me off the hook.

Sympathy was one of Greta's strong points.

Thinking again about lunch, I decided my waistline could afford to miss a meal. Anyway, having gotten through the mail, I suddenly felt ambitious enough to ask Henry to print out the month's accounts so I could balance the office chequebook.

As she was doing that, a call came in from an American guy in Glasgow – I didn't know him and when I asked how he got my name he mentioned someone I'd never heard of – wondering if I knew a way he could legally get Cuban cigars into the United States. He might very well have been legitimate, but it's my nature to be particularly suspicious, all the more so when suspect business comes in like that. So I reminded him that Cuban cigars were banned in the United States. He said, of course he knew they were banned, which is why he was hoping I could help him. I reminded him that banned meant they were illegal and that I was a lawyer. He answered, why do you think I'm phoning you? I said sorry, can't help, bye-bye, and immediately started wondering, is someone trying to set me up?

My thoughts returned to Mr Denton.

That's when Johnny phoned. 'Guess what I just found?' He didn't give me a chance to respond. 'On the computer in the newspaper office. They've got the coolest system, with plenty of RAM and all sorts of really neat plug-ins for Netscape . . .'

'What are you talking about?'

'The Internet.'

'Oh . . . yeah, the Internet.'

'So I went into this really cool new search engine that's called Sherlock . . . you know, like Sherlock Holmes . . . and I just started looking up some of those names you asked me to. And you know what I found? All sorts of e-mail. I don't know what any of it means, but there's a whole mess of stuff. I'm downloading it now and I'll put it on a disk and bring it over . . .'

'E-mail? From who?'

'Not just from, but also to. You know, those guys . . . Pincer and DesRocher. A whole bunch of other people too.'

'You broke into their computer system?' If that's what he'd just done, it was an illegal act and I needed to make certain that no one at McBride's place knew about it. 'Is Greystone there with you?'

'No,' he said, 'he's gone off to do a story. But I didn't hack their computer, this is stuff that's on the net. It's just floating out there in cyberspace.'

I didn't understand. 'What does that mean, floating out there?'

'It means . . . I don't know how to . . . it's just out there. Lots of people think that when they send e-mail over the Internet it disappears. But it doesn't. I guess it's sort of like the way you leave an envelope lying around with a letter in it. Yeah. That's what this is. A lot of electronic letters sitting around in open envelopes.'

I wasn't sure that just because someone left an open envelope lying around anybody necessarily had the right to look inside. 'When you download this stuff, is there a record of it?'

'You mean, does someone know that we're reading his mail?'

'That's exactly what I mean.'

'No.'

'Johnny, are you absolutely positive?'

'Trust me, dad. I know what I'm doing.' He sounded very proud of himself. 'There is no way anybody can tell that I found this stuff or that I've read it or that I've downloaded it. Please . . . trust me.'

I wanted him to understand, 'I do.'

'So . . . what now?'

'What now is . . . when you've got it all, get into a taxi and bring it back to the office.'

'There may be a lot more. I don't know. I keep following all these threads . . .' Then he asked, 'You do want me to do this, right?'

I told him, 'Yeah.'

'So . . . do I still have to go to that dumb Parliament thing?'

None of the e-mail messages – forty in all – struck me as being of world-shattering interest. There was a lot of small talk, like a note from Pincer to someone at Kaducee-Pharmacopeia in Switzerland confirming travel plans. There was also a lot of highly technical stuff, like a note from DesRocher to someone at Berghaun Arzneikundlich in Germany discussing a patent that had something to do with erythropoetin, which my dictionary noted was some sort of hormone that stimulates the production of red blood cells. All of the messages contained either the name Pincer or DesRocher – Johnny explained he'd done two searches, one for each name – and none of them mentioned Bickerton.

'I can go back there and do more searches,' Johnny volunteered. 'I didn't think of doing one for him.'

There was no crosstalk between Pincer and DesRocher, but there was a lot of it between those two and T.P. Tsung. 'You can search any name?'

'Any name. It's easy.'

So I phoned McBride to ask, 'Would you mind if Johnny comes back and uses the computer again?'

He growled, '*Mia casa es sua casa.*'

I took that to mean it was okay.

I listed four names – Tsung, Bickerton, Mars and Tyrone – then added a fifth. Denton. Then I added a sixth. 'The fellow's name is Christopher Frederick Donald Bearde. Remember that CD-Rom thing I bought you that has all the addresses and phone numbers for everybody in the States? Have you got any friends who have the same program and can look up a name for me? He lives somewhere in California. At least I think he does.'

'You just want his address?'

'Preferably his phone number.'

'I don't need the CD-Rom. The entire US telephone book, you know, everybody's address and phone number is on the Internet.'

'It is?'

'Yeah. How about e-mail?'

I couldn't get over how much seemed to be available in cyberspace. 'For Bearde? I don't think you'd find his name mixed up with any of these other guys. Although . . .' I thought about that, '. . . you might check to see if there is anything between him and Bickerton.' I started to explain, 'The guy wrote a book . . . or someone else wrote a book about him . . .'

'You want to know about the book?'

'You can do that too?'

'The Library of Congress card catalogue is on the Internet.

'Next you're going to tell me that someday the Internet will replace sex.'

He grinned in a very strange way. 'For some people it already has.'

'I don't think I want to know.' I handed him another £10. 'I'm trusting you that no one will ever be able to track any of these searches back to you because . . . Johnny, this may be illegal. I don't know that it is, but it might be.'

That excited him. 'Are we, like, being spies?'

I answered, 'We're like . . . taking care of business for a client.' I wrote down McBride's address. 'If Greystone or anyone else asks what you're doing, don't tell them. And get a sandwich or something because you haven't had lunch.'

'I'm not hungry. This is too good.' He started to leave, but stopped at the door. 'What about Parliament?'

I gave in. 'We'll worry about it tomorrow.'

As soon as he left I rang Rodney the researcher. 'I've got a bunch of names I need you to check. They're all involved with various companies. Maybe even with each other. That's what I want to know.'

'In botany it's called cross-pollination,' he said. 'No problem.' He promised to get back to me as soon as he could.

He phoned back a couple of hours later. I wrote down everything he told me and when he was finished, I drew seven circles, one for each name – Pincer, DesRocher, Tsung, Mars, Tyrone, Denton, Bickerton – then tried to connect them according to what Rodney told me.

Bickerton didn't link to any of them, except through the ERP. Denton tied into the others through the ERP, but Rodney had also uncovered a link to Tsung.

One of the people listed as a director of Tsung's lab, Deoxydev, was Dr Piers Stafford. He in turn was listed as the director of a company called Alpha-Helix, on whose board were Eric Schluter and Rosemary Schlessinger. Schluter's directorships included several US companies, among them, Taptech.

At the same time, Schlessinger was on the board of a French pharmaceutical company whose non-executive chairman was Raoul DesRocher. That company, GenSeq SA, showed up on British records because it listed, as one of its assets, a thirty per cent share of SciSecGroup, which was a UK-based company involved in high-tech security for the scientific community. The owner of that company was none other than Carl Denton. And SciSecGroup's chairman was none other than T.P. Tsung.

I rummaged through my notes, pulled out the photo taken at Bickerton's going away party, and put it in the centre of my desk. Then I went back to linking all the circles.

Pincer. DesRocher. Tsung. Mars. Tyrone. Denton.

I phoned Rodney again. 'More cross-pollination,' I announced. 'Try Piers Stafford, Rosemary Schlessinger and Eric Schluter.'

Again, he promised to get back to me.

When he did, I drew circles for those three.

Now I had ten.

Bickerton was still the odd one out, but the others were all interlinked.

I reached for the newspaper photo and stared at it for a very long time.

The more I looked, the more convinced I became that at least one of the people in the photo was guilty of murder.

Chapter Thirty-Three

Johnny phoned to say, 'There's good news and there's bad news.'

I suggested, 'A wise man begins with the good news.'

'So the good news is that I've got a whole slew of stuff from all those names you gave me. And some new names too.'

'Is one of the new names Schluter? And another Schlessinger? And another Stafford?'

'Hey, how do you know?'

'Good news travels fast. Who do they talk to?'

'No,' he said, 'first you have to tell me how you know.'

'Lucky guess,' I answered. 'So, who do they talk to?'

'No soap. Tell me first. Let's see how lucky you can guess this time.'

I figured, 'Pincer and DesRocher?'

'Aw . . . too bad, Mr Barolo. I'm afraid you have not won the car or the ski chalet in Aspen. But if you'd like to try for the consolation prize . . .'

'Tsung?'

'Wow . . . Mr Barolo, if you will look this way . . . you have won the vacation of a lifetime, a round trip for two on the Hudson River Day Line . . .'

'The Hudson River Day Line?'

'It's only the consolation prize,' he said. 'Come on, how did you know about those names? And don't say, lucky guess 'cause it wasn't.'

'I'll tell you all about it when you get back. So, what's the bad news?'

'Bearde. Nothing. I even tried spelling it without the 'e' at the end. There are lots of Beardes in America, but none with all his names or all his initials.'

'It was worth a try,' I conceded. 'When you finish up there . . .' Then I remembered. 'Hey, what about the book?'

'Oh yeah. I found it in the Library of Congress catalogue. It's called, *An Inventor's Life*. The author is C. F. D. Bearde. That's him, right? It was published in 1975 by Redwood Scholars Press in Santa Rosa, California.'

'Good work. You and Megan hop into a taxi and we'll go somewhere for an early dinner.'

'She's not back yet. I guess I should wait for her . . . I think . . . I mean, I'd like to. And maybe while I'm waiting for her I can keep looking for stuff.'

'Sure. And when you get tired of playing the computer, see if you can find one of the reporters who knows something about Parliament . . .'

'Hey, Dad . . . I've never been that tired.'

I hung up with him and wondered if I shouldn't just go bang on Tsung's door and ask him who killed Roger Bickerton. Instead I dialled information and asked for the number of Redwood Scholars Press in Santa Rosa, California. The British operator found it, then reminded me, 'You'll need to dial zero, zero, one, for the United States, and then seven, zero, seven, followed by the seven-digit number.' I said thanks, started to make the call but didn't get past the area code.

Seven, zero, seven.

'Just like the jet plane,' I said out loud, and grabbed the manila envelope that Clare Prout had given me. Bickerton's notes. The page with the numbers. There it was, the large 707 and his drawing of an airplane with seven digits locked inside a doodled rectangle.

It wasn't the same seven digits as the one for Redwood Scholars Press, but I dialled it anyway and when a man answered, I took a shot at, 'Mr Bearde? Christopher Frederick Donald Bearde?'

'Yes? That's me. I'm him.' He sounded very old.

'Mr Bearde . . . good morning . . .' That's when I realized California was eight hours earlier than London . . . 'Ah . . . Mr Bearde . . . please forgive me for phoning at this hour . . . I hope I haven't awakened you . . . I hope I'm not calling too early.'

'Who is it? Yes . . . that's me . . . I'm him . . . but you'll have to speak up.'

'My name is Barolo . . .' I spoke slowly because when you're talking to someone who is that old, slow works just as good as up. 'I'm ringing from London, England about your book.'

'My book?'

'Yes. Your book, *An Inventor's Life*? I've been trying to find a copy of the book . . .'

'Oh . . . well, I don't sell copies . . . I wrote the book many years ago . . . maybe if you check with a good bookstore . . .'

'Actually, sir, I was wondering . . . you see, I'm phoning from London, England . . . I'm hoping to find a copy of the book . . . can you remember who might have published it over here?'

'London, England? I enjoy London, England. Mrs Bearde and I were there many years ago.'

'When the book was published?'

'Can't recall when the book was published. But it was many years ago.'

'I meant . . . were you in London for the publication of the book?'

'No, wasn't published in London, England. I'm American. It was published in America.'

'This is the book about the never-ending light bulb, right?'

'I don't know what book you're thinking about but that's the only book I ever wrote. Not the only invention I ever invented . . .' He asked, 'Do you know about my invention?' Now he chuckled. 'Pretty good invention, huh?'

'I heard about it . . . which is why I wanted to find a copy of the book.'

'But there are copies on sale somewhere. Must be.'

'You mean, copies on sale in England?'

'That's what I just said. I know because when the fellow called some time ago also from London, England about my book . . .' He stopped. 'Well, not exactly about my book but about something I'd mentioned in my book. Like I told him . . . I can't recall his name because it was some time ago . . . he also phoned me from London, England.'

I tried to jog his memory. 'Could his name have been Bickerton? Roger Bickerton?'

'Might have been,' he said. 'So you know him? He lives in London, England too.'

'He does,' I said, sticking with the present tense because I didn't want to confuse the issue. 'What was it you mentioned in your book that he wanted to know about?'

'He wanted to know about the dedication. Yes. That's what he called me about.'

'The dedication?'

'The dedication.'

So now I asked, 'Who did you dedicate your book to?'

He laughed. 'Fellow named Alberik.'

'The monk?'

'You know who he was?'

'Well . . . I noticed the name.'

'He wanted to know more about Alberik.'

'Do you talk about him in your book?'

He snapped, 'Dedicated the damn book to him.'

I asked gently, 'Do you happen to remember what you said in that dedication?'

'Of course I do.' He repeated it like a proclamation, '"This book is for Alberik. We are his disciples."'

I grinned. 'Did you write anything else about him in your book?'

'Just told you . . . must have a bad line . . . I dedicated my book to him.'

'Yes, must be a bad line,' I said. 'Well, thanks anyway. Maybe someday if I'm ever in California I'll come to visit you.'

'Let me invite you first,' he said, 'goodbye,' and hung up.

As soon as he did, I rang Johnny at McBride's. 'You and your Internet. The name is Alberik . . .' I spelled it. 'I want to know whatever the Internet knows about him.'

'Didn't I look him up once?'

'So, look him up again. We're talking about the know-all Internet, right?'

'Dad, it doesn't work like that.'

'Hey. You were the one who said to me it's just like the Jersey Turnpike. So, somewhere on the Jersey Turnpike there's a billboard with the name Alberik on it. All you have to do is find it.'

'Dad,' he reminded me, 'there are no billboards on the Jersey Turnpike.'

'Then turn off at the next exit, make your way over to Broad Street and try there.'

'Broad Street? Where's that?'

'Newark. There are lots of billboards in Newark.'

'Newark? When was the last time you were in Newark?

You know how dangerous that town is? You can get killed there.'

I hurried through my notes and found the photocopies I'd made at the British Library. 'From *Lives of the Benedicts*,' I read to Johnny. '"Alberik. 1622–1684. French Benedictine monk falsely credited with having formed the basic tenets of genetics." Got it?'

'I got it,' he said, 'but don't hold your breath.'

'Hey,' I asked, 'what kind of a kid would want his father to turn blue?'

'Hey,' he retorted, 'what kind of a father would let his fifteen-year-old kid drive alone in Newark?'

Henry announced, 'I'm out of here for a couple of hours. Personal time.'

'Personal time?' Looking at my watch I noticed that it wasn't yet four. 'Where are you going on personal time?'

'The reason they call it personal time,' she explained, 'is so that I don't have to explain where I'm going.'

'Who calls it personal time?'

She made a face. 'Don't you ever watch *NYPD Blue?*'

'Oh,' I nodded, 'yeah, that's right. That's what they call it at the 15th Precinct. Except, around here we call it where are you going?'

'If you must know,' she said, 'the hairdresser.'

'You never go to the hairdresser.'

'Well, today I'm going to the hairdresser.'

'What for?'

She demanded, 'Why are you prying?'

'I'm not prying, I'm curious-ing.'

'Is that supposed to make everything different?' She turned and headed for the door. 'It was Megan's idea.'

She was gone before I could mumble, 'Oh shit.'

As long as Henry wasn't going to be there to answer the phone, I put the machine on, figuring I'd screen my calls. If it was Johnny, or someone else I wanted to talk to, I could always just pick it up. Otherwise, what I really wanted to do was spend some time going back over Bickerton's notes. I was slightly annoyed at myself for having missed the 707 reference. Now I wanted to see what would happen if I dialled those other numbers.

But that turned out to be easier said than done.

There were three strings of numbers on the same page with the drawing of the plane. I had no reason to assume that they were all phone numbers – just because one of them was Bearde's – but if the other two were, I was anxious to find out who'd answer. Except, phone numbers in the States consist of ten numbers. In Britain, when you add in a long distance dialling code, you can sometimes have as many as thirteen. The first string on the page only had eight – that was the one where there were periods separating every pair of numbers – and the one on the bottom had letters mixed in.

I couldn't figure out how to dial either.

I stared at them for a long time – long enough that had they been words, they would have started to look misspelled – and began to wonder if maybe my initial assessment had been correct, that they were some sort of scientific equation. Then I noticed a small line, as if Bickerton might have dragged his pencil off the page, and I thumbed through the other pages to see if it continued there. Clutching at my elk-foot magnifying glass, sure enough, the line matched another on a second page. That led me to the firm conclusion that the two pages had been facing in his notebook. But after congratulating myself on such impressive forensic skills, I had to confess that it was pretty useless information.

I was still getting nowhere by the time Johnny and Megan arrived.

'It was great,' she gasped with excitement. 'Katy got all the shots with a long lens from the roof of the house across the street . . . I mean, right through the window. Except that it wasn't Sting.'

Johnny insisted, 'I told you it wasn't Sting.'

I asked, 'Who's Sting?'

'They never knew we were there . . .' Megan said. 'It was so cool.'

Johnny shook his head. 'You should have known better. I mean, why would Sting pose for some naked calendar?'

'It doesn't make any difference,' she snapped, 'because it wasn't Sting.'

'But you thought it was.'

'Because she said it was.'

I dared, 'Who was it?'

Megan faced Johnny. 'I could see it wasn't Sting. I know what Sting looks like . . .'

He snapped, 'Not naked you don't . . .'

'Hey.' I stopped them. 'I don't even know who Sting is when he's dressed. So who was it?'

Johnny said, 'You wouldn't know him either.'

'Try me?'

Megan answered, 'George Michael.'

'Who?'

'He's very famous,' Johnny said.

'Very,' Megan answered.

'As famous as John Hoyland?'

They said, almost in unison, 'Who?'

'Just because you never heard of him, it doesn't mean he isn't famous.'

Johnny said, 'I guess not,' but Megan cut in, 'Yes it does.'

I smiled. 'I rest my case.'

They didn't get it.

I pointed to Johnny. 'What about Alberik?'

He tossed a floppy disk to me. 'It's all there.' Licking his finger, he marked a line in the air. 'One point for JB.'

'Okay, JB,' I tossed it back to him. 'Set it up so I can read it.'

'Trust me,' Megan said, 'George Michael is very famous. Where's Drew?'

'Drew?' It took a moment before I understood. 'If you mean Henry, she's gone to have her head painted so it glows in the dark.'

'She did it.' Megan's eyes opened wide. 'I didn't think she'd have the guts . . .' She poked Johnny. 'I told you she would.'

He glared at her. 'Just remember that I bet you my dad would tell her to get it washed out.' He turned to me.

I shrugged. 'It is a free world.'

'See?' She poked him again. 'I told you your dad is cooler than you think.'

'Thank you.' I smiled at Megan, then made a funny face at Johnny. 'You don't think I'm cool?'

He said, 'Yeah, okay,' with obvious reluctance, 'you're . . . well, you're cool,' sat down at Henry's desk and booted up her computer. 'I just hope you can stay cool when you see Henry . . . or Drew . . . or whatever she thinks her name is.'

The phone rang. Before the machine could take it, Megan had already answered it. 'Law offices,' she said imitating a British accent. 'May I help you please.' She glanced at me and winked. 'May I tell him who's calling please? Thank you, please hold . . .' She mouthed one word to me. 'Greta?'

I picked it up, nodded to Megan that it was all right to hang up, and when she did said, 'Hi.'

'They're beautiful,' Greta said. 'But you shouldn't have. And I'm very concerned for Johnny. Have you had word from him? Are you going back to the States . . .'

'He's here,' I told her. 'He showed up . . .' I almost said the word yesterday, but decided the fewer the details the better my play for sympathy. 'He's here. With me. I guess he'll stay for the week . . . but he gave us a pretty good scare.'

She wanted to know how he got here and when he got here and if he was all right. I promised to fill her in on the details when I could speak. 'And who,' she now asked, 'is answering your phone with that terribly British accent?'

'Johnny's friend Megan.'

'Sounds as if you have a flatful.'

'If that's the same as a houseful, I'm afraid I do.'

'Are you going to have a flatful or a houseful next week too?'

'Would you care to make a reservation? I can take your booking but you will have to guarantee it with a credit card.' I spun around in my chair so that neither Megan – who was listening – nor Johnny could hear. 'I'm sorry about last week.'

'I understand,' she said. 'I waited . . . I even got angry . . . but under the circumstances . . .'

'I'll make it up to you.'

'My anger or my patience?'

'Whatever emotion you care to . . . emote? Is that the right word?' Then I asked, 'Unless you want to come to the fights Friday night. It's Hambone's big night.'

'A boxing match?' She said, 'Sure, why not.'

I told her she'd have to meet us there but that I'd arrange to have a ticket waiting for her at the front door. 'It's at the E&C Sports Centre . . . a couple of blocks from the Elephant and Castle tube stop.'

'You certainly know some classy venues.'

'First fight's at eight. Hambone is number three on the card.

Figure sometime around nine. But it could be later if the first two run the distance.'

'Shall I bring my own beer?'

'No, we can provide all of that stuff. Cigars too.'

'Thanks again for the flowers,' she said.

'I'll see you Friday night.' Hanging up, I spun around in my chair to find both Megan and Johnny staring at me. 'Who's Greta?' he wanted to know.

'Who's Alberik?' I asked.

'Right here,' he pointed to Henry's computer.

I walked over there and after he hit a few buttons on her keyboard, some text came up on her screen.

'It was on a tiny database called Crooks,' Johnny explained. 'Some sort of on-line encyclopedia owned by the International Mystery Writers' Association.' He shrugged, 'This isn't downtown Newark, it's like a side street in Perth Amboy.'

All it said was, 'Alberik: seventeenth-century French monk who defrauded the church with his falsified studies of genetics and on whose work the early geneticist Gregor Mendel originally based his own studies. Alberik's swindle was the model for early scientific fraudsters.'

'Hah.' I read it twice.

'You want me to print it out?'

'No. Let's see all that e-mail stuff.'

'That I do have to print out,' he said. I nodded. He hit a button on the keyboard and within a few seconds pages were spilling out the printer. Megan brought them to me in small batches. And the more I read the more these messages confirmed what I already knew. That all these people were living lives of entangling alliances. That Bickerton had somehow gotten in the way of one, or several of them. That one, or several of them had crushed him.

Sitting back, I announced, 'I know how to find out which one.'

'Which one what?' Megan asked, as Henry appeared in the doorway.

'Da, da,' she trumpeted her own entrance.

'Great,' Megan screamed with delight.

Her hair was bright green.

'So?' Henry asked me.

'Isn't it just the best,' Megan exclaimed.

'So?' Henry asked again.

'So . . .' I didn't want to risk losing Johnny's approval of my cool. 'How permanent is that?'

'How permanent do you want it to be?'

'Me? I love it.'

'Do you really?'

'Yeah.'

'I love it too,' she said, almost as if she was trying to convince herself.

'Tell you what. How about if I give you five quid for every day you wear it without someone saying, why did you do that?'

'And if someone does say that?'

'You put it back the way it used to be.'

'You'll make a fortune,' Megan promised.

'It will be washed out within three days,' Johnny mumbled.

I was betting she wouldn't last that long. 'Deal?'

'Deal,' Henry said.

Megan chided Johnny. 'I told you your old man was really cool.'

He stared at the two girls for a very long time.

I started making plans.

He told Henry, 'You stand here.' And he told Megan, 'You stand here.' Then he took a sheet of paper from the printer and put it on his head, positioned himself between them and said, 'Now bend forward.'

I glanced up.

He proclaimed, 'It's the Italian flag.'

I laughed but my mind was elsewhere.

I could hear Bearde's voice.

We are his disciples.

Chapter Thirty-Four

If the never-ending light bulb scam worked for Bearde, it could work for me too. And even if that's what got Bickerton murdered, I reckoned that with a little luck it would flush out his killer.

That night I phoned Sherman Straw at home and asked if we could meet as soon as possible. He apologized that he couldn't do anything before tomorrow afternoon and suggested we should meet at the hospital at three. I told him I'd be there.

Wednesday morning, Johnny and Megan announced they weren't going to the office with me, that instead they were going to take a guided bus tour around London. He was wearing a pair of training shorts and she was wearing a long tee-shirt and by the way they kept looking at each other I could tell that guided bus tours were just about the last thing on their minds. And maybe if my mind wasn't filled with thoughts of Alberik and those who followed I would have insisted they come with me. But I had things to do and I didn't know how much time I had to get them done. So I said, have a good bus tour, and then just to clear my own conscience, I phoned the tour company to find out how often the buses ran. 'You better hurry,' I warned, 'or you'll miss the nine thirty.'

I forgot to tell them there was another at ten.

'When do I get my first fiver?' Henry wanted to know as soon as I walked into the office.

'One every twenty-four hours.'

'That's this afternoon.'

'If you make it that far.'

'I will.'

'How do you know?'

'People with green hair know a lot of things that people who don't have green hair can't even begin to imagine.'

'That,' I said, 'is probably one of the world's great truths.'

'The tickets arrived.' She held them up to show me.

I tried to recall who I'd already promised them to. 'Greta. Giovanni. Give me some for McBride . . .' I took three. 'I'll deliver them myself. See you later.'

'Where are you going?'

I reached for three more. 'Come to think of it, I'll deliver these as well.'

McBride seemed in an unusually happy mood. 'Three tickets? All for me? Am I supposed to bring a date?'

'You like ladies with green hair?'

'One ticket will do.'

'I need to borrow Greystone and Katy.'

He reminded me, 'When someone borrows something they intend to return it.'

'I do.'

'There's no need to.' He bellowed, 'Greystone?' Then told me in a softer voice, 'Katy's out.'

Greystone appeared. 'Hi. Where's Johnny?'

'You might say he's seeing the sights.' Then I asked, 'Can you write?'

McBride interjected, 'Debatable.'

'Sure I can,' Greystone insisted.

'The man asked if you can write . . . not if you can overwrite.' McBride turned to me. 'Terse, short, tight writing, that's what good journalists do. Pontificating, overwriting, that's what he does.'

Greystone gave McBride a sorrowful look. 'I can write.'

He thought about that, then took a small step backwards. 'Let's say you're getting there.'

It brought the smile to the kid's face.

I sat with Greystone at his desk and told him that this was a tale of entangling alliances. I didn't mention Bickerton. But I filled him in on Pincer and DesRocher and the gang from the ERP. I told him I had some of the notes he'd need, but that he'd have to dig for the rest. I also told him that if everything worked out the way I thought it could, he'd have a really good story to write by the weekend.

'I can write,' he said, 'and I'll prove it to him.'

I thought of saying, McBride means well. Except, he didn't. Instead I advised Greystone, 'You don't have to prove it to him, you have to prove it to yourself.' I left a note for Katy to ring me, then headed for the Cypriot's betting shop.

'I need to borrow your phone number. Have you got a private line?'

'Yeah . . . what for?'

'Someone will call you in the next few days.' I told him what that person would say, and wrote down what Homer was supposed to answer. Then I handed him a ticket for Hambone's fight.

'Hey, that reminds me . . . what about those odds you were looking for . . .'

I whispered, 'The heat's on.'

He asked, 'What's that mean?'

I winked. 'See you at the fights,' and left him there wondering what I was talking about.

Next stop was his brother's place. I knew it was a couple of blocks off Soho Square, but I'd never been there and couldn't bring myself to ask directions. How do you say to a perfect stranger, where's the Erect Lion Sex Shop? So I walked around for nearly twenty minutes until I found it and then made certain that no one saw me go inside.

'I already gave Giovanni the money,' Ulysses said. 'You selling again or buying this time? I'll give you a good discount on whatever you want. We've got a special on . . .' He reached for a huge, inflatable doll. 'They don't come already blown up like this . . . I pack 'em in a pretty discreet box . . . unless you want to walk out of the store with it already blown up . . .'

'I don't think so.' I couldn't believe how unlifelike the doll looked. 'She's horrible.'

'You think I sell these things to Tom Cruise?'

'Listen . . . I need to talk to you. Somewhere private.'

'Come with me.' He led me behind a doorway that had multi-coloured plastic strips hanging down to separate the hall behind it from the shop. In his tiny office, there were a dozen more dolls already inflated sitting on the desk.

'I need to borrow your phone number. Do you have a private line?'

'Yeah, sure, Mr Barolo. But can I know what this is for?'

I told him the same thing I told his brother. He thought about

it, shrugged, said he'd be glad to help out and I handed him a
ticket for Hambone's fight. 'Thanks.'

'Fifty off on the dolls,' he called after me as I poked my head
out his front door to make sure the street was empty.

I then went to see Giovanni and told him I needed to keep
a table free for a meeting. He said, no problem. So I dropped a
ticket on him. Finally I stopped at One Hung's and asked if he
would keep a table free for me. Sure, he said. I just said thanks
because the last time I gave him free passes to a fight he sold
them to his own waiters.

I walked upstairs in time to take a call from Katy. 'I need
you to shoot some pictures.'

'When?'

'I don't know.'

'How many?'

'Probably just one. Or a couple. I don't know. Have you got
a motor drive? Run off a half a dozen.'

'Of what? Or of who?'

'It's a who but I don't know who. At least, not yet.'

'Close up?'

'No. Megan told me you have a long-distance lens . . . This
will be maybe from across the street. Or maybe through a
window. I'll take you to where it's going to happen and you
can work out whichever way is best.'

'Down and dirty, eh? That's the best way. I'll meet you at
your office at five.'

When I hung up with her I asked myself, can this really
work?

After I thought about that question for a few minutes,
I began to worry, and what happens if it does?

'How's the current Miss Westerberg?' I asked, stepping into
Straw's office.

'Hope springs eternal.'

I reminded him, 'I'm going to get the two of you out to dinner
and negotiate a reasonable settlement. Then, you invite me to
the wedding and I'll bring a present, you know, something in
a big box that you'll never use.'

'Presents are good.'

'Which reminds me . . .' I handed him two tickets to the
fight. 'Bring her along.'

'Boxing?' He read the ticket. 'The Elephant and Castle?'

'She'll be mightily impressed when she sees what a classy guy you are.'

He made a face. 'The closest the current Miss Westerberg has ever been to boxing is the day after Christmas.'

I grinned. 'I'm here because I need a favour.'

'Tell me.'

'Genetic ligature. I need paperwork. Back up. Whatever it takes to make someone believe I've got the formula.'

'What formula?'

'The formula for a genetic ligature. I don't know, the code. Whatever you call it. I want to make someone believe that I have the link between human chromosome 5 and human chromosome 13 . . . that I have the key to the FAT gene.'

'I assume you're referring to someone who would know it was the real thing when he saw it?'

'Someone who would think it was the real thing when he saw a little bit of it.'

'How little?'

'Only just enough. It's Pincer and DesRocher. I need one of them to think I have Bickerton's papers.'

'Ah. This may not be as easy as it sounds. If they don't get enough, they'll be suspicious. If they get too much . . . because we don't know what Bickerton's papers contained . . . I mean, there is his patent . . . but they've already had access to that . . . this has got to be something they wouldn't have seen yet and think they need . . .' He leaned back and stared at me. 'Does this somehow tie into Bickerton's death?'

I nodded.

His expression quickly changed. 'Are you saying that one of them murdered Bickerton?'

'I think one of them knows who did.'

'Wow!' He took a deep breath. 'This is going to take me some time . . .'

'How long?'

'I can't get to it until . . . earliest this evening. I'll have to dig through a lot of data. I can use the computer here . . . it will take me a few hours . . .' He wanted to know, 'How are you going to send it?'

'What do you mean?'

'If there's a diagram . . . are you mailing it to them?'

'E-mail.'

'So I need to give it to you on a floppy disk . . .' He started thinking out loud again. 'The Russian study for G-CSF . . . perhaps if I can confuse it with something I recently saw about interferon . . .'

'You've already convinced me.'

He explained, 'There's a Russian doctor here who showed me a study that has to do with the granulocyte-colony stimulating factor. As far as I know, it hasn't been published in the West. I don't know that the study itself is of any real importance, but if I can use that and maybe lift a few things out of a research project I saw about six months ago . . . We'll have to hope that Doctors Pincer and DesRocher don't spot the seams. I'll phone you when I've got it . . .' He stopped. 'That is, if I get it.'

Katy arrived on time, paid due homage to Henry's hair, then asked me to show her where I wanted the pictures taken.

On the way to Giovanni's, she never stopped asking questions. Black and white or colour? One person or two? Close up face, bust shot or full body? I told her black and white was fine, said one person and close up, but then changed my mind. A close up of one and maybe a shot of two people, I said, you know, the target and me handing the target an envelope.

She didn't like the lighting in the restaurant. 'Lighting is everything. What time of day will this be?'

'Late afternoon, I hope.'

'How late? Dusk is bad. Night is terrible.'

'I'm aiming for five.'

'And if it runs later?'

I told her the truth. 'I don't know.'

She decided the only suitable place was the first table near the door. Giovanni was slightly worried about what might be going on, but he was willing to humour me. We then walked back to One Hung's. Katy found a table at the side of the room that, she said, offered the best possibilities through the window from the doorway across the street.

One Hung told me, 'Whatever you want,' and put a reserved sign on the table while we stood there.

I said, 'It's not for today. It's like, maybe tomorrow or the next day.'

'It's okay. I charge you by the hour.'

I patted him on the back and reassured myself that he was only joking.

Johnny and Megan eventually appeared.

'How was your bus tour?'

'Great,' she said.

'Terrific,' he told me.

And the two of them continued talking at the same time, as if they needed to make me believe they'd actually been on a bus tour. Except, the only thing they remembered seeing was Big Ben.

'Here's the deal,' I said to Johnny. 'I've got to send two e-mail messages. Sort of the same message to two different people. I won't have the bulk of the text until maybe tonight at the earliest. Once I have it, how long will it take you to send it and when will they get it?'

He said, 'To send a message takes however long it takes to type it and push a couple of keys. To receive it, they get it right away.'

'So the guy who gets it knows right away . . . ?'

'No. The guy who gets it gets it right away. If he doesn't check his e-mail box for six months, then he doesn't see it for six months.'

'Ouch.' It only just dawned on me that there were probably a lot of things I hadn't thought of.

Chapter Thirty-Five

Louise phoned Wednesday night, demanding to know when I intended to return Johnny. I told her he'd be on a plane Sunday.

'Do I really have to go?' He started shaking his head. 'I want to stay here with you and Megan.'

I reminded him, 'She's going with you.'

'Maybe,' she said. 'It's not as if I have to be in school, or anything. At my age, I've got to keep my options open. If I stayed for a little while, could I bunk here with you? You know, until I got a place of my own.'

'The only options you've got is which airport you want to land at. A is Kennedy. B is Newark. There is no C, none of the above.'

Taking care of that was the first thing I did when I got to the office on Thursday. They'd come over on a cheap charter and the return was two weeks away. Those tickets were a write-off. So I started calling bucket shops and after fighting my way through a maze of rudeness, stupidity and general inefficiency, I managed to buy two seats out of Gatwick to Newark.

Once that was settled, I dug up my notes on the gang of nine – Pincer, DesRocher, Mars, Tyrone, Tsung, Schluter, Schlessinger, Stafford and Denton – threw them all into an envelope and sent them to Greystone with Johnny and Megan. He said he'd help Greystone dig through the Internet and Megan said she wanted to hang out with Katy, and I said that was fine, as long as they remembered that Johnny still had a term paper to do.

'Try to get to the House of Commons by two,' I said. 'You know, to get a good seat. Then when Question Time comes, make sure you keep your eyes open. Every now and then you may have to duck.'

Once they were on their way, I started digging myself out from under the work I hadn't been doing.

A fax had come in overnight from Los Angeles, from a lawyer I'd never heard of, representing a record company I'd never heard of, asking if I could handle a deposition in a lawsuit for a musician I'd never heard of, who'd written a hit song I'd never heard of, that got stolen by someone else I'd never heard of. Except, if you say who's that, you lose the job so I faxed back, 'His music is great, it would be a pleasure.'

A FedEx arrived from Sandy Miller at Great Lakes Reliance with a two hundred and thirty-six-page document that a British firm had filed in a US court trying to collect on a $35 million claim for a shipment that they said had been lost somewhere at the Port of Dover, despite port records showing that it never got there. 'Bogus may be a needle in a haystack,' he wrote by hand, 'so where is it?' I faxed him, 'Needles in haystacks are our specialty.'

Then Fuzzy White phoned. 'The deal is off, as of last night.'

'What deal?'

'I gave you until Wednesday to put your kid on the card in Birmingham.'

He was so predictable. 'So you're calling me now to tell me I'm too late and there is no deal.'

'That's right.'

'How about if I say, gee Fuzzy, I forgot all about it, I'm sorry, and I accept?'

'You can't. I mean, you can but not under last week's terms.'

'What are this week's terms?'

'They're queuing up for the spot. Best I can do is two and a half if he wins, two if he loses.'

'And what was last week? Three win, lose or draw?' I started to laugh. 'I presume the line is so long that it stretches all the way to the nearest phone booth. How about if we discuss it after the fight Friday night?'

'Why? You think you're going to get a better deal? If your kid loses there's no deal at all.'

'And if he wins?'

'Say . . . you got any spare tickets?'

'Fuzzy, we're not talking the Royal Albert Hall here. This is a seedy gym at the Elephant and Castle. Sneak in the back door.'

'No good . . . they lock that door.'

I'd no sooner put down the phone with him when Henry announced, 'This should go in here.' She was carrying a large piece of white cardboard, on which she'd drawn a grid, and in each square she'd put a number: 5–10–15–20. There must have been ten lines up and ten lines across, because the last box had 500 written in red, with an exclamation point to emphasize it. 'That should buy me a very nice holiday in Sydney.'

'You never take holidays.'

'Just because I can never afford to go any place doesn't mean I'm not supposed to go.' She decided it looked best tacked onto the wall behind my door. 'I've decided to let you off the hook as soon as you've paid for the trip.' With her magic marker, she crossed off the first box. 'Five quid down. Only another ninety-nine days to go.' Then she curtsied and went back to her desk.

That's when Sherman Straw phoned. 'I've got it.'

'You do? Great.'

'I may not have Miss Westerberg much longer, but I've solved your problem.'

'What happened?'

'I was here all night.'

'I'm going to take care of it. Where is she? Give me your address.'

'What are you going to do?'

'Just give me your address.'

'She's at work.'

'So, give me her office address.'

He did. 'What are you going to do?'

'I'm going to square everything with her. Trust me, I'm very good at squaring things with ladies who've seen their dinners get cold. Now . . . what does it look like?'

'I'll have to explain it to you. This is complicated stuff. Can you come by?'

'I'll be right there. But tell me something first.' I asked him, 'Do you want to marry this woman?'

'Why?'

'You're under oath. Yes or no will do.'

'Okay . . . yes. Now tell me why?'

'I'll see you in half an hour.' I hung up, dialled the florist, put six dozen roses on my credit card and asked them to be delivered as soon as possible to the current Miss Westerberg. I dictated the card, hoped I'd just done the right thing, and went downstairs to find a taxi.

The note with the roses simply said, 'I love you. So please marry me. S.'

He was waiting for me in his office with two single sheets of white typing paper and one floppy disk. On one page he'd written out a string of letters and numbers that, for all I could tell, could have been the US Navy's nuclear go-code. On the other, there was a spreadsheet with numbers, and then a small box that looked like an oscilloscope with a lot of wavy lines. And on both pages, there were several dark spots, almost as if the computer he'd used to print this stuff had blacked out the most important parts.'

'This is pretty damned obscure,' he promised, 'and I think it should do the trick.'

'You don't sound totally convinced.'

'I can't be . . . no one can. We don't know what Bickerton knew. Nor do we know what Pincer or DesRocher know about what Bickerton knew.' He took a deep breath. 'So what we're left with is the bikini axiom.'

'The what?'

'The bikini axiom. What you see is nice. What you don't is important.' He handed me the floppy disk. 'Just download it.'

'I owe you one.'

'Or maybe two or maybe three.'

I patted him on the shoulder. 'Thanks, Sherman.'

His phone rang.

He nodded to me, 'Any time,' and waited a second, as if he was expecting me to leave before he answered it.

I moved towards the door.

He picked it up – 'Dr Straw' – listened for a second, then looked at me with the strangest expression.

I smiled, winked and walked out just as he said into the phone, 'And I love you too . . .'

*   *   *

Johnny and Greystone were sitting next to each other at the back of the newsroom, using separate computers, hurriedly typing away – and chattering at the same time – so engrossed in whatever it was they were doing that neither of them noticed I was standing right there.

I watched my son manoeuvre his way easily through what I consider to be the embarrassingly confounding world of information technology. The screen in front of him was attached to a little box filled with wires and that little box was somehow attached to the entire world . . . and how that was, baffled me.

I didn't understand when Johnny told me that the computer on his desk was faster and far more powerful than the one that put Apollo XI on the moon. I didn't understand when he said that someday, all the world's libraries and all the world's television programmes and all the books ever written and all the movies ever made would be instantly available on everyone's home computer, no matter where on earth they lived. I didn't understand when he claimed that the day was fast approaching when arithmetic, algebra, geometry, trigonometry and calculus would become obsolete – banished to the same irrelevance that we now give Latin – because computers the size of a wristwatch will, among other things, instantly solve every equation we can come up with.

I didn't understand where I was when the world I grew up in stopped being a simpler place and yet I remained a simpler person.

And even if, in weaker moments, I would wish to revisit those simpler times – at least for a little while – I do not wish those times or my own simplicity on my son. Yet, I would feel much better about how the world is changing so fast, if only I could convince myself it's all being done with mirrors.

'Hi.' Johnny finally came up for air. 'Wait till you see this.' He punched a few keys and pointed at the screen. 'This is more e-mail. It's endless. We're getting everything.'

Now Greystone motioned for me to look at his screen. 'They're all in bed together . . . all these people . . . look at this . . .'

There were lists of names – mostly the nine I'd given him – but others too. I didn't recognize them, but that didn't matter. He and Johnny seemed to know what they were doing.

I was hoping that I did too.

'There's a file on this that has to be e-mailed.' I handed the floppy to Johnny. He took it, punched a few more keys, saved whatever he was working on, put the disk into the computer and brought Straw's two pages onto his screen. I then took two sheets of paper and wrote out this message: 'All around the scientist's bench, the scientists chased LRB's equation. Pop goes the FAT gene. A real investment opportunity.'

On the first one, I added Homer's phone number, and told Johnny, 'This gets e-mailed to Pincer.'

On the second, I added Ulysses' phone number, and told Johnny, 'This gets e-mailed to DesRocher.'

He sent the two messages right away. I then made a note for myself – Homer/Pincer, Uly/DesRocher – patted him on the back and left.

There was nothing to do now but wait to see which one of them swallowed the bait.

Chapter Thirty-Six

Homer didn't call.

Ulysses didn't call.

Henry didn't change her hair colour – that cost me another five quid – and Johnny didn't get to Parliament.

'I don't have to go,' he announced. 'Greystone's been there and he gave me a copy of a series he wrote about it, all four parts, and Katy gave me some really neat pictures she took there once and with that I'll be able to explain everything.'

I reminded him, 'Everything except what you personally saw and what you personally heard and what you personally felt. Other than that, it's an eyewitness report.'

'Come on . . .' He held out his hands as if he was begging me to see it his way. 'This is not really a term paper. It's Mr Wilson's way of saving face.'

I wasn't going to admit he might be right. 'Or your way of staying in school.'

'I'm going to do it . . .' Now he poked me. 'How many term papers did you ever do when you were in school?'

'College?'

'Try high school.'

I still wasn't going to admit he might be right, so I changed the subject. 'You're positive that the e-mail got sent properly and that it's just a question of . . .'

'They got it,' he said. 'They got it. There's no way they couldn't have gotten it. This is not like a mailman who's too afraid of your dog to deliver your Reader's Digest. You'll just have to wait.'

And that's what we did.

We waited all Thursday afternoon.

And we waited all Friday morning.

Hambone rang twice, both times very nervous about the fight, and both times I did my best to calm him down.

'It will be all right.'

'It's not going to be all right unless you're in the dressing room with me.'

'What does Moe say about that?'

'I don't care what Moe says about that. I say I need you, man.'

'All right. Count on me.'

'6:30. I'm counting on you.'

I took Johnny and Megan to the deli, mainly to show Johnny off to Barney and Bernie. Megan stuck to vegetables, but I ordered salt beef sandwiches on rye for Johnny and me, which Johnny agreed was a good idea, until Barney came over to the table to say, 'We're outta rye bread.'

I wondered, 'How can you be out of rye bread?'

'What?' He looked at me as if I was crazy. 'This isn't a free country? So, today we're outta rye bread. So, tomorrow, I'll try to be outta white bread. How's that?'

I cancelled the sandwiches – there ought to be a law forbidding delis to serve salt beef sandwiches on anything but rye bread – and after conferring with Johnny, we settled on a couple of bowls of soup and a piece of boiled beef.

'With my mustard,' I demanded. 'You'd better not be outta that.'

'Lucky guy, your father,' Bernie said to Johnny. 'He's got a son who isn't like him.'

I smiled. Except, somewhere in my mind I was beginning to wonder if the fact that these guys ran out of rye bread – which they probably hadn't ever done in the past twenty years – was some sort of omen.

There was no call from Homer or Ulysses by two.

There was nothing from them by three.

And now I knew, it wasn't going to work.

And that's when Homer called. 'I told him . . . he rang me . . . five o'clock at Giovanni's.'

It was Pincer. He'd swallowed the bait. He was sending someone to look at Bickerton's papers.

'We're on,' I screamed to Johnny and Megan and Henry. 'Quick, get Katy on the phone and tell her it's Giovanni's.'

Pincer, I kept thinking. Of course. It makes perfect sense.

Then Ulysses phoned. 'Hey . . . a guy just rang me . . . he wants to meet. I told him where to go . . . like you said, Lance's place . . . the Chinese . . . he'll be there at five.'

'What?'

'Some guy called, just like you said he would, so I told him just what you said I should . . .'

DesRocher. He'd taken the bait too.

Now I said, 'Holy shit.'

'What?' Johnny wanted to know.

I told them, 'Hold on . . . let me think . . .' I tried to figure out what this meant – that both of them responded – and how I was going to be in two places at the same time and how Katy was going to be in two places at the same time. 'Give me two large manila envelopes,' I said to Henry. 'Then open anything . . . a phone book, a newspaper, whatever, put it on the photocopier and make two dozen copies. Then put a dozen pages in each envelope and seal it up with tape.' While she did that, I called Katy. 'We're on for five. But it's both places. They're not far away. Can you get to both or do we need someone else?'

'Down and dirty,' she said. 'As long as I know when it's happening.'

'What do you mean?'

'I do whichever one goes down first, then run to the other, but I've got to know where to start.'

'Okay,' I said. 'Get here as soon as you can.' I hung up, tried to work it out in my head, then dialled Signorelli. His phone rang once, then twice . . . I said nervously, 'Please be there' . . . three times, then four. And finally he answered it. I explained what I wanted to do. He said he'd stop by and kit me up.

When Signorelli arrived, I introduced him to Johnny and Megan. Then I waited for him to ask Henry why she did that to her hair. But he didn't. He told her, 'I love it.' Henry extended her palm. I dug into my pockets, handed her five one-pound coins and she checked off another box on the grid.

'Who gets wired?' Signorelli wanted to know.

Instantly, Johnny and Megan both said, 'Me.'

It wasn't a bad idea. There was nothing dangerous about this. All they had to do was hold onto the envelope until Katy took the photo of whoever showed up. 'Okay.'

So Johnny and Megan both got wired with a tiny transmitter

– 'When it goes down, you just say in a normal voice, he's here – and when Katy showed up, he gave her an earpiece. When you hear someone say, he's here, you'll know where to be.'

He also gave me an earpiece so I would know what was happening too.

By that time it was four twenty.

Katy already knew what to do. I briefed Johnny and Megan that all they had to do was hand the target the envelope. I said, 'Don't get into any conversation. Don't wait there while the fellow opens it. When someone walks up to you and asks, have you got something for me, you say yes, offer him a seat, wait until he's sitting, then hand it to him and walk away. When you leave the restaurant, come straight back to the office. Henry will be waiting here. Got it?'

They both said they did.

I took Johnny to Giovanni's – whispered in Giovanni's ear, keep an eye on him – and sat Megan down at the table in the window at One Hung's. I planned on watching her from the kitchen.

Henry made the rounds to see that everyone was in position and poked her head in One Hung's kitchen to tell me everyone was ready.

And then we all waited.

I sat at the big round table, toying with a cup of tea that I didn't want.

My watch said it was four fifty-five.

What seemed like an eternity later my watch said it was four fifty-nine.

Then it was five. Then it was five after. Then it was ten after. My tea was long cold.

It was five thirty. Then it was quarter to six. Then it was six.

I told myself, neither guy is going to show. I told myself, even if one shows we're going to lose the light. I told myself, if I'm not in that locker room on time, this is going to ruin Hambone.

'He's here,' Johnny's voice came into my earpiece.

I tried to hear their conversation but the kitchen was too noisy. All I could make out was Johnny telling the man to sit down and then something that sounded like, 'That's all there is. Just the envelope.' The next thing I heard was like about a minute later when Johnny said, 'Warm up the coffee, mama, I'm coming home.'

Now I moved to the hallway and a couple of minutes later he was there. I hugged him, told him to be quiet and pointed upstairs. 'Wait there.'

'I did it,' he was so excited. 'I did it.'

Megan's voice broke into my ear. 'He's here.'

'Go on.' I pushed Johnny towards the stairs and moved back into the kitchen. I didn't want to make my presence too obvious, so I only dared to peek through the swinging doors that lead the waiters into the restaurant.

Megan told the man, 'That's right.' There was a pause. 'You want it, you sit down,' she said. ''Cause I said so.'

I craned my neck to see what was going on. Jeezus, girl, don't start ad-libbing. All I could make out was Megan standing next to someone . . . a man with black hair . . . and she was handing him the envelope. They weren't sitting down. But it looked to me as if she'd somehow turned him towards the front window.

And then he was gone.

Megan came towards me. I let her step into the kitchen, then hugged her too. 'Great job.'

'He wouldn't sit down,' she said.

'I know. I know.'

'But I faced him right and I could see Katy across the street, in that doorway . . .'

'Great work.' With my arm still around her, I brought her into the office.

Now she threw her arms around Johnny and they did a little dance.

'Your ten quid has gone to better use than my hols,' Henry announced, and whipped out a bottle of champagne.

I told her, 'Why would you want to go play in Sydney when you're having all this fun at work?'

'Here.' She handed me the bottle to open while she ran downstairs to borrow some glasses from One Hung. She came back upstairs with Katy.

'Got him,' she said. 'Down and dirty.'

I popped the cork.

Megan applauded.

I poured five glasses and we toasted to our own success. 'What a bunch of spies,' I said.

'Barolo's angels,' Henry proclaimed.

Megan challenged her, 'Who are you calling an angel?'

Johnny took a big swallow. 'I'll drink to that.'

'Go easy,' I said to him. 'Here's to down and dirty.' I toasted Katy. 'Thanks.'

'Down and dirty,' Megan said. 'Sounds better than being an angel.'

Johnny took another swallow. 'I'll drink to that too.'

'How soon can you get some prints?'

Katy said, 'I'll go back and do them right now. Where are you going to be in an hour?'

'Oh shit. Pardon my French.' I finished my glass. 'Let's go.' I gave Katy the address of the sports centre, told Henry, 'Give her a ticket,' saw that it was now nearly seven, locked up and herded everyone out of there.

Downstairs, I gave £10 to Katy. 'This is for a taxi back to your grandfather's. And then a taxi to the fights.'

'I'll take a bus,' she said.

A taxi came along. 'No you won't.'

Another was just behind it.

I hailed them both, piled Johnny, Megan and Henry into one, told the driver, just a second, and put Katy in the second.

'How many prints do you need?' she asked.

I called back, 'A couple of each guy,' and started to get into my cab.

'What are you talking about?' she shouted as her cab pulled around past ours. 'It was the same guy.'

Chapter Thirty-Seven

It took twenty-five minutes to get to the sports centre.

For the entire ride, I grilled Johnny and Megan on what the fellow looked like.

I didn't know who he was.

And the fact that he made both stops confused me.

We rushed into the centre, almost didn't get in because I forgot which pocket I'd put the tickets in, I screamed to Johnny to secure ten ringside seats, and went to find the locker rooms.

When I finally located Hambone, sitting in his shorts at the far corner near the showers, he was a wreck.

'Man, I thought you weren't coming . . . I've been waiting . . . I've been watching every minute of the clock since six thrity . . .'

It was one big old locker room for all the fighters. So I reminded him that Davey McGraw was in there somewhere too and tried to settle him down. I nodded to Moe and he came over and together we somehow managed to restore some calm. But I was worried about him because my being late had sapped some of that good nervous energy that an athlete needs to get up for the big game.

A guy came in and called for the first two fighters and I told Hambone it was time to get taped.

He looked at me with those big eyes of his and I gave him a hug. 'Win it before you even get into the ring.'

He looked at me with those huge eyes of his.

I moved up close to him, stared into those eyes and whispered, 'Do that!'

Moe put his arm around Hambone's shoulder and took him over to a table with some tape. I went into the arena to find Johnny.

McBride and Greystone were both there. So was Giovanni and a couple of his waiters. So were Homer and Ulysses. Then Greta showed up. She looked around, mumbled, 'What a swell place to spend a Friday evening,' and I introduced her to Johnny and Megan.

Next, Hambone's mother arrived with a whole troupe of people, and Rufus showed up too, with his entire family – new baby and all – in tow.

Then Sherman Straw walked in, with a truly beautiful, slim young woman on his arm. 'I'd like you to meet the current Miss Westerberg.'

I shook her hand. 'I'd just like you to know that over the course of this evening you will meet some very seedy people. All of them are very dear friends of Sherman's.'

She laughed.

I sat her down next to Greta.

'Thanks for the flowers,' he whispered to me. 'She said no . . .' then added, 'at least not yet.'

I patted him on the back.

The bell sounded for the first fight. It lasted two rounds.

The second fight was as brief, and as bad.

And then it was time.

Just before the fighters were announced, Fuzzy White walked over to say hello. And Katy arrived with the photos. I got rid of Fuzzy – 'He wins tonight and the price goes way up' – and showed the photos to Sherman. 'Know him?'

'Sure.'

'Who?'

He said, 'Tsung.'

'Ladies and gentlemen . . .' The announcer blared as his microphone squeaked. 'A middleweight contest of eight rounds. In the white corner, wearing white shorts with a red stripe . . . weighing eleven stone six pounds, from Wimbledon, Day . . . vey . . . . Mac . . . Graw.'

The crowd of maybe two hundred and fifty gave him a mild welcome.

'And in the red corner, wearing red shorts with a white stripe . . . weighing eleven stone four and a half pounds . . . from Lambeth . . . Derek . . . the Equalizer . . . Hannover.'

He got a similar welcome, but those of us on the Hambone

benches screamed and yelled and made enough noise for twice as many people.

Moe and Charlie and an old friend of Charlie's were working the corner. They stood with Hambone while the referee told the two fighters that he wanted no holding and clean breaks and reminded them that three knockdowns in the same round would end the fight. They touched gloves, Hambone danced back to his corner, Charlie gave me a thumbs up, Moe kept talking to Hambone, the bell sounded, Charlie pulled the chair away and out he came.

Hambone moved into the centre of the ring. McGraw went left. Hambone threw a right. And in a flash, McGraw caught him square on the side of his face.

Hambone dropped to the canvas.

I went pale. 'Get up,' I yelled.

I could hear Father Mac screaming at me, '*Chutzpah.*'

'Get up.'

The count was two. Three.

'Get up.'

Four.

He started to struggle to his feet.

'Get up.'

Five. Six.

He was off his knees.

Seven.

'Get up.'

Now he was up. The referee looked in his eyes, nodded, and told them, 'Box.'

McGraw came in, moved Hambone against the ropes and then Hambone did what he always did whenever he was hurt. He went into a crouch and stayed that way until the bell sounded ending the first round.

Hambone fell onto his stool and sat there while Moe and Charlie wiped him down and talked to him.

In the second round Hambone did the same thing. He crouched up and let McGraw hit him.

When the bell sounded for round three, he was already two rounds down.

Moe started screaming at him.

Then we joined in. 'Go get him, Hambone.'

We started making noise.

'Go, Equalizer.'

He came out throwing some punches. He stayed off the ropes but none of his punches meant anything. Then McGraw landed another one. Hambone never saw it coming. It rocked him. But he somehow managed to stay on his feet. McGraw tried to follow up. And Hambone went back into his crouch.

The fourth round was just as dismal.

Then something very odd happened. Hambone was sitting on his chair getting wiped down, when he looked over at me. I clenched my fist. He just stared at me. The bell sounded. He kept staring. Charlie shoved him off the chair. I jumped up. Hambone kept looking at me. Now I pointed at McGraw and said very loudly and very sternly, 'Do that!'

Hambone nodded.

The ref shouted, 'Box.'

Now he moved into the very centre of the ring.

McGraw came forward, trying to get under Hambone's jab, and stepped into a hook.

It didn't hurt him, but it sure surprised him.

He came in again.

This time Hambone missed with an uppercut.

McGraw pounded one, then two shots into Hambone's chest.

Hambone seemed to falter. He stepped back. McGraw moved in, but he came in straight ahead and now Hambone planted his feet and suddenly he unleashed a furious combination. He hit McGraw with his left hand, stunned McGraw with his right hand, then brought his left up from nowhere and landed it square on McGraw's chin.

We were all off our seats.

McGraw thumped onto the canvas.

'My God, he's got an uppercut,' I screamed.

Hambone stood there for a second, looking down at McGraw, until the ref shoved him into a neutral corner and began his count.

Two. Three. Four. Five.

McGraw struggled desperately to get to his feet.

Six. Seven. Eight.

His legs couldn't take it and he slumped back onto the canvas.

Nine. Ten.

The ref waved him out.

And we went wild.

I jumped into the ring and started hugging him and he did a little dance, and the Hambone benches started screaming, 'Ham . . . bone . . . Ham . . . bone . . .'

The euphoria continued all the way back into the locker room.

Everybody piled in. Greta was mildly uncomfortable. The current Miss Westerberg was very uncomfortable. But Megan and Katy and Henry all took it in their stride. Even Hambone's mom thought it was the proper place to be. 'With my boy.'

I told Hambone, 'That was the worst uppercut I have ever seen.'

'I caught him . . .' he said, obviously just as surprised by the punch as McGraw had been . . . 'I caught him real good . . .'

Out of the corner of my eye I saw McGraw come in and go silently to the other side of the locker room with his corner guys. So I snuck away and walked over there to tell him he fought good, to say I hope he wasn't hurt, and to wish him luck.

On the way back, Fuzzy came up to me. 'Four if he wins.'

'Five . . . win, lose or draw.'

'No way . . . my boy isn't getting that.'

'McGraw got away lucky tonight. All that hanging on the ropes. Five . . . win, lose or draw.' I knew how to taunt him. 'And an extra hundred quid to say your boy doesn't last as long as McGraw.'

'Yeah . . . okay . . . sure.' He started nodding. 'Okay. But why don't you and me make it five hundred? Still so cocky? How's that for a deal?'

'Five grand for him . . . five hundred for me . . .' I looked back at the crowd Hambone had collected. 'And . . . one other thing. The black kid over there with the baby.'

'Rufus Winger?'

'Yeah. You put him on the card.'

'Rufus Winger?'

'That's right. He goes on the card or Hambone doesn't.'

'What kind of a deal is that?'

I told him, 'The only deal in town,' and went back to Hambone.

After a while, Moe wanted Hambone to take a shower, so we all left him alone. Giovanni said we should all go back to his place to celebrate. I said that sounded like a good idea. So some of them left for Giovanni's but Johnny, Megan, Greta, Sherman and the current Miss Westerberg stayed behind with me to wait for Hambone.

We were hanging out in the corridor outside the locker room when someone tapped me on the shoulder. 'Remember me?'

I turned around to see Hal. 'Where the hell have you been?'

'Been out there to watch your kid do real good.'

'No, I mean where have you been for the past few weeks?'

'Oh . . . I've been trying to stay low key . . . you know what I mean.' He pulled me aside. 'About those tapes . . .'

'They're gone. I told you I was getting rid of them.'

'You sold them, right? I mean, you got me some money, right?'

'I got you . . .' I looked at him, sighed, and figured, what the hell. 'I got you £250. But that's all. I told you I was throwing them out. That was the best I could do.'

'You got me £250? They were worth like . . . ten times that . . .' He shook his head. 'Done in by my own lawyer.'

'I am not your lawyer.'

'Okay. Okay. Let me have the money.'

'What, now? I don't have that much on me. You'll have to stop by the office next week . . .'

'Next week?' He waved me off. 'Not a good idea to be in London next week. I've got to think of my health. I'm heading for the sunshine.' His voice got softer. 'Help me out here, will you. Let me have the two and a half and throw in an extra two and a half. I'll pay you back.'

'How much?' I mumbled. 'You're lucky I'm giving you two and a half.'

'Hey . . .' He held out his hand. 'I'm a little stretched . . .'

I glanced around for the Cypriot but he was already gone, then told Hal, 'You know Giovanni's restaurant near my office?' He said he did. 'All right. Go there right now and wait for me. Giovanni's holding some money for me. Tell him I said to give you two fifty.'

'Yeah . . . sure . . . okay . . . thanks . . .' He squeezed my arm and left.

I moved back to Johnny, trying to hear what Sherman was saying to him, when someone else tapped me on the back.

Turning around, this time I found Denton.

'What the hell are you doing here?'

'Running a little errand for my mate,' he said. 'What kind of a stunt was that this evening?'

I pulled myself up to my full height. 'What kind of a stunt was what?'

'Passing off envelopes filled with newspaper photocopies. You think maybe my friends don't tell me what's happening? You think maybe I let my friends down when they ask for help? You think maybe you're invisible and too hard to find?'

I motioned to Johnny, 'Is this the fellow you saw trying to break into the apartment?'

Johnny was hesitant. 'Ah . . . it kinda looks like him . . .'

I challenged Denton, 'First you break into my office. Then you try to break into my home.'

Hambone, Moe, Charlie and the rest of them came out of the locker room.

Denton smirked, 'Prove it.'

'What do you say, I prove it sometime next week. Just you and me. Face to face.' I reminded him, 'Tonight I'm busy.'

'Let me tell you something, Barolo . . .' Denton stood his ground. 'You've been getting up the noses of a lot of people lately. Next time we meet . . . just remember what I told you about life.'

'Right. The guy coming up from behind.' I said, 'So I guess that means you forgot what I told you about boxing?'

'Right. The guy in front.'

I took a deep breath, moved away from him slightly and looked at Hambone. 'Derek, remember what I said to you in there? Remember how I said that was the worst uppercut I have ever seen?'

Hambone looked at me with a very confused expression. 'Huh?'

I took one half-step forward, said, 'It's done like this,' brought up my right hand and threw my entire body into the punch.

Denton's head snapped back and he was literally lifted off his feet. He crashed against the far wall and sank like a dead weight to the floor.

Johnny and Megan screamed, 'Way to go.'

And as the pain shot up through my fist, I smiled, 'Hambone, that is an uppercut.'

Chapter Thirty-Eight

I spent the rest of Friday night in a hospital emergency room, getting my hand x-rayed and taped. I introduced Sherman Straw to everyone as my private physician. Johnny, Megan, Greta, Hambone and all the others stayed with me. If there was a victory party at Giovanni's, we missed it.

On Saturday morning, with my hand badly swollen, I phoned Giovanni to apologize. He made the pain go away by telling me that my friend Hal had done exactly as I'd asked him to do – collected my share of the bet on Hambone.

'My share? I told him two fifty.'

'That's not what he said.'

'You gave it all to him?'

'That's what he said you wanted.'

The best I could do was try to console myself into thinking that Hal might show up again, one of these days.

As for Denton, he spent the weekend in the hospital. I learned later that when one of his friends suggested he file charges against me with the police, he firmly refused. Just in case he planned on showing up again one of these days, I phoned a solicitor friend to tell him I had a dozen witnesses who would swear that my altercation with Denton was self-defence. He asked if any of my witnesses were Italian. I said they all were. He assured me, I believe them already.

Because it was their last day, I took Johnny and Megan to Portobello Road, along my regular route, and introduced them to all my various connections. At the back of one stall Johnny found an old Louisville Slugger baseball bat and a Duke Snider signature outfielder's glove. The guy who had it wanted £15 for them. I offered him £5. The guy said, this is England and baseball stuff is rare. I reminded him, this is England and baseball stuff is useless. We settled at £8. Under a pile of junk at another stall, Megan found an ostrich-plumed Tyrolean hat. The woman who had it wanted £20 for it. I offered her £8. She said, this is England and ostrich-feathered Tyroleans are rare. If we were in the trade, she said, the best she could do was £15. Megan wanted it very badly, so I said, we're in the trade and gave her £15.

Then I piled them into a taxi and took them to the Houses of Parliament – at least so they could see what it looked like from the outside – and bought Johnny a guidebook filled with colour photos, at least so that he could see what it looked like on the inside.

We did a pub lunch and on a whim I suggested we take the boat down the Thames to Greenwich. We had tea there, saw the clock – I bought them both souvenir wristwatches – and got back to the apartment in time to have a meeting about where to eat supper.

All of a sudden they both turned coy.

I didn't understand.

Megan suggested we might find something in the neighbourhood, which was all right with me, but when I said let's leave, Johnny said he wasn't hungry yet. So I said we could wait until he got hungry or until I got impatient, whichever came first.

Fifteen minutes later I declared myself the winner.

Hustling them out the door, I suggested we head up Portobello but they wanted to go down towards Notting Hill Gate and before I realized it we were standing outside Patel's place.

'How about here,' Megan wondered, 'because I'm a vegetarian.'

'No way,' I said, 'because I want to live to tell the tale.'

But Johnny said he loved Indian food and she took my hand and before I could do anything about it, Patel was there opening the door to welcome us.

'Why, Mr Barolo, it is always such a pleasure to serve you and your companions.'

I whispered to him out of the corner of my mouth, 'If you put lamb vindaloo on the table, I will personally plaster it all over your flocked wallpaper.'

'Welcome to the Taj Mahal of the India Gourmet,' he said to Megan and Johnny, as he led the three of us towards the back.

I mumbled, 'Gourmet my ass.'

Then someone yelled, 'Surprise.'

Charlie and Hambone were there. So was Hambone's mother. So were Giovanni and Moe. Rufus Winger was there too, with his wife. So was Henry. And her hair was now back to its regular colour.

Greta was standing next to an empty chair, looking at me and smiling.

So we had Hambone's victory dinner after all.

The party broke up pretty late – Greta said, see you soon and even though everyone was watching, she kissed me goodbye – and when I got home I invited Megan and Johnny to join me for a nightcap. I mixed it while they stood watching, horrified. And after they smelled it, they refused to drink it.

I toasted, 'Here's to your grandmother who taught me how to make this. And here's to you too. Both of you.'

They flew home the next morning.

I took them on the train to Gatwick and stood with them while they checked in. There wasn't much time before they had to board so I walked them to the security checkpoint and tried to make a joke. 'You know the one about the fellow who gets onto the plane with a duck on his head and when the stewardess says, you can't come onto the plane like that, the duck answers, get him off my ass and I'll sit alone.'

They both laughed politely but Johnny's eyes were red and when I looked at Megan, hers were too.

'Hey, I'll see you guys soon.'

'Thanks for everything, Dad.' He hugged me, and finally started to cry. 'Can I come back here to go to college, like you said?'

'Yeah,' I said, fighting back my own tears. 'Yeah. I'll square it with your mother. But first . . .' I tried to make another joke, 'First you've got to rewrite Greystone's story on Parliament.'

Megan reached over and hugged me. 'He loves you a lot,' she said in my ear.

I wanted to say, don't hurt him, but managed to soften it with, 'Be kind to each other.'

She nodded, took his hand and the two of them walked away. When they were gone, I hurried to the men's room and only just got there before the tears began running down my face.

Back home, the apartment suddenly seemed very empty.
I moped around.

After a while I dug through the carton with those boxing tapes
that Uly didn't want and tried to find something I hadn't seen.
I settled on some early Ken Norton bouts, which was okay, but
it didn't make me feel as good as I felt when Johnny and Megan
were here.

At around six, someone started ringing my bell and for one
brief instant I kind of hoped they'd missed their plane.

I opened the door to find Greta standing there. 'I forgot to
ask, what's Bass River?'

'Don't you mean where?'

'Okay. Where is it?'

I pointed behind me. 'In the hallway cupboard. Waiting
for you.'

She walked past me, opened the cupboard and pulled out
the plate. I shut the door and followed her.

'Whatever happened to Sam and Sophia?'

'I'd like to think that they will forever live in the glow of
those nights at Bass River.'

'Just one plate?'

'When you're in love, you don't need the whole dinner
service.'

'I'm not sure that's correct,' she said. 'But I think you should
lock the door and put the phone on the answering machine. I
thought we'd make up for last night. And last week. And maybe
you shouldn't plan on going to work tomorrow.'

I didn't.

Johnny and Megan got home safely and soundly. I know
because he sent a fax to the office saying as much, which
Henry found Monday morning and – after explaining that,
from now on, she was going to call herself Megan – she read
it to my answering machine.

That machine stayed on for the rest of the day.

Tuesday, Greystone's article appeared, detailing Tsung's
relationship with DesRocher and Pincer. Katy's photo of
him looking terribly sinister appeared alongside. Greystone
also enumerated on the various conflicts of interest he'd
uncovered linking Mars, Tyrone, Schlessinger, Schluter and
Stafford. Tuesday evening, Terry Dunn – the press guy at the
ERP – released a statement denying the facts that formed the

basis of Greystone's story and blamed Fleet Street for starting a smear campaign.

Wednesday, *The Times* and the *Telegraph* both picked up on the story.

The following day, the *New York Times* ran a large piece about Pincer and the possibility that Government grants awarded to Taptech had been misused. Thursday evening, Terry Dunn issued another statement, this time to announce that, with much regret, Professor T.P. Tsung had resigned from his seat on the ERP board to pursue private interests.

The next morning, the *Guardian* reported that the French had begun to investigate DesRocher's relationship with the CNRS in Marseilles – it turned out, his services were contracted to them through a private management company called Bio-Patronat SARL, which he happened to own. At best, it was highly irregular. At worst, the *Guardian* said, it was criminal deceit.

That same afternoon, Raoul DesRocher announced his early retirement. Then Terry Dunn reappeared to say that, with much regret, the European Research Project was announcing the early retirement of Dr Hans-Dieter Mars.

On Saturday, the *New York Times* revealed that Kaducee-Pharmacopeia had filed suit in Switzerland against Pincer and Taptech and that the Swiss police were looking to interview Tyrone and Mars. The London *Sunday Times* carried a lengthy exposé on the giant pharmaceutical companies, and implicated DesRocher in a scandal that was just breaking in Germany over the marketing of a drug based on erythropoetin. Tied into it were Doctors Schluter and Schlessinger. And the Sunday *New York Times* published an exposé on Taptech, tying Pincer into an offshore company that was supposedly secretly owned by DesRocher's Bio-Patronat.

On Monday, the *Washington Post* broke the news that a full-fledged FBI investigation was underway, and buried deep in that story was a list of companies that they wanted to know more about. According to the report, obviously leaked by someone at the FBI, one of the mysterious offshore entities they wanted to know more about was called Monachus SA.

The name jumped off the page.

I got Rodney on the phone right away. 'The company is

called Monachus. I don't know what it means. I don't even know where it is. Except it's an SA.'

'*Societé anonyme*. But if you want to know any more,' he said, 'you've got to give me a clue, such as, where it's incorporated.'

'How's the Caribbean?'

'Too hot this time of year. Got any numbers?'

'Numbers?' I told him to hold on, took Bickerton's notes and found the word Monachus. It was the page with the faint line that stretched to the three sets of numbers. 'How about numbers with a bunch of letters in it?'

'Sounds better. Give it to me.'

I did. He promised to get back to me. And within twenty minutes, he did. 'Luxembourg. Shell company. Opened and closed within the same week. No record of the owner. No record of any transactions. No record of any business. It doesn't exist. It's gone. Evaporated into thin air.'

I had no idea how it tied in to the murder of Roger Bickerton, but I felt the least I could do was call that cop Lascasse in Guernsey and tell him about it. 'Are you still handling the case?'

'It has not yet come before the coroner,' he responded gruffly, 'so yes, technically, it is still considered to be open.'

'But no body has ever been found.'

'Probably won't be.'

'What would you say if I told you Bickerton was murdered.'

'What makes you think that?'

'I have reason to believe that he was trying to get even with some people he worked with. People he figured were screwing him. I think he got in way over his head and one of them, or all of them, or maybe just a couple of them, decided to do him in.'

'And who would these people be?'

I gave him the names, and told him of the various scandals that now surrounded them.

'Sounds to me,' he said, 'that your client has indeed got even.'

I mumbled, 'I guess he has.'

'Unless you can do more than theorize . . .'

I pointed out, 'There is motive. One, or all, or at least some of them had a good reason to kill him. And there is opportunity. One, or all, or at least some of them could have arranged it with a single phone call. I suspect there is also conspiracy to murder here because I doubt very strongly that it was just one of the group.'

'That's still not enough. How about, as you Americans like to call it, the smoking gun?'

'If the obvious is that he's dead and the unobvious is that his murder was made to look like a suicide, what's left?'

Lascasse answered right away, 'One low-mileage Renault Laguna. Nice motorcar.'

I wondered, 'Why would you say, low mileage?'

'Because he didn't drive it very far.'

'How low is low?'

'As I recall, under three thousand miles.'

'So it's basically a new car.'

'This year's.'

Now I asked, 'Mr Lascasse, do most people buy a new car if they plan on committing suicide?'

'Still no smoking gun, Mr Barolo.'

'What happened to the car?'

'We have it. But a claim has been put in for it by someone . . . I recall it was a lawyer representing the next of kin.'

'In Paris? Acting for Ghislain Cesari?'

'That sounds right.'

'Has the lawyer said what he was going to do with the car?'

'Mr Barolo . . . I can understand that you're trying to make a case for your theory . . .'

'I mean, did he say he planned on selling it in Guernsey or has he asked that it be shipped back to England?'

'What possible difference could it make?'

'What's anyone in Paris going to do with a right-hand drive car?'

He started to laugh. 'You should have been a cop.'

'I kinda once was,' I said. 'In a previous incarnation I was an assistant district attorney in Brooklyn. Crown prosecutor, you'd call it.'

'Well, Mr Barolo, that explains a lot. But there's no need to worry about your client's motor because it's a little diesel cack-hander. It should suit Parisian traffic just fine.'

'Cack-hander?'

'Left-hand drive.'

'Huh?' It didn't make sense. A guy who lives in England buys

himself a new car with the steering wheel on the wrong side and
drives it all the way to Guernsey so that he can commit suicide.
'You say it's a diesel?'

'That's right. Oh, and just for the record, because you're
obviously interested in this sort of thing, I recall that it's pale
blue, with CD and stereo, air-conditioning and leather seats.'

'Are you positive?'

'Mr Barolo . . .' I could hear him take a deep breath. 'I'm sure
you mean well. But even if the case is officially open, it's really
closed. What I'm trying to say is, if you ever find the smoking
gun, let me know. If you want to know more about a Renault,
call your local dealer.'

'I might just do that,' I said. 'Thanks, Mr Lascasse. Have a
good life.'

'You too, Mr Barolo, have a good life.'

I dialled the first Renault dealer I found in the phone book.
'I'm looking for a Renault Laguna, diesel, left-hand drive with
air-conditioning.'

The salesman wanted to know, 'This for export?'

'Export?' I pondered that. 'Why, is there a difference?'

'Export, someone else gets the commission.'

'Okay, how about if it's not for export. Laguna. Diesel.
Left-hand drive. Air-conditioning.'

'If it's not for export, why are you making life so difficult
for both of us?'

'What do you mean?'

'You want a Laguna? I can sell you a dozen different colours
with a whole range of options. I can even do diesel. But left-hand
drive? And why do you want air-conditioning? This is England.
The whole country is air-conditioned.'

I thought about that. 'Yeah . . . you're right. Listen . . .
ah . . .' I lied, 'I've got to take another call. I'll get back
to you.'

Hanging up, my mind flashed back to Brighton. My meeting
at the fire department. The fire at Bickerton's lab. Was it
Raymond or was it Chorley who said to me that they'd
smelled accelerants? That the fire was accelerated with diesel fuel.

Rummaging through my notes, I found Ghislain Cesari's
number in Paris. I dialled it and let it ring for several minutes.
There was no answer. I thought about how I could get in

touch with her. Then I remembered my new friends at the George V.

The hotel operator obviously knew who they were – I wasn't surprised – and she put me straight through. Crosby answered, '*Bonjour là.* Hello, there.'

'It's your lawyer,' I said. 'How's Paris?'

He said gleefully, 'Tell us you're here.'

'Not quite. Are you having a good time?'

'If you only knew the half of it.'

'I trust it's a half that won't get you arrested.'

'You have to do something about that Italian macho streak . . .'

'Listen . . . I need a favour. Have you got half an hour?'

'For you?'

'For me.' I gave him Ghislain Cesari's address on the rue d'Italie. 'Take a taxi. I'll reimburse you. Bang on the door. Or ask her neighbours where I can find her. I need to speak to her as soon as possible.'

'Don't be silly. You don't have to reimburse us . . .' Crosby cupped the phone and explained – I presume, to Sam and Doris – 'It's Vincent in London. He needs our help, desperately.' Then Doris said to me, 'We're on our way. I'll personally call you back with a full report.'

An hour later a breathless Crosby was on the line. 'Moved. Picked up. Gone.'

'What?'

'Ghislain Cesari . . . the rue d'Italie . . . don't you just love how French sounds . . . well, there is such a place but there is no longer such a person. Left town. *Au revoir.*'

'Where did she go?'

'No one knows.'

'Who did you ask? Who did you speak to?'

'Everybody. You know, Doris speaks very good French and Sam and I are both picking it up . . .'

Sam got on another extension. 'Did Crosby tell you? Sorry, but it seems the lady has left.'

'Oh my God,' Crosby exclaimed, 'was this a lover's tiff?'

'No,' I corrected him. 'Strictly business.'

Crosby was suspicious. 'You know, Vincent, if you ever want to nurse your sorrows . . .'

'Thanks anyway. It's that Italian macho thing.'

I went back through my notes and found the French lawyer's name – Jean-Pierre Rosso – and phoned his office.

That he was on the place d'Italie; that Ghislain Cesari had been on the rue d'Italie was a coincidence that did not escape me. That I got an answering machine with a man's voice in rapid French merely frustrated me. Then I realized that Paris is an hour ahead of London, and I understood that the rapid French answering machine was telling me the office was closed for the night.

I asked myself out loud, what do lawyers do when they shut the office for the night? And answered, they go home. So now I asked directory inquiries in England for the home number of Jean-Pierre Rosso – *avocat*, I knew that much – in Paris. The operator put me on hold, came back to ask if *avocat* meant lawyer, and promptly gave me his office number. No, I said, I want the home number, and after a few more minutes she came back to ask if I had an address. 'There are loads of Rosso, J-P in Paris. Perhaps if you had a street name . . .' She stopped. 'How are you spelling the word for lawyer? Is it with a "d" as in advocate?' No, I replied, it's a–v–o–c–a–t. Well, she said, there seem to be two Rossos J-P who are a–v–o–c–a–t . . . one of them is on the rue Malsherbes and the other is on the rue . . . I'll spell it . . . M–E–S–N–I–L . . .'

'Mesnil?' Why did that ring a bell? 'What number on the rue Mesnil?'

'Number twelve,' she said.

I knew it from somewhere. 'What's that phone number, please?'

She gave it to me, then reminded me that the code for France was three-three and that the code for Paris was one, followed by an eight-digit number.

The instant I heard eight digits, I thought of the number in Bickerton's notes, on the same page with the drawing of the airplane. The eight digits, where every two were separated by a period. And the instant I saw that those numbers matched Rosso's, everything fell into place.

I said out loud, 'Rosso lives with her,' and dialled the number. A woman picked up the phone. '*Oui?*'

I asked right away, 'May I please speak to Joelle Peltier?'

'Joelle Peltier?' she answered in English with a lovely accent. 'But it is now Joelle Rosso. Who is this?'

And just like that, I hung up. There wasn't anything to say. I'd figured it out. With hindsight, perhaps, I might have told her, I'm kind of glad that your cousin got his revenge. Or, I think it's nice that he's back with his wife. Or, tell him for me that I hope he has a good life. But I didn't think of it then. And I guess I'm glad I didn't. There was no need to get into a conversation with her. I mean, what was there to speak about?

An offshore company that purposely disappeared into thin air?

An arson deliberately intended to make it look like files were gone for ever?

A suicide that was supposed to look like murder?

The FAT gene that may or may not exist?

The never-ending light bulb?

Maybe I could have told her that the word *monachus* was Greek for monk.

But, in the end, I didn't say anything. Which was the right thing to do. After all, I'd cashed his cheque and helped him to get even. And if everyone else thought he was dead, that was what they were supposed to think. As far as I was concerned, the man was still entitled to client-attorney privilege.

Epilogue

Johnny's high-school team made it into the State finals and when he called me to say they were playing the best of seven for the championship, I told him, 'I'll be there.'

They lost in six but he came up with two great catches and he scored in every game, knocking in nine runs to win the batting title. His mother showed up for a couple of the games, so did the trumpet player, but they sat together on the third base line and I sat alone on the first base line.

Notably missing was Megan. Johnny said she'd moved to Nashville. Something about answering a calling to write country music and, in the meantime, she was driving a taxi cab.

Oh well, he sighed, it was fun while it lasted.

He took it better than I thought he would.

Somewhere around game four he introduced me to Francine, a girl in his class, who had short blonde hair and a bright clean smile, and who giggled every time he made bad jokes, which he seemed to do whenever she was around.

The night before I left, Johnny said that Louise wanted me to stop by for dinner. I wasn't sure I should – I knew I didn't want to – but he said he'd like it if I did. So I went.

We were just getting through dessert – Louise made apple fool, which I felt was appropriate, what with the trumpet player sitting at the head of the table – when she announced that as soon as Johnny graduated high school, she and the trumpet player were taking off for Florida.

I said, 'That's next June.'

Louise said, 'That's right.'

I asked, 'What's Johnny supposed to do?'

And Louise answered, 'He can go live with you.'

So this time when I got on the plane to come home I was

in a really great mood. I mean, I figured I was immune to numskulls.

But American Airlines got me again.

I was just getting settled into 19A – that's the second row in tourist class, on the window, right next to the galley and the bathrooms, which means it smells like liquid hand soap and industrial-strength gravy, and it's also just behind the bulkhead seats that they always save for screaming kids, which means it's got to be the worst place to sit on the plane, which is why I chose it. Not even a numskull would want to sit next to me as long as there's a better seat free somewhere else.

Except, just before they closed the doors, some guy threw himself into 19B and started babbling away.

In a panic, I realized I had nothing to bury my nose in because I'd been feeling so good I forgot to buy any boxing magazines.

He said to me, 'So, what do you do?'

I told him, 'I'm in scaffolding.'

And he got all excited. 'No kidding, I'm in fasteners.'

'Fasteners?'

'Yeah, fasteners. You know, like nuts and bolts. We do stuff for scaffolding.'

I looked at him. 'You're joking, right?'

He slapped me on the back. 'Hell, no. It sure is good to meet another guy in the business. Tell me, what's new in your end?'

New? What could I tell him about a subject for which no discussion should be humanly possible. 'Not a helluva lot.'

'Well, then, I guess it's all happening on my side, huh? Especially with the advent of DWS.'

'DWS?'

'Yeah. Dry wall screws.'

'You're putting me on.'

'Hey. Dry wall screws are the future of the human race.'

'What the hell are dry wall screws?'

He leaned closer, as if I was supposed to hang on his every word. 'You know how when you put a picture on the wall, you first have to drill a hole and throw a molly in there? One of those little plastic plugs. You sink your screw into the molly because it wouldn't hold in the wall otherwise. That's all changed now. DWS . . . you go right into the wall. Let me tell you, my friend . . .' He grabbed my arm. 'Mollies are dead. I'm going to own the world!'

So I said, 'Hey,' and reached into my pocket to pull out one of my cards. 'You got a patent for that thing? Listen, if you ever need an American lawyer in Britain, call this guy. He's new to patent work, but he's good.'

He took the card, studied it, then repeated, 'I'm gonna own the world.'

That's when I stood up, stepped across him, tossed my pillow and blanket onto the last empty seat in the middle row, and told the numskull, 'Not me. I'm gonna settle for a flat full of chairs, some boxing tapes and my son.'